Portland Mercury staff:

LACK OF APPEAL

Thank you for review consideration! :)

D1617099

NICK VALENZUELA

Thank you for review consideration! :)

Copyright © 2018 Nick Valenzuela

All rights reserved, including the right to reproduce this book
or portions thereof in any form.

This work is a semi-fictionalized portrayal of two days in the life of a civil rights investigator. Identities, situations, and events have been changed or invented for literary effect.

Cover art by : Tim Barber of Dissect Designs

ISBN: 1981141081
ISBN-13: 978-1981141081

DEDICATION

For my father and brother, and my family, friends, & experiences.

And to my wife, who saved it all…

LACK OF APPEAL

He remembers sitting on a beach, in a 1970s-yellow t-shirt and who-knows-what-color shorts, or swim trunks…lazily, languidly using his plastic kid-shovel to scoop up sand, and then concentrating on putting the spilling ploughs into a small plastic kid-bucket. It was almost in slow-motion. The sun and the sand were very warm, and he was doughy-faced, and doughy-limbed, the only time he'd ever be that way in his life as an otherwise-abnormally-thin male. And he was in Florida. Not that he specifically remembers that he was in Florida, but it had to have been there: your typical Kentuckian, whether from one of the few urban cities or one of the countless rural communities, vacations in Florida. He should know, he's almost 100% half-Louisvillian; and, he lived in Louisville off and on throughout more of the 1970s than he did any other city in the United States.

The beach scene wasn't even a memory until he saw a different photograph of himself from the 70s in a completely different setting: dressed in a brown, dandy, toddler, police-detective-kinda coat, he looked dumbfounded and amazed and drunken and idealistically at an autumn, red-and-yellow-and-brown-and-especially-orange leafy tree. He looked like he had just done a double-take. It was about the same time in his life, so he guessed that it triggered this other memory of him at the beach. He was just as plump, his hair was still black, still longer, and girly-curly androgynous. And, he was wearing jeans. After college, fashion-conscious or not, he'd stop wearing them.

And this fall memory was just as pleasant as the other memory. And he just wished that he could actively recall more memories. And, remember any nighttime dreams. And, he just wished that he could enjoy the present more.

Because he was bombarded by the present and the future, his life was all under

r
e
c
o
n
s
i
d
e
r
a
t
i
o
n
.
.
.

CHAPTER ONE

1:53 a.m.

The clock radio is black, with red digital font, and a red dot is not on at the top right of the screen (or at the bottom-left of the time).

***

4:21 a.m.

The clock radio is black, with red digital font, and a red dot is not on at the top right of the screen (or at the bottom-left of the time).

***

(5:05 a.m.)

(In defiance, I will *not* look at the clock.)

God-I-hope-it's-4:40 a.m. I'm sick-and-tired of being sick, and tired, of not coming close to sleeping seven or eight hours a night. And I haven't woken up to an alarm in months.

Each night, I'm in bed looking at things online by 7:30 p.m., and sometimes even earlier: each night, I'm just lazing there, intentionally, consuming local and national news. Each night, I only just check social media, watch an internet-streaming television show or two, or watch half of, or no more than, a two hour movie. Researching vacation packages online, because, this time, it's *my* turn to choose where we go, and it's *gonna* be Europe or South America…well, or Canada again. All the preparation in the world for the next business day's work. Eyes shut at around 9:30 p.m. Falling asleep usually within twenty minutes, but then the hourly open-and-shut case of insomnia after a long night's nap.

Part of the problem was this typical past weekend. Saturday meant the same awaketime as the workweek, around 5:45 a.m., of course despite no alarm set, followed by running around doing chores, going shopping for perceived-essentials…neurotic with the anxiety of the threat of termination from such domestic employment. It all had to be done. Dinner reservations brought reprieve and a decent evening, however, and then in bed again relatively early, before Sunday, YES, FINALLY, Sunday, sleeping in, until 7:05 a.m.

But then, more running-and-chores, like shopping-and-laundry. Talking by telephone with extended family. Surface cleaning. More virtual touristing online laying on the bed, in between laundry loads, giving a little rest, but long-gone are the days of staying inside my own apartment, turning down the windowshades, dimming the lights, and laying on the couch all Sunday in front of the television after having fun partying all night, recovering…all…day…

So, this morning, I'm tired. So, *so* tired, and of *course* there's a Complainant coming in today for a difficult interview, and two testers coming in…then, the afternoon presentation about fair housing, then intake duty back at the office, and then home for another microwaved meal, before *then* going *back* out to the university for the monthly meeting. Of *course* it's today, not tomorrow when, watch, I'll have had a good night's sleep. I do everything right, everything to prepare to be the best for the following day's seriousness at work. No caffeine after the second cup of coffee after breakfast before work. No strenuous activity the evening before. No smoking a cigarette in five years. No alcohol in *six* years. No weed or any other drug in seven years, and that was intermittent anyway if you don't count college.

But no. No good sleep. They say you sleep more than you think when you get a bad night's sleep, I'm begging that's the case, because I'm *tired.* It's doom. It's really hanging over me. I do everything right (!), *why does this happen to me?!*

Maybe it *was* the alcohol. The mostly-collegiate drugs, maybe…? The moving every few years, mostly involuntarily, growing up with a dead mother at age nine and jumping around the country back and forth to the same four cities. Signing on as a near-middle-aged adult to the stability of a family with kids, a dog, and a house, and suffering ongoing allergies to all three…

And, of course: the job. Aside from the traumatic nature of the business, it's at least partly Brenda, no question. I've given all the professional and mission-based soul that nearly twenty years of competitive, constant, motivated career work could give, including my sanity, into making that dump-of-an-agency the past dozen years into the best in the nation (!), and, after years as a fixer-upper elsewhere doing the same work. I've *believed* in what I was doing--what I'm still doing. The agency was under internal audit before I got there, with a Director forcibly-resigned in disgrace…they didn't know *what* the hell they were doing until I got there, AND, figured it all out for them, *yet again* as a self-starter. And then-Assistant-Director Brenda was there. I wish she was a tyrant instead of a nice-enough personality, 'cause at least then I'd be permitted my venom without any guilt whatsoever. But, she *is* a polite bully, she can't manage a staff, and, she's underhanded. She's only interested in "getting her name out there," as she said once in directing me to attend time-wasting meetings in the community (like the one set for this afternoon), and having other people do *her* work for her (also said once with matter-of-fact pride). She's a bureaucrat and a politician, and she has no business directing this agency if there's no meaningful public service component. The Director of a major municipal government agency has a second job, for god's sakes (!), teaching a community college course. She might be great as a community college teacher for a class…only.

And, she worked to pass me over for multiple promotions I was qualified for, earned, and should've been *immediately* appointed to, working to do so individually, and with Human Resources, in favor of lesser-qualified candidates. Underhandedly.

And, she's inexplicably, and continuously, backed by the Mayor's administration.

I guess she was on the scene first, before me…

***

5:23 a.m.

The clock radio is black, with red digital font, and a red dot is not on at the top right of the screen (or at the bottom-left of the time).

Wait, is the alarm on for a.m., and not p.m., on the cell phone? Yes, of course it is…(!)

Just get up already…

In the dark, I reach over the opposite way and grab my cellular flip-phone from my side-table. Lightning-quick, like a thirteen-year-old with a smartphone, I thumb the buttons on the 2005 keypad with one hand and scroll through the options to turn off the cell phone alarm set for 5:25 (a.m.!). I exhale sharply and with contempt, almost, but not quite, trying to be quiet about it. It's warm in the room.

Where's Tivoli? Good: he's not here staring at me waiting for me to get up so he can torture me, with his punching right-leg paw-claws, and his big head rubbing up and down the side of the bed to go outside, or play, or whatever it always is with him…

I feel for my glasses with my right hand and put them on and get out of bed, and Jenny deep-sleepingly rolls over the opposite way. In the dark, I walk over to my section of the chest of drawers, open a bottom drawer slowly to try to not make any noise, and I get out the pair of boxers I set on top of the others in the drawer, ready to color-code with the dress shirt and pants I ironed yesterday and will wear today.

(This may change if the tie that's up next in rotation matches the color of the underwear that *would've* come up in the rotation but was bypassed, just as the shirt & slacks had come up in their rotation and will have to be brought together by a tie. So, I may go back later and switch boxers, depending. This is *very* important…apparently…)

I walk over to the bedroom closet door and grab the previously-used bath towel hanging on the doorknob. The towel is on Day Two of the three-day use rotation. I go out of the barely-ajar bedroom door, step two feet across the hall, and I'm right into the adjacent bathroom. I put my boxers on top of the bathroom cabinet, then drape my bath towel on top of the open shower curtain rod. I close the shower liner and curtain, again wondering if they should be closed to begin with to avoid mildew growing on them, or, if they should be kept open to avoid mildew growing on the wall tile.

I turn the shower knobs under to the left, both with almost equal turnaround, and water immediately soft-screams out of the showerhead above. I push the shower head diagonally-up towards the wall tile to avoid the potential for water shooting out over the bathtub, repositioning it since everyone else in the house always aims it too close to the liner, and I take off my white undershirt and boxers worn since the previous day. They go on the floor, not the bathmat that's only been used a few times since the regular Saturday replacement. I take off my glasses and put them on the windowsill, then walk back over to the shower to check the water temperature. It's still cold. I check the left knob, and it seems like it's turned over to the left enough…better move it just a hair. It's taking longer to heat up today, especially considering it's summer--oh wait okay there we go (!). I then get in.

Instead of the dandruff shampoo (the name-brand and/or knock-off-brand that I've used for 25 years now), today I'm gonna use the salon non-dandruff nice stuff. Well, as nice as a national grocery store chain might carry. On clearance. But it *is* nice. And then conditioner. At least the conditioner is dandruff-version. If only the body wash was unscented... *Wait, is this Day Three for the towel, or Day Two?*

I get out of the shower after five minutes, which should have taken ten, but I'm just so damn tired (and defeated), and then I dry off, put on my new boxers, and then cotton-swab the right ear around-and-in the canal before doing the same for the left ear.

I've thrown the towel on the floor instead of placing it on the shower rod, so it must be Day Three.

I go back over to the bedroom and immediately kick on the light with the wall switch before throwing the towel and the finished boxers across the room into the hamper near the far window. With contempt. I do not look at Jenny sleeping in bed.

Opening curtain-covering wall-shelving, I grab my deodorant, looking up and away and probably cross-eyed with its use, and then I spray cologne in the air towards my chest, walking slightly away and then turning-twirly quickly to get my back after my front. I put on my house pants, which are former dress-casual slacks damaged by the office work desk on one leg and unraveling at the cuffs on both legs, and then I grab the manual razor and shaving cream before turning the bedroom light off and going back across to the bathroom, ignoring Jenny.

I shave my face and only elicit two small blood cuts: putting my index finger to my tongue, I then furiously back-and-forth-wipe the two red spots until they disappear, waiting a few seconds to see if they re-form. They don't, so it's then back over to the bedroom. I put away the razor and shaving cream and grab my keys from a wall-ledge, and the flip-phone from the side-table, and I stuff them in respective pants pockets.

"Jennifer, it's time to get up," I say with professional directness.

Slowly-stirring, Jenny mumbles at me lovingly, "Okay, sweetheart..."

Pause.

"I'm going down*stairs*, Jenny," I say like a parent.

"O*kay*, I'll be *down*...(!)" she forces, sleepily-frustrated.

And the routine continues. Always the routine.

Lumbering step-by-step down the loudly-creaking Victorian-era hardwood staircase in the silent house, left hand along the banister handrail, I make my way to the first-floor kitchen and start the extra-strong drip-brew coffee that only I drink in the household. I pull-tab open a can of Tivoli's wet dog food, grab one of the odd-shape-out forks from the kitchen utensil drawer, scrape out the can contents into the kitchen-floor bowl, and put the empty can on the counter. His water dish has two tablespoons of water left, so I'll refill that after I walk over to get a scoop of supplemental dog kibble while Jenny comes down and starts the cooking. I dump Tivoli's kibble in a dry-splash onto the food bowl, then I use tap water to swirl out a once-over cleaning of his water dish before filling it and placing it next to the food.

It's now on to the living room to contemptuously bring in the one used cereal bowl & spoon; one used fork & small plate; and, one used glass, all from Jenny's kids' use, which I know are going to be there before I even officially look. I don't turn on the living room chandelier light, just going by the light from the kitchen. (Oh, look, they added wrappers to…something (!), maybe role-playing game card packets, or…food (?), as well.) Tivoli's there in the living room, on his bed near the unused fireplace, head down flat, eyes wide-awake and watching. Nervous that he'll startle-up from his bed and want my attention, I proceed with a little frustrated caution getting the living room after-party devastation picked up for the kitchen, delicately exiting the room with a delicate scowl on my face.

I set the breakfast table in the dining room for all four of us, a few trips back and forth, and then I sit on a stool in the kitchen, looking down towards the floor at the other side of the refrigerator, away from Jenny, again defeated, and halfway seeking Jenny's attention. Awake-but-not-awake, and waiting, while Jenny keeps cooking today's eggs and pancakes with a side of raspberries in small ramekins.

And Jenny knows what's coming. And she's not gonna say anything. Yet. We both know what's coming, so, Jenny looks like she's just gonna get it over with.

"Did you sleep, honey?"

"No, of *course* not--"

"--*Okay*, jeez…(!)"

"This is the busiest day I'll have had in months, and of *course* I didn't sleep…"

"Why don't you *just* call in sick, Alex…"

"I *can't*, Jenny. If this were any-other-day, I would, but I *can't*, I have too much going on today, *and* tonight…"

"Maybe you need to get counselinnnnng, or use the Employee *Assistance Programmmmm*, or go to the doctor *again*, or--"

"I don't want to hear it," I say firmly.

"Listen to the way you're speaking to me, I don't talk to you like this," Jenny defends with a little attack. "Maybe you should just go ahead and get an apartment, and be alone, and live your life back that way again, with no kids, no dog, no people to frustrate you…"

I don't respond, not giving an inch with any emotion but rationally-aware of the shame I *should* feel from what she's saying.

There's a moment of silence.

Aaaaand here comes Tivoli. A hundred pounds (well, 92 pounds, on-the-record, but probably heavier now) and scraping his legs in a senior-dog walk across the house hardwood floors, stopping to hind-leg-scratch his neck where the collar is fastened **clink-clink-clink-clink-clink**, then stretching both his hind legs while yawning, before then briefly wagging his big tail looking at me and Jenny in the kitchen with the smile of a toddler. He then slowly, slower than all of time, lumbers while breathing heavily to the side dining room, oafishly does almost two full circles-of-a-walk around, and then collapses down in a huge exhale huff, front legs forward, to watch the action in the kitchen, at attention. Waiting.

The kitchen assembly-line routine just keeps on going. Breakfast goes just a minute too long in the preparation stage for me, and Jenny's yelling upstairs for younger child Corinne is too much for me, too. Older child Michael storms down, inadvertently, after one call, as he always does. He heads for the downstairs restroom after reaching the bottom of the stairs near the front door, silently-singing the opening theme song of a British science fiction TV show, words indecipherable, but it seems like there might be a melody there.

And Corinne's not coming down, like she always doesn't. The three of us downstairs come together to go ahead and start eating at the dining room table in our usual, reserved spots, full plate and empty seat where Corinne usually sits when lightning strikes.

After a few minutes of our silence, Jenny gets up from the dining room table ("*Oh jeeeeez…!*" she snaps) and marches upstairs, yelling Corinne's full name two more times.

"Corinne: last call!"

Silence.

I hear Jenny try Corinne's bedroom doorknob, and the big resistance-clunk means that it's locked, of course, which is against Jenny's house rules, and Corinne knows that. Jenny knocks loudly and yells again, and "…*okay*…" is acutely, but sleepishly, projected from behind the bedroom door. Jenny comes back downstairs.

We three continue eating in silence this morning, me re-reading the Sunday local newspaper national professional sports statistics, Jenny looking through a Victorian-era museum jewelry collection library book, Michael surfing the online content inside his head in tandem with his focus on his meal. Michael scarfs his food down efficiently and then excuses himself in silence by taking his plate with his fork to the kitchen (leaving his empty juice glass), humming his way back up the stairs. After he's gone, I then see my chance to sort some of the impending drama out.

"So Jenny, can you text Michael today and make sure he walks Tivoli by the time I get home for dinner, I gotta eat *real* quick and then head back out. I don't wanna have t'come home and Tivoli is all--"

"*Yes*, we already talked about that…don't worry, I'll remind him," Jenny says defensively before a pause. "And, just *tell* him to walk him if he hasn't done it, Alex."

I roll my eyes, exhaling a little, yet again. Breakfast is then pretty much done.

The kitchen is cleaned up, with Jenny doing the washing off and me doing the item-shuttling back and forth from the dining room to the counters and the dishwasher. One more cup of coffee poured for me while Jenny gives Tivoli his daily egg in his dish, causing him to explode up loudly from the dining room hardwood floor and lumber over to engulf it before then just licking his wet dog food. Jenny starts the dishwasher, we wait for Tivoli to stop his morning snack, and then she puts his leash onto his collar while I get my keys ready. Jenny wrangles Tivoli while putting her light jacket on. Michael, carrying a bath towel, tries, but fails, to collide with us on his way to the bottom of the adjacent-to-the-front-door stairs in making his way to the downstairs bathroom shower as I open the front door into room-temperature sticky humidity outside. Me, Jenny, and Tivoli makes three to exit the house.

Tivoli pulls Jenny down the brownstone-ish front steps of the house in stuttered double-time, before trotting to the closest dirt patch segment in the sidewalk along the house. I bring up the rear by looking out and around the street, seeing that there's no troublesome activity at the dead-end cul-de-sac gate closing off the end of our urban street. I then lock the front door, pulling the door quickly twice to check its closure with two resistant thuds. It's now mostly-light outside, and I again look around the area for suspects as I single-step down our house concrete stairs. A Transit Authority bus air-blasts before rumbling and roaring on like a lion from a stop on the other side of the gated curb. Way down the block towards West Ormsby Avenue, a guy is walking along our side of the street on the sidewalk towards us, and he looks like a regular, but I'm not taking any chances and I'm in no mood this morning.

"Let's cross the *street*, Tivoli," I say firmly like a parent to the dog, as a not-so-subtle cue to Jenny.

"Come on, Tivoli," Jenny lovingly says to her third child. He starts to trot over across the street but then quickly yanks and pulls Jenny back to the curb: he's found some of the partially-breaded fried chicken bones that intermittently litter the surrounding neighborhood streets in the vicinity of a dollar-chicken-piece fast food start-up. Jenny yanks him away with a "Tivoli-no!" and we cross the road and get to the other side, in between the lines of parallel-parked vehicles.

We walk slowly down the block, Tivoli walking a shimmy much peppier than his otherwise-senior retirement days would have anyone not in our family to believe. It's a patchwork partnership on the walk on who leads who, with all three of us giving equal direction for us throughout the dog-walk trek. We watch as the 7:00 a.m. city-government-tattooed compact car turns onto our residential street and drives our way towards the no-parking-anytime section of the block back down by our house, where only two vehicles are parked in violation of the posted signs this morning. Crickets, mockingbirds, blue jays, pigeons, and cardinals aren't sleeping in the summer humidity saturating the tree-lined, small-yard 1800s mini-mansions along the block.

We then reach the grassy No-U-Turn-sign section of the intersecting corner forming one corner of Tivoli's neighborhood cage: our street and West Ormsby Avenue. Tivoli squats down to do his business, thankfully respecting our forced routine on him this morning and not saving it for when we both are on our way out the door for work. Jenny uses a small leash bag to clean up while Tivoli trots away three steps before then standing stoic and proud to the neighborhood, only kicking his hind legs through the grass one time each. I meanwhile keep watch on all sides of the streets. Tivoli then eagerly tries to lead us away down West Ormsby the opposite way beyond the corner boundary, but "*Nooooo…!*" from me and Jenny, or, really, Jenny's leash, brings him our way to cross the street the other way so we can walk back along our street back towards the house.

Still walking slowly in silence from conversation, I finally give in.

"I'm sorry I feel so awful, Jenny."

"Al*right…*"

"If I can just get through today, I don't have *any more* meetings in the evenings for the month, and I can rest in the evenings, and I can call in sick if I have to, if I don't sleep again, whatever…"

"O*kay*, Alex…"

I pause.

"I can't wait 'till we're on a plane together again…"

I lean over to give Jenny a kiss, and she puckers up with instant, receptive automation but her eyes look away from mine. After what might be a make-up, we move on.

Walking towards the house, Tivoli looks up and sees only that the giant *clock radio is black, with red digital font, and a red dot is not on at the top right of the screen (or at the bottom-left of the time)*. Then, in defiance, he does *not* look at the clock.

Jenny forcibly butts the side rump of her body against Tivoli's stone butt in order to push him towards his impending doom of back-in-the-house. But, he's giving even more resistance than normal. Since I refuse to wait around in my frustration, slight make-up with Jenny or not, I go ahead up the stone house steps, unlock the front door, enter and then close the door behind me. I head straight past the hissing shower coming from behind the closed downstairs bathroom door, into the kitchen to get my cooling cup of coffee, and I hear Jenny emerge behind me from the front door creek with a maternal and peppy "Come on…!" followed by a scratchy **clink-clink-clink-clink-clink.**

I drink another gulp from the coffee cup and then Jenny and I hike the steep hardwood stairs back up to the second floor, Tivoli lapping up his water dish in his unchained freedom and likely to scout the kitchen, try the locked garbage can, and then admit defeat by pawing at the remaining kibble in his bowl. Both of us heading for our bedroom, Michael's bedroom door is wide open with the light on and National Public Radio talking about something to do with the Texas legislature.

Jenny gets into bed again and lays as if to go back to sleep. I pitch my flip-phone and keys onto the mirrored bedroom wall ledge, I get on the bed with my netbook that I bought off of Corinne about a year ago after her birthday laptop upgrade, and I look at e-mail and bank accounts; news of police-involved shootings and protests in other cities on a major news website; and then, inadvertently, the posts and comments for the incidents on social media, and, quickly, one national "expert" commentary opinion.

Hmmm…

I debate and judge quickly the news events in my head. Another friend or two is likely going to be a dropped-casualty of mine on social media in the current culture wars.

Since I'm again not paying attention to Jenny before we go to work, the result is rekindled tension, because we both know that she wants me to cuddle up with her for a few minutes. I consider it, realize that I *should* do it…but I don't. I'm too tired and wired for the workday and the workweek ahead.

Jenny then exhales in frustration and gets up, goes around and out the bedroom door, proceeding on down the short hallway to Corinne's bedroom door.

Knock-two-three-four-five. "Corinne…get--" *knock-two-three-four-five* "--up!"

"Okay…"

"Open the door, Cori…Cor…! Open the door!"

"Okay--I-said okay…!" I hear Corinne's door unlock, but not open up. I then hear Jenny open the door and I know that Corinne's back in bed, magically teleporting back from unlocking her door as if she'd never gotten out of it.

"You have *got* to get up when I ask you to," Jenny instructs. "We're *all* done with breakfast and yours is down there getting cold, Corinne. Get up! Get…up. Get up (!)"

Silence.

"Corinne: Get! Up!"

"Look at the way you're yelling at me (!), you're yelling at me like I'm a *dog*," Corinne pleads, only a second before her just-like-her-mother defense-mode kicks in within her to retaliate. "That's the way you *treat* me, Jenny!"

Uh, nooooo, even stubborn, cantankerous Tivoli would've gotten up after no more than three calls for him.

Take. Away. Her. Electronics. For god's sake, Jenny…

Calmer, and not too surprisingly, Jenny tries a different approach than the *Corinne, We've Talked About This* logic that I know won't work.

"Do you have band practice after school this afternoon?"

Pause.

"No," I hear in a muffled rustle, "but I have Quick Recall practice."

"Okay, that's right. And Michelle's mom is still taking you home, right?"

"Yeah…well," with more rustle, "I think so," Corinne exhales. "I don't know. I'll text her."

"Okay, let me know as soon as you can, I have meetings this morning and if I need to pick you up, I just need to coordinate everything, I don't want you taking Transit Authority to get home today. Go ahead, and go downstairs, and eat breakfast, Cori. Cori-Cor. C*orinnieeeee…*"

I then just roll my eyes with a log off of the netbook with a few clicks and a snap-of-a-fold shut. I get up from the bed, internally shaking my head as I go back to the bathroom to brush my teeth, use mouthwash, walk back over to the bedroom to take my asthma/allergy medication, use an eyeglasses cleaning cloth, and then start to get dressed. I hear Michael come back upstairs, his song briefly dialed up loudly for one or two extended-word high-notes hissing during all his humming, and then he's back in his bedroom, door closed, National Public Radio apparently now talking about Asian shrimp farming's impact on the world economy. After I leave the restroom to use the laundry room the next room over as a partial dressing room, Jenny sneaks into the shower.

The rotational dress shirt is on, the rotational tie is on, the rotational dress pants are on, and I forego a suit vest since it may clash with today's random color scheme. And because it's allegedly going to be sweltering today. I look in the mirror four hundred twenty-six thousand times to make sure that the outfit I ironed is coordinated, looking in mirrors in the bedroom and the bathroom across the hall both, to see the contrast in two different lighting scales. The tie doesn't quite work, so it goes back on top of the tie pile in exchange for the next one in line. Thankfully and atypically, it just takes the second tie to match the shirt while adequately bringing together the dress pants. (I *think*. I'm probably dressed nerd-chic but more nerd.) There's at least comfort and security that the rotational handkerchief today is white, so it goes with anything.

Just the act of trying to coordinate an outfit has wiped me out in exhaustedness. I collapse seated back onto the bed, back onto the netbook to just stare, and to hope for some miraculous rejuvenation. While Jenny still showers, I hear stirring and eventual emergence of a younger teenage child from her bedroom. Corinne stumbles down the hardwood floor stairs to enjoy her cold pancakes and orange juice, leaving half of her eggs and all of her dishes in the dining room for us to clear for her, of course.

I lay there cynical of having strength to get through the twelve-hour day, zoned out. I continue to hear Michael continuing his routine like clockwork, as he goes downstairs to pack a lunch, drink a small glass of water, and then head out the front door, without a goodbye to anyone, to walk his three-quarters-of-a-mile to his urban high school. Tivoli then fights his old legs up the stairs panting, and he pokes his head into our bedroom from the slightly-ajar door, standing there. I don't make eye contact. Tivoli then snorts and pushes through the door to wobble his bad hind legs inside the room, sneezing twice in frustration for reasons only he understands, before he walks in barely a circle slowly, slowly, slowly, slowly, four times, collapsing down with front legs forward down on the bedroom carpet instead of the hardwood…panting, and looking towards the wall.

Ultimately, after Jenny gets out of the shower and dressed, I get up and grab the flip-phone, I grab my keys, I grab my wallet, I sling my black work bag over my shoulder after sprinkling it with a day-and-a-half's worth of cough drops…I go downstairs, I grab a plastic container and fill it with a plastic microwave burrito, I grab an apple, and I'm out the door after a formal, routine see-ya to Corinne and a bye-I-love-you hollering to Jenny up the stairs. And, a weapons-check of my pockets: phone, keys, wallet, handkerchief. Front door locked, me locked-and-loaded-and-disoriented.

I stand on the front porch and again look around the streets, and no one appears to be threatening. In fact, no one appears to be around at all, which is odd for such an urban, fair-weathered Monday. Even the #25 Transit Authority bus waiting at the stop a couple dozen yards away at the cul-de-sac gated street seems to be questioning the lack of pedway traffic. I still look around as I make my way to my car parallel-parked across the street.

I jump in and start my compact car while simultaneously locking the door and putting on the seat belt in one almost-graceful motion. With the factory-installed compact disc player turned off, I immediately turn the cd player on and click the buttons to try to forward from the middle of a song that *was* playing, into the next one on the album: thankfully, it's a great track on the rotational queue, great since I won't have to start rationalizing skipping tracks on the disc in my internal obsession of finishing things that've been started. And I turn the music up to a tinnitus-level volume, but not exactly full blast. The wall of chaotic sound can be embryonic comfort for the commute on days like today, and it may be the only way I can get through this day, ringing ears or not.

And I drive the increasingly-urban streets a short ten minutes and 1.2 miles to the eleven-story office building downtown on West Chestnut Street, consumed in the tornado-vortex of loud music and competitive road-rage inside, despite no traffic to really speak of, and before calming down a brief moment at my destination: I wave once to the accepting nod of the attached parking garage attendant, Walter, who's been there for about six months now, every weekday morning. He must be able to hear the swirling, echoing music going on inside the car, and I try to turn it down sometimes, but today the volume stays up. It may be my only life support since the coffee and familial support are not at hand during the workday. I need carry-over music radiation for my being.

I drive up into the cave-of-a-structure attached to the office building, steeply ascending the antique-paved ramp in my eleven-year-old vessel, immediately veering to the second level to the right. A few cars are already peppered about spaces, but they don't appear occupied, so I finish listening to the song in my unassigned, usual garage parking space that's again open, *just* intoxicated enough with the angst, the drive, and the professional-enhancement challenge that the previous two-song minutes gave me on the way into work.

Sometimes, the music is more raw energy of chaos, sometimes it's tinny-electronic, sometimes it's dangerously-close to being lyric-based; this morning, however, it sounds of a giant supernatural dog wailing in a deafening, dark thunderstorm, a moaning-roar howl rather than a primal rage against the world that's kicking-and-screaming-and-pounding-and shrieking. I beggingly need energy, and I hope the adrenaline has increased within from the music for the day, instead of sapping it from me, as I fear it well might have. I'm in cautious-warrior mode today, and I hope this doesn't help channel an animal out of me any more than necessary to continue being the best *ever* at my job description, even if I *am* on death's door. Maybe I should go back to listening to sports radio to provide my brain with direct, corporate-style communication skills, eliminating the abstractness of music, for the preparatory commute into downtown.

I walk down the ramp of the garage and go to pay Walter in his booth. I gave up on a monthly parking discount a year or so ago after starting my grievances against the Mayor's administration: if I get fired today, then I'm not out the rest of the money for the month. One day at a time, just-for-today. One hour at a time, a few *minutes* at a time, because, right now, it's 7:48 a.m.

"*Well*, good *morning*, Mr. Alex, how are ya today…?"

"I'm fine, how are you, Walter?"

"*Oh*, I'm fair-to-middlin'! haha…Did you have a good weekend this time, did ya--did ya get ya sleep you was lookin' for?"

I hand him cash, a combination of bills and coins.

"Yeah, it was alright, I didn't get enough sleep and I have a *huge* day today…"

"Oh yeah? Well…Sure hope it goes okay for ya, then. Uh-huh …yeah …"

"Sorry I have to give you some quarters with the dollar bills this morning…"

"Aw, well, you know, that's *okay*, that'll spend, too…haha!"

I slightly laugh and wait for him to lead the conversation today, as I almost always do. But even more so this morning since I'm standing there at attention visibly tired.

"It's gonna be a hot one to*day*, they say…"

"Yeah, no doubt."

"Talkin' 'bout, the whole week's gonna be hot, ain't it…"

"Yeah, probab*ly*..."

"Yeah...well...Did you see there, on the news, they was talkin' 'bout another police officer, gettin' shot, all that...?"

"Yeah..."

"This time in, uh...uh...'round...'round Philadelphia?"

"Yeah..."

"Is' a shame, ain't it?"

"Yeah..."

"Yeah...well...I mean, these *young* people, I mean, they have no--they just don't wanna...you know, get along, you know, live in peace, with people, like they used to...I tell ya, it's gettin' so it's to be dangerous, where people just wanna get together and fight all the time. I know *I* used to be a little wilder in *my* younger days, but I know that God wants us to live in peace, *you* know...live--live without bringing up all this stuff."

"Yeah..."

"Violence, and all that. You know, my son, he--he lives up there in Chicago, and they're havin' a *terrible* time up there right now. He works with attorneys up there, and I call him, and I tell him, you know, 'Be careful,' you know, with all that's goin' on. You know, this, this Ferguson, and Philadelphia...uh, Chicago. And people, tryin' to make it all out to be a race thing, with all this riots, and destroying things, and really it just all needs to go away, and just...just, try to get *along*, you know?"

"Yeah..."

"Get *along* with people, *you* know...I'm 'bout to hit seven-three years old, and I'm just lookin' to maybe...retire, and all that, and maybe move back out to the country, back to where I used-to live, when I was younger, growin' up. I mean, *I've* been discriminated against, treated unfairly sometimes, but most of these--those big-time racists, those kinda people, they died years *ago*, you know...they're all dead. Most of 'em, at least..."

"Yeah..."

"Well...well, o*kay* then...well...you're lookin' sharp to*day*, I know you're busy today, haha, so, I'll let ya go, let ya be, then. You have lots 'a meetings today, or...?"

"Yeah, I got a lotta meetings inside *and* outside the office today," I say with a single slight-laugh. "It's gonna be brutal, non-stop today. But I'll get through it, I guess…"

"Yeah, well, yeah, that's all we *can* do, you know, is…is keep prayin', and keep goin' on, I suppose. You know, they don't know how lucky they *are*, have you work hard, keepin' on comin' in, and doin' the job, making things go, workin' it all out. Just like my bosses, they keep talkin' 'bout rollin' back *my* hours, givin' 'em to the lady who come in, in the afternoons here. I wanna feel good for her gettin' all those hours, all her hours, but she comes in late half the time, half the time sayin' it's the bus letting her off at the wrong stop, makin' her--pickin' her up late, all that kinda stuff. And she smokes all them cigarettes and leaves 'em all over the ground, like right out here, every day, and I come in, in the mornings, and I have to sweep 'em up instead 'a her doin' it. I worked…30 years, at the truck plant here, my supervisors there, they never woulda put up with that kinda stuff. We all had to show up on time, we had to…had ta…you know, *work*, you know, get the job done…"

"Yeah…"

"So, I just don't understand it. She lets her boyfriend, man-friend, he hangs out here, and sometimes he gets here before she does."

"Yeah…"

I struggle to hide a yawn with my pink eyes half-closed and my eyelids warm.

There's a pause.

Walter can probably tell that I'm struggling with the empathy of conversation.

"Well, all *right*…well, I hope--hope ya have a good day now, there, Mr. Alex…"

"Thanks, Walter--"

"--Don't work too hard--"

"--Yeah, you too, Walter."

"--Try to--try to take it *easy* now…!"

"Yeah, you too, man…!" I manage to pep-out, haggardly.

We both smile and slightly-laugh, slightly-awkwardly, in completing our morning routine. It might be the healthiest two-way respect I'll have with someone all day.

I now march into the office building, one hand holding the black work bag strap already wrinkling my ironed dress shirt at the shoulder, and I lead with my caffeinated head on auto-pilot. The middle of the three elevator doors is open with no light on, but the elevator car to the right is open for business, just waiting. I walk in, I hit the "5" button with a closed index finger, and I look out onto the lobby and the street in a pose, hoping no one tries to make a mad dash to get on with me. The elevator door slowly, slowly closes, and despite no one around, I act like I don't see anyone coming on board. Taking the elevator to the fifth floor means looking again at the 2013 inspection certificate…<*ding!*>…the elevator doors open.

As the rickety curtains open, I stand there looking ahead with a tired, defeated, sarcastic scowl on my face: I'm right in front of the secure, office entrance front door of the Louisville Metro Civil Relations Commission.

He remembers his mother around her early mid-thirties, driving him and his younger brother to their separate kindergarten and preschool in the morning. He thinks it was Lexington, Kentucky, 1978 or so, and the song on the radio sounded like a pied piper calling for all the little children to follow: first, the charmer laid the groundwork with a repetitive piano; next, marching drums to follow the vocal call; and, finally, some flute notes, three steps up and then one step down, to mesmerize the carpool.

He gets the sense that contemporary music taste was important to her. It was she who introduced him to the latest hits, buying him 33⅓, 45, and 72 RPM vinyl records of pop-rock and movie, television, and book tie-ins. He played most of the records over and over, and he couldn't get enough of the sounds: retro-1950s teen Americana romance film soundtracks, disco film soundtracks, cartoon-animal disco music parodies, and kids' music book companions to animated halfling fantasy-novel television-movie adaptations. He's guessing that he's his mother's son in that way, though he actively stopped listening to most new music for a period of at least a dozen years following his mid-twenties…

The number one song according to some of the United States music charts the week of his birth had both a radio cut and an epic, eleven-plus-minute deep cut: lyrics and music evoking a slice of urban social ill of inner-city family-structure destruction. Many of the real-life versions of the story would enter his office daily to file complaints after termination from employment; bans from places of public accommodation; disputes with neighbors elevating to dangerous levels of hate; and, evictions from rental housing. Not that he is, or at least should be, casting any stone: he's certainly been no stranger to chasing women and drinking.

CHAPTER TWO

The front receptionist area lobby lights are on, so Janice and/or Roberta must already be in there.

Scanning my Louisville Metro Government identification card, <*bleep-bleep*>, I open the door <*dong!*> and Janice is walking behind the counter to the lobby front desk reception area, coffee mug in hand, ready to tend bar for staff and the public.

"*Morn*ing, Alex!"

"Morning, Janice…!" I muster with half-legitimate enthusiasm through my one-quarter-closed eyes.

"How's ya weekend…?" she asks pleasantly, placing a sheet of paper on the counter bar near the wall cross-section.

"It was alright," I already start descending.

"D'you do anything special, or--"

"No, not really, just rested and chores again."

I take the chained inkpen on the counter bar between us and start to try to write, but swirling it in a patch near my name won't make the ink come out. I then grab a loose ink pen next to it there and start writing with success my break times for the day, my lunch hour, and my out-of-office appointments on the staff timesheet Janice just placed down.

"Well, whatcha got goin' on this morning?"

Janice can tell I'm tired and wound up, and she grabs an ink pen and a notepad.

"Today is gonna be *brutal…*uh," I sigh, "Okay: Ms. Tamara Johnson, a Complainant on a sexual harassment case, should be coming by about 8:30 in a few minutes, and then Scott, and Liz, are scheduled to be here later this morning, but you know how they are--"

Already smiling and nodding, Janice affirms. "Yep…"

"--and then I'll go to lunch at the regular time, then I have to give the presentation at the Regional Housing Center at 1:30--"

"Oh, okay, that's right…"

"--so, I'll take the city vehicle, and then I'm on intake starting at 3:30, hopefully I'm not late but I should be here by then. They have a board meeting scheduled for after the presentation at the meeting, so they won't wanna hear me drone on for too long…"

"Okay…"

"If we get a walk-in during intake and it's housing or a hate crime, and I'm not here, just go ahead and give it to Agnes for review…"

"Okay, *you* betcha--"

"And tonight is the Disability Action Network meeting at the university, so it's gonna be a rough one."

"Oh okay, you got that goin' on again? All righty…" Sipping coffee from a United States Department of Housing & Urban Development mug, Janice finishes writing her notes. "So, Roberta's not in yet…she--"

<bleep bleep>

<dong!>

Not Roberta, it's Ron, a Minority Contract Analyst. Janice and I say good morning as Ron politely-smiles a silent hello, but he doesn't stop heading to the first office lair down the hallway, to the east of the receptionist desk, that he probably claimed with the Civil Relations Commission during the agency move to the current location about sixteen years ago. Almost, but not quite, out of earshot to him, Janice tries to give me the latest as he makes his left into his office and shuts his door.

"Oooooh, you missed it! Friday, Roberta was up at the switchboard, and the Budget Division was calling for Ron, and Agnes, and then--"

<bleep bleep>

Janice stops the gossip while looking through the door side-windows, and I turn to look, and we're waiting…looking…at the front door.

<bleep bleep>

locked door struggle thump

<bleep bleep>

locked door struggle thud

<bleep bleep>

Janice grabs a remote control for the front door, aims, and pushes a button.

<bleep bleep>

<dong! thud>

Success, at last, ungracefully brings in Sherry, the Commission's other Minority Contract Analyst, who immediately looks to take the frustration out on me and Janice…by half-laughing and exaggerated-fake-stumbling over her encumbered office plant, lunch bag, purse, and garment bag.

"*See*…(!)" she laughs.

I smile and give a half-laugh and Janice full-laughs, taking the bait that Sherry's throwing out there.

"Sherry," Janice starts. "Sherry-baby…(!)…want some coffee, Sherry?…Sherry…(?)…" Looking at me in the eyes, she points out, "That's *Sher*-ry…*Shar-ruh*…*Shurrr*…!" Janice continues and holds her HUD mug perfectly-surrounded in both hands, looking more comfortable than any Director at the Civil Relations Commission has ever looked. Or currently is.

Sherry smiles in her pleasantry to me and her joking, ignoring rejection of Janice.

"Did you have a good weekend?"

"Heh, it was alright…"

"How's Jenny, how're the kids?"

"Never--"

"*--better*!" Sherry exclaims out sarcastically in unison with me.

I smile and slightly-laugh in my humbling say, "Yeah, here we go again…"

Sherry laughs once and then quickly asks, "You have a busy day today?"

"Yeah, it's gonna be a looooong day…" I exhale. I struggle to hide a yawn with my pink eyes half-closed and my eyelids warm.

"Tired already, huh?" Sherry says. "Testers coming in?"

"Yeah, Scott and Liz are supposed to be here this morning. Then I gotta give a presentation at the Regional Housing Center on fair housing, then back here for intake, and the Disability Action Network meeting tonight. And a Complainant's coming in here around 8:30…"

"What kinda case?"

"It's a housing sexual harassment case. I dunno about this one, the Respondent said that she was late paying her rent four times in the past year-and-a-half, she had an unauthorized occupant in the house, all that, but the Respondent's not responding to requests for additional information or a site-visit for the investigation. We'll see, the Complainant is real nice…? We'll see what witnesses she has, I guess."

"Okay, then…" Sherry starts up. "*Alex* is on the case…"

"*Heeeee*'s on it…" Janice quips.

I immediately start smiling and provide a sarcastic smile smirk.

"What happened with the one case?" Sherry seriously asks. "The one, I forget: the boyfriend, she and the boyfriend were trying to rent the house…?"

"Oh, yeah, the--the *Cartwright* case…yeah, that case is still Probable Caused with the County Attorney, in litigation…Laura Beck told me that a hearing's scheduled for next month. That one makes me nervous, 'cause it was definitely Probable Cause, no question, the Complainant had all these text messages showing her conversations with the white Respondent landlord, about how he offered to rent a house to her, and then, allegedly, after he saw that her boyfriend was African-American, all of a sudden the property wasn't available anymore…the Respondent allegedly made racial statements to her about the neighborhood when showing her the house originally by herself, then, when showing it to both of them, her boyfriend brought along this white maintenance guy friend and the white maintenance guy told me in an interview that the white Respondent landlord was racist by ignoring the African-American boyfriend, only speaking to *him*, the maintenance guy, when the boyfriend was asking the Respondent questions, that kinda stuff…"

"Uh-huh…" Sherry politely says.

"What makes me nervous is the Respondent first offered to rent to her a *different* property before this subject property, but the Complainant allegedly wasn't qualified because of her income, so then he offers her that second house and said it was being renovated, and that then the rehab for it cost more than he thought…so, I worry that the hearing officer will latch onto language under the ordinance about requiring a Complainant to show an ability to pay, trumping a refusal-to-rent discrimination issue."

"Uh-huh…"

"I mean, don't get me wrong, it *totally* shoulda been Probable Caused," I continue methodically, "she has three witnesses including herself, the second house was *available* then *not*, right after the boyfriend was first seen, and the Respondent allegedly sold that subject house four days after receiving the HUD complaint notification. So, I mean, I think it's about a 70% victory for the Complainant. We'll see though, they may still conciliate the case and then that's the end of *that*, anyway."

"Uh-huh…"

"I just wanna see it litigated, create case law, from a selfish standpoint. I can't *stand* conciliation agreements…(!)"

"Yeah…well…good luck (!)," Sherry smiles.

Janice smiles, too, and then a pause, before she again looks back up, this time to Sherry. "Oooooh, Sherry, you missed it…!"

I look at the reception area wall clock, 8:06 a.m., and start to hurry on down the hallway to my right of the receptionist bar, unfortunately seeing the Mayor's picture prominently posted on the wall next to the mailroom near the sign-in/sign-out sheet. It almost ruins the good morning greetings I've had.

"…Budget was calling for Ron, and they couldn't get…Agnes… Brenda," I hear from Janice as I walk in focusing trying to get to my office. Labyrinthine hallways on this side of Civil Relations Commission offices, the east wing, are better for staff gossip support than on the other, more-open, west wing side, but you can still eavesdrop, intentionally or not, on what's going on at the front desk if your office is down the main hallway like mine and Ron's. Halfway down the long hall, I reach my office after passing Ron and Sherry's, and I flip on the light switch in almost the same motion as unslinging my black work bag down onto my office desk.

I turn on my office computer, see that there's no voicemail-message indicator diamond lit up on the office desk telephone next to it, I dig into my deep-drawer to the lower right in my wrap-around hardwood office desk to dig out an empty, used, slightly-crinkled plastic water bottle, and then I proceed to take my lunch from my work bag. The office kitchenette further down the east wing hallway and around two jagged bends, I lumber while flicking on light switches along the way. I put my plastic-container lunch in the telephone-book-magnet-adorned refrigerator and then walk further past vacant workstations, around to the end of the east wing, flicking on light switches along the way.

Laying on the lower tray of the dual copier/facsimile behemoth are about 30 printed pages face down, which I pick up and review briefly and interpret were printed out by Bonnie, the other, part-time-reduced-budget fair housing Investigator. I then place them back to where they were, face down. On the top tray, face up, is a one-page fax advertising palm trees and a toll-free telephone number for the excitement of a Caribbean cruise, only $399 for "*Three nights! Air Included!! (*restrictions may apply)*"

(!!!!!!!!!1!!)

I grab the party-fax off the machine and carry it with me back to the sink in the kitchenette. I fill the crinkly water bottle with the morning's potion from the tap, and at least the water coming out today is cloudy-white and not corrosive-brown. I walk back down around the jagged turns and down the long hallway past my office towards the front, past Sherry dumping things in her office on the right, and then go into the mailroom on the right located just before the front receptionist bar area. I shove the fax in the mailbox marked "Director." Then, I check the mailroom's gigantic printer/copier queue for any stored electronic documents I forgot to release from print-hold on Friday, following the prompts and entering in my debit card pin number code which doubles for my access code. No print jobs waiting. I then walk back towards my office, passing Sherry opening and closing office desk drawers loudly, and I sit in my oversized office chair taking a swig of the crinkled bottle water refill.

I look at the computer monitor with confidence and more energy than I thought imaginable just an hour ago, thanks in large part to more than a decade's work familiarity in the same small office location, though still not what I'd imagine I'd feel like at 100% like I was, say, ten fiscal years ago. My username is already saved in the city government system login, so I enter in my password of the title of the most recent great movie I've seen, mixed with a few symbol characters, and much of my world of civil rights, mainly fair housing, with Louisville Metro Government, and on behalf of the federal government, begins again.

I start opening my e-mail program. While it loads, I immediately check for updates on my computer's document viewer program and updates to the general operating system, the latter eliciting Louisville Metro Government's only-administrators-have-privileges message…once in awhile, the administrator screening is offline. Looks like only three e-mails have come in since Friday: two from a national fair housing advocacy listserv, both consisting of nationwide non-profit congratulations for a $35,000 settlement on an emotional-support-animal housing discrimination complaint case in Massachusetts; the other a "have-a-good-weekend-but-hey-how-are-your-dad-and-brother" e-mail from a friend in metro Toronto I met playing online games about a dozen years ago. I delete all three e-mails after quick scans, but leave the e-mail program open for "instant messaging." My true instant messaging account with the city has a permanent "busy" designation so I can just not deal with the rapid-fire distraction of all two users who might use it in the entire 6,000+ workforce. I also notice that MyCallNavigator, an online program to process voicemail messages through the computer system, is not loading and looks to be offline again.

<bleep bleep>

<dong!>

I hear the usual staff arrivals out at the front receptionist desk, this time the second wave that arrives each day technically-late, but just at, or after, Louisville Metro Government's grace period. Chad, the Civil Relations Commission's newest Investigator for employment and public accommodations; Julia, the new city police Ombudsman; and Ronita, the Commission's Office Manager, are here. Chad starts scuttling down the hallway my way, walks past my office, and, since today is apparently an odd-numbered day, he doesn't say "morning" when passing.

I pull up my word processing program, click-ly scan through my various file folders to "*Johnson v. FMD*," and pull up the file "*Johnson v. FMD recom memo*" before scanning through "Complainant Allegations" and "Respondent Complaint Response" summaries I typed up a few weeks ago.

"Good morning, Janice! Good morning, Sherry!"

Here comes Julia…

I hear a collective "morning" response much lower in volume than the always-animated Julia.

Her footsteps are approaching…

"Good *morn*ing, Alex! How are *you* this morning…?!" she loudly asks while walking past, ready to load the east wing kitchenette refrigerator with bags of lunch and snacks and beverages.

"I'm fine, morning, Julia…" I struggle to pleasantly say. Possibly no one's ever been more kindly giving to me at the Civil Relations Commission than Julia, which is why I'm *almost* fighting to overcome illegitimate hellos to her today in response to her daily, morning cheerleading.

I struggle up from my chair to go over to the 1970s-era small file cabinet inside my office in order to get Scott and Liz their testing assignments ready, but then briefly look out the office window down to the street. There's early-morning downtown calm down there on West Chestnut Street. I then get back focused and grab two of the prepared stacks of housing discrimination tests resting on top of the file cabinet, placing them in my cheap plastic inbox-outbox tray on top of my office desk. I pull up my world wide web browser and check for updates (<*administrator-blocked*>) and then quickly type in "*louisvillemarketplace.org*" before then navigating on to the "Real Estate" search section. I'm about to type in keywords but then hear **locked door struggle** at the front door, a pause, and then <*ding…tone…*>.

It's 8:18 a.m., according to the computer clock. I don't hear a sound at the front desk, so Janice & Sherry must be back in Janice's office fueling up on communal coffee and/or chatting the weekend away.

Pause…silence.

<*ding…tone…*>

I quickly grab two cough drops, dropping one in my front dress shirt pocket and put the other in my front right dress pants pocket. I grab an ink pen for the ready, like a weapon, and sit there with my ear ready.

Pause…silence.

<*ding…tone…*>

In a Lexington, Kentucky kindergarten, he was allowed to caress the pantyhose-tight legs of an attractive, younger teaching assistant as she sat in a chair in front of the closely-gathered class during afternoon storytime. Always front and center for the sessions, he once made his way slowly up her skirt, both with his eyes and his usual eager hands, as she sat reading to the class the adult paperback version of a halfling fantasy novel.

Trying to explore a different, older classroom teacher's shin as he laid on a cot during naptime caused her to jump back in surprise disdain and reprimand.

***

In Louisville's first grade, he had a female classmate come over to his family's apartment bedroom to play dolls, and to play domestic games. She accepted his several pecks on the lips, but she was focused more on how dinner would be prepared for the two of them and on how their house furniture needed to be rearranged.

***

In L.A.'s fifth grade, a female friend walked up to him during recess on the vast, chained-in, blacktop playground; slapped him hard across the face; and then apologized by saying that she didn't know why she did that.

***

Also in the fifth grade, a quiet female acquaintance-friend sitting next to him at a world-class Los Angeles music hall during a field trip surprised him by laying her head of long, silky-black hair on his shoulder during an abridged-for-kids production of a Chinese opera.

***

In Louisville's fashion-challenged 1987, he had to embellish his mild fever in order to get sent to the nurse's office after being chastised by classmates for not dressing up enough at the eighth grade dance. A nice female classmate-acquaintance kindly agreed to stay with him as he laid on a countertop in the office until a counselor arrived.

***

In Louisville's high school, he only lied about his intimacy once. (Because his friend asked him about it, point blank.)

***

In Louisville's college, he was too busy having fun with substances to gain sober or intoxicated confidence in being with a girl after a party, a date, or an intimate invitation. More or less. But mostly less, though age nineteen was his not-quite-perfect but at least minimally-satisfactory breakthrough.

***

In Indianapolis retail jobs during and immediately-after college, he had a few dates with female co-workers.

***

His first apartment, shared in Louisville upon invitation by a platonic college acquaintance, brought out possibly the worst challenge to his "manhood" before or since. When things quickly started breaking apart early on between them, her weapon of choice against him during the progression of the year's lease agreement was her former, and especially current, experience; his weapon against her was a cocktail of verbal deconstruction, intentional silence, constant avoidance, a few head games, and an entry-level Louisville career. Mostly avoidance, however, and saturated with insecurities, ignorance, and continued, slower cognitive development towards intimacy with a woman.

***

At a doom-generation sensory-chaos bar he contemporaneously frequented by himself downtown, both for adventure and for escape, he once didn't give the right answers to the advanced, predatory solicitations of two hyper-alpha, hyper-smirking, about-to-twilight erotic medusas who approached him as he sat alone at the bar: one asked the questions of him, while her siamese twin licked her lips holding up a clear, plastic bag of torturous late-night fun-to-be. They quickly smelled the fear within him, just as his roommate had…but, after the onslaught, they did sincerely tell him to have a good night before writhing away, continuing their wide-eyed hunt.

***

When he responded by telephone to a newspaper advertisement of a two-bedroom apartment for rent, the elderly-female-sounding-landlord asked if the apartment was for him and his wife.

"No, it'd just be for me and a male roommate," he said.

"Oh. Oh, no, no, I can't have that, no," she told him.

Concluding the call, he stunningly vowed to do something about the unfair treatment against him, and he immediately drafted a housing discrimination complaint to send to the United States Department of Housing & Urban Development.

Which he never filed.

***

The pioneer land rush of late-1990s internet dating swept him into online chatting and long-distance relationships, as he cautiously, unconsciously, continued to develop his craft while juggling the progression of a professional and alcoholic career in both Lexington and Louisville. There was almost nothing like hearing a flight attendant announcing in English and French that the plane was about to land at an international airport, knowing that after a few nervous minutes of customs-declaration, an idealized woman would be presented behind opening automatic metal doors to take him to a downtown hotel for a four-day long weekend. The puppy-love immersed him into being okay with her refusal to take him to her small hometown and/or residence two hours away; he respected her wishes to protect her two minor children from the relationship, at least for the first few years.

***

His female Director in Lexington advanced his career tenfold by using her connections, and by using him for her political ambitions, to turn him into a bigger fish in a medium-sized pond. She succeeded in becoming mayor, and he became a board-of-directors veteran. When he moved on, to live back in Louisville and to work for the Commonwealth of Kentucky, his working relationship with females continued to progress with not only a supportive female Director, but a great team of more than 40 females to his sole maleness at their offices. (There was almost nothing like hearing the occasional competition for his attention during the workday. Not that he solicited such, as a professional.)

***

After a three-year Louisville domestication with a devoted angel He may have sent to him, he couldn't completely devote himself to Her and went off on his own, tied down only to his career, his father and brother living a few hours away, and his continued love affair with drinking. Subsequent regular visits to the exotic dance club located almost directly across the street from the front of his downtown office building meant that he had to covertly wave to the occasional bartender or dancer sitting or standing out front smoking during the business day. He entered the doors of the establishment almost exclusively on weekend evenings, making sure that he saw no lights on in the building windows along the row of his office floor. He prided himself on buying drinks for the working girls for drunken conversation only, never once buying or eliciting a paid lapdance, or more. One time, though, he gave a significant amount of cash over to a friendly regular dancer/ bartender, just because she asked, and she then asked to go home with him (and maybe she did so even because he didn't specifically ask her to).

***

One of the highlights of his dating career was when he found out that one fling-in-progress was a formerly-married-to-a-woman, Jewish witch, then possibly in her beautiful prime at thirteen years his junior. As a 36-year-old, it was impossible for him to keep up with her. He pondered the morality of objectifying her with such a description based on such demographics, but he justified it with his recollection that, in public, she once grabbed him firmly, confidently, and authoritatively by the back of his salt-and-pepper head of hair when telling her self-styled "lesbian friends" that he was her current boy-toy. He decided that there was almost nothing like hearing that welcome objectification.

***

He had, and continues to have, Probable Cause for marriage and partnership with the only wife he's ever had (including countless conciliation agreements executed between the parties to resolve complaints).

CHAPTER THREE

I scramble to get Ms. Johnson's file from the four towering walls of case files piled up on top of my office desk, I quickly write down "*8:20am*" on an 8½" x 14" yellow legal-style blank notepad, and then I get up and walk out of my office towards the front receptionist desk. Halfway down the hallway, I see Janice flying out from behind the west wing wall to the receptionist area, coffee mug in hand. I stop with a scrape on the hall carpeting and then retreat back to my office. I then hear Janice's elevated "Push the Button…" and then her "Can I Help You" greetings at the receptionist desk, followed by the fast-food-drive-thru-intercom sound of response of "*I'm here to talk about my case*" from someone sounding female.

"Okay…your name?"

"*wah-wah Ms. Johnson, Tamara Johnson…wah-wah I'm here about my landlord…*"

"Okay…"

I write "*Johnson v. FMD*" as a header on the yellow legal pad and underline the case name. Then, it's "*C. interview at CRC @ 8:30 a.m. appt.*" next to the "*8:20am*" note already written on the first line below.

<dong!>

"Hel*lo*…!" I hear Janice say to her.

"Hi, I'm here to talk about my case…?"

"O*kay*, you here to see Alex?"

"*Yes*, uh-huh, I think so, it's about my landlord…?"

She sounds very pleasant.

"Okay, yep…he's expecting ya. Just have a seat, and I'll buzz him and let him know you're here…"

The telephone in my office rings like anything other than a standard buzz, because it's back to its mysterious over-the-weekend volume increase blare that almost jars me out of my office chair. Or maybe it's my nervous lack of sleep. I've never been able to figure out who turns it up in my office, or if it just sometimes resets to some default thanks to some Louisville Metro Government remote communications specialist. Either way, I leap to reduce the volume back to the minimum decibel, hitting the volume-down button rapidly and repeatedly.

"Hello-this-is-Alex," I say professionally into the receiver, even though both Janice and I know that I know who's calling in on the interoffice line, and for what reason.

"Al *lex*, your appointment is here to see you…"

"Okay, I'll be right out…"

I hang up the phone receiver, put the yellow legal-sized notepad inside the *Johnson* case file while holding an ink pen, and clickly password-lock my computer settings with the computer mouse after noticing another fair housing advocacy listserv e-mail come in. I get up and exit my office, walking back up towards the receptionist desk, and while I hear my office desk telephone ring behind me, I see Ms. Johnson looking through Civil Relations Commission brochures placed on top of the bar-wall separating the desk from the public. Ms. Johnson doesn't see me coming towards her, or she makes it appear so.

"*Hi*, Ms. Johnson…?"

"Yes…" she looks up and half-smiles.

"*Hi*, I'm Alex…? Nice to meet you, thanks for coming down…"

I don't offer to shake her hand. Sometimes I do offer, depending on how germophobic I feel that day, or with what I think the member of the public might want for them. But, today, it's a no-go, and Ms. Johnson seems fine with it anyways.

"I've got us all set up across the hall in our conference room," I say in directing her with a nod of the case file. "Let's go ahead and go back out, over here…"

"Okay--" Ms. Johnson says before my disjointed interruption, and the front door interruption.

<bleep bleep>

<dong!>

It's Agnes, arriving slowly for work with an equal mix of lethargy and inquisitiveness of the front desk area activity right now.

"Oops, excuse us, Agnes, we're just headin' across the hall this morning," I explain to both Agnes and Ms. Johnson. Agnes says nothing in her slight frowning, and she slowly proceeds on with her bags, one in each hand draped down, towards the west wing office area.

Ms. Johnson then follows me out the front reception area, ten feet over to the Civil Relations Commission conference room door across the main office hallway, close to the elevators and far away from the end of the long, carpeted hall of vacant-office doors lining the rest of the fifth floor of the building, heading east.

"Okay, *here* we go," I say as I start fumbling to unlock the door with my conference room door key that I'm sure the Mayor's administration regrets me now having from years ago. "Did you park on Chestnut Street at a meter?" I ask as I kick a plastic dollar-store door-stopper under my opening door, in order to keep my view open to the outside hallway and Civil Relations Commission offices.

"No, I had a friend drop me off, so it's fine."

"Okay, great, I just don't want you to get a ticket if we need to spend a lotta time here this morning going over your case, but it sounds like it doesn't matter."

"Okay," she slightly smiles.

I flip the light switch on inside the doorway to the left to activate the slightly-humming fluorescent lights above. "Lemme know if it gets too chilly in here, or if you need me to turn down the heat at the thermostat here," I offer.

"No, you're fine," Ms. Johnson says without looking at me, checking out the large, somewhat-impressive conference room table in the middle of the room adorned with uninspired adequate-only upholstered chairs.

"Please, sit wherever you like," I say as she's already placing her Commission brochures from the front lobby onto the conference table.

I sit diagonally-across from her on her end of the table, and she takes off and puts her light sweater around the closest chair in front of her before sitting down. It's time to begin the always-awkward beginning, especially when I lead the way after substandard sleep and lots of caffeine, but we should be able to get to where we need to go.

"Okay, so, thanks for agreeing to meet with me today," I begin. "I wanted to go over your case in detail, and give you an update on the status of the case."

Ms. Johnson pleasantly looks at me as I start rolling.

"So, if you have any questions I can try and answer for you, please just ask me at any time."

"Okay…"

"Do you have any questions, or--"

"—No…no, not yet…"

"Okay, well, please, Ms. Johnson, just let me know if I can try to answer any for you this morning. We can take as much, or as little, time to go over things, but I do have some questions, and some of them may be kinda sensitive, so feel free to answer or not answer anything you feel is appropriate or inappropriate…"

"No, okay, you're fine."

"Okay, so, um: We received a written response to your complaint from the Respondent, or, your landlord, which was submitted to us within 30 calendar days from the Respondent's *receipt* of the complaint notification, which is required under local ordinance. Basically, the Respondent *denies* unlawful discrimination based on your sex, or, specifically, sexual harassment."

"Okay…"

"And, as you might imagine, it's not uncommon for our office to receive written responses denying unlawful discrimination occurred. So, we just go ahead and go on with the investigation process regardless, and so, this morning, I'd like to conduct a formal interview with you to supplement all the good information you've provided previously…"

"Okay…can I see what he wrote? What did he say?"

"Well, generally, I like to keep the details and information confidential, so I can tell you that there was a general denial of unlawful discrimination from him. Just as we keep your information confidential, we keep almost all information confidential during the course of the investigation, unless there's an imperative need to disclose information or exchange information between the parties. That covers you and everyone else, and allows folks to speak freely and provide information."

"Okay."

"Also, it avoids building a foundation for the investigation based on hearsay. That way, we can piece together everything on the back end to try to determine what happened, based on the information and evidence that we're able to gather."

"Okay."

"Again, we can take as much or as little time as you feel comfortable with to discuss the case, and that'll go a long way towards getting to a conclusion to the investigation, and for the Civil Relations Commission to make a determination based on the merits of your complaint. *If* it gets that far, because later I'll ask you about potential ways to attempt to resolve the complaint prior to the Commission exhausting our resources and completing the investigation."

"Okay."

"As far as jurisdiction, our office is investigating the complaint, but it's also dual-filed with the United States Department of Housing & Urban Development, or 'HUD,' since it appears that there's federal jurisdiction, so it's filed under federal law, as well. But you only have to work through our office, since we dual-file the complaint with HUD, and we keep them updated on the status of the case. The only time you *might* get contact from HUD is a complaint notification letter confirming that the complaint was filed with them, but it *should* reference the Civil Relations Commission as the investigating agency. And if the house you rent from the Respondent receives federal funding, then maybe HUD would contact you directly…"

"Yeah, I do use Section 8 for the house."

"Okay, great! I'll have some questions about that as we go along."

Pause.

"So," I start repeating too much, "Any last-second questions before we begin, or…?"

Pause.

"No," Ms. Johnson again says. "No…I can't think of any off the top of my head…?"

"Okay, well…there's a few different ways we can do the interview. I can just start asking questions, and you can answer…or, I can just let you go ahead and tell what happened, and I'll just start taking notes and ask you some questions along the way. I just act like a journalist for the interview, except that we don't publish the results in the media, of course. The information you provide remains confidential during the course of the investigation. However, I have to tell ya that the parties *do* have the right to request a copy of the final investigative report at the conclusion of the investigation, which has a detailed summary of all the information we gather. And, if we find Probable Cause for the case, and legal proceedings commence, then there are always legal proceedings that *could* make information public, depending on what happens. *But*, in a sensitive case like a sexual harassment case, we have an obligation to keep lots of sensitive information confidential even beyond your typical housing discrimination complaint record."

"Okay…"

"I say all this because sometimes it depends on which way the wind blows when the County Attorney's Office, which is the agency that provides responses to open records requests and is our--the Civil

Relations Commission's, litigation division, they respond to information requests from the case file. The County Attorney assigned to respond may have different ideas on what should be provided to the parties, so I *have* to make this disclaimer. Sometimes, they just provide the final investigative report like they should do under state and federal law, but other times they provide too much information, like copies of documents and things like that. Anyways, I just say all these things to let you know how the system works, and what your rights are, but, like I said, your case would have a little more privileged information, in theory. But I'm happy to try to answer any questions you may have about any of this..."

"Okay..."

"Anyways, the Civil Relations Commission is a neutral, impartial, investigative agency, since we're a department of city government, so we don't represent you like an attorney, or an advocate, would...*But*, I wanna provide you with good customer service, and if I do *my* job right, we should be able to gather a minimal amount of information to go ahead and make a determination of Probable Cause, that unlawful discrimination likely *did* occur; or, No Probable Cause, that, based on the information we're able to gather, unlawful discrimination likely did *not* occur. If No Probable Cause is found, then the case is just dismissed. But, at that point, you could still file a lawsuit in court based on the discrimination allegations in the complaint."

"So, what happens when you find Probable Cause?"

"Well, when-and-if we find Probable Cause for the case, that's when our agency's role changes a bit: the County Attorney assigned to the case would work with you in preparation for legal proceedings, barring any quick negotiated settlement for the case, which usually doesn't happen right away but it could. The County Attorney technically doesn't represent you, like your own private counsel would, but, from a *practical* standpoint, the County Attorney and the Commission would work with you and litigate the case, the Charge of discrimination that's levied on your behalf and in the public interest. Sort of like a second investigation, because that's usually when depositions occur, documents are subpoenaed, discovery requests are formally made, stuff like that."

"Okay..."

"So, keep in mind that, at this point, we just have an open investigation, and we make no predetermination on the merits of the complaint. *But*, we take your allegations seriously, and I wanna do a good job investigating this, as far as it goes."

"Okay…okay, that's fine," Ms. Johnson somewhat-frown smiles.

"Any other questions I can try and answer for you…?"

"No…no, not right now…? But maybe later…?"

"Sure! Just ask me at any time, and we can put things on hold, whatever you want to do."

"Okay then," Ms. Johnson half-smiles.

"Well, how about--why don't you just tell me what happened, and I'll just take some notes. I promise that I'll do much less talking and listen more and take some notes as we go along here…"

Slightly-smiling, Ms. Johnson then takes a breath, pauses, and explains her position quickly with reserved demeanor.

"Well, Mr. Alex: I rent this house in the South End, me and my two kids, and my landlord started making comments to me, and then he brushed up against me, and he said--he told me if I *wanted*, we could just call us even on the late rent he said I owed him, and he did this at my house. So, that's when I called HUD, and then you all called, and then I came in, and signed the complaint…"

I begin writing on the yellow legal notepad but then stop quickly. "Okay, great! So, maybe you could try and start from the beginning, and I'll document it as we go. So, if you could maybe start chronologically on how you found out about the house for rent, and then I can just go from there, and if you go out of order, it's fine, too, no problem. It just helps me in my notes to go from the beginning, but please just take your time explaining. I may interrupt you sometimes to ask for some clarification for my notes, so I apologize in advance…"

"No, that's okay…So, well, I found out about the house because my sister rented from him before, not *that* house, but somewhere else he had…"

"Okay, so, what's the name of your sister, if you don't mind?"

I launch into jotting my own brand of shorthand notes, quickly, strongly, and diligently, and on autopilot despite my lack-of-full-sleep hangover.

"Keisha."

"Okay…is that spelled K-E-I-S--"

"--S-H-A, yes, sir."

"Okay, and what's her last name?"

"Harris…"

"H-A-R-R-I-S."

"Yes, uh-huh."

"Okay-great. And who's *he*, your landlord?"

"Yes, Mr. Forrest…Forrest Davis."

"Okay, and his name is--his first name, is spelled F-O-R-*R*-E-S-T?"

"Yes sir…"

"Okay, great!…And, Davis, is pretty self-explanatory…And, real quick: this may sound like a 'duh' question, but I'd like to document specifically for the investigation what the sex, or gender, is, for each person identified for the case, since sexual harassment falls under the sex protection under fair housing law. So, you mentioned Mr. Davis, I assume he's male?"

"Yes…yes sir."

"And your sister, she's female, I assume?"

"Yes, yes sir…"

"Okay, great. The other reason I ask about this is because I wouldn't be a good investigator if I didn't specifically ask you about it, then document the response. Probable-Cause or No-Probable-Cause, I could be called on to testify about this in a hearing or in court, so I wanna make sure I document all the relevant stuff…I've had cases petitioned to the United States Supreme Court, so I need to cover myself, much less *you*, and the Commission," I say with a single slight-laugh.

"Sure," Ms. Johnson says, slightly smiling in response.

"Okay, great! So, you heard about this house from your sister--Ms. Harris…"

"Yeah, she told me that he had this *other* house for rent in the South End that used Section 8, so she gave me his number to call him and I called him."

"Okay, so, when was this?"

"Um…uh…*hm*…"

"Approximately. Just your best guess, you don't necessarily have to provide the day, or even month, but at least around what year…"

"Okay, um, this was…this was in about…I'd say around… January…of…2014…? I know I was looking to move after I was staying with my mother, through Christmas, through Christmas 2013, and I needed my own place, for me and my kids."

"So, you called for him--Mr. Davis, and he accepted Section 8? And by 'Section 8,' you mean 'voucher,' as in 'Housing Choice' voucher, what most people still call a 'Section 8' voucher?"

"Yes, Section 8 from the Housing Authority."

"Okay great, just checking. Most people still call it 'Section 8,' HUD just changed the name of it a few years ago, and no one else seems to call it what HUD now *wants* it to be called. And there's also project-based Section 8 subsidy tied *to* the property to help pay rent, where you're just certified on-site at the apartment complex, instead of a voucher from the Housing Authority that's portable and you take it with you as long as the private landlord accepts it. Just so you know, vouchers are not typically considered federal funding to the landlord, where HUD would look at other federal laws that our agency doesn't have jurisdiction to enforce and then make a separate determination on the case from us. That may be neither here nor there, and HUD's typically hands-off anyways (!), but it basically means that you'll likely just work with our office exclusively for the investigation…"

"Okay…okay, so, I called Mr. Forrest, and he said that, yeah, he had this house available for rent, and that he'd rent it for 900 a month, with a 7-50 deposit, and that it was Section 8. So I said, 'Can I see the house?' and he said, 'Yeah, I can show it to you tomorrow,' and so he told me the address, and he said to meet him there the next day, I think it was in the afternoon."

"Okay, so what was the address of the house?"

"1469, Rosebank, Court."

"Okay, and that's here, in Louisville Metro?"

"Yes, where I live now."

"And it's a single-family house, not an apartment, or a multifamily property?"

"Yes, uh-huh. And so, we meet at the house, and I'm there with my sister, and the three of us look at the house, and we're excited, 'cause it's big enough for me and my kids, the rent is not too high with Section 8, and the location is good for both my kids' schools, and their daddy can get there by Transit Authority some weekends for visitation. And I can get out from my mother's place, 'cause she's got a small house, and it was cramped with all of us there. So, I faxed Mr. Forrest the application, and he approved it, and Section 8 approved it, and so I got to move in about three weeks later with my kids."

I continue writing and note-taking. "Okay, so, I have an optional question for you to answer, about your kids. What you *can* do, if you like, is list them as aggrieved parties for the case, since they're also allegedly damaged, just like you've alleged *you've* been damaged, and you all live together at the subject property. I realize the sensitive nature of the fact that they're minor children, so it's optional on whether you wanna do that …"

"Well, yeah, that would be fine…will they need to provide interviews? 'Cause Martez saw Mr. Forrest doing it."

"Okay, well, honestly, that's up to you, Ms. Johnson. And them. I gotta tell ya, cases like this can be he-said/she-said sometimes, and I generally do *not* want to involve a minor child in the investigation process…but, if you think it'd help, and that the case may hinge on it, we might agree to interview him…?"

"Okay…"

"You don't have to decide on that this instant moment, but it *is* something to think about. You can leave here today and think about it, talk things over, and all that…"

"Okay…"

"So, then what happened, after you moved in?" I continue writing.

"Well, everything was fine, I paid my rent every month until a few late payments, but I was never too late in paying. I might've paid on the tenth a couple times, but I was never evicted…"

"Okay, so, what day was the monthly rent due?"

"The first of the month. And I did pay by the fifth of the month, almost every month."

"Is that when the grace period was due, the fifth?"

"Yeah."

"So, when was the first late payment that you made to the Respondent?"

"Well, I'd say…about…about maybe June? June, 2014. And then again in July, but not again until just this past January, and February. But Mr. Forrest started doing what *he* did last summer."

"Okay, so, let's talk about that. I know it's kinda sensitive, but it'd be helpful if you could describe in detail what Mr. Davis did that caused you to want to file this complaint."

"Okay, so: when I started paying late, Mr. Forrest said that he needed to come over to do repairs on the house. I mean, like, I didn't think anything of it, because he came over, and he looked at some things, and some things *did* need repairs, like from before we moved in. But, then, he came over in…I think it was…August? Yeah, August, last August, 2014. 'Cause he said that he wanted to look at the closet in the master bedroom that he fixed when the closet door came off the hinges again, and he asked if I was going to be late paying the rent again that month, and I said no, and he called me over--I was standing in the bedroom doorway, and he was leaned over looking at the closet door track, and messing with it, and he called me over to look at it, and while he was bent over there, he was all--he started to back up against me, up and down for a second. I mean," she slightly scoffs, "I stepped back, not thinking it was intentional, like, not that he *meant* to do it, but then he got up, and he turned around, and he started looking at me, and then at the bed, and then at me again. I thought, 'This is strange…' and I could tell that he just thought that I didn't think he meant what he really *meant*, and so he said that he would fix the closet track again the next time he came over to make repairs. See, he doesn't have a maintenance man, he does it all himself, he has, like, four houses he rents out, and that's his only job, I think…"

"So, as far as you know, he has four total properties he rents out? Do you know if they're all single-family houses?" I continue quickly note-taking.

"I think so, I think that's what he said one time, but, I dunno…"

"The reason I ask, is because, in general, four or more total 'dwellings,' as federal law calls it, are covered under the federal Fair Housing Act. If there's less than that, then it's *still* covered under local ordinance, anyways, though…"

"Okay…"

"Okay, great! …So, I have some sensitive questions to ask about the maintenance incident. Did you call him to come fix the closet door, or anything else, that day? In around August, 2014?"

"No, he called *me*. I mean, he had called about coming over to winterize the house before, ask if the toilet was running, things like that, sayin' he was tryin' to save money on his bills since he paid the water. But he called me, and then *this* happened with the touching and all that…"

"Okay…So, could you tell me again, what he said, and did, when he called you over to him?"

"He said, 'Here's your problem, right here,' and he was all bent-over, looking at the track for the closet door," she says, moving her head to hunch over slightly. "And I came over to look, and it was off the hinge, and he backed up against me while getting up, which I think was intentional, and he spun around into my face, like, also intentional, and that's when he said he'd fix it, but he was lookin' at me, then looked at the bed, then he looked at *me* again, and, like I said, I was thinkin' it was strange, and then he said he'd fix it next time he came over. So, that's all that happened that time. Yeah...and right before he called me over, he'd asked me about the rent."

Still quickly writing, "Were there any people in the house at the time, besides you, and the Respondent--I mean, Mr. Davis?"

"No, no, this was during the day, and my kids were at school, I think, 'cause school just started. I didn't tell anyone about it right away, I just told my mother about it, after it happened again."

"Okay, so, then what happened, after this incident?"

"Okay, so, the next time, was when he came over about a week...yeah, I think it was about a week or two weeks later, to fix the closet--and this time my kids were home, 'cause it was in the afternoon--I came home from picking them up from daycare late in the afternoon, and when I got back to the house, his van was already there, and he had called that morning saying that he was gonna come by to look at the furnace."

"Okay, so, approximately what month and year was this, then, again...?"

"Uh, it was still August...September--well, maybe. I still--I think it was still August."

"2014?"

"Yes, still 2014. And he--he was sitting in his van in the driveway, talking on his phone, when I got back to the house with the kids, and so we said 'hi' and all that, and we all went into the house. Mr. Forrest looked distracted when me and the kids got out of the car and maybe it was because we had to park on the street since his van was in the driveway, and Martez and Montavius ran inside, and Mr. Forrest went into the basement, I guess to look at the furnace. So, Mr. Forrest then came to the bedroom where I was putting away the new shoes I bought, I hadn't been in there a *second* while he was in the basement, I was mostly in the kitchen and the living room getting the kids' things all taken care of and put away, so I was in the bedroom, and, like I said, for just a second, so it was almost like he was waiting for me to go in there, and then he said, 'Here, lemme take a look at the closet again,' and he walked up on me behind me, and I had to step back from where I'd just put the shoes away in there, and then he looked down at the closet track, and then he got up and he looked me in the eyes, and he got a weird look, and then put his hand on my shoulder. And he said, 'If you want, we can have rent taken care of,' something like that. And *then*, Martez came to the door, and he saw how when Mr. Forrest saw him, Mr. Forrest jumped back real quick. Like, jumped his hand back, like this," Ms. Johnson imitates, "and Martez *saw* it…"

"Okay-great," I continue rapidly note-taking while trying to affirm receipt of her information. "Did anyone else see what happened?"

"No, Montavius was in the other room, and my mom wasn't over, but I told her about it."

"When did you tell her about it?"

"Well, I called her that night and I told her about it, and she said that I needed to call Section 8 and report him."

"So, did you call the Housing Authority?"

"No, I did call them, but not after *that* time. I just thought maybe that was it, but then he did something like that again, like…in the end of February. Yeah, February. Or maybe it was March: 'cause he said--sorry, March 2015. 'Cause he called, and he said that he wanted to talk about me giving him rent in person from now on, since I did pay late, in January, and February. It was in the morning, so Montavius and Martez were at school, and Mr. Forrest came over, and we talked about it. He wanted me to pay rent in person with a money order from now on, and I said okay, and then he asked if there were any things I needed fixing again. I said no, not that I know of, and he asked about the closet again, and I said no, it's okay…but by the time I was saying all that, he had gone back again to the bedroom, and I just waited in the living room, even though he was talkin' all loud, saying he thought he knew what the problem was, or something like that. So he came out when he knew that I wasn't gonna go back there, and then he said--he asked, 'Okay, so, we have a deal on the money order?' And I said, 'Yes, Mr. Forrest,' and that's when he put his hand out again, I thought to shake, shake hands on it, but--well, he did, we shook hands, but he got all--he kinda, grabbed my arm, moving his fingers, like, all touching me up on my arm, and then he grabbed around with his other hand--" Ms. Johnson imitates, "and he put his other arm around my waist, like this. I pulled back real quick, and he looked like he was embarrassed, but that he might try to reach out for me again, 'cause he was lookin' at me in the eyes, but I guess he didn't do it then, and then he said 'Okay, okay,' and then he left." She slightly exhales. "So, I called my mother again, and she started yelling and sayin' that, 'You need to call the Housing Authority!' and 'If you don't do it, I'm comin' down there and takin' you over there!'"

I pause my writing while having my tired hand catch up. "So, then…is that when you called the Housing Authority?"

"Yeah, I did, and that's when they told *me* to call HUD."

"Did you call the Civil Relations Commission about it before calling HUD?"

"Yeah, 'cause my mom also told me to call you all, so I did that first, and I left a message about it but no one called me back."

"*Oh*, okay, well…uh, if that happened, and no one called you back from *our* office, I apologize on behalf of the Commission. We need to provide good customer service, obviously, so…"

"Well, yeah, I did call HUD then, after that, and then you all *did* call me back after that. Miss Janice was real nice calling, and saying to come down, and sign everything, all that."

"Okay, great, that's good, then…So, *then* what happened, after the around-March incident?"

"Well, okay, so, then…the last time, was when he called me a month or so ago. He called, and he said that he needed to come over to see if the thunderstorms had done anything to the trees at the house, since he was worried about the tree at the back, this one oak tree that's back there, and he got frustrated asking me why I called the city on him, which is when he got your-all's letter, he was saying that 'We didn't need to go through all that,' something like that. He said he needed to come by, and so I said it was fine, and he came by later the next morning, and the kids were at school, and right away he was all, like, 'Look, we don't have to go through all this, I'm not trying to put you out or *anything*…just think about it, you could live here without paying next month,' and then, he--he said, 'the next two months.' I was all, like, oh my god, this is--I mean, this is *crazy*. It's all…"

Ms. Johnson sighs deeply, shaking her head slightly. She's not crying, or appearing about ready to cry, but she's not smiling, or half-smiling, with something withdrawing within her that seems to be confusing her as she looks diagonally-down at the conference room table. She's stopped. And a little stunned.

"Okay, great," I bridge after a pause, trying to convey a lower, more sensitive voice, still writing but seeking her recovery. "I just wanna reinforce my notes on all this…you're doing a *great* job on this so far, by the way, Ms. Johnson…seriously…"

"Okay, good, Mr. Alex," she says with another sigh and a pause. "It's just all, so…so…you know, like, I don't know why he would do this, except to try to take advantage, you know? I didn't tell him I wanted to do anything with him…I have a boyfriend? My babies--my kids' father, he tries to pay his support on time, but sometimes he can't, and so *I* have to try to pay Mr. Forrest on time, but I don't have anyone living with me, or helping working, or anything with me right now…"

"It's just you and your minor children there, living there?"

"Yes, it's just us. And my boyfriend doesn't live there like Mr. Forrest told me he thought, one time. My boyfriend has his own apartment, he has his own lease, everything. I mean, he comes over, but he doesn't spend the night there all the time, he works second shift, and he has to sleep in, the days, and all that, to get ready for work. But I pay my rent, I was only late just a few times…"

"Okay, great! …Got it. So, also, just to let you know, retaliation for the filing of a housing discrimination complaint is illegal under local ordinance and the federal Fair Housing Act. So, if you believe you're suffering from harassment, intimidation, or coercion, *because* you filed the complaint, just let our office know, and we can work to address that. We could draft a separate housing discrimination complaint from the original complaint, and you could even get No Probable Cause on the original complaint, but Probable Cause on the retaliation complaint. Or both Probable Cause. Well, or No Probable Cause, both, but just sayin'…let us know if you believe that's happened at any point…"

"Okay…so, can he evict me over all this?"

"Well, if the Respondent subjects you to eviction, contact us to look at retaliation, but also contact Legal Aid. Legal Aid can look at representing you in the eviction proceedings in court, concurrently while we investigate the discrimination and/or the retaliation complaints. Legal Aid looks at local landlord-tenant law, which would be separate from what we look at, and they're more of an emergency-services-type response agency for eviction actions--One of the systemic dysfunctions of fair housing law for us here is that we won't intervene with prompt judicial action…like, intervene with a court order to halt an eviction while we conclude the investigation. I mean, legally, we *could*, it's just that the County Attorney's Office has advised us that they *won't*. They want only things like that after Probable Cause, which takes so long to establish on our end, with investigation, and legal reviews, that usually the damage can be done already by the time of the eviction. I'd get in trouble with supervisors for telling you that, but that's a problem we have here, and the Commission is also to blame for not pushing this. But also, I guess you can contact the Housing Authority to look at a grievance with *them*, regarding the federal subsidy terms--the terms of the voucher subsidy, and Housing Authority lease provisions. And, also, you're welcome to contact a private attorney."

"Well, I can't afford to have an attorney, that's why I went to HUD."

"Okay, sure…well, what you could also do, is contact the Bluegrass Fair Housing Council. The Bluegrass Fair Housing Council is a private, non-profit, fair housing advocacy agency, and they can represent you in the complaint proceedings with our office. Or, they could just offer advice, or advocacy, off the record. But always for free. They're based in Lexington, but they do work in the entire state, including here. And they only work with fair housing issues, they get grants from HUD specifically to work on housing discrimination enforcement and education."

"Yeah, Miss Janice gave me their number when I came in to sign the complaint, I was thinking of calling them…"

"Well, we work with their office extensively, so they're real familiar with the work that we're doing, and what rights and responsibilities you would have…Okay, so, you mentioned our agency, and HUD…did you attempt to file a complaint about the harassment with any other agency, by the way? Like, in court, or with the Kentucky Commission on Human Rights?"

"No…no, I just called HUD, and then I guess they sent it to you all, and then Miss Janice called me, and I came down and signed it…"

"Did you file a written complaint with the Housing Authority?"

"No, no, I didn't…like I said, they just told me to call HUD. I didn't file a grievance with them, and as far as I know, they didn't call Mr.

Forrest. Unless that's what he meant by 'Why did you go and call the city on me,' instead of you all, but I don't think so…"

"Okay-great…and no lawsuits?"

"No. No, I never called an attorney, I just thought I'd let HUD handle it, or you all to sue him, or something."

"Okay, great. Sort of as I mentioned before, this is an ongoing investigation, so no litigation proceedings have commenced, at this point. It certainly *could* happen, but we have to conclude the investigation, and then, when-and-if Probable Cause is found in the case, there could be a lawsuit filed by the County Attorney's Office, or an administrative hearing, sort of like a trial."

"Sure."

"Okay, so…we may have kinda already covered this, but as far as witnesses for the investigation…"

"Yes…"

"Besides yourself, and, obviously, Mr. Davis, you mentioned Martez saw him jump away, and all that. Did Montavius witness anything?"

"No. No, not really. I mean, Montae was in the next room that one time, and he saw Mr. Forrest at the house sometimes, but he didn't see him actin' on me. I told my mother about it, though, but she wasn't there, either."

"Okay, so, would you like to give your mother's name for the investigation? Even if she didn't directly witness anything, she might still provide an interview that could provide some relevance for the case…"

"Sure, her name is Beverly…Johnson."

"B-E-V--"

"Yes, E-R-L-Y."

"Okay, great…Would you like her to contact me, or would you like me to try and contact her?

"I'll have her call you, she should be fine calling you. Do you have a card, or…?"

"Yeah, sure, here," I say, and then get a business card out of my wallet from out of my dress-slacks left front pocket. "If she has any questions, I'll be happy to try and answer any of 'em. I can even send a letter in advance, just a generic letter, inviting her to contact me as a potential witness for the investigation. I can just call, as well, but some people have a fear of government, some people have a *hatred* of government, so I sometimes just try and send a letter briefly explaining the reason for the interview request, and how it's voluntary, and confidential, and all that, and that way they have something in writing to explain things first."

"No, no, that should be fine, I'll talk with her tonight and she should call you tomorrow or this week or something."

"Okay, great! We have some time, so it doesn't have to be tomorrow, but, in the interest of moving things along, maybe if she could provide the interview within the next seven business days?"

"No, no, I'll tell her, I'll tell her to call you, she should."

"Okay, cool, and maybe you could think about whether Martez could provide an interview for the case, since, like you said, he's the only other person present who witnessed some of what happened?"

"Okay, yeah, he can, I'll talk to him, too."

"Like I said, I hesitate to involve minor children in things like this, but since he may have extremely pertinent information as a witness, it might be good to speak with him. I mean, one thing about providing an interview is that the Commission accepts interviews in just about any format. We accept interview statements in person, over the telephone, written interview statements by fax, e-mail…again, we try to keep information confidential throughout the course of the investigation, but you're welcome to be present if he provides a statement, since you're his mother and all, either in-person or even in a conference call."

"Okay…okay, that sounds fine…"

"And what about your sister Keisha--Ms. Harris?"

"Yes, she could be a witness, I can talk to her, too."

"Okay, great, and let me know if you want me to try to contact her directly, too. So…okay! So, do you have any other information to provide, at this point, for the investigation?"

"No…no, I can't think of anything. I just can't believe it, Mr. Alex. I didn't try to respond to him or *any*thing. And, I mean, he's *married*, so I can't imagine his wife…"

"Oh, *oh*, okay, so…" I react with a single half-laugh, still writing notes.

"Yeah…"

"So--so, did he, Mr. Davis, did he ever come over to the property with his wife, or…?"

"No…no, I never met her. He just mentioned that he was married, I never seen her."

"Oh ok…and, I assume, she was not a witness to any of the incidents, right?"

"No, no, she wasn't at the house."

"Okay, great…so…So, anything else that you can think of?"

"No…no, not at this time, no…"

"Okay, well, as far as any documentation, do you have a copy of your most recent lease agreement that you can provide for the case? I can make copies of documents here at the office free of charge, as long as they're relevant for the case."

"Yeah, I do, here…" Ms. Johnson says, opening her purse.

"Okay, great! Incidentally, did you call for police about any of the incidents with Mr. Davis?"

"No, no I didn't," Ms. Johnson says, handing me a folded set of a few papers.

"Okay, that's fine…Well, if you could give me just two minutes, I'll run back across the hall and make a copy of the lease for the case file. Is everything okay for you, time-wise?"

"Yeah, everything's fine, I'll call my friend when we're done."

"Okay, great…I'll just be a minute, and when I get back, we can go over one or two more things, and then that's probably what we need for today. So…okay! Be right back…"

"Okay, thanks Mr. Alex…"

I fold up my yellow legal notepad and Ms. Johnson's lease agreement into the case file before cradling it under my left arm over to the main offices.

<bleep bleep>

<dong!>

Janice looks up at me in the eyes while talking on the receptionist desk telephone, pen in hand. I go into the mailroom and open the giant top-loading copier, cursing internally that Ms. Johnson's lease is stapled and would be more of a hassle to remove the staple to just form-feed the three pages quickly through the copies in one swipe. I grab my dress shirt pocket cough drop with one hand, pop it, then throw the wrapper in--*miss*, the trash can. I copy each page individually by hand on the copier after grabbing the wrapper off the floor and getting it in the trash can, making sure to double-side the copies from the single-sided originals, and I again think about how I'm the only person in the office who does what budget-fisted Ronita instructs us to do in order to save

Louisville Metro Government, and our department, money on printing costs. I then throw the lease originals and copies into the case file and head out of the mailroom. Waiting for me, Janice, now off the telephone, interrupts the flow.

"Al*ex*...Roberta called in sick, and Agnes says that she has to go to a meeting at 1:00, and you said you were on intake when...?"

"Well, I'm on from 3:30 to 5:00, but I have to go to lunch at the normal time 'cause I've got that meeting outta the office, before coming back. What happened to Chad?"

"Well, he said he has interviews on the telephone at noon, and that he can't do intake well enough yet. Same with Briana."

"Well, we just won't have intake coverage, huh," I say with a heavy-sigh eye-roll. "I'll be here when I'm supposed to be here...(!)"

"Yep, me *too*, it's all you can *do* around this place..."

"Yeah, for real..."

"Oooooh, Alex, you know how I was gonna tell you about Ron--"

"--Well, Janice, yeah--hold-up, lemme get back over there..."

"*Oh*, yeah, okay, sure...I'll tell ya when you get done..."

"Okay cool."

I speed back over to the conference room across the hall, and Ms. Johnson is talking on a cellular telephone.

"Yeah, yeah, he said--okay--wait--lemme--lemme call you back, I'm with--okay, call ya back. Bye... Sorry, Mr. Alex..."

"No, that's okay..."

"I called my mother, and she said that she'll call you later today."

"Okay, no problem...I *am* scheduled to be out of the office some this afternoon after lunch, and then when I'm back in the office I'm on intake, which may take me away from the call, but if she leaves a message, I should get back with her by no later than tomorrow. Unless my job description changes by then, which, working in this place, certainly *could* happen...(!)"

"Okay, that should be fine..."

"Okay, so: I've made a copy of your lease agreement for the case file, here's your original..."

"Okay, thank you..."

"And, uh, any last information that you can think of, for today?"

"No...no, no, I can't think of anything, else..."

"Okay, great! Well, there's one last thing that I'd like to go over for the case, separate from the investigative record…So, HUD regulations, and, by default, local ordinance, state that the Civil Relations Commission should make the parties aware that *conciliation*, or what most people would call 'negotiated settlement,' is an option to attempt to resolve the housing discrimination complaint. Conciliation is a *voluntary* way for the parties to try to resolve the complaint, prior to our agency making a determination on the merits of the complaint, and it has no bearing on the investigative record, and it's concurrent with the investigation tract. So, if you like, you can submit a written proposal for the Civil Relations Commission to present to the Respondent to attempt to resolve the complaint…as long as there's nothing illegal in the proposal, we'll send notice of the proposal to the other side, for response."

"Well…what would be illegal?" Ms. Johnson asks quizzically.

"Well…say, for example, that you propose a bag of *cocaine* to attempt to resolve the housing discrimination complaint. Obviously, we couldn't convey that proposal."

Ms. Johnson exhales a non-enthusiastic half-laugh as I continue.

"I mean, that's an extreme example, and I wouldn't expect you to propose something illegal, but it *has* happened with our office before. Well, not the cocaine part, I mean, we had a Complainant one time who proposed something that we couldn't convey to the other side. In that case, the Complainant proposed something she probably--she might not have *thought* would result in discrimination the other way, but after a legal review and recommendation, it would've been unlawful to have an agreement with a discriminatory provision."

"Okay…"

"Anyways, so, it's something to think about. Many investigators with agencies like ours try to use conciliation to coerce the parties into a resolution to a complaint, but I don't do that, and we *shouldn't* do that, since it's all voluntary. We just keep on investigating the case until we make a determination, or until the parties agree in writing to resolve the case. But, we *do* have a firm policy that all conciliation proposals have to be submitted to our office in writing. We used to take verbal proposals, and call, back and forth, by telephone relaying whatever the proposals were, but about ten years ago, things went horribly wrong with that. And it wasn't my case, thankfully (!), it was another investigator's. A

Respondent's attorney threatened, or filed, litigation against the Commission after the parties allegedly agreed to some money amount, but then the Assistant Director at the time refused to sign off on it, saying it wasn't a high-enough dollar-amount to the Complainant. Even though the parties had supposedly agreed verbally, and maybe in writing, to something specific, something like that, and then the Assistant Director told the investigator to refuse it. All before a determination of Probable Cause or No Probable Cause was made on it. So, ever since then, we have to have everything in writing…"

"Okay…"

"And it doesn't have to be today if you wanna think about things. I mean, we still have a little time before we likely have to make a determination on the case. If you do submit one, I can usually turn around the notice to the other side, to go out, within a business day or so. At this point, the Respondent has *not* submitted a proposal to the Commission to convey to you, otherwise, I would've done so within that business day or so."

"So, how long does it take to investigate the case?"

"Uh, that's a good question. Local ordinance states that we should conclude the investigation within 100 days of the Respondent *receiving* the discrimination complaint notification. But the federal Fair Housing Act says that we should, in general, complete the investigation within 100 days of the *filing* of the complaint. So, we try to go by the most restrictive standard, and get it all done within 100 days of the date you filed it, which I'm showing…is…uh…June 10th. So, ideally, we'd like to make a determination on the merits of the case by about mid-September or so, next month. Sometimes we have to go beyond the 100 days, but, these days, we're doing really well with that part, we make most determinations within the 100 days. Some years, we don't do so good. Like, if you'd have filed this complaint five years ago or so, I estimated at one point that it took approximately three *years* from the date of the filing of the complaint just to make a *determination* on it, much less if it went Probable Cause and got into legal proceedings."

"Oh my god…"

"Yeah, at one point, it was just me investigating all housing and bias-related crime complaints for the agency, so I had 55 *active* investigations at the same time, and no help. And other job duties."

"Oh wow…"

"Yeah…so…so, yeah, we're doing really well on that part right now. We're still short-staffed, and yours is certainly not the only case we have (!), but I'm cautiously-optimistic, as of today, that we can conclude the investigation within the 100 days."

"Okay…okay, that sounds good, I'll just keep waiting, I guess, 'till I hear from you all…"

"But, like I said, this interview today goes a long way towards helping us make a determination on the case. And if we need any additional information for the investigation, I'll contact you, of course."

"Okay."

"So, anything else you can think of, that we need to talk about…?"

"Well, only--what do you think my chances are in the case?"

"Well, I'll be honest, Ms. Johnson, I really can't say. We make no predetermination on the merits of the case, like I said. I *do* make a recommendation on every case, but the Director of our agency makes the ultimate determination of either Probable Cause or No Probable Cause. There've been times that I've recommended Probable Cause, and the Director makes a No Probable Cause determination; and, times I've recommended No Probable Cause, and she's rendered Probable Cause. So, honestly, I can't speculate on what the ultimate outcome of the case will be."

"Oh okay."

"But, if *No* Probable Cause is found, there *is* an appeals process, what we call the 'reconsideration' process. I can go into all the potential outcomes of a case in detail, in general, if you like…Regardless, we'll send you notice of the determination, in writing, via certified postal mail. And we take your allegations *seriously*, Ms. Johnson."

"Okay…okay, well, thank you, Mr. Alex. I'll just wait to hear from you, I guess …"

"Okay, great! …We'll try to get this case where it needs to go, as soon as possible."

Both of us begin rising from the conference table.

"Okay…okay, thank you, Mr. Alex. I just don't want him to do this to anyone else…"

"Sure! Yeah, that's understandable…Okay, well, have a good day, Ms. Johnson, I'll get to processing all this information, and then we'll go from there. Just lemme know after today if you have any questions, or need to provide any additional information…"

"Okay thanks, Mr. Alex."

I walk over to the thermostat, turning it from "*auto*" to "*off*" while wondering which staff person it was *this* time who left it on over the weekend (again…and again in violation of office procedures to save money), and then I walk to the conference room door entrance and kick out the door stopper towards the bookcases on the wall with my right foot. After I pull the conference room door shut with a thud, I double-tug the door knob and confirm that it's locked. I then turn to Ms. Johnson, who's on her cell phone again waiting for the elevator with a down-arrow button lit up in front of her. I raise my eyebrows when mouthing "Bye" to her and she juggles doing the same in focusing on her call and the elevator. I don't struggle to hide a yawn with my pink eyes half-closed and my eyelids warm after I turn away.

Minor anxiety lifts as the interview for a sexual harassment housing discrimination complaint is over, but I'm on the way to crashing from the energy of the meeting as I head back into Civil Relations Commission offices.

<bleep bleep>

<dong!>

"This may be filed about sex, but we all KNOW this about race…!"

His boss whispered to him with a toothy grin of excitement, too close to his ear, in one of the few things Mason Keller, white/Caucasian, said to the young investigator during the whole trial. While sitting apart from each other in the gallery pews, Mr. Keller couldn't contain himself when scooting over to offer him the barest of commentaries and assessments of how things were going for them (that's what he deserved for making eye contact with Mr. Keller, a boss he always had to keep an eye on). Now almost 70 years old, Mr. Keller had the hardened, beaten look of 40 years' experience going through these state court trials time and again, though maybe not within the past ten or fifteen. But Mr. Keller was still a youthful, idealistic 1960s advocate. From the 1940s or 1950s. 490 years old in dog years in 1997.

By the end of his three-year internment as Mr. Keller's petty-officer housing discrimination Test Coordinator for Kentucky Housing Opportunities Made Equal, he'd heard from current loyal staff, and elder current and former community leaders, that Mr. Keller was forced from Commonwealth of Kentucky government dictatorship of the same civil rights agency he had co-founded and ran for 25 years. It'd take years to learn that when municipal government agency directors go out to pasture, they often chair boards of directors; start their own non-profit activist agencies; or, arrange for a combination of the two. And that government, whether local, state, or federal, is about individual personal control; the politics of the deal; and, most especially, making problems go away, irrespective of ideology or intent to reform, and irrespective of personal justice mission.

And, above all, that government was about maintaining "confidentiality."

But Mr. Keller was a little different.

"I grew up during The Depression," he felt compelled to explain when ordering only a single beef burrito for lunch ("Nothing else, you understand…just the beef!"), when the understaff of twenty-somethings, hand-picked for young energy, young ideology, and young obedience, escaped Kentucky-HOME offices for fast food during the workweek. Mr. Keller continued to gadfly, continued to push, continued to study, continued to wage a war, that at times was nineteenth century, at times still currently, relevant: civil rights to Mr. Keller was about civil law enforcement and use of media, combined, and not bureaucratic regulatory review. And, to Mr. Keller, as with many civil rights advocates past and present, it was about socially-engineering the demographics.

Sitting in the near-empty 1997 gallery for the state court trial was not like what he'd seen in the movies or on television: it was much, much different. It was shorter. It was more entertaining for the subject matter, but it was more boring for the procedure. Things didn't seem so formal. Unfortunately, housing discrimination lawsuits didn't get much of an audience back then, as the number of jurors seemed just as sparse as the professionals and the spectators involved. Not that things would change much in the 21st Century, of course.

For the instant case, the Complainant, an African-American female, approached Kentucky-HOME and alleged that she was not permitted to rent a fourplex apartment unit because the Respondent landlord, a white/Caucasian male, told her that he instead preferred that a male rent the dwelling; she alleged that he told her that the other three units of the fourplex were already occupied by single females, and that he therefore preferred having a male in the fourth, currently-available unit in order to help with maintenance for all the units. Just a landlord preference against renting to a person based on their sex, much less an outright refusal to rent based on such, was against local, state, and federal fair housing laws, in general. Kentucky-HOME reviewed the Complainant's allegations and, instead of filing with a municipal or federal fair housing investigative law-enforcement agency, immediately filed on her behalf in state court based on the strength of the case. Or the strength of her race, depending on which KY-HOME staffer you asked.

In court, the Complainant testified. Then the Respondent testified, who must've grown up during The Great War but was ahead of his years in energy, similar to Mr. Keller, and was well-represented by counsel. And then, Kentucky-HOME had a few questions for him.

As the Respondent remained on the witness stand waiting for cross-examination by the Test Coordinator's much-older contemporary, supervisor, and teacher, the 29-year-old Jason Rolek, white/Caucasian, the Respondent sat looking comfortable, friendly, and accessible as Mr. Rolek arose from his counsel table notes. Mr. Keller may've been an attorney, albeit a semi-retired one, but Mr. Rolek was the professionally-trained fair housing litigant that would lead the Kentucky-HOME charge.

"Mr. Schlusser, good morning, how are you…?"

"I'm good, sir."

"Okay, good…" Mr. Rolek said, gearing up. "Mr. Schlusser…we appreciate your testimony this morning. Would you please state for the court what your sex is?"

"Yes. I am a man."

"Okay, good. Mr. Schlusser, would you please tell the court the incorporated name of your business…"

The questions, or lawyer-statement-questions, went on quickly. The white/Caucasian judge sitting on the bench was slumped over a little to his right while using a computer mouse, looking intently up-and-down the computer monitor screen. Our Honor only interjected a few times to say things like "sustained" and "overruled," seemingly with little authority, and he only once looked away from his monitor. This judge knew the routine. As did Mr. Keller, who was now slumped over a little to his right dozing in the pew a few yards away.

The Test Coordinator waited anxiously, watching the question-and-answer session but not doing much active listening since the fear of his first court testimony loomed. He was to represent Kentucky-HOME on the stand as a witness to the agency's "frustration of mission" and "diversion of resources" segments, to explain how the private, non-profit agency, too, was damaged by the Respondent discrimination against the Complainant. A seemingly heavy burden at the time for someone who'd never went to law school, never took a civics class, and, at age 24, never, ever thought he'd get into the business of enforcing fair housing.

"Mr. Schlusser, I notice that you have an accent," Mr. Rolek projected in his Rust-Belt-big-city, slightly-nasally dialect after his two-year Louisville accent was quickly shorn. "Would you please tell the court where you're from…"

"Here. Here in Louisville."

"Well, I mean, I notice that you have a foreign accent, like, someone would have from a foreign country. Not from the United States…Would you please tell the court where you moved to Louisville from?"

"Ohio."

"Okay, okay, Ohio then," Mr. Rolek continued with a slight laugh. "Okay, now, where did you move to Ohio from?"

Pause.

"Germany."

"Okay, so your accent is German, you're from Germany? Originally?"

"Yes."

"Were you born in Germany?"

"Yes."

"And what did you do in Germany? As a profession."

"I was a business man."

"Okay, and what did you do before you were a business man?"

"I worked in a plant. A plant making vehicle parts."

"Okay. And what did you do before you worked in the plant, making vehicle parts?"

Mr. Schlusser paused again.

"I was conscripted."

"'Conscripted?'"

"Yes."

"'Conscripted'…like, 'conscripted' into an army?"

"Yes."

"The German army…"

"Yes."

"Okay, and what year were you conscripted into the German army?"

"1941."

"Okay, 1941. And what did you do in the army?"

"I worked on military vehicles."

"Okay. So…who--who was in charge, when you were in the army?"

"My commanding officer was named Sorge."

"Okay. Okay, so, who was in charge of officer Sorge…like, his commanding officer?"

"Mr. Strobel."

"Okay. And who was in charge of Mr. Strobel?"

"Adler."

"Okay, Adler. And, who was the commanding officer for Mr. Adler…?"

Mr. Schlusser paused.

"Mr. Kahler."

"Okay…Mr. Kahler. So, then, who was the commanding officer…"

The questioning went on up the chain of command, leading to inevitable names, those first known by likely only a few historians but then gradually on up to the most infamous of dictators, well-known to anyone in the general public. It was one of the few moments that the judge looked away from the computer, though his hand remained firmly on the mouse, always ready at attention to his commanding monitor.

And then came time for the Kentucky-HOME foot-soldier to finally testify for the court and his own commanding officers there. His nervousness pushed aside any thoughts he'd had of asking for a different, non-religious swearing-in for his upcoming testimony, his normal church-versus-state activism in those days now getting a pass. Despite the sparseness of attendees in the gallery, he eyed the place as wide but as covertly as he could. The judgmental stares of the jurors bothered him most; the eyes of his co-workers, next-most (though Mr. Keller looked like he was about to doze off again); and, the eyes of the judge, the least, as it was finally revealed to the Test Coordinator when sitting in the witness stand that Justice was using his mouse to play factory-installed computer solitaire.

As a postscript, the Test Coordinator noted that after the case suddenly resolved for not even a few thousand dollars in conciliation/negotiated settlement proceedings prior to a jury verdict, Mr. Schlusser introduced himself and his accompanying wife to him, and the couple seemed impossibly friendly and nice. The Test Coordinator guessed that fair housing enforcement really was all civil stuff…not criminal, like many people make it out to be, or want it to be. Even when the alleged discrimination is committed by the nicest former-Nazi he'd ever met.

***

In Louisville's middle school, a white/Caucasian teacher quickly responded to a white/Caucasian teen classmate's language in describing another schoolchild as "some black kid."

"What's 'black' got to do with it?!" the teacher snapped.

***

In his high school days, he accompanied three white/Caucasian friends in walking the streets downtown, trying to find the car after Thunder Over Louisville's mass migration from the fireworks finale ended. Under one narrow stretch of covered-sidewalk construction street, he brought up the rear of the party while ignoring teenage shouts seemingly against him from behind. After having enough, and taking the bait, he stopped and started to turn to the offenders, but he was barely-caught by a black/African-American fist to his jaw while another black/African-American male continued jawing insulting challenges at everyone ahead, not just the party, inviting the taking of all-comers on the streets while perplexed onlookers all watched the teens then break off into the night as quickly as they had appeared.

"Don't worry," one friend was compelled matter-of-factly to tell him, inside the closure of the car. "There's blacks…and then there's niggers."

He remained silent in the second stunning moment of the evening.

***

Drinking with mostly-white/Caucasian friends in 1997 could inadvertently bring out some "cultural appropriation" beyond the typical, fashionable, popular, "urban-contemporary" music of the day, whether from their own self-study or from the friend's study at the University of Louisville.

"You see," his friend said devouring a mouthful of food, "Slaves used to eat collard greens when the Master wouldn't give out things like meat, and potatoes, and all that, in the South, working in the fields. Greens have iron, potassium, vitamin C, they're like superfood…They make you strong, so you can keep going, keep your stamina up, all on their own, they're amazing…!"

***

He was there when a fellow discrimination investigator, black/African-American, was terminated that day. The ripple effect of shock was evident on the entire non-administration staff, even though most probably knew in the back of their minds that, family or not, the investigator flaunted his intentional laziness to management.

"I ain't workin' for black folk NO MORE*!" another African-American investigator proclaimed in contemptuous response to administration supervisors, regarding her good friend's departure.*

***

At 12:54 a.m., January 1, 2008, the white/Caucasian male leapt into the dining room of the house party and announced, "3…2…1…Happy CPT New Year!!!"

When the joke was lost, since everyone was silently confused, the jokester tried to help everyone in the room understand his meaning.

"It's Happy New Year…Colored-People-Time…!"

Everyone remained silent in response.

***

At the gentleman's club near his downtown Louisville apartment, he was drinking and watching dancers, television, and, inconspicuously, patrons, at the bar. An early-twenties dancer came up to him between dances upon their eye contact and she sat quickly right next to him to talk…she spoke fast, and cheek-to-cheek, in his ear.

"Hi, my name is Monique," she said with a play-innocent, eyes-engaged, pouty-lipped demeanor that complimented perfectly her baby-fat youth. "Will you buy me a drink, it's okay, I know you don't want to, I know, you don't, it's okay, it's because I'm black, it's okay…I know, it's okay…I know, it's 'cause I'm black…it's okay…"

"Stop saying that!" he exclaimed with a slight snap, though not as loudly as he thought he would, or should, say, all things considered.

He then bought her a drink.

***

Drunk again at the not-normally-this-crowded Louisville strip club, he decided to go outside to have a cigarette since the girls weren't allowing indoor violation of the smoking ban…some days, if everyone chipped in $5 each to pay any potential fine if the bar was caught by Louisville Metro Government inspectors, patrons were permitted to blaze up right there like in the good ol' days before 2008. A few others also went outside into the sticky summer night, including two black/African-American males who approached him and asked for some money. Looking at them in the eyes and using his standard "I Don't Have Anything, Sorry" response was not accepted by the duo, maybe because he wasn't going to hide his impairment from anyone that night.

"What about that ten you got in your pocket?" one asked, while the other started swelling with anger, and slight huffing, and not breaking eye contact with him.

"Sorry, man, it's all I got," he slight-laughed back to them.

"We just got outta Corrections," the talker then said, the huffing of the friend leaping to panting in his stare at him.

"Sorry, man," he said to them again.

"It's okay," the talker then said in switching gears, before tapping the friend with the back of a hand to the friend's chest in appearing to go against the wishes of the not-breaking-a-stare. "We'll go with God…Come on…"

And the two were off.

Later in the evening-turned-almost-early-morning, he was blacking in-and-out a little at the bar when the red lights suddenly turned to fluorescent white blaze. The microphone announced closing time, and it didn't appear that any dancers were going to go home with him this time. His eyes opening and closing slowly, he regained consciousness outside just enough to sense the various shadows and figures moving around under the street lamps outside the club. One male yelled from a distance away at another male more near him, with all the remaining bodies and silhouettes from the closing venue scattering in all different directions. He was rocking back and forth in an urban concrete ocean.

"Come on, you need help getting home…?" one of the figures asked him.

"No…naw…I live, right over there…" he feebly responded.

"Come on, I'll walk ya home," the now-black/African-American male said.

Too drunk and unaware to fight off the assistance, the two walked across the vast, well-lit, striped blacktop parking lot into a usually-familiar covered downtown parking garage area. An elevator should be there to lay in wait for transport to the parking garage roof, which, in turn, would hold a stairwelled back-door entrance to his high-rise apartment building. Walking past the parking garage vehicle entrance bar, the volunteer assistor led the two from a good distance ahead, on into the covered garage while he struggled to catch up to the new friend waiting near a lighted section revealing the elevator. Slowly shuffling past the parking garage vehicle entrance bar into the garage, a white/Caucasian male security guard then teleported in front of him to investigate.

"Is he bothering you?" the security guard asked him.

"No…" he feebly told the guard, regaining focus to what was ahead of him.

"You sure…?" the guard asked again, close to him, and looking him in the eyes, waited for the starting gun.

"No…" he said again, and he managed to catch the volunteer assistor far past, behind the guard, with the raised eyebrows of an open-mouthed frown of horrored disappointment.

The security guard then subsequently blocking the view of the assistor, or his own drooping eyelids doing such, he then got into the elevator, pushed the "up" *button, and leaned on the left wall as the doors closed on the night.*

***

On his lunch break reading online local news, he liked to read crime reports and look at mugshots of the alleged perpetrators. He noticed that, sometimes, there was inconsistency in the descriptions of persons based on their race; some suspects and/or victims had their race listed, some didn't.

However, on one particular day, the online television news article writer seemed eager to reinforce the newsworthiness of the demographics. The picture of an African-American-looking male identified and arrested for the heinous crime was accompanied by the location occurring at "the 2400 black of West Muhammad Ali Boulevard" in the West End of Louisville. He decided to report it to his Director, because he couldn't see the reporter having anything else but race on the brain in writing the story: the "a" and the "o" are located on opposite sides of a standard QWERTY keyboard, of course, so how could it be an innocent typographical error?

CHAPTER FOUR

<bleep bleep>

<dong!>

Sitting at my office desk, I turn my ear slightly as I listen for who arrives at the front door this time.

"Janice…hehe!…*Jan*ice…!"

I hear Janice laughing in response at the receptionist desk as Bonnie rustles her bags while getting in, followed by Bonnie's weekend update about her oldest son and something about her youngest grandchildren. After having hit the staff men's restroom only once so far this morning instead of the three times I typically do, likely today due to dehydration from lack of sleep, I text a belated message to Jenny.

cant wait till the weekend :x

I've put Ms. Johnson's information from this morning, wrapped up in the case file, on the left side of my desk. Normally, this left-side case file placement would remind me to timely-enter the required data entry and case novelization into HUD's online tracking system, but I'm just too busy today to give it more than a fleeting thought. The case, at least for today, is just going to sit.

Since it's near the beginning of the month, two dreaded e-mails have come into my e-mail inbox: one calendar request to attend an investigative unit meeting, another calendar request to attend the general Civil Relations Commission staff meeting. Despite the usual temptations to send back "cannot-attends" and "maybes" in revenge for wasting my time, I click on the confirmation tabs for both, handwrite the asterisk-starred meetings into my desk calendar, then highlight the entries with yellow highlighter for an hour's worth of time down the calendar pages for both. The unit meeting will likely last about a half-hour; the staff meeting, until the hour of my death.

Three more fair housing advocacy listserv e-mails have also come in, and they'll remain unread for now.

"Hey, what's up, Fat*eeeee*ma!"

Bonnie cheerfully goads Sherry, standing in the office doorway right before mine. I also hear that Monica, Commission Education & Outreach Coordinator, reveals herself to be sitting in Sherry's office, and Monica fights Bonnie back with mocking formal office etiquette.

"*Now, see, that's all bad for office morale, Bonnie.* I'm tellin' Brenda. That's discrimi*na*tion. And Brenda told me to *tell* you that, too…!"

"Hehe…Brenda's got all up-'n-crazy in *here*, now, hasn't she (!)," Bonnie says as Sherry and Monica continue the ball rolling on laughs. I then hear Janice rolling around from the receptionist desk and swooping in to Sherry's office, too, and if I wasn't so busy, I'd be seriously tempted to get up from my desk, walk over next door, and join them for the fun. All four of them, carrying on, and making me laugh when I get the privilege of eavesdropping on their playing, their messing-with-each-other, all the socialization that I too-infrequently join in for. It was so much easier to do all of it when I first started working for the Civil Relations Commission, back when we were adequately-staffed.

Instead, I jump back online from my seat and pull up *louisvillemarketplace.org* before noticing a voicemail-indicator diamond lit up on the office desk telephone that I apparently missed from earlier. I see that MyCallNavigator is still offline on the computer operating system, so I pick up the office telephone receiver, dial Louisville Metro Government's voicemail access extension, and then enter in my four-digit, fifteen-years-running automated teller machine pin number. The system speaks in 1990s robot Limited English Proficiency.

"*You. Have…One. New. Voicemail. Message…To-listen-to-your--*"

Contemptuously finger-punching "5" on the telephone keypad, I then hear, "*First. Message.*"

A sleepy Liz is testing me again on a Monday morning, asking me in a crackly voice and telephone line, both, to call her back.

"*I know we were…we're supposed to meet this morning, but I was calling…I was calling to see…if we could meet later today…or tomorrow…you can call me at--*"

Hitting "7" on the telephone keypad, I then hang up the phone receiver. I take one of the two stacks of the prepared housing discrimination tests from my inbox-outbox tray, put them back in the pile on top of the file cabinet, then look out the office window again down to West Chestnut Street: still Monday morning, as only a shopkeeper sweeping the weekend sidewalk trash is visible yet down there, before the lunch rush begins. I sit back in my office chair again and then quickly realize that I should get my Disability Action Network meeting folder (volume 2014-15) ready. Oh wait: better hold off on putting it in my black work bag, I need to get brochures for the Regional Housing Center presentation first, grab at least one copy of local ordinance…I think that's all I'll need for the afternoon presentation…

Bonnie now starts to walk past, "Morning, Alex," and she's about out of my office doorway view when she stops with a turn back and an "Alex..."

"Yeah, hey, morning, Bonnie...?"

"Hey, how's your weekend?"

"It was alright..."

"Okay cool, hey, lemme ask you something..."

"Yeah, sure...?"

"Ok, lemme-tell-ya what's goin' on," she says lightning-quick, with a just-as-quick seat in the door-closest of two chairs in front of my office desk, bags from home to her side. "Okay, I have this Respondent who won't respond to my letters, I've asked him to send in additional information, about comparables, you know? And he told me once over the phone that he *would*, but after I got the initial complaint response: *nothin'*."

"Hm, okay..."

"Okay. *So*: the Complainant, she's all over the place. You know--you had, you ever have Ms. Rucker?"

"Oh, *jesus*...yeah...(!)"

"Yeah, exactly. So, she filed again, sayin' that she was evicted based on her race, but she admits that she didn't *pay*, December *or* January. She just said that she had some friend at some other apartment there, this white girl, who didn't pay three months, and the Respondent let the friend stay. She said she was gonna have the friend call, but then I didn't hear anything, and so I called for the friend, and sent the friend a letter, and she hasn't responded either way. Ms. Rucker keeps callin', and callin', and callin', and I said, '*Baby*, you've got to be *patient*, it takes at least a hundred days to investigate the case.' I keep telling her to call Legal Aid and she says they don't do anything and they tell her to call over here. So, *I* dunno. I dunno *what* I'm gonna do. Whadda *you* think, what should I do? I don't know."

I pause.

"Well, I guess--uh, have you...have you asked for a site-visit from the Respondent yet?"

"No. But you know what? That's what I'm gonna do. I was waitin' on the witness, 'cause then I could just write it up as Probable Cause maybe, if the witness says that she wasn't paying, herself, and not evicted, but yeah--"

"Yeah, I'd just send the Respondent the site-visit proposal letter and sometimes that gets 'em goin' to give you some more information," I yawn-out from tiredness.

"Yeah..."

"Sorry, Bonnie--Yeah, so, otherwise, I guess we just have to gather what information we *can*, like the Complainant's information, and any alleged witnesses...documentation. And if the witness never responds, then we just go from there..."

"Yeah, right, huh..."

"So who's the Respondent in the case?"

My office desk telephone starts ringing, and I shoot a quick glance by turning my head just enough to see which line while still showing attention to Bonnie.

"You gotta get that?"

"No, no, that's okay," I dismiss. "It's outta-the-office, they can leave a message..."

"Okay, the Respondent is Allen--Mark. Mark Allen. Gaslight Properties, you ever had them? Out in J-Town?"

"Uh...*yeaaaaah*, I think...? Maybe...? Jeez, I can't even remember anymore, Bonnie..."

"Too much goin' *on*, huh? Hehe..."

"Yeah, no doubt. Uh, I'll see--lemme see if I can find anything in my files, I may've tested them before, anyways. I'll check. I mean, I guess it could be different treatment if we could find out that Ms. Rucker was being subjected to eviction but not others, but the tests would just show availability to rent and that's it, we can't do in-depth testing by submitting rental applications and signing leases, of course. I'm just lucky to get the damn tests *done*."

"Yeah, I know. I mean, she keeps not paying her rent, Ms. Rucker keeps getting *evicted*. Even if the Respondent *doesn't* respond, if we can't get that friend to call in, then it's outta here (!)," Bonnie says with a loud whistle-sound.

"Yeah, no doubt..."

"Okay cool." Bonnie pauses. "Okay, so, lemme ask you somethin' else: What do you think about Chad? I mean, he's-nice, he-really-is..."

I think Chad walked past my office to the restroom, previously, so I'll go ahead and speak up as if he's out of earshot.

"Yeah, he's alright...?"

"Yeah he's cool. He doesn't talk much, though, huh?"

"Yeah, he's always back in his office."

"Yeah I know, he's just like all the other guys who've had that office."

Slightly-laughing, I agree. "Yeah, I dunno what it *is* about that…"

"Hehe. Yeah, Robert, Donald…"

"Yeah, really (!), both of them, too…"

"Yeah but he seems--Chad seems nice. *He's* young. I don't think he's worked with black folk before, though, you know? Not that I'm sayin' he's a bad person or anything, I'm just sayin' that I don't--you know, I don't think he's worked with many people that way, you know?"

"Yeah, maybe not…"

"Yeah, he's new, too, *you* know…He's-nice."

"Yeah, and at least he's working on a couple of Probable Cause cases (!)"

"Hehe, oh, yeah, you're talkin' 'bout Robert again, huh?"

"Yeah…Chad's been here, what, about, fourteen months, just over a year? Robert was here four-and-a-half years and not *one* Probable Cause case…?"

"Yeah, it's ridiculous, right?!"

"Yeah it's pathetic! I mean, I've had a year, *maybe* two, with no Probable Cause cases, but that's just in the housing unit. In the employment unit, they usually have three *times* the number of cases *we* have, on average, so you can't *tell* me there weren't some Cause cases in there."

"For real (!)"

"I mean, Bonnie, you and I have all these Cause cases…ah forget it, never mind, I'll just go nuclear again, and I have a *long* day to go to start doing *that* already…"

"Hehe. Yeah, what-you got goin' on?"

"I'm goin' over to *your* friend's office this afternoon, the Regional Housing Center."

"Oh, *LORD…*"

Bonnie drops her home bags she's holding on both sides down onto the ground.

I start quietly laughing. "I'll tell Mary Korsak you'll be there at the next Fair Housing Network meeting--"

"--Okay, *look…*"

I still quietly laugh, leaning back in my office chair and putting my hand over my mouth.

"*Mary*...Lord Jesus...Okay: I *like* Mary, she means well...but at *that* meeting, she was just...you know, she was all trying to make it out to be a racial thing, with the placement of Section 8 housing all in the West End, and nowhere else. But that's not *true*, it don't matter if you're black, white, yellow, green, whatever: some people just don't pay their rent, some people just don't *wanna* work, you know what I'm sayin'?"

"Yeah..."

"I mean, we find discrimination here all the time, and it's got *nothin'* to *do* with *not payin'* your *rent.* Mary just gets these reports, with the Louisville Metro Housing Authority data, and just turns it all into race, when it's not always that *way*..."

"Yep..." I frown upwards.

"People make up all *kinds* of crazy stuff, that don't mean it's discrimination. You *gotta* look at the prima facie case elements, look at those comparable situations, and if they're not met, you know, it's outta here, we got too much to do here...!"

"I know, huh..."

"So, what's Agnes and Brenda havin' you do over there today?"

"Mary asked us to give a fair housing presentation to Regional Housing Center membership, so they're making me go over there and give it to all *four* people who'll probably show up, and then I gotta run back here so I can be on intake. Then I gotta go to the monthly Disability Action Network meeting tonight 'til 8:00..."

"Man, you're all booked up today, aren't ya?"

"Yeah..."

"Well, okay, then (!). So, how's ya' dad, how's your brother?"

"They're fine, still the same, as always..."

"How 'bout your wife, she okay, how's she doin'?"

"Yeah she's doing really well, the library is the *good* department of Louisville Metro Government administration these days ...(!)"

"Hehe alrighty-then, huh...Well, I catcha later...I *am* gonna go ahead and send that site-visit letter to the Respondent, but I'll call--I'll call him first, one more time."

"Okay that sounds good, just give me 'till tomorrow on the testing..."

"Oh yeah, no problem! I'll get back wit'cha."

"Okay cool, thanks Bonnie…"

"No problem, Alex."

Bonnie picks up her home bags from both sides and leaves my office to make her way on down the east wing hallway to her office. Yelling down the hall "Ron-ny! Ron! Whatcha doin' back in there…!" arbitrarily backwards towards where she had just came from, since his is the office past mine between the receptionist desk and Sherry's office. He doesn't respond, but she has to mess with him, of course, even when she forgets to do so previously.

Sitting in my office chair, I stop for a second to collect my thoughts. Trying to shake my head of the tiredness and overwhelming feeling of the day, the day still to come, I pop another cough drop and then look back towards my computer. Fair housing listserv e-mails that have come in will have to wait. I see my Toronto e-mail for the morning, titled "*Moanday Mourning*," and the body contains only "*??????????????!*" Since I couldn't start the morning conversation by e-mail like I do almost every workday, and since it's twice as bad today since I didn't respond to her last Friday e-mail, I just delete today's message from my friend and will let her believe that I called in sick today. If only I could or would have… (!)

I still have Scott's tests to create, so I jump back on *louisvillemarketplace.org* and type in keyword searches "*no kids*" and "*adult*," send the first two search-result rental housing advertisements to the mailroom printer, and then pull up Liz's contact information from the "*Testing*" folder via my computer's word processing program. I then make the call grabbing the office telephone.

"Hello…?" she asks, more awake.

"Hey Liz, this is Alex, how are you…?"

"I'm okay…" she says, sleepy-tentatively. "Um, hey, I was calling to see if I could reschedule our appointment, I know I'm supposed to come in today, but I dunno if you have anything available for tomorrow or Wednesday…?"

"Well, yeah, that's alright, I can switch it to tomorrow or Wednesday, depending on what time you wanna come in…?"

"Well, tomorrow, I can come in--what time do you get there tomorrow?"

"I'm scheduled to be here at 8:00 a.m."

"Okay…how about…okay, and you said we could do it Wednesday, too?"

"Yeah, tomorrow, or Wednesday, that would be fine. I could even leave the test information for ya if I'm not able to meet with you, and you can drop off the old tests if I'm not around…"

"Okay well, tomorrow, I have class at 9:00, and I dunno when I'll get away from campus…how about…Wednesday? I have to work, but I get off at 4:00, and you work until 5:00?"

"Yeah, but as long as you can get here by 4:45 at the absolute latest, we can do the debriefing real-quick and then be gone…"

"Oh yeah, no, let's do Wednesday, the place where I'm temping right now is on West Muhammad Ali, close to downtown in the West End, so I can get there by 4:30."

"Okay that works, let's shoot for Wednesday, which is September 2nd, at 4:30 p.m. I'll have everything ready for ya…"

"Okay, thanks Alex…!" Liz says with all the young, earnest gratitude of a hungover 24-year-old. God, I miss those days sometimes.

"Okay thanks Liz, see ya then…"

"Okay bye."

Hanging up, I put a circle around, and then an oversized "*X*" through, Liz's asterisk on my office desk calendar for today, before flipping the pages to Wednesday and handwriting the asterisk-starred meeting now for the 2nd at 4:30 p.m., highlighting it with yellow highlighter for half an hour.

I grab the Civil Relations Commission's 1990s microcassette tape recorder and put a cassette tape in it noted with "*S.E.K. 2014-15 testing*" on the body in scraggly ink pen. I place Scott's tape recorder on top of the tests already waiting in the plastic inbox/outbox combination tray on my office desk, wondering if today'll be the odd-numbered day he shows up for his testing at a time we don't have scheduled, as opposed to the 11:00 a.m. or so appointment actually agreed-upon last week.

10:28 a.m. means that it's almost time for my ten-minute-allowed break, so I wrap up my office paperwork phase and roll into my online-news-update phase. Time to check the local newspaper website for local civil rights news or, better yet, Louisville Metro Government administration scandal, and if I have time, maybe a check of another national news website. Looks like Courting Our Racial Equality ("CORE") has issued a statement condemning local police for an officer-involved shooting in Old Louisville last week, and their press release is no coincidence locally to other activist group events now, nationwide. And the sentiment is echoed in a separate announcement by grass-roots Louisville non-profit Open Connections, stating that OC's mission of civil rights for persons based on sexual orientation and gender identity is not mutually-exclusive from the civil rights African-Americans currently struggle with in combating police aggression.

"*Alex...*"

Janice comes to the office door, ink pen and papers in hand. News update time is over just as quickly as it began. Janice sits in the same chair Bonnie just vacated a few minutes ago.

Janice sighs.

"Got a call this morning from a lady who said that her neighbor--she got into it with her neighbor...well, it's a lot of things. Okay, so, this lady who called, she's white, the neighbor's African-American, and the lady says that the neighbor and the neighbor's boyfriend threatened her--it--it's--" sighing again, "--it's all over the place. The lady said that she and the neighbor used to be friends, like they would watch each other's kids, they live in the same apartment complex in Shively...The lady said that she and the neighbor got into an argument a couple months ago, because she--hehe--she said that she was seeing the neighbor's boyfriend, but not this *current* boyfriend of the neighbor that also threatened to beat her up, it was this *other* one that was some *former* boyfriend this neighbor had, ex-boyfriend. And the caller, she admitted, you know, she admitted that she was seeing the neighbor's *old* boyfriend behind the neighbor's back, and then, when the neighbor found out about it, the neighbor--hehe--beat up the *old* boyfriend, with the new boyfriend..."

"Oh, *jesus*, here we go..." slightly shaking my slumping-over head, eyes closed with a sarcastic half-smile.

"And--and then, the neighbor's boyfriend was charged with assault, but not the neighbor. But then the caller said that whenever the neighbor sees her out, you know, in the apartment complex, the neighbor ignores her, until the *new* current boyfriend is around *with* the neighbor, then the two of them, they just start calling her 'white bitch' and saying 'we're gonna get you, white girl,' and all that kinda stuff. So the caller said she talked to the apartment management, and said that the manager tells her to call the police, since it was a criminal thing, and so she said that she *called* the police, but that they won't take any action against the neighbor, or the new boyfriend, because they, the police, didn't see it happen, and they told her to go file a warrant…"

Getting winded, Janice sighs again.

"Okay, so, I started drafting it as a housing complaint, but…well, what do *you* think, should I draft it as housing, or a hate crime, or wha--what should I…I dunno …"

"Well, I mean, it could be drafted as both, *if* the apartment complex won't do anything about the neighbor, and management knew that racial slurs, or race-based statements, were made against the Complainant. And, a bias-related crime complaint could be drafted against the neighbor *and* the neighbor's boyfriend, based on race. The neighbor and the boyfriend would probably argue that it wasn't about race, but about the old boyfriend, but the Complainant could argue that it was *elevated* into a bias-related crime once the race-based statements were made repeatedly, even if the original dispute was *not* about race. Like, that hate crime case we had with Ms.…uh…what's her name…Ms.…uh…Ms.--Ms. Broadus. Did you do that intake?"

"*Yeaaaaah* …yeah, uh-huh, which one was that…?"

"That was the one a few years ago, where the Complainant and her family were African-American, and the neighbors, a married couple, were Caucasian, and the neighbors put up the Confederate flag, like, *conditionally*, whenever the families got into it, and then the Respondent husband allegedly posted signs, handwritten with anti-African-American racial slurs, then there was a fight between them, like, physically, and the Shively--yeah, this was also in Shively, *that's* right…the police didn't make any arrests. Because the police had been to *both* residences a bunch of times, but we argued after the investigation that the matter escalated into a hate crime when the race-based stuff came into it. Multiple times."

"Yeah okay, I remember you talking about that…"

"Yeah, and we issued Probable Cause based on the witness statements, and the Respondents in that case, at hearing, the Respondent wife admitted that he--her husband, was obsessed with the Confederate flag, having shipments sent to him here in Louisville from Alabama, where they were originally from, and he just denied in the hearing to the hearing officer that *anything* took place between the families, so the hearing officer ruled in the Complainant's favor. *Finally* got one of those cases through to a full hearing (!). You can have those mixed-motive type cases, it just depends on the evidence, you know?"

"Okay, so, you're saying, draft a housing and a hate crime, both…or, two--hate crimes, for both, and not housing."

"Yeah, based on what you said, she--the caller, the potential Complainant, could do that. Up to two hate crime complaints, one each against the neighbor and that new boyfriend, and then a housing complaint against the management company if she says that the landlord refused to deal with it knowing that race was an issue."

"Okay…o-*kay*, I'll call her back, and I'll tell her, we can do housing, and a hate crime."

"Yeah, or, you know, whatever the combination would be. And then if I'm not here to review the complaint drafts, you can just give 'em to Agnes, or…if it can wait, it may not be 'till tomorrow, but I can review 'em."

"Okay, that's fine, I'll call her back…okay *thanks…*"

Janice is up, off, and out, and I decide to abandon online break time. I *have* to go get those fair housing brochures and things for the presentation this afternoon.

But before I get up to head down the hallway, past the kitchenette, to walk around towards the very back of the east wing, I see the e-mail arrive from Assistant Jefferson County Attorney Laura G. Beck:

> "*Brenda/Agnes/Alex,*
> *I write with an attached final, executed Housing Conciliation Agreement between the parties in the matter* Cartwright v. Rutherford*. After the three of you sign, date, scan, and return the Agreement to me, the County Attorney will proceed with closure based on the terms.*
> *If you have any questions, please let me know. I'll be in touch with Briana to contact the Kentucky Office of the Attorney General hearing officer to cancel the hearing scheduled for next month. Thanks.*"

And the brochures will wait.

I eagerly open the attached Housing Conciliation Agreement in the e-mail and see that, aside from epic waivers of liability and standardized tough-sounding language clarifying all kinds of jurisdictional matters, the bottom line is that Respondent in the case agrees to pay the Complainant $4,500. The Respondent also agrees to "self-certify" studying some courses on fair housing law, but there's no other remedy specifically for the public interest.

The United States Department of Housing & Urban Development *should* be upset with us at audit time for the latter provision…or, at least, that's what HUD's audit paperwork checklist for agencies like ours indicates. HUD will prorate our payment for the case, docking us money due to the lack of meaningful public interest enforcement in the resolution. That is, until the Civil Relations Commission appeals HUD's partial-compensation withholding from us; then, we'll likely get the full amount, *if* there's even a question over our compliance with HUD policy by our assigned HUD monitor.

I'm disappointed in this resolution to the case emotionally, or maybe it's because I'm so tired today, but my better reasoning is pretty much on board with the end result. Not that the Complainant should've necessarily received more financial compensation in the settlement, but, aside from the alleged Respondent refusal to rent to her based on her race association with her African-American boyfriend, the year-and-a-half time it took for me to investigate the case and go through legal proceedings, including being present for depositions of the Complainant and the Respondent both, and the intimacy I've held of investigating and monitoring one of the Civil Relations Commission's all-too-infrequent Probable Cause cases, it all just starts to leave me.

I've conducted full investigations of hundreds of discrimination complaints, thousands when including limited, partial, and inconclusive inquiries, but the Probable Cause cases, those not only recommended and then dismissed in disagreement with the County Attorney's Office and/or Director, *and* those that actually get through to legal proceedings, are the ones that help hold my sanity in this angry, exhaustive business. Objectively, though, this resolution is in the ballpark of being about right: absent a court or hearing officer judgment on legal discrimination occurring, affirmative remedy against the Respondent is negotiation-limited in the conciliation. I guess. I rationalize. Oh, well.

I send the Agreement document to the mailroom printer.

Instead of heading for the mailroom printer, however, and rushing over to talk with Sherry & Janice about the coincidence of the Agreement arrival when we were just talking about the case this morning, I launch into stride the opposite way down the east wing hallway, winding around past the kitchenette, to walk to the very back of the wing. *I've got to get those damn brochures*, my caffeine-head neurosis and attention deficit say in unison.

But rounding the corner to try to get to the very back offices, and trying to ignore her in order to maximize my efficiency-time, I hear "*Alex!*" from Briana: Commission Secretary, HUD liaison, and occasional staff interrogator. Somehow, she snuck past me earlier in the morning to get to her office work desk in the last station before the very back area.

"Morning…" I say as I give in and stop to speak with her. "I came back here, 'cause Brenda's been lookin' for you, she's *pissed…*"

"Nuh-uh, you lie, quit all tryin' to be like me…(!)"

I slightly-laugh and try to breeze through.

"I gotta get brochures for the presentation this afternoon. This is gonna be a looooong day…"

"Uh-huh. You-takin'-the-car?" Briana pointedly, and loudly, and quickly, asks. She's in her interrogation mode already, I better be careful, and reactionary.

Here we go.

"Yeah," I respond.

"Where you *goin'…?*"

"The Regional Housing Center. I'm gonna give a fair housing presentation."

"You gettin' *brochures…?*"

"Yeah."

"Pens?"

"No, just brochures."

"Magnets?"

"Nope."

"Bookmarks?"

"Nope."

"You ain't gettin' no magnets!?"

"Nope."

"Why not? Alex! You should get *magnets*, we got billion of 'em…"

"This is just a presentation for the membership today, no *real* people from the public will be there…"

"You should still get *magnets…!?*"

"Briana," I sigh, "no, we gave those out to--*Bonnie* goes to their monthly meetings, she gave some out in--back in April, I think. National Fair Housing Month."

"So give out more!"

"Briana…(!)"

Briana loudly-laughs.

"Oh my *god…*" I dread out loud to the world.

Again, Briana loud laughing.

"Alright, I gotta get these brochures," I say to no one around me.

"What-you speakin' on?"

"Just on what we do, fair housing. And the Supreme Court decision on disparate impact."

"What-Supreme-Court."

"The U.S. Supreme Court, the recent decision on how disparate impact is valid under the federal Fair Housing Act."

"You mean in Kentucky, that Supreme Court?"

"Briana…(!)"

Loudly-laughing again, Briana concedes, "O*kay*, Alex. You got you-meetin' tonight, too?"

"Yeah, it's the last Monday of the month, so I'll be there…"

"How late you workin' tonight?"

"Probably 'til 8:00 p.m."

"Dag…!"

"Yeah…"

"Take some magnets, then!"

"Ohhhhh mah *god--*"

Loud-laughing Briana.

I knew I shouldn't have mustered the strength today to let her joke around with me. I'm about to just bolt, but then I can't help myself.

"Wait, Briana: did you see Laura's e-mail just now?"

"*Nooooo*, what e-mail? What e-mail you talkin' 'bout, I didn't get no e-mail--wait, lemme see," Briana says, turning to her computer. "I didn't get no e-mail…?!"

"Oh ok, well, Laura just said that the *Cartwright* case just settled. The Complainant gets $4,500, the Respondent gets *marginal* training, all that. I guess I'll sign it, I'm assuming Agnes and Brenda will sign it, then you'll need to cancel the hearing set for next month. Laura said that she'll get with *you* on it…"

"Oh ok…Well, she didn't e-mail me about it. Is she gonna create the Order, the Order for the case?"

"Uh, I dunno. She'll probably tell you how she wants it worded."

"You sure?"

"Briana," I say with a single tired exhale-laugh, "I mean, I guess so, you can have me look at it, too, if you want, I dunno…(!)"

"Because you did it that last time, you remember? You remember you did that…?"

"Uh, yeah, maybe…sure…"

"Okay. I'll just wait to hear from Laura, then. And maybe you do it."

I see Sherry walking back towards us with a pen and a clipboard, so I know she'll be up to bat against Briana next.

"Alright," I ease out, "I *gotta* get these brochures, Briana…Go mess with someone else, like your friend *Sherry*…"

Sherry's game. "Aw, *naw*, see…(!)"

Briana and Sherry both laugh their own trademark laughs and I continue on back to the Civil Relations Commission's 1970s-orange file cabinets, which seem to reach for the heavens with Minority Contract file folders from the 1980s; standard HUD fair housing and home mortgage predatory lending informational brochures, both circa 2007; and, various sets of Commission brochures, individualized with explanations of rights to action according to Commission-jurisdictional complaints, printed from federal fiscal year funds in 2004-05 and 2014-15. I grab a stack of about 25 fair housing brochures printed last year in English, and five in Spanish, and then one each in Bosnian, unidentified Chinese, French, Korean, Russian, two types of Somali, and Vietnamese. Since it's a low-income housing advocacy crowd this afternoon, I'll forego the Commission employment discrimination, public accommodation discrimination, bias-related crime complaint, and police ombudsman brochures in either of our two languages printed, English/Spanish.

I then curse under my breath (in English and Spanish) while grabbing a stash of fair housing magnets printed in English, and then one magnet each in Bosnian, unidentified Chinese, French, Korean, Russian, two types of Somali, Spanish, and Vietnamese.

Walking back past Briana and Sherry, both ignoring me for their conversation together, and then after walking the hallway past my office, I circle to turn into the mailroom but see that the copier-printer is being used by Ron. I sneak away from the mailroom door entry in order to avoid his detection, circling back to land back in my office chair, frustrated.

The computer clock reads 11:43 a.m. Looks like Scott is late, or not showing up again. In the few minutes before lunchtime, I pull up a synopsis for *Texas Department of Housing and Community Affairs v. The Inclusive Communities Project, Inc.* to study the recent United States (not Kentucky) Supreme Court decision narrowly-affirming a disparate impact allegation of discrimination under the federal Fair Housing Act, as amended. The Court held that discrimination can be an impact without specific intent--

My office telephone office rings again. Out-of-office line.

Barely-professional enthusiasm kicks in with, "Louisville Metro Civil Relations Commi--"

"*Bluegrass Fair Housing Council, Max speaking…*" the mockingly-stuffy voice says.

"Hey, Max…" I try to inflect positively.

Back in his normal voice, Max legitimately asks, "How are you…"

"I'm *tired-as-hell*, and I have to work until 8:00 p.m. tonight, you?"

"I'm good…just calling about the *Cartwright* case--"

"*Yeahhhhh*, I just got Laura's e-mail on that. So, you all settled it?"

"Yeah, Ms. Cartwright just wanted it over with, I think."

"Yeah, I can understand *that…*"

"Laura and I thought it was worth much more than that, though."

"I actually think it was about right, for conciliation, I guess. But I always wanna see these things go to full hearings or court, establish case law--"

"Yeah, we all know *that--*"

"I mean, I just worry though that the Respondent woulda seized upon local ordinance language that the Complainant wasn't qualified financially at first, when he had the first house available for her, and she didn't have enough income for it, and then he cited renovation costs for the second one he offered, in needing him to increase the rent after he first offered that second house to her, and he documented that… allegedly--"

"Yeah," Max litigates, "but he offered her the *second* property at one amount, she accepts it, he then sees the boyfriend is African-American, then all of a sudden it costs more, and then he ignores her after she agrees to pay the higher amount. In writing, with her text messages. And he made racial statements in his stories to her when showing the property to her, and he later ignored the boyfriend when they were there, and the Complainant's boyfriend's maintenance guy friend was a witness to the Respondent ignoring the boyfriend's questions, talking only to him, the white maintenance guy…you know? I think it's a good case, Laura and I liked our chances at hearing."

"Oh yeah, I know," I quickly agree, "and four days after the Respondent receives the copy of the HUD complaint notification, he sells the property. Instead of continuing to renovate it and rent it…Well, allegedly. I mean, I agree, I just worry about a hearing officer seizing upon that ability-to-pay language in the ordinance anyways. But, hey, conciliation is voluntary between the parties, so, that's that…"

"Yeah, I always wanna advocate for our clients, but HUD's on us now to insert more training, advertising, follow-ups with Complainants, that kind of stuff. When they audit our HUD grants, we have to document all of that or get cited, they're looking into things more these days."

"Yeah, same here, we have to insert all that 'affirmative relief' for *you* guys, and your Complainants, whether pre-Cause or post-Cause, and it makes things difficult when a Respondent doesn't wanna do it pre-Cause, 'cause they never did anything wrong in the first place, obviously…"

"Yeah…"

"So, I just draft conciliation agreements without those provisions if there's a stalemate between us inserting too much and the Respondent refusing it, HUD can dock us on the payment on the case, I don't care."

" Your bosses Brenda and Agnes will care…!"

"I know, but the Complainants and the Respondents come *first*, obviously. I mean, if they agree to something, pre-Probable-Cause, and we make no determination on the case of Probable Cause yet, they can pretty much resolve it any way they want, unless it's illegal or something."

"*Dude*…you're crazier than half the crazy Complainants I represent, you know that, right?"

"Yep…okay, dude: lemme let you go for today, can I call you back tomorrow, I gotta go to lunch, and then the rest of the day is messed up…"

"Sure, I was just calling to check in," Max says, "but we also have a case coming your way, Janice'll tell you about it."

"Uh, okay man, sounds good, keep 'em comin', as always…I'll call ya back…"

"Okay bye."

"Later, man."

Almost slamming the telephone receiver into its mold, I jump up from my office chair, bolt out of my office, and again check the mailroom…no one's at the copier-printer, so I launch into the "*hold print*" section of the prompt, enter my ATM pin number, select the applicable printer tray tables and paper sizes, then print out the *Cartwright v. Rutherford* Housing Conciliation Agreement. I grab an ink pen from the mailroom sorting table, quickly sign the Agreement with a little contempt of *whatever*, and slide the Agreement through the printer form-feed for a copy; then, I put the original-signed Agreement back into the form-feed, navigate selections, and scan a copy into an electronic document in the machine that will make it available in a shared electronic directory folder for staff. I then place my signed original Agreement in Agnes' mailbox, leave the mailroom, and head on past the now-vacant receptionist desk for Ronita's office in the near west wing.

"Hey, Ronita, you mind if I get the city vehicle key from ya…?"

Sitting in her office desk almost in the dark but surrounded by papers, Ronita silently and patiently goes into her top left desk drawer and hands over the key, almost without making any eye contact. Usually about 90% business, I get the "*Here you go, sweetie*" ten-percent response from her today that some on staff have only heard rumors about getting themselves. I grab the key from her and retreat with a simple, hurried *Thanks, appreciate-it* and I struggle to hide a yawn with my pink eyes half-closed and my eyelids warm.

I swing past the still-vacant receptionist area, proceed on to my office ("*Alex, I left the intakes in your office*," Janice yells out from Sherry's office and I throw back a passing acknowledgment), I dump the Agreement copy on my desk, grab the empty water bottle and an air freshener aerosol while listening to the office desk telephone ring again (*Not getting it*), and I head on down the east wing hallway back to the kitchenette refrigerator. I pop the plastic top to the container of my plastic lunch ration, I nuke it in the cheap new "retro" microwave I bought six months ago to replace Janice's 1970s-era artifact I was lucky enough to short out, I fill the water bottle to help kill the 1:15 microwave timer clock, I grab the lunch after the ding and spray a quick blast of the air freshener, then I head back to my office dodging potential staff chatting roadblocks ("*Hey, hey…!*" and "*It's lunchtime…!*"), shutting my office door behind me. I dig into my deep-drawer desk for a rubber-banded, half-eaten bag of family-size seasoned corn chips, and I get out a mostly-full can of grocery-store-brand unsalted peanuts. Arms flailing for a few seconds, I arrange everything for a space on the office desk before crashing into my office chair, which dumps down a notch from its regular seat-adjustment setting.

I breathe an abbreviated breath. It's 12:00 noon, and it's time for a shortened lunch hour.

It wasn't until age 35 that he first held an infant minor child in his arms. Sitting in his girlfriend's one-bedroom high-rise apartment in downtown Louisville, she agreed to watch her niece while her sister and brother-in-law had an evening out. The baby was fine when the parents were around, but as soon as they left, the terror built up into a blood-curdling, purple faced, open-mouthed scream that no one but the parents could console into calm. Once again, reinforcing his unwillingness to ever have children of his own…to the extent that he had any control over that.

He couldn't help thinking at the time, though, of how his father told him how colicky he was as an infant, so much so that his father smashed a chair in frustration. And a co-worker also once told him when discussing a child discrimination case that, incidentally, he was a colicky adult, much less probably was a colicky baby. He's the first to admit, however, that he himself was the child he never had.

***

He'd never changed a diaper in his life.

***

He'd never visited a maternity ward at a hospital in his life.

***

He'd never been an uncle in his life.

***

He'd never house-trained a puppy in his life.

***

At age nineteen, one of his best friends led him to a small apartment party hosted by his friend's girlfriend's older brother. The late-thirty-something attractive blonde stranger with the tummy bulge in the living room circle there had to have been around eight-and-a-half months pregnant, and she sat passing around a seemingly endless go-around of marijuana joints, smoking a chain of cigarettes when not her turn for a hit. When she easily convinced him to drive both of them out to the liquor store in order to get some bourbon for the party, she explained during the ride that she quit heroin and cocaine for the health of the baby.

CHAPTER FIVE

It's 12:20 p.m., so that gives me about ten minutes to go to the office staff men's restroom and brush my teeth, use mouthwash, put on my not-city-government-color-schemed official city government name badge, and make sure my salt-and-pepper hair looks especially "distinguished" for the afternoon presentation. I grab my office toothbrush, housed in a plastic travel case, out of the deep desk drawer; a red plastic party cup in use for swishing for months, I think since the last Kentucky Derby staff lunch event; and, a travel-size mouthwash container, half-full from this past Friday's refill from the large bottle also in the drawer that's too cumbersome to take down the hallway. Halfway down the hall I stop in my tracks, double-back to my office, and dig into my black work bag to grab the forgotten-already name badge. I try again down the hall towards the west wing and successfully get done with the lunchtime restroom routine, with no one still at the front receptionist desk since Janice went off to lunch and Roberta called in sick.

The fair housing brochures now in the black work bag, along with a copy of *Texas Department of Housing and Community Affairs v. The Inclusive Communities Project, Inc.*; an 8½" x 14" yellow legal-sized notepad; and, the prized fair housing magnets, I'm out the front door with sunglasses on. Instead of the front elevators, I walk down the fifth-floor hallway east to the South 4th Street side-elevators. Since it's most of downtown Louisville's lunch hour, I've given myself five extra minutes to account for the tied-up elevator on the less-used side of the building, which will have people coming and going in singles and groups all at around the same time. But of course the elevator car arrives almost right after I push the down button, and no one's inside, so there was no need to stand to one side, away from the opening elevator doors, to let people out or have them adjust their close quarters to let me in.

Out on 4th Street, alive in a different way now that I'm out of the office and feel the heat and humidity, I dive into sparse pedestrian traffic and make the short walk to the next building over. A parking garage pedestrian entrance and an inside elevator car being pulled by a hamster bring me to the top roof area, where Louisville Metro Government tattooed compact car number 423 sits. I walk around the vehicle and see that two of the four tires appear under-inflated; there's a crack in the passenger-side side mirror; and, rust spots have continued to spread here and there throughout the white vehicle body. With an eye-roll and a frown, my informal inspection passes, and I unlock the driver's side door and get in, locking the door manually right away.

I see that there's about half-a-tank of gasoline according to the fuel gauge, correct with a benefit of the doubt I've incurred after the last department vehicle ran out of gas on me with a quarter-tank reading. I remove my sunglasses and exchange them for the normal glasses in my black work bag on the passenger seat, I get out a small note pad out from the bag's zipped side-pocket, and I write down "*59995*" after turning the ignition switch and cranking up the air conditioner, which of course blows out hot air. In order to try to keep my brain sharp, there's no music for the commute, and I don't turn on the radio for any kind of talk for the drive (and, I don't use the cassette tape player…or use the cigarette lighter). I flip open the ashtray to reveal a plastic parking pass entry/exit scanner card, and I ready the card in my left hand, ready for quick use at the parking garage exit bar to accommodate any tailgaters riding me on the way down the garage ramps.

Now, I'm *really* prepared to take my life in my hands, thanks to the antiquated maintenance of the city vehicle; the antiquated driving habits of most Louisville Metro drivers; and, the antiquated health I suffer from today. I back the car out of the parking space, looking incessantly in all directions despite half the roof parking being unoccupied, and I begin to drive the constant stay-to-the-right unmarked ramp lanes winding down out of the parking garage. The rooftop floor may have decent visibility today, but the next four floors are tightly-packed and bring most of the caution. There's also a lack of striping and signage in this quasi-Louisville-Metro-Government-operated garage, including no designated prohibition on oversized vehicles parking on the corner turns so that visibility and navigation space can be sufficiently unblocked.

I always slightly-worry about the general public calling in on me to answer "How's My Driving!?" ever since Brenda called me into her office after my first run in the car a dozen years ago: someone called the office of Mr. Two Mayors Ago and alleged that I was speeding through a school zone while snaking in and out of traffic. So the Director at the time had then Assistant Director Brenda to investigate. I had to explain that I did the speed limit, which was permitted since it was a few minutes after the school zone time expired the reduced speed; and, that when people stopped in the left of two-laned traffic to turn left from

Bardstown Road, it was customary, née, *mandatory*, to go around the turn-waiting car, to the right. (It was one of only two times I'd ever been "in trouble" on the job, though the other time, I actually *did* the minor infraction I was accused of. In order to be with a girl. And, concurrently, to get out of a ridiculous federal fair housing conference lunchtime *interpretive dance* production that I did *not* sign up for, when I took all other conference breakout sessions seriously. My fault for getting caught by supervisors on that one, I guess.)

Maybe since it was the heart of lunchtime on a Monday, I only narrowly-miss hitting a pedestrian once on my way down to the parking garage exit bar, and there's no vehicle riding my bumper. I fumble my left-handed garage scanner card, start lowering automatically the rear driver's side window by mistake in pushing the wrong driver's side door button, then get it all together to scan out and drive out of the garage exit. I drive out to the edge of the long parking garage entrance/exit sidewalk area and switch out to the sunglasses in the bright, humid, summer day again at the South 5th Street crossing.

Using turn signals, slow lanes, and speed limits, my professional persona quells the *enfant terrible* within that would've otherwise used car horns, cursing, and hand gestures to assist getting me to Regional Housing Center offices located a dense 1.7 miles away from the Civil Relations Commission. I arrive at the RHC-housed three-story office suite building on the east edge of downtown and park the car in free, flat-lot-space-style parking at 1:00 p.m. I gather my things, exit the vehicle, lock the driver's side door with a driver's side button before throwing the door shut, and then head inside. At the elevator, I push the only visible button to go up. The elevator door opens, no one exits, and I enter the elevator car and push for the second floor. I then get out of the elevator and head three offices down the hall to suite #217, where a Regional Housing Center logo of hands around a generic home symbol adorns double-doored glass. I pull the right-hand door latch and the door stays shut with a locked tremble…then, I notice the "*push*" sign right near the latch. I regroup to follow the instructions and Renee is there to half-smile at me from an ovalish receptionist desk.

"Hi, may I help you?"

Renee's pleasant, but I can't tell if she recognizes me from the annual RHC meeting they had last summer, where we initially met and made small talk for about ten seconds.

"Hey, yes…My name's *Alex*, I'm here to give a presentation at 1:30, on fair housing…?"

"O-*kay*, are you with the Human Rights Commission?"

"Well, the Civil Relations Commission, yeah, as opposed to the Kentucky Commission on Human Rights…"

"Okay, yep, we're ready for you, it's at 1:30?"

"Yeah, I'm here early to set up and all…"

"Okay…let me…let…me…see, if they're back from lunch, yet. You can have a seat, and I'll check around, *okay*?"

"Okay sure, thanks…" I half-heartedly smile, but do so wide-eyed to try to force through the tiredness.

"Just one moment…"

While Renee picks up an office telephone and starts scrolling through what might be an online shared office calendar on the desk computer, I look at the lobby walls and tables, squinting with my chin out, instead of immediately sitting to wait. Equal housing opportunity posters, statements, and logos from HUD; homelessness resource directories and stickers, in Regional Housing Center partnership with a statewide coalition advocating for the rights of homeless persons; local rental tenant association how-to brochures in partnership with Legal Aid; and, know-your-federal-subsidy-regulation-rights booklets in tandem with HUD and the Louisville Metro Housing Authority. All the materials surround the RHC's signature bounty of grant-funded annual reports and special reports on the status of low-income housing in the city, which tie housing into the cost of maintaining utilities, child care, and transportation. The RHC is the crossroad of affordable housing and fair housing, which, to me, are oftentimes mutually-exclusive things. At least, legally, and, locally, from a housing discrimination standpoint.

I then go ahead and sit in a lobby chair, black work bag on my lap held as if I'm waiting humbly for a job interview. I dig through the work bag to pop a cough drop, since the menthol may last me the hour-or-so time for the presentation, and I ready another cough drop in my front right dress shirt pocket for quick-draw, as needed. I go over the planned syllabus for the presentation in my head, with my pre-presentation jitters relatively mild but causing scattered, racing thoughts, and anxiety, as always, anyways. I have with me an electronic version of a generic Civil Relations Commission fair housing presentation on a flash drive, but I'd much rather wing it with the speech, and then just dive into questions.

Some people can give a talk and then respond to audiences with a lot of nothing-speak; I'm a know-it-all, if it's fair-housing-related, so I'd rather try to be on point in a response to an audience member question. Well, more or less I know my stuff, I have been known to get convoluted…

1:10 p.m.… 1:11 p.m.… the black seconds-hand of a 1980s white circular wall-clock behind the receptionist desk goes around to 1:12 p.m.…

I struggle to hide a yawn with my pink eyes half-closed and my eyelids warm.

I then see through the glass front doors Mary Korsak walk up to the offices' doors, laughing with two other persons I've seen around at conferences or local community meetings but haven't formally met. I smile my slightly-insecure smile from my seat as they enter.

"Alex, hi…!"

"Hey, Mary…!"

"So, yeah…this is it! We're on to talk about fair housing this afternoon!"

"Yeah, we sure are…"

"Alex, have you met Emily Kneller, she's a board member with RHC?"

"Well, I've definitely seen you around, Emily, hi…" I say as I extend my hand.

"Hi," Emily says with a quiet, maybe-shy smile, barely shaking my hand by just putting her hand out.

"And this, *this*, is Roger Cowan, also a board member--"

"And Sergeant-at-Arms, Mary just won't let me keep watch anymore, nice to meet you, Alex…" he says with a business-firm handshake, making me lose control of the black work bag shoulder strap.

"Hi, nice to meet you, Mr. *Cow*an…" I acquaint with adjusting my black work bag over my shoulder again.

"Take whatever Roger says with a grain of salt, he's our board jokester," Mary segues. "Come on into our conference room here, and we can wait for the others to show up."

We're all shuttled down the office hall by Mary and I awkwardly-mouth a silent "*thank you*" to Renee along the way, though Renee's looking down at something on the receptionist desk and doesn't see me. Mary kicks on the lights in the Regional Housing Center conference room, which is about twice the size of the Civil Relations Commission conference room and, likewise, has at least twice the up-to-datedness of technology for presentations. Mary's local media campaign, her message on low-income housing advocacy, and her political connections all elevate the RHC's community presence from fringe gadfly status to more of an institution on the level of a municipal government department in Louisville Metro.

"Alex, I think we can have you set up over…here," Mary parades, "…and then we have about a dozen board members who RSVP'd that they'd be here this afternoon."

"Okay, cool," I say, unslinging my black work bag onto a side-table in front of a standing podium at the head of the large conference room table. I unzip the bag and then dig out the fair housing brochures, magnets, large yellow legal-sized notepad, ink pen, and *Texas v. Inclusive Communities*. Ms. Kneller and Mr. Cowan take what appear to be their regular, formally-unassigned seats.

"And you'll talk about the protected classes under fair housing, is that right?"

"*Yes*, well, yeah, I can. And about the Supreme Court decision on disparate impact under the federal Fair Housing Act, is that right?"

"Yes! Important, historic decision! Our board is eager to hear about that."

"Okay, I can do that…"

"But they also can use a refresher course on the protected classes, and what the Civil Relations Commission does with fair housing and housing discrimination issues."

"Well, we can do a whole lot *more*, I can tell ya that, Mary…"

"I'll tell Brenda you said that, Alex," she slightly-laughs.

"I wish you *would* (!)" I say as exuberantly as Mr. Cowan's handshake.

"Do you have an electronic presentation?"

"No…no, Mary, I was just gonna wing it, unless you want me to do the electronic stuff. I'd much rather get into questions and answers from the crowd."

"No, no, no need for the visual aids. We'll just wing it, like you said…"

"We may not take it easy on you, though, Alex," booms Mr. Cowan.

I exhale-laugh once. "I'd expect nothing less, Mr. Cowan, sir…!" and I start walking around and passing out the brochures by handing them out to the attendee or placing them on the table, whatever the respective persons present or not-present seems to give me. Rounding back to the front area, I then see HUD walk into the room.

"Hi, everybody," Pauline Smith says, friendly-but-more-politely-and-matter-of-factly, while keeping her head down on the hunt to choose a seat.

"O-kay, *HUD* is here today…that's always a good thing," Mary ribs. "Pauline, you brought the grant money with you today, I assume?"

Pauline stops and tilts her head down diagonally to shoot Mary the look in the eyes. "Yeah, it's why they're transferring Louisville Program Office staff supervisors to Florida and leaving me *here*."

"Well, and you know, Pauline, you can chime in on this presentation today, too," Mary says. "We're gonna talk about the Fair Housing Act, and disparate impact on protected classes."

"O-kay, Mary, we'll be here," Pauline deflects, as she scoots herself into a seat at the conference table.

Then, into the conference room enter a group of two, followed by one, then another pair, of likely board members who I may or may not actually have seen before at various conferences or education & outreach events. I scramble to finish distributing the fair housing flyers.

"Hi, these are for your records…" from me to the strangers elicits the barest of thank-yous and half-smiles from the new arrivals.

"Let's give it two more minutes, for those hopefully on their way," Mary prompts to the room after looking at the black seconds-hand of a 1980s white circular wall-clock go around to 1:30 p.m.

I'm now removed from the rest of the group, standing near the podium with my hands folded down in front of me to be ready at a moment's notice. I have anxiety and self-consciousness that replaces my usual neurotic mindset. The only way to get the confidence is to begin, by diving right in, and, it may go well, where I speak with clarity and explanation; or, it may not go so well, where I garble words, look uneasy, use clichéd phrases incorrectly like "*it's raining like hotcakes*," and mumble "*uh*" way too many times. On my yellow legal notepad, trying to kill time and nerves, I write the header "*Regional Housing Center*" and then underneath "*1:30 p.m. @ RHC, 1:15 p.m. -   p.m.*" The next line I write "*# of attendees:*" and count nine people currently in attendance, including myself for number-padding, so I then write "*9*" next to it.

Mary sees that it's now a couple minutes past the half-hour, so it's time to begin.

"O-kay, well, everyone…Thank you all, for attending the meeting… I wanted to have this presentation before the regular monthly board meeting, which we'll have at around…oh…no later than *2:30*, let's say. I wanted to have this meeting beforehand because recent developments with the Supreme Court, as well as issues we're having here locally with the Housing Authority's proposed relocation of families from Walnut Court, and Berrytown Plaza, and Newburg Square, bring up a lot of discriminatory potential with our housing stock here in Louisville. Today, we have," gesturing, "Alex…Calderon…with the Commission on Civil Relations…"

I wild-eye smirk an almost-goofy cartoon smile out of humbleness, gratitude, and nervousness, all at once.

Mary continues.

"He's here to talk about these issues, and how these issues affect persons who are in protected classes from discrimination. As you all already *know*, we've been working on these issues with the Housing Authority, and the Mayor's office, but as it stands today, the Housing Authority relocation plan for families in those affected projects--*developments*," Mary catches herself, with a slight laugh and leaning over to Ms. Kneller. "It's better to call them 'developments,' not 'projects,' shame on *me*…the Housing Authority relocation plan is *not* a one-for-one replacement of the housing units, much less an increase in the number of units, after they tear down the old development. The result is going to be less families housed in public housing, with Section 8, in Low Income Housing Tax Credit properties, and what *have* you, reducing the already substandard housing stock availability around Louisville, *and*, fostering *more* segregation of persons of color, families with children, single mothers, et cetera. It seems the more we talk about this issue over the years, the more it stays the same," Mary says, looking around at all attendees. "The RHC continues to try to work with our local elected officials to stop the discriminatory practices that affect protected classes, including those practices that are facially *neutral*, but have a discriminatory *effect*. The U.S. Supreme Court just made a decision on this issue, disparate impact, which says that, statistically, when a policy affects people in those protected groups in an adverse way, it's discrimination. *Even* when there's no intent to do so. You all *also* know that we've looked at mortgage lenders over the years, and how African American and other persons were refused loans because they live in African

American neighborhoods, were refused refinancing, and how where your zip code is located should *not* define your creditworthiness, and so on. We've looked at the foreclosure and vacant property crisis in predominantly African American neighborhoods over the past ten years or so, and how it continues today…We've looked at utility deposit disparities based on credit scores, access to public transportation for single heads of households with minor children…*All* of these issues we hear about, study about, report about, here at RHC. And, *so*, we have Alex here to tell us about that, and we want to hear from him, about how *all* of this is going to be fixed by the end of his presentation. Alex…?"

The board members and HUD give minor laughs, and one more attendee enters the conference room quickly and covertly to take a seat at the conference room table.

"Thank you, Mary, so much," I exhale in a single-laugh. "And the answer to all of that, is that housing discrimination based on protected classes is illegal; unfair housing is immoral; and, affordable housing is…*radical*?"

Mild polite laugh from the crowd, barely audible.

"*Crucial*, is what I meant, 'crucial,' not 'radical.'"

That joke attempt bombed.

I lean into the small crowd and mock-secretively continue with my right hand up covering my mouth on one side.

"Since I'm wearing a city government badge, I *have* to be a political agnostic. Or at least I *should* be, I'll probably abandon that quicker than a 2007 fly-by-night predatory mortgage lender and really upset my bosses, *and* the Mayor's administration, but oh well…"

The second part of my jokey icebreaker didn't really work, either, just as my tired attempt at the alliteration and wordplay to start didn't. Looks like it's another mixed performance-to-be for Alex today, at best…

"So, *yes*, my name is Alex, and I'm an investigator with the Civil Relations Commission. We're a department of Louisville Metro Government, and we're different from the agency most people think of with civil rights here in town, the Kentucky Commission on Human Rights. We're the *city* civil rights agency, and we do similar work to the Kentucky Commission, only our jurisdiction's in Jefferson County slash Louisville Metro. We're chartered to investigate employment, public accommodation, bias-related crime, and, yes, housing discrimination complaints, under local ordinance, among other related services. So, if you believe that you've been discriminated against here in town *in* housing, you can file a complaint with us to investigate. You could technically also file most of these complaints with the state instead, or with Pauline over here…"

"Oh *jesus…*" she defeatedly says.

Smiling, I'm still trying to hit a stride.

"But, we here at the Civil Relations Commission realize that you have your *own* discretion on where you want to *file* your complaint, so we appreciate your business. And we try to help out Pauline and the United States Department of Housing & Urban Development, or 'HUD,' out…well, you all know HUD, I can use that acronym with this crowd, DUH. We try to help HUD out by dual-filing those housing discrimination complaints that also meet federal jurisdiction, filing them at the same time as the local complaint, with HUD. That way, Complainants and *Respondents*, or, those who're served with the complaint as alleged to have discriminated against the Complainant, can just work with the Civil Relations Commission investigation instead of filing with one agency, then another. And HUD pays us to do their investigations with all of that beautiful, juicy HUD money we all love, so…"

"*Mm…!*" Pauline throws out, and almost up.

I don't really stop my roll.

"*So*: I know I'm dealing with an educated crowd here on housing discrimination issues, but I do wanna to blow quickly through what's covered under local ordinance and, mostly, also under state and federal law. Local ordinance here in Louisville Metro protects persons from unlawful discrimination, in housing--by the way, with our bias-related crime cases, or what most people call 'hate crime' cases, I'm the only hate crime investigator with the office, and most hate crimes involve housing issues, too, we look at civil remedy for hate crimes while the police and the FBI can look at the criminal stuff--*So*, the protected classes Mary mentioned include race; color, which is separate from race, like if someone light-skinned discriminates against someone darker-skinned; religion; national origin; sex, or gender; disability; familial status, which specifically means the presence of minor children in the family, not adult aunts, uncles, brothers, cousins, etc.…those are the seven *basic* protected classes, which also are covered under state and federal law. Now, local ordinance *also* covers two additional protected classes from discrimination, not covered in-and-of-themselves under state and federal law, though with the receipt of federal funding there can be Executive Orders and policies from the President's administration covering them. The ordinance *also* covers sexual orientation and gender identity, which most people here locally still call the 'Fairness Ordinance.' But, the feds have recently re-interpreted the 'sex' protection under federal laws to include many sexual-orientation-based complaints, and most-all gender identity complaints, based on the issue of different treatment and stereotypes based on sex or gender. It's controversial, and it's emerging case law nationwide, and *kinda* unsettled, so we, as an agency, have to sort out all this jurisdictional stuff when we intake a complaint."

I pause briefly. My racing thoughts are close to tripping me up.

"Uh, *so*: we investigate the complaint by intaking, basically, any good-faith allegation of discrimination, so long as we have jurisdiction and it's timely-filed. We certainly have taken in some questionable allegations once in awhile, but my experience as an investigator is that, even though we always pre-judge a case--which is natural, we're human, of course--we *need* to investigate it, because just when I think that a case is *junk*, all of a sudden the evidence builds up and it's, like, 'Oh, ok, jeez, I guess the Complainant *wasn't* crazy, I can *see* why they filed…' Or, just when you get the most egregious allegations on the front end from a Complainant, with some evidence appearing to back it up, then you get the full investigation done and it's a case where it's just fraud by the Respondent to everyone, and not discrimination; or, a comedy-of-errors leading to what could be perceived by *anyone* as being discrimination, when it really wasn't; or, the Complainant falsifies evidence against the Respondent; that kinda thing, it turns out that it was some other issue. So, we investigate, and then, unless it resolves through what we call 'conciliation,' or negotiated settlement, voluntarily between the parties, then we make a determination on whether or not to go forward with litigation. And this is all civil stuff, so there's no criminal component to *any* of it. If we find Probable Cause, then a housing discrimination case is filed in court or, supposedly quicker, it goes through an administrative hearing process. The Jefferson County Attorney's Office then litigates the case on behalf of the Civil Relations Commission, working with the Complainant. And the Commission itself can *be* a Complainant, sometimes…we can file Commissioner complaints in the public interest where there's suspected discrimination. For example, online message board advertisements are a plentiful *bounty* of discrimination, usually by mom-and-pop landlords based on familial status against kids, right there in overt wording in the ads. We've also found disability-based discrimination overtly in ads, and we have a small housing testing program to test for discrimination in Louisville Metro, such as for race, national origin, disability, familial status...we have part-time employees hired only for the purpose of doing the testing, for a few hours a week. And that's helped generate complaints, also."

Bright-eyed Mary nods down diagonally with "Intriguing...!"

The rest of the crowd, maybe not-so-intrigued.

"So," I re-group, "that's the barest-bones way I can put what we do, or are *supposed* to do, at the Commission. Statistically, we get about an even number of race and disability discrimination complaints filed in housing, while nationally it's overwhelmingly disability these days as the number one basis for discrimination complaints filed...over 50% of all complaints. Second, with us, would be familial status complaints, then sex-related complaints. National origin would be a distant...fourth, and then we've gotten only a handful of religion and color complaints since I've been with the Commission for the past thirteen years. Most surprising to *me* is that we also rarely get any sexual orientation or gender identity complaints filed in housing, which is odd considering how much attention these issues get in the media and with activism these days. But, we *have* had some egregious sexual orientation hate crime cases, housing-related, with documented evidence, and I've certainly recommended Probable Cause on some other cases that just get dismissed with No Probable Cause. In housing, the most Caused cases I've worked on the past dozen years or so with the Commission have been disability and familial status, followed by an alarming number of sexual harassment cases by male landlords against female rental tenants, and then there were some religion and national origin cases that didn't get through. And there've been a few race cases, too: the only full hate crime hearing we've had was a victory for the Complainant and the Commission, where neighbors were going at it and the white family posted the Confederate flag, made signs with racial slurs, things like that, to intimidate African-American neighbors. Another hate crime case that did *not* go to hearing, because it settled first, was with a white female Complainant who provided video she took of the white male Respondent who lived across the street yelling," animatedly, "'Tear up that nigger-lover's driveway!'

when calling his white friend over in a monster truck. And you see these gigantic monster-truck tires peel out on the street, kicking up the road blacktop, and soot, and all that. It was pretty horrifying to watch in the video. The white female Complainant had two biracial white/African-American daughters…so, I gotta tell ya, this is not the *1950s*; this is not Mississippi, or Alabama, or California, or Idaho, or Texas, or somewhere in the Northeast…this is *your* Louisville. Jefferson County, Kentucky. In the past five years…"

My mouth is getting dry with even more dehydration. Better wait on the cough drop though.

"…And that's just what's reported and filed with us. I mean, I've read in local media about hate crimes alleged when alleged African-American teens beat up an alleged white male using alleged racial slurs, likely in a housing context, and other cases of alleged discrimination, things that don't seem to make it as complaints to our agency. I mean, I could go on with statistics, but I try to view what the Commission *should* do with this kinda stuff is enforcement. As far as I'm concerned, this stuff we do is a peace-keeping operation, at least the civil component of it. When you're talking about human *behavior*, education and outreach only goes so far. I'll probably get in trouble by saying that I can't *stand* education and outreach, in general. Though, I guess I'm a hypocrite since I think what we do is not well publicized, as far as the enforcement aspects. And, I'm here giving a presentation, here, today, so…"

I give a slight, single-exhale laugh.

A pause before Mary.

"Gosh, Alex, that's…fascinating. I had no idea about those cases…"

"Yeah, I mean, people can *claim* discrimination all they want when things don't go their way, but sometimes it's not true, whether they know it or not. Right now, we're in a new era of civil rights, not just with the activism needed for enforcement efforts, but also in an era of establishing or maintaining the integrity of civil rights, in some circumstances (!). But of course, sometimes it *is* true that discrimination occurs, and that's where the morality of the public interest is at stake. Like the writers of the ordinance in the 1960s said, discrimination, quote, 'menaces our democratic institutions,' unquote, much less affects our physiology as an individual who's singled out for unfair treatment, based, in whole, or in part, on what society has deemed those arbitrary demographics when it comes to securing housing. Again, I'm an investigator for a living. Not an activist for a specific group of people, but an activist for the system to actually do its *job* for a change. Systemic impediments with government agencies like mine, to me, that's the *real* civil rights issue for today…people marched in the streets and got laws passed decades ago, the laws are there, for the most part. *Now*, it's the enforcement system that's the problem. People can get comfortable and fat in their roles with government, they can overanalyze things, they can just want the case to go *away*, they can be overwhelmed by lack of help and resources…those appointed citizens to advisory boards and commissions can be afraid to go against the administrations that appointed them…government legislative branch city council members can be subservient to mayoral administration executive branches…there's a million incentives for real cases of discrimination to fail."

"Wow, you're very passionate about this, Mr. Calderon…" says an unidentified board member, who I think works with the local women's voting rights advocacy group.

"Yes, and opinionated (!)," cross-eyed Mary quickly adds. "It's all very complicated, and bureaucratic. But I *would* like to say that there *is* also a place for history in all of this, the legacies of discrimination that persist, from generations and generations of government-sanctioned policies. The histories of those who fought for civil rights when there *were* no protections, the histories that we'll be condemned to repeat if we're not reminded of the work that they've already done--well, rather, that we *are* repeating, and how to model our current efforts at change after those successes that came before…"

"Well, I have to agree with Alex, here," chimes in another, who I also don't know but she seems, or seemed, to look like another academic…until she speaks. "I mean, I go to a lot of these events that are put on, and it's always the same, it's always the 'history,' always the same ol' Family Reunion of people making the circuit. And they act like they--some will even *tell* you that there's no one doing anything now, or that no one's done anything, about civil rights after, like, 40 years ago. I mean, you don't want to disrespect the elders, and their achievements, all that. But, on the other hand, you don't march and hold up signs for some things today like you did back then, you have to use the government agencies and fix them when they don't do anything."

"That's *right*," I say, with a mental pounding-of-the-table. *Study history, but don't live in it, for god's sakes...*

"Like the EEOC," my new best friend continues. "The Equal Employment Opportunity Commission has been called a 'paper tiger' by a lot of folks, because it *appear*s that there's a federal agency watchdog out there for employment, but you can file complaints with them that go *nowhere*, into a black hole, and you don't even know what leads to them dismissing the case."

"Yes, and that's where activism for, against, and *within* the systems of civil rights law enforcement come in," I say, steering the conversation back to housing. "You know, HUD, these days, is like night-and-day compared to where it was ten years ago or so." I lean forward to say, "Thank you, Paul*ine*..."

"Alex, lord..." Pauline slightly-laughs. "You know, I guess *I* was the one who called you the 'boy wonder' when you came around all this fair housing stuff, but *who's* y'alls *HUD* monitor now, Glenda Jackson? I'm calling her, there's somethin' *wrong* with you..."

"See...everybody, I know how HUD works," I lighten. "But seriously, HUD is a model now, more than it's ever been, for federal agency civil law enforcement. Compared to its peers, at least. They do a decent job of keeping agencies like mine in check, making us timely-investigate these cases like we should, withholding *lots of money* if we don't do what we're supposed to do. The Civil Relations Commission works today like a private, non-profit agency within Louisville Metro Government, but ironically we're also the city cash-cow, not just for our department but for city government in general, with these case closures generating incredible revenue from HUD and going back into the city coffer. And government is increasingly the biggest private corporation these days..."

Now maybe *I'm* getting off track.

"So, Alex," Mary steers, "why don't you tell us about the Supreme Court case out of Texas, and why that matters..."

"Okay," I pause, gearing up for a complicated, hope-I-can-get-this-right summary, and the inevitable controversial editorial. "Okay," I sigh, "So, the *Texas* case...A little while ago--lemme see if I can get this right. Basically, the Supreme Court--the *U.S.* Supreme Court--just ruled, or affirmed, that disparate *impact*, which is different than intentional different *treatment*, may still be discrimination under the federal Fair

Housing Act, as amended. Basically, when someone files a housing discrimination complaint, they usually say that 'so-and-so housing provider treated me unfairly'…on purpose. With intent. But what was in doubt to some, for decades since the Fair Housing Act was passed in 1968, was that disparate impact was a valid legal theory. Disparate *impact* is when a housing provider policy is neutral on its face to a protected class of persons, looking like everyone was treated the same, but that the effects end up having a negative impact on the protected class. So, despite no *intent* to discriminate, discrimination occurs."

"Yes…" Mary says quietly nodding.

"So, the Supreme Court *now* has ruled that it *is*, in fact, a valid theory under the law, with the intent of Congress that fair housing be affirmatively furthered in the United States, not just in fighting intended discrimination by housing providers, but also where that discrimination *without* intent has occurred."

"Yes…" Mary continues.

"A lot of fair housing advocates had been arguing that this theory existed for decades, not just in the language of the statute, but also in case law in different parts of the country, which was almost unanimously accepted in local circuit courts, things like that. A lot of those advocates were scared that the Court would roll back these perceived protections, then were thrilled when the Court affirmed it, narrowly, 5-4."

"Yes!"

"But, there's a big, *huge* caveat to all this. If you read the decision, it really gives a lecture on the business justification possibility to trump a disparate impact effect on a protected class. The Supreme Court said that even if discrimination is the result of an unintended policy, a business justification can trump the outcome if there's not a less-restrictive means available to achieve the end result, *and*, meaning 'also,' it doesn't impede furthering the intent of fair housing. And that burden, like all discrimination complaints, lies with the Complainant to prove."

It's quiet in here.

"So, Mr. Calderon, wait: what does that mean? I don't understand."

"God, not another attorney…"

"Jefferson County Public Schools text-message alert: *School counselors help students learn communication skills to solve problems, enroll now!*"

No one says any of this, but everyone, except Mary, thinks this, if I'm reading the blanks stares, and cellular-telephone-checking, correctly.

Mary was an attorney for Legal Aid years ago, and I know she gets what I'm saying, though she'll certainly express an opinion on it in a few minutes to counter what she likely doesn't want to hear.

"So, Alex," Mary concerningly says after the pause. "What's an example of what *would* fall under this, what would be discrimination in the eyes of the court, under the law?"

"Well, honestly, I don't know if I can say, the Supreme Court just sent the *Texas* case back to the lower courts, I think. Everything is going to be subject to an individualized assessment. But I'll guess--here's what I think would be a valid disparate impact case: a housing provider has an apartment complex designated for persons only age--I dunno, let's say, only age 48 years old and older allowed to live there. A complaint is filed, alleging that they discriminate against families with minor children. The housing provider says 'Hey, we don't have anything against kids, *specifically*: kids are welcome to visit and all that, we just wanted a more mature tenant base, and that includes no twenty-somethings, no thirty-somethings, because our business model shows that they party more, they're more transient…' stuff like that. And not in a pretextual context, either--in other words, lying for the real reason being that they just don't want minor kids: they legitimately appear to have all this statistical evidence on their end that it's more profitable to rent to, maybe even implicitly, singles and couples age 48 and older. So, the intent may not be *specifically* targeted at kids under age eighteen, but the obvious impact is that no kids are gonna be allowed to live there, since they're all under age 48. I think under the Court's interpretation, this'd be illegal, because even if the housing provider could show financial benefit from this kind of policy, neutrally-enforced to families with, and without, children based on that age, the Fair Housing Act specifically says no discrimination based on familial status, and the impact would go against the intent of the protection, regardless of whether it was more commercially-profitable to do so. That's when the fairness part of the law comes in…"

"Mr. Calderon…"

Mr. Cowan…?

"I'm a developer here, and I can tell you that when we look to place low-income housing units in different parts of town, we have city councilmembers who ask us--or, rather, *advise* us, to have age restrictions on some of these places. They say that when we seek to get the tax credits, we have to put age limits on who can live there, in order to qualify. So, now *you're* saying, you're telling *us*, that it might be discrimination if we do that…?"

"Well, honestly, Mr. Cowan, it probably always *was* illegal to do that, *if* it was an age other than 55 years and older, or 62 years and older. Then otherwise it may be okay. There's a senior housing exemption from fair housing laws for those two age brackets, only regarding minor kids. In general. I mean, it gets kinda fact-specific and stuff. Otherwise, like, age 48, stuff like that, it'll certainly be open to liability under fair housing laws. But one thing I should mention also is that the Supreme Court very clearly said that you can't just rely on statistics based on demographics to make the case, and it must carefully weigh the commercial enterprise involved, permitting the free market to do what it does…I gotta tell ya, I was on the fence about disparate impact as a theory before the decision, but I think they knocked it right outta the park: it preserves the morality of fair housing, permitting *some* of these kinds of cases, but it's also fair to the housing providers to a large extent, only getting involved in a mostly *reactive* way to address the societal interest. I mean, the overt discrimination stuff is overt, the different treatment discrimination is different treatment with intent, and those will continue to be the obvious cases of discrimination here. This recent case just tries to sort out when a bunch of data is, or isn't, illegal discrimination. Only a geek like me might think this, but it truly *was* a good decision for a rare Supreme Court review of fair housing law. The private market is likely still free to do most business-justified things it seeks to do in a commercial enterprise."

"Well," Mary reservedly says, "we here at RHC certainly care about this, as well as how this all ties into affordable housing and what needs to be addressed."

I can't help myself, as the storm of nervousness, sleeplessness, and maybe the morning caffeine or withdrawal from such vortexes me ahead.

"And it's also gonna go against the practices of some fair housing activist agencies, incidentally. Some non-profits and fair housing attorneys have been filing large-scale complaints against major mortgage lenders nationally, and in multiple major cities, based on demographics by zip code, such as by race. And in a few cases, municipal governments have joined them. They've alleged different treatment in property maintenance of bank-owned foreclosures in what are viewed by the advocates as 'minority-majority' neighborhoods, and I think the disparate impact decision comes into play here, just as much as a different treatment theory. They've filed court cases, then had huge settlements without decisions at trial, with both sides probably afraid of what the decision would ultimately *be*, just as they all were nervous with the Supreme Court case--oh, even more on point, here in *this* city, the Civil Relations Commission tested this back about a dozen years ago, with the Section 8 voucher program. There was an apartment complex here that accepted the vouchers, which is voluntary to accept here…in other parts of the country, you have to accept them under those local non-discrimination laws, source of income isn't protected here like those areas, though…So, the apartment complex alleged that the Louisville Metro Housing Authority was late in paying the federal subsidy supplement of the voucher to them, so they said, 'You know what? Forget it, we can't run our business if the government checks aren't coming in on time,' and they stopped accepting vouchers and it forced those current tenants *with* vouchers to possibly vacate, since they couldn't afford the market rent amount. So, kinda like a constructive eviction from their apartment. Well, four Complainants argued that the disparate impact was based on race, as a vast majority of the voucher users were persons of color, and a majority of them African-American. So, I investigated and recommended *No* Probable Cause, because all the evidence was not really in dispute, it was just all about the law. The County Attorney agreed, but my supervisors believed that it *was* discrimination based on disparate impact. Well, the case went to court after they Probable Caused it; the Complainants and Civil Relations Commission lost, then appealed it to the Sixth Circuit Court of Appeals, and, in a big-deal *en banc* ruling, they lost again. The Commission did not appeal it to the U.S. Supreme Court, the final step, fearing, quote, 'bad case law,' unquote, with another loss. But it goes towards the issue, in my mind, of what is *fair* housing, and what is *affordable* housing, which can be two different things. You know, both *can* be immoral, just in different ways. See, I'm a purist on the fair housing thing, I'm not looking at income inequality, that's too much out of the scope of my job description, and expertise. I look at whether two millionaires are given different treatment, and one is because of race. Or sex. Or whatever protected class it is. Or two people with the same low incomes treated differently, obviously. You know, there's a National Fair Housing Training Academy operated by HUD, and a teacher there--who was otherwise sharp as *anything*, a real genius with much of the law--he once said that discrimination isn't rational…but, the counterpoint, is that the law *is*, and you're gonna have to prove intent in 99% of these cases, the business justification will likely trump it, otherwise…or, you can always hope for politics to intervene. Or to get an irrational judge or two," I almost laugh out. "Another way to look at this, too, is that the Supreme Court just threw these cases back to the lower courts for decision individually, meaning even *more* gridlock, of course. Disparate impact is where the rubber meets the road for the great, vast divide between reparation ideology based on statistical demographics and discrimination against individuals on a case-by-case basis."

There's almost another pause.

"Remind me to charge *Mr. Calderon* a higher security deposit the next time he tries to rent my townhouse," Mr. Cowan says.

Hearty laughter erupts from everyone, who are certainly *all* treating me the same.

"Hey, steering is illegal discrimination, too, but way-underreported, so feel free to send me to your worst unit…" I say, as a know-it-all, back as a joke.

Mary is amused, as well, but she's taking some of the assault on affordable housing personally, and I'm not surprised in the least.

"And," I have to get out of my system, "never underestimate the reality of self-segregation by people based on their own, or *perceived*, demographics. It's not something people wanna admit to, or agree with, but some people *do choose*, in fact, to live with other people of, quote, 'their own kind,' unquote, whatever that demographic may be to them. Or, sometimes, intentionally *not* their own kind, which could foster its own segregation. Freedom of choice and association comes into play here, too, sometimes…the elephant in the room may be, in some circumstances, that someone chooses that housing route on their own, and is it fair to impede that choice, whether we agree with it or not, whether it's bigoted, or narrow-minded, or against the public good, or not…? If it's the homeseeker's choice, not forced onto them by a housing provider."

People are shifting in their seats, and I don't know if it's my opining or if they're just ready to have it all end out of disinterest, disagreement, or boredom.

After a pause, Mary addresses the group with the standard "*So, are there any questions?*" line that continues to deflate the afternoon engagement (even if it was one-sided) and is taken to just let things lie.

"Well, Alex…this is a lot of helpful information, it shows a lot of the issues at play in fair housing, and how affordable housing is tied into the work that we all do. I have to disa*gree* a little bit on the statistics part of things, the data is all there, and it's been there, to show different treatment, intentional or not."

More to the group, she continues.

"What I'm hoping for, is for all of us to incorporate fair housing into the quest for affordable housing, and that means working with our elected officials *before* the individual acts of discrimination can occur, making positive changes to our laws and regulations that impede our housing choice. Starting our work in the planning processes, in the development stage of affordable housing, from securing the funding, to zoning issues--as we've talked about here, time-and-again, zoning is legally-sanctioned discrimination here in the city when, depending on where you are, there are limitations on the number of multifamily housing units allowed to be placed on a lot, by law (!), *continuing* to enforce in-place segregated housing patterns. So…lots of work to do. Write your Metro Councilmember! Call city government! Be sure to show up to the Metro Council monthly committees on housing, transportation…Okay, so…great, everyone…anything else, any more questions, anyone…?"

I eagerly raise my eyes to the crowd, ready to dive into any tough questions.

Nothingness.

"Okay," Mary says, addressing me and the crowd alternately together. "Well, Alex, we really appreciate you coming down and addressing us…lots of good, interesting, information. *Okay*, I'll walk Alex out, and we can prepare for the board meeting in…oh, let's say…ten? Ten minutes, that should be…is that enough time for everyone?"

No one formally responds, maybe a nod or a mouthed-yes from one or two as the rest turn to each other to talk about anything but fair housing.

"Thanks, you all, appreciate it…" I say to the crowd, trying to make eye contact, but then I quickly gather my yellow legal notepad and items from the table and stuff them all haphazardly into the black work bag. Only Pauline smiles and tells me goodbye in sending me off.

I intersect with Mary as she walks over to meet me towards the conference room exit door. I smile "Well, thanks, Mary…!" and she leads me out of the room.

"No, thank you, Alex, it really was very informative, and interesting. I gotta say, I don't know if I *agree* with everything you said, about the separation of fair, and affordable, housing, I really do think that they're much more intertwined than we realize…"

"Yeah, you may be right, Mary, I dunno. Keep in mind, I've done this work for *wayyyyy* too long…"

"We know, Alex…Brenda always talks about how committed and passionate you are with fair housing."

"Oh, she does, huh?"

"Yes…"

"Okay…" I say, a little stumped, as anyone with their boss hanging over their head would be. "Well, thanks again, Mary, I'm gonna rush back to the office and get to the enforcement part of my job description, if I can. I'm on intake this afternoon, and then I gotta work tonight, too, it's a long day today," I say in quickly digging out the cough drop from my dress shirt pocket.

"Oh, wow, okay…Well, good luck this afternoon, then…" Mary says while pushing the elevator down button for me.

"Thanks, let's see if I really *can* be a political agnostic this afternoon and tonight, instead of a bureaucratic hypocrite…"

"'Political agnostic,' I like that…Okay, well, bye now…"

"Okay bye Mary…!" I say with lifted anxiety as she turns away from me, leaving.

I enter the elevator car, and then the doors close on me.

He was baptized by his Catholic parents at a time he was too young to remember. He doesn't remember whether he went to church services much as a young child, but vividly remembers how he exaggerated being sick on Christmas Eve as an eight-year-old in order to avoid going to mass…it was a lot of work, but his demanding parents finally gave up the crusade. If he's being honest with himself, he really can't explain why he didn't want to go, then or in hindsight; he was just firmly sure then, as now, that church wasn't for him. It wasn't a feeling, it was just absolute.

Years later, in his early to mid-teens, he was forced by his father to go through Catholic confirmation proceedings. All he can remember through the teenage contempt was his chosen confirmation name, "Matthew," and the way that the oil felt when the Archbishop thumbed down and across his forehead at the ceremony.

***

He went to secular public schools throughout primary and secondary education. In Louisville, he sang middle and high school choral songs giving tribute to Christian and Judaic themes.

***

His first dose of LSD was a double-dipped "Jesus print" tab.

***

He went to a Catholic college, under what he felt at the time was coercion by his father but, looking back, was a good choice for him, legacy or not. Armed with absolute atheism, insecurity in societal humanity, and dependency on that same Father, he non-judgmentally and matter-of-factly watched as so many of his fellow students seemed just like him except for the occasional chapel service and ashes on their forehead one Wednesday a year.

Even more tolerant was forgiveness of the school when he gave a speech in a religious history class: his objective exposé on film and religious faith ended with a personal, defiant rant that the country was becoming more and more atheist.

Ironically, he'd soon take acid for the last time.

Sitting alone in the underclassmen dormitory suite he shared as an upperclassman with two roommates, neither of whom were around that Saturday afternoon, he dosed with the usual expectation that he'd live another video game inside his head that would be a little fun, a little challenging, a lot unique, a lot affordable, and excitedly adventurous. Professional basketball playoffs were on from noon until midnight that day, and he watched while sitting on his couch smoking cigarettes, and smoking the occasional weed, waiting for the LSD trip to progress: the slight ache in the top part of his spine and shoulder-blade area creeped in, the fluorescent ceiling lights changed from a radiant white to a glowing yellow, and the television images eventually began to tic. Then, the visual trails seemed like they wanted to appear, but they wouldn't fully emerge: restless, he left his dorm room and went next door to the room where his brother and brother's roommate dwelled; neither were home, but for some reason, he had his brother's key. Sitting for what seemed like only a few minutes in his brother's room yielded the same slight restlessness he'd had in his own room. Returning to his own dorm room, he walked from the living room section into the bedroom area, where it happened.

The bedroom lighting went from the white or yellow sunshine present everywhere else in the building to a greenish, hint-of-tan hue, and it stopped him in his tracks in the middle of the bedroom. Instantaneous awareness of God, a moral order manifesting itself into an entity, and/or a moral order of overall existence, was revealed, and he let out a deep acknowledgement with a jaw-dropping, mouth-opening, eternally-mute "oh…"

He now understood.

"Life was a test, and I am failing" was the non-verbal, consuming revelation.

A terror so real and physiological, so completely outside the scope of his control, and so pronounced, it seemed to have given him no choice but to lay down on the top of his bunk bed and submit to the fear of the ultimate end, all-doubt that he'd be spared. It was real, unending sin.

When he came to, or started coming to, he joined his brother and brother's best friend in his dorm suite living room; how they got in, he can't remember, but they certainly appeared and babysat him in trying to ease his trauma. The looks on their faces indicated that they had real fear for him.

And when he came to, or started coming to, he vowed that he'd never, ever use any drugs again.

And so it was…

(…well, more or less.)

And from that day forward, he was no longer atheist. The dilemma, in a much more "sober" mind, was whether the incident was the manifestation of God; a God; some Gods; the Gods; a god; some gods; the gods; some other divine moral order; some other governing moral order, such as a cosmic or universal or alien order; or, was it just the drug(s), i.e. a hallucination, a delirium, an implosion from his isolation while under the influence. He confidently ruled out mental illness. Was it religion, science, or a combination of the two?

The dilemma was also not about what caused the incident, though maybe he has a pretty good grasp on the effect: but, what was the goal of the moment of truth, if, in fact, it was made to be revealed to him. There was no script, either before or after the incident, on how to live his life within the divine/ordered channel, such as from a religious tome or some other manuscript blueprint for how life should be done…or, at least, that he could cognitively be aware of. If life was about choices, does that mean when involved with society/people only, and/or as an individual when by himself and alone, and just in the most seemingly routine and mundane acts of his daily life, much less those bigger scopes of events?

This level of ambiguity would later be completely identifiable by a co-religious, co-philosophical label that others before him had struggled with, however: based on the evidence that he was able to gather, and that he was able to interpret, there was Probable Cause for him to identify as an "empirical agnostic."

At least, as of the current moment…things could all change instantaneously based on the circumstances, divine or not-divine, or possibly in a brief or an unending appeal of his reevaluation of the nature of overall existence at any time in his life.

In an atheist college friend's challenge to his agnosticism, the friend asked him how could it be proven that nothing of the divine existed, in order to justify the lack of a supreme being's presence. Nothing is nothing, and absence is unverifiable. He felt that his friend reinforced his point exactly, as faith in the lack-of-faith was still a faith, just without the evidence. No one could ever prove to him the lack of evidence of the beginning-of-the-beginning, whether that be the pre-divine era before a God, or a not-divine scientific cosmosis setting everything in order from a measurable-by-humankind study.

His dilemma with living a god-fearing life was that turning his life over to a higher power might mean turning his life over to a predatory segment of humanity.

***

Despite the militant agnosticism in his twenties and thirties, he still attended voluntary alcoholism recovery meetings in order to try and gain control over his ongoing chemical-based anarchy. He thought the act of attendance, i.e. a work ethic, would secularize the addiction treatment, regardless of a higher power, even as he might or might not understand such, and grant him the sobriety that he sought. On one occasion, one of the rare ones where he was either called upon to speak to the group or voluntarily decided to proactively speak up, he was challenged in forceful terms by a fellow attendee to go home, drop to his knees, and humble himself before God.

He gave an even rarer good-faith effort that afternoon, getting on his knees pleading in the desperation of a night-before that involved drunken driving which only a guardian angel could've seen him through. He was hung-over, he was desperate, he was going to try anything, and he was sniveling to the heavens, real or imagined, begging for help. Genetic Catholic guilt, clinical post-intoxication depression, theological damnation…it had all been contemplated before, but this one day was different. He was going to do anything.

***

At the erotic club near his apartment building, he was again sitting at the bar relaxing and drinking, both to excess, when he saw out of the corner of his eye a girl who appeared to be a dancer, no older than her early twenties, fully-clothed in the modest dress of a sweater and bluejeans, placing a foil-covered large aluminum chafing dish on top of the bar. The bartender, a not-so-modest dancer in waiting, talked with the girl briefly, and friendship-hugs were exchanged between them. Then, turning to leave the red-light-soaked bar, the modest girl smiled at him, pausing with at least slight instant attraction, as if to say something to him, and he reciprocated. "Hi" and "hello" were exchanged, and the friendly girl left. The bartender, on familiar terms with him just as friendly as she'd been with the girl, asked him if he wanted anything to eat, to which he politely declined.

"You sure!" She yelled over the music and the red light. "They also ordered pizza for us, it's on the way, if you don't like fried chicken…!"

"No…thanks, though!"

"Okay!…It's free, you know! They're with Blossom House, they're a Christian group…!" she said matter-of-factly, and, without a hint of judgment.

***

He still doesn't know the best reaction to express in response to government-sponsored religious invocations. He tends to just look ahead these days, maybe catching an eye-glance or two in the sea of head-bows, whereas up until a few years ago he'd at least lower his head out of respect for those faithful in the room. Since he most always insisted that church-state separation was fundamentally an all-or-nothing exercise in faith and faithless expression, he lately seemed to be granting reasonable accommodations to the masses.

***

He vowed repeatedly, usually while in church for a girlfriend's mass or for an acquaintance's wedding, that the only time he'd kneel before anyone would be when he proposed for marriage.

CHAPTER SIX

Driving back to the office, I'm full of relief from the presentation being well-done and/or over-with, but I can feel myself becoming more drained. It's 2:30 p.m., it's blazing-August hot-and-humid outside, and I'm scheduled to be on intake at 3:00 p.m. Despite plenty of time to get back, I still need to squeeze a break in before the war-room-dealing-with-the public may or may not begin. We'll see.

Just as cautiously as I drove to Regional Housing Center offices, I make my way back through downtown traffic similar to my way over there, save for a few extra exhaust-exploding vehicles carrying on with their day in front and all-around. I make my way back into, around, and up to the roof of the parking garage also, in a reverse-routine. Luckily, it's still mid-afternoon; any later and I'd be facing careening-full-speed vehicles shooting down the ramps inside the garage towards me, fueled by the euphoria of office workers getting off the clock for the day. I park in the open space on the garage roof where I pulled the city vehicle out from, pull on the emergency brake, jot "5*9999*" on the small note pad, then exit the car to the elevator after double-checking that the vehicle locks. I hit the down button and wait there, listening as the elevator system hums hopefully-upward with the speed of a hamster taking a ten-minute afternoon break. The elevator car finally arrives, I get in with no one getting out, I get down to South 4th Street quickly, and sludge into the office building side-elevator after dodging forced-hellos from the building smokers sitting outside on the building ledge in their afternoon breaks.

<bleep bleep>

locked door struggle

curse

<bleep bleep>

<dong!>

I almost-collapse getting into the Civil Relations Commission front office area, sorta like staff earlier this morning. The receptionist desk is receptionist-less. I write "*2:50 p.m.*" on the sign-in/out sheet and see the Mayor's half-smiling head again on my way to opening the mailroom door…ugh. I look in my mailbox and see an intake-not-taken form waiting for review on top of a small pile; grabbing the stack of paperwork, I'm compelled to shuffle through it in front of the mailboxes: the intake inquiry involves a housing discrimination complaint based on marital status, not covered under local law; a glossy brochure from a Chicago fair housing law school program solicits $750 for a conference on continuing education; a written Respondent response to the housing discrimination complaint *Open Connections, Inc. v. Pathways of Christ, Inc.* is formatted like a United States Supreme Court brief filing; and, a few green United States Postal Service certified mail return receipt cards are coded for my discrimination complaint cases by Commission Secretary & Staff Badger Briana in her signature encryption.

I look over the *Open Connections* Respondent complaint response and see the expected denial of unlawful discrimination based on religion, including constitutional challenges to Civil Relations Commission statutory authority and freedom-of-religious-association arguments from the representative attorney. I then shuffle through the small deck of certified mail return-receipt cards, with none of them particularly-meaningful towards any of my caseload. No time to process anything, everything'll have to wait until towards the end of the week, probably. I place all of the documents back in the mailbox and get an ink pen out of my black work bag. I look at a legal-size sheet cursively-labeled "*city vehicle #423*" resting on top of the wooden mailbox fixture and then write in applicable spaces "*Alex Calderon*," "*none*," "*Regional Housing Center*," "*59995*," "*59999*," and "*yes*."

Moving forward out of the mailroom, I walk back towards my office and, out of the corner of my eye, see Janice sitting in Sherry's office while Monica stands next to Sherry looking over Sherry's shoulder. They're all-work and all-play both right now, and I'm too high-strung to get to a nominal break in my day to stop and join in their fun, which sucks. I put my black work bag down on my office desk, get out the small notepad from the side-zipper pocket and place it on the desk, then take my city government identification badge off of my dress-shirted breast and place it in the bag. I see that the voicemail-indicator diamond is lit up on the desk telephone, but I then ignore it and walk back out of the office heading back past the fun, back towards the front receptionist area. I keep walking around to the west wing, going past Agnes' office, past Janice's office, and across from Ronita's office to the staff men's restroom. I scuff the carpet with a hard stop before I enter the bathroom, turn around, and head to Ronita in her office instead.

A big, dumb, sarcastic, exaggerated, tired smile comes over me as she looks up from her paperwork and I say, "All *right*, here's your key, Ronita…"

"Okay thank you sweetie," she unintentionally-dryly says, placing it in automated fashion back in her top-left office desk drawer, still avoiding eye contact.

I'm then off to the men's staff restroom again, finish and then exit to race back around to the front receptionist desk. But on the approach, I hear Janice and someone unfamiliar talking.

"So, is she expecting you?"

"No, but I keep calling and she won't return my calls, I keep getting forwarded back to the receptionist when I call for her to ask about my case," the obvious-Complainant says to Janice. I silently give thanks that it's probably not a walk-in intake complaint that'll snag me for the next hour.

"Okay, uh-huh…" Janice juggles with her down-to-earth accessibility-to-the-public voice. "Okay, well, Agnes isn't *in* right now, I can take a message and have her *call* you…?"

I quickly, and sheepishly, maneuver the narrow accessway between the Complainant's back and the front door. The Complainant gives me a darting glance before going back to continue to address Janice standing behind the bar-counter of the receptionist desk.

"Okay, is there a supervisor here…?" the Complainant firmly asks.

As much as I want to be the fly on the wall to hear how Janice breaks it to the Complainant that Agnes *is* the supervisor, and that the Director is the supervisor of the supervisor and is also otherwise out of the office, too, leaving *no* supervisor…I get back to my office and see the intake Janice filled out from our discussion earlier in the morning resting in the office chair. I grab it and place it in my inbox-outbox tray to signify my priority to review it, then sit in the office chair to breathe another breath.

After the pause, I log back into my city government workstation computer and try to log on to MyCallNavigator: it logs on now, *finally*, so I see in a menu tree that there are four voicemail messages waiting. I recognize one of the telephone numbers on the limited caller identification of the telephone number listed only, but only as someone who's regularly called me for years. I start playing the messages with online clicks while grabbing my pre-prepared intake documentation for intake duty this afternoon, shuffling through the papers to see if I really am, in fact, prepared with paperwork for a walk-in from the public at a moment's notice. I don't recognize this first telephone number.

> "*Uh, hi, this is Beverly Johnson, I was asked to call, by my daughter, Tamara Johnson, about the…about talking to you, about the case she filed, against her landlord. I'd like to speak with you about this as soon as possible, my number is 5-O-2…5-7-4…6-3-8-0. It's important that I speak with you, provide the…the interview, about her landlord, Mr. Forrest, Davis. 5-7-4, 6-3-8-0. Thank you…*"

I click on the voicemail message weblink in the MyCallNavigator program and choose the option to save it electronically. I clickly scan through the file folders to "*Johnson v. FMD*" and save the voicemail message to the folder. Not deleting it from the MyCallNavigator server, I click on the next voicemail message weblink, and I don't identify that telephone number in advance, either.

> "*Mr. Calderon, hi, my name is Jordan Fordham, I'm an attorney with Funkhauser, Bates & Mitchell here in Frankfort, my telephone number is 5-0-2, 5-7-3, 0-0-4-6. I represent Pathways of Christ, Inc. in a complaint that your office filed, complaint number C-0-0, H…it looks like an O, dash, 4-8-8-2… If you could please give me a call at your earliest convenience, my client is concerned about why the Commission would take it upon itself to file this case. Our client is not discriminating against anyone based on sexual orientation, anyone is more than welcome to participate in Pathway programs, and that's aside from the fact that it appears that there's no real victim alleged in this complaint, which is--and the complaint, incidentally, is quite vague, the allegations state that my client engaged in discrimination, but there's no property involved, Pathways doesn't lease apartments or sell housing, doesn't even offer housing, only residency in their addiction recovery programs. So, again, Mr. Calderon, this is Jordan Fordham, Funkhauser Bates Mitchell, 5-0-2-5-7-3-0-0-4-6.*"

I click on the voicemail message weblink in the MyCallNavigator program and choose the option to save it electronically. I clickly scan through the file folders to "*Open v. Pathways*" and save the voicemail message to the folder. Not deleting it from the MyCallNavigator server, I click on the next voicemail message weblink and I don't identify the telephone number in advance. Concurrently, I open my e-mail program to see what the latest news or job assignment is or might be.

> "*Hi, Mr. Alex, this is Tamara Johnson. I was calling because--we met today, and I talked to my mother, Beverly Johnson, and she should be calling you. Also, I wanted to go ahead and have my son Martez give an interview, for the investigation. I'll talk with him about it tonight, but he should be okay with giving the interview for the case. I'll call you tomorrow after talking with him tonight, and see when we can come back down again and have him speak to you. It would have to be late in the afternoon, 'cause the bus doesn't usually drop him off here until about 4:00. So, I'll call, I just wanted to let you know, so we can keep…moving on the case. Thank you, Mr. Alex…bye…*"

I click on the voicemail message weblink in the MyCallNavigator program and choose the option to save it electronically. I clickly scan through the file folders to "*Johnson v. FMD*" and save the voicemail message to the folder. Not deleting it from the MyCallNavigator server, I click on the last voicemail message weblink and I know who it's going to be based on the telephone number.

> "*Uh, yeah, hello Boss…This is Bakari! Hehe…Uh, yeah, I'm calling, to let you know, that I won't be in this afternoon…I'll be in on Wednesday, around…9:30…9:30 or 10:00. You can call me back at 5-0-2, 4-5-6, 3-2-5-0…Wednesday, 9:30 or 10:00, this is Bakari…4-5-6, 3-2-5-0. Okay. Have a blessed day…*"

I click on the voicemail message weblink in the MyCallNavigator program, select "*delete*," and minimize the program into the operating system lower tray in order to get it out of view. Bakari wasn't really scheduled to come in for his tester debriefing today anyways, but at least I know that he's on track to be here at a now-certain day and time, and I won't scramble to get his housing test materials ready until the morning.

More e-mails have arrived from the fair housing advocacy listserv, and instead of deleting many of them upon scan, I just decide to keep them in the e-mail program inbox and sort them through later. I also see an e-mail from this attorney Jordan Fordham, with an attachment titled "*Civil Relations v. Pathways of Christ*," so it's probably another copy of the Respondent housing discrimination complaint response he mailed in already. Electronic paperwork piles up today just as the hard-copy paper trail piles up today; usually, I at least have a clean e-mail inbox, and just a pile of paperwork on the left side of my desk waiting for processing, not all over the desk, and at least in a neat stack.

I look at the bias-related crime complaint intake form Janice put on my chair while I was out. The summary of Complainant allegations is too sparse, so I get out a red ink pen from my office desk flat underdrawer and concisely state in a few sentences that the Complainant alleges racially-based statements made against her in the two Respondents' harassment and assault. I also mark to Janice that only one of the Respondents was listed, so to go ahead and add the second one if the Complainant intended to do so. I mark my initials on the intake section marked "*reviewed by*," write in "*intake ok to draft*" and "*complaint draft changes*," leaving the "*approved*" section blank, then get up from my desk and try to get to the mailroom again. Janice is still in Sherry's office, so I place the paperwork in her mailbox instead of going directly to her and then I scuttle back to my desk.

I suddenly remember that I need to get materials ready for the Disability Action Network meeting tonight, so I open my black work bag, take out the few remaining fair housing brochures and the rubber-banded-together undistributed fair housing magnets, and place them all in my inbox/outbox tray. Since the meeting tonight will have persons with limited vision, I'd better get at least one large print copy of the fair housing brochure, as well as one large-print copy of the Civil Relations Commission's last annual report. I jump on the computer, scroll through file folders, and format the print jobs to increase document size and assign the corresponding printer-paper-tray. I grab Disability Action Network meeting folder volume 2014-15 from my bottom-left desk deep-drawer and put it in the work bag.

Then it's back-and-forth to the mailroom again, where I hear the front receptionist desk telephone ring on my way out. Janice and I pass each other along the short way.

Back at my desk, I fold up and paperclip the large-print fair housing brochure and the annual report, respectively. The office desk telephone then rings its transfer-from-another-Metro-telephone-line double-ring.

"Louisville Metro Civil Relations Commission, this is Alex…?"

"Uh, yeah," a female-sounding person begins slowly. "I was told this is where I could call, to get help with my landlord…?"

"Sure, well, possibly…why don't you--If you could tell me what's going on, we'll see how we might be able to help ya," I say, shuffling through my pre-prepared intake paperwork to find a housing discrimination complaint intake form. I also get pen and the cardboard from an empty yellow legal-sized notepad ready for notes.

"Ok, well, see: I rent this apartment in Old Louisville, with me and my three kids, and my landlord won't fix anything, I called and they said--they send maintenance out to try to fix things, but they don't do a good job, and I pay my rent every month, and they just let this place--it's falling *apart*, there's roaches, and ants, comin' in, there's holes in the walls, in the ceilin', the lock don't work, you…you just have to see all what's going on over here…"

"Okay…well, our office investigates discrimination complaints, including in housing…do you think that you've been discriminated against by your landlord with all of this?"

"Well, I don't know, the apartment is falling apart, there's holes in the walls, the lock on the door won't catch, and I reported it when we did the walk-through, when I moved in, and I told them that there's crime here in Old Louisville…and half the time, they just don't respond, or when they *do* show up, they just put that cheap plaster on the wall, they don't wanna fix it, and then I gotta go down to the office, and they ignore me when I complain about it, it's just--I mean, someone's gotta do somethin' about this, it's…I…I-don't *know*…!"

"Okay, well, our office investigates discrimination complaints in housing, but *discrimination* is defined as unfair treatment based on your race, color, religion, national origin, sex, minor children, disability, sexual orientation, or gender identity. Do you think one or more of those bases is involved?"

"Well, I don't know, they say that they're gonna fix everything, or then they ignore me when I call. I got the--I don't have the money to fix it myself, it's--it's *crazy*, there's holes in the walls, and in the kitchen, there's bugs and roaches all over, in the cereal, and the toilet keeps running, and it won't turn off, there's holes in the walls…piece 'a ceiling fell, *hit-the-baby-in-the-head…*"

I choke one laugh uncontrollably out loud.

"Well, ma'am," I recover, miraculously-quickly, filing away the caller's last line in my head for Janice and Sherry and Monica later, "uh, do you think that this is because of one of those bases I just mentioned, like, you're treated differently than the others there?"

"Well, I don't know," the now-doomed Civil Relations Commission caller says. "They just don't wanna fix anything, they're slumlords, they don't do anything around here..."

"Okay, have you called code enforcement, which is the city department of Inspections, Permits & Licenses, for an inspection?"

"No...no, my friend at church, she just told me to call you all..."

"Okay, well, if you're unsure if discrimination has occurred, you might start with the Louisville Metro department of Inspections, Permits & Licenses. They're the city code enforcement agency, so if your apartment is in substandard condition, like a health and safety issue, then they can send a code enforcement officer out to your apartment to inspect, and then they can cite the landlord for any violations. They're a department of city government, just like we are, the Civil Relations Commission, and we're the city civil rights agency, but we'd look at different treatment based on race, religion, stuff like that. So, if you like, I can transfer you to Inspections, Permits & Licenses for intake with them, or just give you their number to call if you think that's the best starting point for an inspection, and discrimination is not evident, at this point...?"

"Well, yeah, like I said, they don't wanna--they won't fix anything. I got three kids, I can't *live* in this apartment like this, somebody's gotta do somethin' about these people, it's crazy..."

"Okay, well, let me transfer you, and if it looks like discrimination is involved, where it doesn't necessarily appear evident right *now*, just call us back and we can look into it and assist you with the filing of a discrimination complaint. But based on what you said, Inspections, Permits & Licenses might be the best starting point--oh! Also, you might wanna contact Legal Aid, since they're Louisville's, sorta, landlord-tenant-law review agency. They may be able to give you some advice on how you might deal with the lack of maintenance you're talking about, like, see if it's a violation of local landlord-tenant law. I can give you their number, too..."

"Okay, that'd be fine. You said Legal Aid?"

"Yeah, they can maybe help. Their number--oh, do you need to get paper and pen, or--"

"No, I'm ready…"

"Okay…so, Legal Aid, can be reached at--they're here in Louisville, so, area code 5-0-2, 5-9-5, 2-3-4-0."

"Okay…"

"Okay, and Inspections, Permits & Licenses can be reached here in Louisville, of course, at 5-7-4, 3-3-2-1."

"Okay…"

"And I can transfer you to IPL right now, if you like…?"

"Okay, yeah, that'd be fine…"

"Okay, and then, real quick, for tracking purposes, can I ask you for your name, and telephone number, and who your landlord is, for this inquiry? We ask that information on a voluntary basis, and log it in, where it just sits in a book, and we can reference you calling if you need to contact us in the future, like, if you file a complaint with us later on. We don't act on it, and we don't contact the landlord or anything like that…"

"Okay, no, yeah, that--that'd be fine…"

"Okay, so, what's your name, ma'am?"

"My name is Charlene…Hampton…"

"Okay…"

"Okay, and my landlord is Metro…Metro, Properties…"

"Okay…"

"And my number is area code 8-5-9, 2-5-2, 0-0-7-1."

"Okay, great," I affirm in wrapping up some notes on the cardboard. "Appreciate it, and, like I said, we don't act on any of this, but you can contact us later on, and reference this call if you need to. Okay, so, I'll go ahead and transfer you over to Inspections, Permits & Licenses, and we appreciate you callin'…"

"Okay, well, thank you, I just need them to fill these holes and fix the lock and get the bug exterminator over here again, we can't keep livin' like this…"

"Sure, that's understandable…okay, well, thanks again, Ms. Hampton, I'll transfer you now, just one moment…"

"Okay, thank you…"

I hit the "*Conference 3*" button on the desk telephone, the name of which means absolutely nothing like it should mean when it puts Ms.

Hampton on hold, then I dial extension 3-3-2-1, then again hit the "*Conference 3*" button before hanging up the receiver in transferring her over to IPL. I look through my pre-prepared intake paperwork and pull out an "*Inquiry Not Taken*" form (a misnomer, of course, since we took the inquiry, we just didn't take the *complaint* for investigation, but, whatever, not my call on semantics…<*cough-Brenda-cough*>…). I complete handwritten information then get myself back into the mailroom, scan the form into electronic format on the copier-printer-now-scanner, get back to my office, go to the staff-shared directory online for staff documents, click the "*Scans*" folder, pull up my randomly-assigned number of gobbledygook for the file made by the scanner, rename it "*Hampton v. Metro inquiry not taken 8-31-2015*," then move it into the shared directory folder "*Inquiries Not Taken.*" I put the hard-copy of the inquiry in a file of paperwork near the office window overlooking the street that includes all kinds of miscellaneous paperwork never to be looked at again, at least until recycling purges it about five years from now. I look out over the street and see bustling below, in addition to a car and a pickup truck parked at two back-to-back parking meters, both with lime-green ticket envelopes under the driver's-side windshield wipers. It's now 3:05 p.m.

Oh, wait, but I forgot: we have to now put Inquiry Not Taken entries into the new City Management System for tracking, as well (!). I dive into the CMS program via my computer web browser, click on various links that even the best investigator, civil or criminal, could never think would make any sense as a gateway to the "*Inquiries*" tree menu, and then data-entry in the applicable requested information, including a summary of the non-Complainant allegations for Ms. Hampton's telephone call. The Civil Relations Commission is where all inquiries into unfair practices, discrimination or non-discrimination, go to die…with near-constant ceremony. The fly-by-night vendor who created the haphazard CMS program during the Mayor's first term is probably an offshore corporation in-name-now-only. The Mayor's pet project of taxing city employee labor with endless hours of statistical collection, under the guise of "open government" in the administration but in actuality just a hobby for the former Economics major playing God with his new toys, continues with the documenting-of-the-document's-documentation; I can't wait to see the exploding head-vein of a new

Mayor-elect when scrapping the ridiculousness of all this in one fatal blow.

And that's when Chad makes his every-other-day appearance at my office doorway.

"So, what's goin' on, man…?"

"Not a lot, man," I say in a tired, as-if-Friday-afternoon, long-work-week mustered earnest. "Just puttin' out fires again, what about you?"

"Nothin' much, just checkin' in…? Did you see the Dodgers last night, they almost beat Houston at Houston, I watched that game…"

"No…no, can't say that I did. I was doing chores yesterday, resting, all that good stuff. I'm so damn domesticated anymore, it's not funny."

"Yeah, I watched all kinds of sports this weekend. I met up with two of the guys at that meetup group I was telling you about, on Wednesday, the Louisville open-thinkers weekly meeting. We hung out Friday night at the soccer game, the stadium's really nice. We watched that game, then last night met up again for drinks and baseball, so it was…kind of the start of a *long* weekend for me…"

"Cool…" I say with a short-laugh.

"But it was cool, we watched games, talked a little bit about girls, and did a lot of philosophical discussion. We talked a lot about the 'In God We Trust' license plate court challenge that you and I talked about, one of those guys is planning on filing an application with the state to have an atheist specialty plate."

"Yeah, you know what, speaking of which, I have to call back this attorney for one of my new cases, a housing discrimination complaint filed by Open Connections based on sexual orientation…something tells me it's gonna be a difficult discussion. I should try to get *you* to do it, since you're our resident sexual orientation or fairness liaison…" I joke.

"Oh yeah?"

"Yeah, Open Connections filed an agency complaint against this Christian-based rehab facility, that they allege harasses and coerces participants to reject homosexuality if they're gay, or bisexual, stuff like that. The Respondent, uh, Pathways of Christ, is allegedly part of a national Christian denomination, operating this program. And so, it's a housing complaint because it's a residential facility, where participants live there for at least a year, according to their website. And participants pay, quote, 'tuition,' and fees, and fill out this huge application, and the Respondent asks about sexual orientation, sexual activity, all kinds of things that'd cross the line in a housing discrimination context if you look at it in a rental housing context…"

"Hm, okay…"

"Yeah, the biggest issue for me is the fact that Pathways gets judicially-mandated referrals from the criminal justice system…so, like, if someone is a non-believer, like, say, non-Christian, or is non-heterosexual, and a judge orders them into the Respondent program as part of their sentencing or disposition of their criminal case, then it has fair housing problems, I think."

"Well, yeah, duh (!), it's indoctrination, then…!"

"It certainly can be, if you're not a believer, and you're not voluntarily signing up for the program. I mean, Pathways will argue that it's *not* a housing provider, just like colleges and universities have argued that under fair housing law, but I think they *are* housing providers for such long-term stays. They're also arguing that they're exempt from fair housing law as a religious entity, citing the religious exemption under fair housing law, but that argument *completely* fails, 'cause the law says that they can be exempt if providing housing specifically for their congregate, or for their religious order of membership, but not when they open it up to others…once you open it up to all, it becomes a commercial enterprise if you're charging annual or monthly 'tuition,' fees, all that kinda stuff, if it's not some nominal operating cost. But see, on the other hand, you also have the First Amendment, and that might trump fair housing laws…local, state, *or* federal, so…"

"No way, then if I'm atheist or don't believe in God, then the First Amendment would then support *me* not being subjected to all that, though…!"

"Well, freedom of religious association can come into play here, with Supreme Court--United States Supreme Court--case law on all this. And then there's Kentucky state law regarding religious…'*restoration*,' unless there's a compelling state interest to trump the religious exemption or discrimination, too. This is an interesting case, it's classic church versus state stuff, obviously."

"Well, that place can't be allowed to discriminate and engage in harassment if you're gay or not Christian…"

I half-laugh in summarizing, "Faith-based versus non-faith-based, yeah…"

"I'll have to talk with Jim Lucas," Chad says in unintentionally name-dropping the Open Connections director.

"Yeah, actually, I'll probably ask to interview Jim on this for the case. I think the big issue on their end--don't tell them I told you this! Or, well, actually, you can, if you want, I guess, but I wouldn't. Open Connections filed this as an agency complaint, and the issue of qualified standing for the agency is a question to me, too. Ultimately, they're gonna have to possibly prove damages somehow, because organizational and associational standing gets challenged with these kinds of agency complaints, when there's no bona fide Complainant, but they can be successful if they have witnesses, documentation…stuff like that. But the Pathways website has a lot of information about the program already, with a lot of the religious-based stuff evident right there. Open Connections will just have to prove the coercion and stuff, if it actually *is* happening, and how they suffered resource damages as a result. The question for us, as an agency, though, too, is that if we were to go by the letter of the law--I mean, fair housing law, on the religious stuff--then, is it a doomed complaint based on the Supreme Court associational-standing issue, where that case law and the First Amendment supersedes the fair housing law we would enforce under our lesser statute language?"

"Wow, well, I'm gonna have to look at their website, that's messed up…"

"Oh, wait, but now that I think about it, maybe it'd be that a court-ordered participant would have the burden to bring up a religious objection in court for this kinda referral. Like, request an accommodation for the person's religion, or lack there*of*, to not be ordered into Pathways' program. Not that I expect many people would know on the front end about the religious nature of the *program*, and to request that accommodation, but still…(!). Anyways, yeah…so, I dunno, that's what's going on with me right now…"

"Yeah, well," Chad pauses, conflicted on whether to go on chatting or not. "I guess I'll let you get back to doing that stuff, then…"

"Yeah, no, it's a long day for me, I gotta work the Disability Action Network meeting tonight, so I'm in the middle of a marathon today."

"Yeah I have a meeting with Open Connections next Tuesday night, so--no, that following Tuesday night, two weeks, I think."

"Cool, maybe I'll have more of an update on the case by then, right now we only have the Respondent complaint response denying unlawful discrimination."

"Well…*okay*, man, I guess--I guess I'll check ya later on…"

"Okay sounds good man…" and Chad heads on towards the front office area.

Okay, fine, I'm gonna roll the dice and call back this Jordan Fordham, which I normally wouldn't do in order to keep my telephone line open for any inquiry calls forwarded to me while on intake duty, and to be ready at a moment's notice for any walk-ins from the street. Maybe because I'm tired, maybe because Mr. Fordham is obviously trying to get me to talk to him right away, maybe because of the freshness of the thinking-things-through with Chad, maybe because it's divine order, I abandon my better nature and standardized plan.

I get the yellow 8½" x 14" legal notepad, write "*Open v. Pathways*" as a header, get out my long-distance dialing log book from the bottom right desk drawer, and fill in the blanks to identify the case name on the log. I read quickly word-for-word the hard-copy written Respondent complaint response for the case, and the summary I made earlier in my head is about the same gist of things as what I read now, and there's no conciliation proposal from the Respondent to the Complainant to attempt to resolve the housing discrimination complaint, so that makes things much easier to deal with for the call. I open and read the attached e-mail Mr. Fordham sent, and it's just the copy of the same written response sent via U.S. postal mail.

I pick up the office desk telephone and dial 502-573-0046, wait two seconds and then hear a long tone…after the tone ends, I enter my four-digit ATM pin number, then immediately hang up the receiver due to the mistaken code I just entered. I grab a scrap of paper with my city government long-distance-calling employee code I've hidden under my Indiana Pacers paperweight that Michael & Corinne, via Jenny's online shopping, got me for Christmas a few years ago, I dial 502-573-0046 again, wait two seconds again, and then hear the long tone again…after putting in the correct pin number, I write down "*3:35 p.m.*" under the case header on the yellow legal notepad. A pause, and as I ready my hand for notes, I hear ringing tones.

"Attorneys…"

What kind of a receptionist greeting is that?

"Uh, yeah, hi. My name is Alex, Calderon. I was returning the call of Jordan, Fordham…?"

"One moment--" the receptionist says immediately, politely, and not friendly.

Pause.

"*You've reached the voicemail of Jordan C. Fordham Funkhauser Bates & Mitchell I can't return your call right now please leave a message after the tone including your name telephone number time of call and reason for the call after the tone--booooohp!*"

(Quick tone.)

"*Uh, hi, Mr. Fordham, this is Alex, Calderon, with the Louisville Metro Civil Relations Commission, at telephone number 5-0-2, 5-7-4, 2-3-9-1. Just returning your call about the complaint Open Connections versus Pathways. I'd be happy to explain the nature of the complaint; the Complainant's allegations in the complaint, at least as the Commission understands them; and, Respondent rights and responsibilities with the complaint. Or, to try to answer any questions you may have about Commission procedure, and the potential outcomes of a complaint. At this point, we're in receipt of your written complaint response, and that puts the Respondent in good standing with local ordinance requiring the filing of a written response to a complaint within 30 calendar days of the receipt of the complaint. If we need any additional information from the Respondent, I'll certainly call you, or send you something in writing, but, at this point, I'm happy to try to answer any questions you may have. Again, uh, Alex, Calderon, 5-0-2, 5-7-4, 2-3-9-1. Thanks…*"

I hang up and write on the yellow legal pad "*Called for R. rep, left voicemail msg ret 8/31/2015 call*"…then I rip the page off, taking half of the "*Open v. Pathways*" header with it. (Great.) I then place the serrated document in the left-hand pile on the office desk with all the other waiting documents.

The telephone then rings its out-of-office ring. I grab the yellow legal pad, quickly scrawl "*3:39 pm*," and then answer.

"Louisville Metro Civil Relations Commission, this is Alex…?"

"Yes, Mr. Calderon, hi, this is Jordan Fordham, Funkhauser Bates & Mitchell how are you this afternoon…"

"I'm fine…?"

"Great, well, thank you for calling me back. I just wanted to talk with you about the complaint your office filed against my client. Pathways of Christ is concerned about why the Civil Rights Commission would file this complaint, especially since there *is* no housing involved, and Pathways doesn't discriminate based on sexual orientation or gender identity, like the complaint accuses, anyone is welcome with its programs…"

"Okay, well, actually, it's important to reinforce that this complaint was not filed by the Civil Relations Commission, it was filed by Open Connections, which is a private, non-profit agency, and the Complainant in the case. The Civil Relations Commission is investigating the complaint, but we're a neutral, impartial, government agency."

"Well, Mr. Calderon, the complaint never should have been accepted for filing in the first place. You know, Pathways has serious concerns about any statutory authority under state and federal law to even investigate this type of complaint, to begin with, constitutional issues--I mean, with all due respect, municipalities, like Louisville, may pass ordinances with these alleged protections for gays, but state and federal law supersede these actions made by local aldermen, and councilmembers--"

"Okay--"

"For example, Kentucky House Bill 2-7-9, the Religious Freedom Restoration Act, passed by the legislature in 2013, it *mandates* that a religious good-faith objection override any alleged compelling state interest with these kinds of things. The state legislature passed this law to address just this sort of *thing.* And there's Supreme Court precedence to shield religious entities from these allegations of discrimination, it's already been tested in the northeast, when a gay-activist group was prevented *by* the U.S. Supreme Court from encroaching on the rights of a Christian-based group, like Pathways, in refusing participation in a parade, when the message promulgated by the offending group conflicted with the religious tenets of the Christian group--"

"Okay--" I note with my own shorthand frenetically.

"I mean, your ordinance may say *one* thing, but there *are laws* to trump whatever your statute says. The country was founded on religious freedom in the First Amendment. And aside from that, since anyone is welcome at Pathways, gay or non-gay, it's not discrimination. And no one is being harassed from being gay, like it says in the body of the complaint--Pathways *is* a Christian-based program operated by a national Christian discipleship, so, there are specific things my client teaches as a part of its mission in these rehab programs for the clients, which admittedly *are* Christ-centric. And Biblical. All teachings are of compassion and in an effort to help these people who *need* help, whatever their addictions are, and whatever they're struggling with. There probably have been gays in my client's programs, but Pathways is not into specifically providing some sort of gay-conversion therapy, or things like that. It *is* expected for clients to follow the rules of the program, and the last thing we want to do is drive somebody out by accusing them of being gay, or homosexual, or for whatever it is that they're suffering with, the goal here is always recovery and life skills, free from drugs and alcohol, gambling, whatever the destructive behavior is that they struggle with. You know, I think this complaint, this Open Connections, I think they read these news articles about Pathways trying to expand their outreach to the community in order to serve more folks, and they just thought all this harassment against gays was going on in the residency programs. But it's not true, no one has filed any complaint with Pathways about anything *like* that. So Open Connections runs to *you all* to file this case, based on all this speculation in the media, when it's just not true. My client is unaware of one iota of evidence of anything improper going on in these residency programs, which are to help the clients--I mean, it's also in the compelling state interest to *have* Pathways *do* this kind of work…my client gets referrals from the courts, which are also part of municipal government. Judges order some of these folks to mandatory participation in Pathways programs for recovery as part of their sentencing and plea-bargaining. In order to try to help them. So, I really--" Mr. Fordham slightly-laughs, "I really--my client is really, really concerned about all of this…"

I've kept up the note-taking relatively-well, and the initial assault is over, it appears, so it's time for my rebuttal--I mean, response.

"Okay," I try to be succinct. "Sure, I mean, Mr. Fordham, I hear what you're saying, your client's arguments, and I have the written Respondent response to the Complainant's complaint, and all of this is duly-noted, loud and clear…and, I'm not an attorney who can render a legal opinion in-and-of-itself *about* your arguments, but our office is statutorily committed to the municipal law that applies here, and any good-faith allegation of discrimination is the standard to what applies for the Commission to accept a complaint for investigation. Or, at least, where we have no information on the front end that the complaint is filed in *bad* faith. This statutory authority is not unique to Louisville, it's modeled after Commonwealth of Kentucky and federal law both, with the Kentucky Civil Rights Act and the federal Fair Housing Act, as amended. This is administrative law, and it's subject to Kentucky administrative rules of procedure, sure, but the ordinance is pretty substantially-equivalent."

"Uh-huh--"

"And, keep in mind, we do have this complaint subject to a current, open, ongoing investigation, with no predetermination on the merits of the Complainant's allegations. If we need *any* additional information before we make a determination on the merits of the Complainant's complaint, we'll contact you, but, you're welcome to contact me at any time with any questions, or to check on the case status, or anything like that--"

"I mean, this is costing my client money to call you, to file these written responses, the work to get you all the information you're asking for, and all while you all are building some kind of case *against* my client…"

"Well, I mean, if we do our jobs right here at the Commission, we *should* just be gathering the minimum amount of information in order to make a determination of Probable Cause or No Probable Cause, under this lowest-legal-standard that's supposed to apply here, and without too much of an administrative or financial burden on the parties. Ultimately, from a legal standpoint, the burden of proof is on the Complainant in the case…"

"Yes, but with the Civil Rights Commission's help, you understand, again: you're building the case…"

"Well, we're the Civil *Relations* Commission," I exhale a single-laugh, "not the Civil *Rights* Commission. And I hear what you're saying, other Respondents have said similar things--I might feel the same *way* if I was your client, there certainly is a burden of *production* that applies to these things, for a Respondent to respond to the complaint, codified by the ordinance. But, again, if we do our jobs right--and sometimes we *don't*," I exhale another single-laugh, "and, usually, that's not gonna be one of my calls these days--then, again, we should gather only the minimum amount of information we need in order to make that preliminary determination of whether to go forward with the case, or to just go ahead and dismiss the complaint. Also, if the Respondent believes that the Complainant has filed this complaint in *bad* faith, then there's a provision in local ordinance to address that. In theory, the Civil Relations Commission can make a determination on a bad-faith filing allegation alleged by a Respondent, in tandem with this procedure, and if there's Cause determined on the bad-faith filing, then we're supposed to create an order against the Complainant, providing reimbursement of reasonable fees that a Respondent expends in response to the investigation process. So, if you submit something in writing detailing the reason for a bad-faith filing allegation by the Complainant, we can review that, and make a determination on it on behalf of your client, as well."

"'Bad-faith filing,' okay, we may do that. Okay Mr. Calderon, I guess my next question would be, 'Can we see what alleged evidence Open Connections filed with you all in order to justify this complaint.' I mean, my client has information and records that I expect your office would want to see, and will ask for, at some point...but, we feel that if it's going to be a fair investigation, we should be permitted to see exactly what it is that Pathways is being accused of, in this 'harassment, coercion, and/or intimidation,' as it says here in the complaint."

"Well, Mr. Fordham, I gotta tell ya, we try to maintain confidentiality throughout the course of the investigation, for the most part, in order to preserve the rights of the parties and encourage participation with this administrative law investigation. I'm not personally qualified to respond to a request for information from a case file, but I certainly don't want to limit your right to ask for *any* information from the case file at any time. We do have a strict policy that all information requests be submitted in writing, and if you were to do that, then I can forward it on for a response, which'll come from the Civil Relations Commission or the Jefferson County Attorney's Office. And of course under the Kentucky Open Records Act, and any other state law not shielding the file from the parties or the public."

"Okay we'll do that. At this point, I know you said it only takes a good-faith allegation to file these things, but without the *proof*, I mean--we feel like it's *Pathways* that's being harassed here, I mean, absent any proof. Open Connections files this complaint, they've demonstrated against Pathways by speaking in public hearings when Pathways was trying to open its third location here in the state, engineering a campaign with some folks in the neighborhood to go against the proposed site, in Louisville, in Crescent Hills--"

"Crescent Hill, uh-huh--"

"Crescent Hills--Hill, and Pathways has the zoning threatened at public hearing, where they may not even be able to open up the new facility at the desired location, potentially costing Pathways even more money. And Open Connections folks hold up signs saying that Pathways is intolerant, when it's Open *Connections* that's being intolerant…my client's just trying to do the good service work it's mission is wanting it to do. Open Connections needs to understand that this is not a huge, profitable venture that Pathways is engaged in, you understand--in fact, it's another reason why this complaint should be dismissed, on its own. Pathways is *not* a commercial entity operating for-profit in the rehabilitation program, it's the intent of fair housing laws to address housing for commercial purposes, which this is not. Pathways charges nominal fees, no rent, there's no landlord-tenant relationship here, no signed lease agreement between the participants…only paperwork agreeing, on a mutual, voluntary basis, for participation in the program to address addiction. Except for these court-ordered clients, and, in which case, it's all for compliance with the terms that the court--the secular court--deems necessary."

"Uh-huh…sure. I mean, *duly-noted*, for sure, Mr. Fordham, I certainly have it all down, and I've taken a few notes based on everything we've talked about right now…it should be *very* clear for the investigative record."

"Okay, well…alright, I appreciate your time today, Mr. Calderon. I guess we'll just wait to hear from you all."

"Sure…and please, you're welcome to call or e-mail back any questions, or any inquiries on the status of the case, any questions about rights and responsibilities, anything like that, at any time."

"Okay Mr. Calderon, you have a good day."

"All right, thanks so much…"

"Okay bye now."

"Okay-bye."

I hang up, exhaling, and the minor adrenaline charge is now keeping me tiredly-going. Soon, I'll crash from it, since I'm a morning person, and this afternoon is an afternoon that'll go on until possibly after 8:00

p.m. tonight thanks to the Disability Action Network meeting. I pop another cough drop.

The telephone in my office then rings again, but on the interoffice line.

"Hello-this-is-Alex…?"

"Um, Alex," Janice says, in her tentative, they-are-right-in-front-of-me voice, "there's a gentleman, and his wife, here, he's--he's speaking Spanish, neither of them seem like they can speak English, but I think they're here to ask about something, maybe a complaint…"

"Okay…"

"Could you--could you come out here and maybe see--it may be an intake, I'm not sure…"

"Okay, sure, Janice, I'll be out in a moment, thanks…"

"Okay bye," Janice says quickly, hanging up.

I sort through the intake paperwork and dig out Spanish-language employment and housing discrimination complaint forms, standardized respectively from similar Equal Employment Opportunity Commission and HUD intake forms; we don't have them in any Commission-drafted format, much less any intake forms at all for public accommodations or bias-related crime complaints, so, of course, watch it be a discrimination complaint combination of the latter two that I'll have to draft somehow. I don't know how I'll get a full intake or two done with Limited English Proficiency Complainants, including drafting a complaint, or even two of them, by 5:00 p.m.

I jot down "*4:23 pm*" on the 8½" x 14" yellow legal notepad, then grab the pad, an ink pen, and the paperwork and leave my office to head down the hall towards the front receptionist desk area.

I see a male and female standing at the front desk looking ahead, likely at Janice, and I hear Janice explaining to them in a slightly-raised voice, almost like a parent, that someone will be out to see them. I walk towards them and try to shift my brain into a communicative mode that I've struggled with for most of my life, but have found that if I stick with it, I can sometimes get a point across…

Drinking a Highball and smoking a menthol cigarette in 1980's Louisville, his maternal grandmother, an American with Louisville lineage since at least the 1800s, told him the story of how she lived in Lake Tahoe with his paternal grandmother, who was a first-generation American born in Arizona on the way up from Mexico. Sitting regally and dignified in F. Scott Fitzgerald fashion, yet humbly, she explained to the seven-year-old how sad it was to her that when she walked along the sidewalks there, "Indians" (also known as "Native Americans") would step into the street and avoid all eye contact with her when they walked her way. Despite being so young, he felt empathy with her empathy.

***

In 1980s Los Angeles, his paternal aunt and paternal grandmother switched from English into Spanish mid-sentence frequently when speaking to each other. And his grandmother did so when speaking to him, and to all his non-Spanish-speaking cousins.

"Grandma loves you, mijo…"

***

Around age eleven, he, his brother, and his cousin blew up coconuts with M-80 firecrackers at a trash heap mountain on the outskirts of Tijuana, Mexico, with the assistance of their animated Mexican uncle. When dusk set in, the fun ended, so it was time for bed.

In the morning, the telephone rang endlessly in the room where the young troublemakers slept, with no answer nor answering machine taking the call. After the uncle sleepingly yelled a few times in English for one of them to get the phone, the uncle stirred with a Spanish-language curse, answered the phone, and quickly did away with the call.

In the dark, still half asleep and not hearing anything more from his uncle, he then heard a hiss and saw a small reddish jumping light onto the hardwood floor in center of the bedroom.

bang!!!!!!!!!!!!!!

***

As a freshman in Louisville's high school, his Spanish teacher, non-Hispanic/Latino American, couldn't understand how he had the worst grade in the class.

"What's the matter with you, this is in your blood…?!"

Maybe it was the teacher's challenge, maybe it was because he matured through the next few years, maybe it was because it was his favorite teacher he ever had, with just the right mix of accountability, accessibility, and confrontational humor…he aced his Spanish classes by the time he graduated.

***

Louisville high school diversity was an unexpected topic of conversation in his junior year math class.

"Everyone here is all the same," one student said to the teacher, "…well, except for" him.

Backpedaling with expletives at what just came out of the student's own mouth, the student begged him for forgiveness and said that it'd be no surprise if he beat the student up.

The thought never crossed his mind on something like that, but maybe it should have; in a half-hearted macho-attempt reaction to the student apology, he snapped his pencil in half with the right hand that held it to save face in class, feigning outrage that, in all honestly, really wasn't there.

***

In his senior year of high school, his non-Hispanic/Latino American English teacher went off-script talking about the British literature assigned to the class, and she evidently took it for granted that there were "no great works from Latin America." After she explained a few weeks later how she'd been to Mexico herself and found that "it was a dirty country," he took enough offense and arranged for transfer out of her class to another. When he asked her to speak with him out in the school hallway and he gave her notice, including an explanation why, she instantly judged that such a decision was "narrow-minded."

When he explained to his new class the details on why he was now a classmate, the non-Hispanic/Latino African-American student sitting immediately in front of him nodded once at him in stoic affirmation.

***

While an eighteen-year-old freshman in college, he seemed to be the only one in the crowd offended when the administration-invited Hispanic/Latino activist author explained in keynote autobiography that the activist's pride came in becoming an American through "assimilation." The perceived affront to his Mexican-American heritage by the author was too great for him to contain, and his fellow students around him, non-Hispanic/Latino Americans, were visibly taken aback at his reaction right there in his seat voicing expletives in the perceived dismissal. Despite the activist qualifying the talk by saying that continued homage to one's heritage shouldn't be abandoned, he only heard the activist judging him with requests of conformity that rejected Hispanic/Latino lineage. That's what he heard…

***

In a post-college and pre-professional time getting service at an Indianapolis car dealership, the non-Hispanic/Latino American maintenance technician who gave him his car keys back asked him what his name was after a moment of small-talk. Upon disclosing his first and last name both, the service station associate responded earnestly, "Well, you sound educated, and…" wished him well with the start of his new job in Louisville.

***

"Oh wow, what kind of name is that?"

"Mexican," he said sensitively while signing his name and avoiding eye-contact, with the slightest of fears that he might be questioned further, or turned away, by the non-Hispanic/Latino American poll worker at the polling station.

***

He adopted his father's pronunciation of Los Angeles as Lohs Angeles, not Lahs Angeles.

***

A non-Hispanic/Latino American friend routinely called him "spic" with the utmost, legitimate brotherhood.

***

He and his Filipina-American girlfriend had fun trying to "out the Filipino" when looking at people in feature articles online, at actors & actresses in movies and television, and in the general public.

Her family also guided him through a vacation to the Philippines itself, providing a profound, non-stop tour of a portion of the beautiful country's urban and rural populations and landscapes.

"The Philippines and Mexico are similar…they are not the same, but they are similar…" her father explained. He would have to agree.

***

The non-Hispanic/Latino American city government co-worker was flippant and resentful when she explained city government hiring & promotion politics to him. "Because of your last name, you probably will get the chance to be promoted like others around here, not me…"

***

"Part of the reason why I hired you was because you're Hispanic…"

***

"Do you think maybe you were passed over for promotions with city government because you're Hispanic?"

***

When completing online surveys for airline travel reward miles credit, he was almost never given an option to select something in between the demographic identification request of "Are you Hispanic or Latino," "Yes" or "No."

***

He occasionally received business solicitations in Spanish via United States Postal Mail, despite never signing up for anything in such language.

***

He sometimes describes his ethnic heritage as "half-Chicano."

***

According to one DNA test, he was identified genetically as being approximately 75% European, 20% Native American, 3% West Asian, and 2% African; politics aside, it was a broad conciliation for a person's alleged-by-nature-and/or-god makeup. Never an absolute, empirical science, the Irish, Italian, and Yaqui genes seemed to him to be the most pronounced, while the American culture dominated (with a Mexican flavor now and then).

CHAPTER SEVEN

"Uh, hola, uh...me llamo Alex, uh...por favor," I say to the couple's stares. "Aquí," I continue in extending my hand towards the Civil Relations Commission intake room cubby-hole, which is attached to the side of the wide-open space on one side of the front lobby receptionist desk area. "Okay...?"

"Sí," the male of the couple says, helping to guide the female to the intake room.

Janice gives me a forced, polite smile and is grateful for me taking the baton.

By hand, more than by my quiet-mouthed word "aquí" again, I direct the couple to sit in the two chairs on the opposite side of the computer-adorned small folding table while I sit on the other side with the computer monitor and keyboard ready. I place the intake paperwork and yellow legal notepad down on the table in front of me, my ink pen ready for action. I see that both have copies of the Civil Relations Commission fair housing brochure in Spanish, taken from the front bar area of the receptionist desk. Shame on me for not bringing with me Briana's Spanish-language magnets.

"Perdoname, pero, yo no puedo hablar español mucho, solamente un *poquito*," I say with too-annunciated, stiff pronunciation as the male sits stone-faced but the female slightly smiles. "Por favor, que es el--la razón, para sus visitas--visitan, hoy?"

The male then goes into quick recitation of what brought them down to the Civil Relations Commission, I think, while I sit hopefully not too-stone-faced and ready to write on the yellow legal pad...just as soon as I can get an idea of what the complaint is all about. I catch the words "policía," "telefono," "criminal," "discriminación," and a few other words in the rapid-fire Spanish monologue, but I can't tell if the issue really is criminal, civil, housing, or exactly what the nature of the grievance is. I wait until he completes his explanation, history, and venting, like I do with almost all potential Complainants anyways, and then I try to start a process with the Commission.

"Okay...uh, unfortunamente, yo no puedo comprender exactamente qué usted es hablando, por que, yo, no es--yo no soy...qual-if-fi-ca-do ...Perdon, yo no puedo hablar Español muy bien. Y, unfortunamente, no es una persona con mi agencia, el Civil Relations Commission, ahora, que--quien hablar Español. Pero, si ustedes puedo—puede…uh…'give'--dame, sus nombre de telephono, es posible que nosotros puede--podemos a llamar ustedes con un, *interpreter*? Es okay, a llamar?"

"Sí, bueno…" the male says.

"Uh, un momento, y yo obtener--obtengo, información de--para ustedes."

"Sí," he says again.

"Okay, un momento…" I smile, a little with relief, and quickly get up. I start to rush over to the west wing of the office to meet my good friend today, Ronita. But right before I get within Ronita's line of fire, Brenda is there standing at a medium-sized paper shredder filing her documents away.

"Hey, Alex," she greets with routine.

"Hey, Brenda," I say as I try to get to Ronita.

"Alex, hey (!), let me stop you," Brenda says, despite my obvious mission to get going on past. "Where are we, with the Disabilities Action Network, and the Mayor's Disabilities Forum…?"

"It's moving along," I say, stopping in my tracks quickly. "I have the Network meeting tonight, and I'm working on the Forum presentation…"

"Okay, Roberta and Janice are getting me the statistics for the Forum on all our cases, if you could get me your information too, then I can plug in the Network information to our meetings we've hand with them and Public Works."

"Okay yeah, I can do that," I say quickly, "but, hey: I have two walk-ins in the intake room, can I get back with you tomorrow on it?"

"Yeah, that's fine, go ahead…" Brenda politely concedes.

Ronita is at her desk, *por dios*, but as I approach with the immediacy and the ear-shot of notice I just gave Brenda, Ronita still doesn't look up.

"Hey, Ronita…?"

"Yes."

She's in dry-mode.

"Ronita, hey: we have a walk-in right now, a couple that only speaks Spanish. So I need to go ahead and schedule an interpreter, but I gotta leave here at 5:00, 'cause I need to go home, grab dinner real quick, and then head back out to the monthly Disability Action Network meeting, so I can't wait around for the interpreter today…"

"You have their number?"

"No, but I'll get it, and then I can give it to you?"

"Yeah, e-mail me their information, I'll send you the interpreter request form e-mail and you can send it back," she says, working on her own paperwork without looking up.

"Okay yeah, I've got it, when you sent it out before to everybody. I'll try to get that to you real quick here before 5:00."

"Okay, do that and then I'll forward it to Mission Charities…soon as they get back with me, I'll have the interpreter call your walk-ins and then we can contract out with MC for the interviews."

"Okay, cool, lemme go run and get them squared away, thanks, Ronita…"

"Uh-huh…"

I quickly get back around Brenda at her shredder, from the west wing to the intake room, where the couple is sitting patiently and quietly.

"O-kay, gracias, perdoname," I say in a flustered sitting-back-down. "Si ustedes pueden dame sus numero de telefono, yo--nosotros pue--podemos, a llamar, ustedes para hablar con sus…situación. Nosotros…uh…nosotros, discriminación, y trabajar con…policía problemas, tambien…"

Both look briefly at each other and then say separately to me, "Sí."

The male then says, "Sí, bueno, el numero de telefono es," and then in heavily-accented English, "fiye-eight-sebben, two-niye-niye-sero."

I write while repeating, "Cinco-ocho-siete, dos-nuevo-nuevo-cero…y, es cinco-cero-dos?"

"Cinco-cero-dos, fiye-oh-two, sí, sí," the male says and the female nods, confirming the Louisville-area telephone area code.

"Muy bien," I say with continuing relief. "Y como se llamas…?"

The male puts an open hand on his chest, "Manuel, Rodriguez. Y ella, ella Maria. Maria Elena, Rodriguez."

I continue writing. "Okay…muy *bien*, gracias. Y me llamo Alex, Calderon. Yo soy un investigator, con la Comisión. Una persona…uh…llamar sus telefono en Español, digan con sus situaciónes. Y…Y, uh…And we will see how we can help you, ayudan usted—ustedes…"

"Okai, muy bien, muy bien."

"Y pronto, por lo--la mañana, probablemente," I say, struggling to provide body language to reinforce that the Commission-contracted interpreter will, in fact, or hopefully will, in fact, call for them by tomorrow morning in Spanish.

"Sí, bueno…"

I get up smiling as earnestly as I can, considering it's just about 5:00 p.m., and I have to get going.

"Gracias," I again say and use my hand to guide them while we walk to the front door. *This is bad customer service*, I think with fleeting guilt. But, we're not an emergency services agency, are we. Still, we'll get in trouble with Title VI of the Civil Rights Act of 1964 for lack of Limited English Proficiency barrier-reduction since we receive so much federal money. If anyone would test us on it.

Commission staff are already walking up the hallway with bags, sunglasses on, doing the slow-walk of killing the last few work minutes before quitting time. Staff slightly-forced, slightly-sarcastic, and slightly-looking-away smiles are there due to self-consciousness for our two visitors in creeping ahead towards the front door, of course. Janice even provides her excellent public relations skills by saying thanks and goodbye to the couple from the receptionist desk despite her encumbrance. The couple exit the lobby without speaking and then wait for the elevator outside the front door.

"Alex, you better hurry…" Julia says jokingly when appearing from the west wing office area. "You need a ride today?"

Walking away towards the east wing, I tell her quickly, "No, thanks Julia, appreciate it, though," in darting down the hallway away from the front door. Julia and Janice start cutting up behind me, then Sherry saunters up from her office with her bags to join them once I pass. I finish the short hallway trek by reading on my cellular telephone that it's 4:58 p.m. In my office, I tear off the brief notes I made for the Rodriguez inquiry and then dial Ronita's extension on the intra-office line of my office desk telephone.

"Yes."

"Ronita, this is Alex, I can't get that interpreter stuff to you today, I'm on my way out the door, but I'll get it for you first thing in the morning…"

"All right…thanks."

"K thanks Ronita, bye."

I not-quite slam the telephone receiver down and see out of the corner of my eye Briana moving past my office towards front-door freedom. I put the 8½" x 14" yellow legal notepad in my black work bag, sling the bag over my left shoulder, hover over the desktop computer, clickly shut-down and snap off the computer monitor with my thumb, then slap off the lights on my way out of my office.

<*dong!*>

I see and hear ahead the slow-but-sure exodus of staff folks who sometimes wait for me to join them, holding the door for me, etc., but today there's probably no waiting since it's late at exactly 5:00 p.m. and I'm so far behind.

<*dong!*>

"Come on, Alex!"

"Yeah, come on!"

The elevator door is closing but the Commission crew shows mercy on me, jarring it back open to allow me to squeeze on as they stand arms to their sides with bags and purses.

"All *right*…" I say, looking diagonally down to both sides of me, to position myself to stand stiff and frozen inside the elevator, to accommodate the overall lack of space.

The elevator door begins closing again and <*dong!*> comes Ron, tote bag over his shoulder and wearing tennis shoes to not-match his business slacks. But he goes past the elevators in his sprint, to take the stairs down to the street instead as we watch without calling for him. And with no jokes about him afterwards, surprisingly.

"You speak Spanish?" Briana says loud, at it again.

"Sí," I say, looking straight ahead.

Briana heartily and quickly laughs before rapid-fire. "Janice say you speak *Span*ish…"

"No, not really," I say, smiling sarcastically and not looking at Briana, or anyone, since it'd cause a collision in the close quarters of the elevator car.

"Janice said you speak Spanish, why you not speak *Span*ish…?"

"Briana…!" both Janice and I yell out at the same time.

Another hearty laugh, but this time from more than just Briana.

"Don't you *listen* to Briana, Alex…" Sherry says, scolding Briana jokingly at the same time.

The elevator stops on the second floor, of course, so we can't go straight down to where we want to go uninterrupted on days like today, when I'm in a hurry. The doors open to the second floor to reveal: no one. My eyes go up into the back of my head in frustration as the elevator doors then take forever to rickety-close again.

Janice, always shocking the crowd in seeking attention, and maybe in order to break the silent pause, then says, "Briana, why didn't *you* eat the *watermelon* I gave you after lunch…"

"*Awwwwww* …" everyone laughs together.

Briana then heartily-caws out with a direct-sarcastic frown, "Ms. Janice, you already *know*, I'm part *I*rish…"

"*Briana*," Janice continues playing, "that don't have *nothin'* to do with that…!"

I surprise myself by joining in.

"Briana, I eat the hell outta that--"

in unison with Sherry "--burrito--"

"--though!"

"Yeah, I was gonna say," Sherry says choking-out a laugh.

"I eat fried chicken…?" Janice questions matter-of-factly in deadpan.

"Ms. *Jan*ice: you-know-you-don't-eat *no* chicken," Briana scowls back.

Julia laughs, slower to respond.

"You all are *crazy*," the Ombudsman says as the least senior of all of us staff aboard, as the elevator finally reaches the ground floor.

I squeeze off and nudge through to the side wall inside and stretch out my hand to hold the elevator door open from the inside, nodding with a humble and slightly-sarcastic smile towards the ladies to exit.

"*Janice* is the crazy one!" Briana says loudly. "She's got a dis-*bility*…In the *head*…!"

"Briana, you--" Janice looks around to tell everyone in the office building lobby, including the afternoon security guard who surprisingly is not outside smoking. "*Briana's* the one with the disability. A *physical* disability: a *peanut head* !"

I'm not busting up laughing on the outside, but in hindsight I will be, and on many other days I'd be falling over participating with the fun. Right now, I'm too tired and high-strung and busy headed to my car, though I do say my byes to the others as they do, to each other and to me.

I walk out into the oven outside, luckily with no pedestrian traffic to navigate, and then on up the parking garage ramp to the left while sticking my hand out in a wave to the unidentified female attendant in the booth, like I'm trying to halt car traffic. I head quickly to my car, the slight adrenaline rush from changed surroundings and the would-be-the-end-of-the-work-day freedom tricking me into keeping me going. Mentally, I'm still so, so drained, and I'd sit and sulk but I need to get this car, out of this garage, and out onto *that* street currently flooding with racecar drivers, sounding horns, illegally-parked delivery vehicles, and cellular-telephoned pedestrians. My road-rage rat-race mentality will compete with my body's physical deterioration for supremacy of whether I actually can get home, get dinner, get back out, get to my meeting, get back home, get back to my family, and, finally and hopefully, get back to my sanity.

I'm so routine-oriented that even in my exhaustedness, I effortlessly snap my seatbelt on, turn all the dials, push all the buttons, and go through all the motions in starting my car, pulling out of the parking space and navigating the other vehicles lining the garage, and the office workers sprinkling out to the garage. I don't turn on the compact disc player yet in order to focus attention on getting out into the rush hour disarray, and to make sure that my out-of-office rush isn't amplified to maniacal levels, especially dangerous when I don't have a clear, rested head.

My car waits on the second-floor ramp while the straggling Briana walks up in a forced hurry, laughing out loud once after I shake my fist at her in mock frustration. Driving on down to the bottom of the ramp, three lines of vehicle traffic have formed on West Chestnut Street and are moving ultra-slowly with no break for me to sneak in, bully into, or careen-into. Rumbling summertime stereo bass and cursed-bravado lyrics protrude loudly out of one vehicle going past in the lane nearest me, from a dark-window-tinted older American car; Spanish-language country music wails out of a non-window-tinted older American car a few lengths behind in the outside lane. My eyes are primarily focused on the left, but I'm also giving darting looks straight ahead at the lined-up vehicles waiting to get into traffic opposite me from flat-rate parking spaces and the hotel parking garage further back; and, I have to keep an eye out on the right for any more office building escapees and general pedestrians.

I wait to be let in, just to make the right turn out of my garage, onto the one-way street. There's still not enough room to creep out yet, as a car is careening maniacally down the inside lane nearest my side of West Chestnut. Technically, that inside lane is a driving lane at this time of day, in order to accommodate traffic, and the car does have the right-of-way for such…it's just a surprise that no vehicle with blinking lights is using the inside lane as a parking space violation today. Cursing with the immediacy of not being able to get out, I wait two more full seconds that seem to be two hours, and then I kick on the cd player. The song that comes on is not a favorite on the disc, and it sounds worse than ever today. I click the forward button on the player, and digitized lines and foreign-looking random characters come onto the screen instead of "Track 7," fulfilling the prophecy of malfunctioning technology to match my malfunctioning body.

Since this *is* Louisville, straggling vehicles in all three driving lanes are just a matter of time and, sure enough, now give me hope down the street to the left in order for me to make a break for getting in line turning to the right. I go for it, hard-right turning too much and I drive slightly over the sidewalk curb with the right side of the car, bouncing onto the street but with surprising acceleration, as always, from my more-than-a-decade-old compact vehicle. I then press the eject button on the cd player and fumble the cd carrying case, which is really a cd-rom vinyl-covered set of half-broken plastic sleeves from 1995, pitching the case onto the front passenger seat with my right hand while I stare ahead driving with the left hand. I thumb through the cd case with the right hand with darting glances deviating from the driving tunnelvision. I see that next up in the cd rotation, according to the carrying case mandate of rotational fate, is the soundtrack from a 2002 Mexican film that reminds me of my ten-year college reunion weekend as much as it does trips to Mexico, oddly enough.

I put the disc in and hear Spanish-language rap/hip-hop with filthy lyrics which are just *not* my *mermalada* (*baile*? what's the slang word in Spanish for "jam," or dance?). Right now, or ever, really. I click the forward button on the cd player and digitized lines and foreign-looking random characters make me eject-then-push-in-again the disc, all while making a right turn onto South 3rd Street. Three beats into the same unwelcome first track, I hit the forward button and it cuts off the cd player to nothingness, not even foreign characters. I curse with one of two Spanish-language curse words I remember, then I try yet again: three beats of the first song play, I hit forward, then there's success with "Track 2," which lays down beats from a traditional version of *La Cucaracha* into a *wiki-wiki-scratch* version for today's kids. It's not a vortex of enveloping sound to comfort me on the short commute home, but it occasionally makes me think of the movie and some of the personal identity of a few past memories I take from it. If not for a lifetime or a minute. And not that there aren't a thousand American-made movies which do the same.

I hit almost every red light on the way, of course, and get stuck behind every slow vehicle, and I'm forced to yield before every haphazard jaywalking pedestrian on the way to the alley connecting to my home street...or at least it seems that way, since the reality is that I hit only two of six red lights; the two vehicles I get stuck behind are doing the speed limit; and, the pedestrians I yield to are crossing in a marked university crosswalk. At the corner of South 4th Street & West Oak Street in Old Louisville, one block away from the house, the summertime urban chaos is organized with persons I perceive to be of all different races, colors, religions, national origins, sexes, physical disabilities, mental disabilities, sexual orientations, and gender identities, roaming and patronizing small businesses, the chain corner-drugstore, and the chain discount store; waiting around for municipal transportation; loitering; or, in some combination thereof. I turn right down the alley from 4th Street, just south of Oak, and a male carrying a brown-paper-bag-enclosed bottle is walking in the middle of the alley coming my way. But, mercifully, he does his duty and moves to the left side of the alleyway street, allowing me to pass while he looks and struts at me driving by.

Reaching the end of the alley, I wait as a small pickup truck coming from the left on my residential cross-street makes a left turn into the alley continuation on the other side of the cross-street. I wait there at the end of my alley segment, with fear that the truck would stop its left-hand turn in not proceeding on, but backing up instead in doing a turn-around by backing onto my residence street in an L-shape. Which is exactly what it does, except, not really, because instead of turning backwards into an L-shape on my home street, it just heads backwards across the cross-street where I'm sitting, waiting. Straight back. My eyes leap up out of my head when I see the back of the truck coming at me with no brake lights, and I frantically try to throw my car gear in reverse while hitting the car horn over and over. I get the horn part right, but not the reverse part.

<bang!>

The back of the small pickup truck hits my front bumper, giving me a small jolt.

Lightning-quick, I fumble the seat-belt and car ignition off, get out of my car and scream out a curse word into the hot air that jars a younger-looking couple as they look to get into their own vehicle a few parallel-parked cars away to my left on my street. Mentally, I'm instantly embarrassed as they stand looking at me with their mouths open; emotionally, I'm not whatsoever. As the offending pickup truck driver gets out of his truck, I look at my front bumper and see no damage.

"Well, it doesn't look like there's any damage," the male driver says.

"I'll be the judge of that," I say back with directness and a slight gnarl.

"Well there's no dent or anything…(!)" he says, sensing my rage and transferring to him.

I look at my car front again while the guy looks at the pickup truck rear.

"No damage," the guy then says firmly and mutedly, walking over with a firm outstretched hand, in surprise to me.

Reeling in the high-strungedness, I shake the firm outstretched hand briefly on instinct and with a conceding frown while contemplating asking him profanely why in the *world* he'd do such a turnaround by backing into my side of the alley without looking. The rage of blame somehow gets tempered by my logic and reason, though with no explanation.

Getting back in my car, I look to see the young couple sitting in their car, still looking at me, their engine not turned on, and they're probably thankful that they were audience to only a minor incident. The pickup truck then drives straight down the opposite-side alley like it should have to begin with, and I turn on my car and right-turn onto my street.

I see the first on-street parking spot open for me to pull right into, right up to the no-parking-beyond-the-sign sign on the utility pole. Sliding in, I turn the car off and sort the cd holder on the passenger seat, putting the old disc exchanged from back at the office parking garage into one of the sleeves, and I put the holder back in the slot under the cd player in the dashboard. I grab my black work bag and exit the vehicle, manually-locking the driver's side door and keeping the keys in my hand for quick-entry into the house. On the short walk out of the street and up the stairs, I curse at the accident that just happened in disbelief and look around at all of the activity around the West Oak Street cross-street nearby beyond the dead-end cul-de-sac, especially at the pedestrians on their way from the two bordering sidewalks onto my street.

Before I can get the front door unlocked with the turn of the key, it startles me by opening from Michael appearing with Tivoli on a leash, complementing my own on-edge nerves of tiredness and car-accident adrenaline. I exchange "hey" with Michael, while Tivoli starts wagging his tail looking at me with his big head and small ears up at attention in seeing me and his thrill of being let out of the house.

"Oh (!) *hey*, be careful, Michael, okay…" I warn, based on my skimming-scan of the neighborhood. "I'll lock the door…"

Michael says nothing, or has audibled something too low for me to hear. He follows Tivoli's toddler-lumber down the steps, and I make it inside the house, locking the door behind me. I turn and look out the front door stained-glass window just in case any trouble is immediate while M & T walk across the street, then out of view. Nothing menacing that I can see, so I walk into the kitchen and see the United States Postal Service mail stack on the stove which'll have to wait for my attention, even though it entices me greatly. The microwave says it's 5:20 p.m.

I put my black work bag down on the counter and open the refrigerator's freezer side-door, looking briefly at the shelves of bagged microwave burritos, hash browns, chopped broccoli, and corn nibblets, as well as boxed ice cream sandwiches and ice cream tubs…finally, I see the expensive, organic vegetarian enchilada "meal" that cost $2.89 on close-out sale at the grocery store from its original $4.79 price. I grab the enchilada carton, flip it over, scan quickly to find the phrases "*slit cover*," "*3 minutes*," and "*1½ more minutes*." I shut the freezer door and open the carton, throwing the carton box into an orange kitchen recycle-bin tub with a crash upon contact with plastic and metal containers like bottles and cans, augmented by the tight construction of the house's 1890s Victorian-era design. I grab a fork from the utensil tray drawer, stab the plastic cover of the meal tray three times in three different areas where the frozen enchiladas aren't encroaching on the plastic ceiling, then place the tray in the microwave. I quickly hit 3-3-3 on the microwave keypad and then hit the start button for a whir of exhaust. I get a plate from the cabinet and set it on the counter, placing the fork on it, and then shuffle the used, empty glasses and empty cereal bowl from one side of the kitchen counter to the other side, closest to the kitchen sink. I can't help myself, so I pull open the dishwasher to see clean dishes still in the machine, which I already knew about since the green light was lit on the closed-tight dishwasher door.

Thumbing through the mail in compulsion while continuing to wait on the microwave, I see my car insurance bill; a Louisville Metro Government notice of a "Community Conversation" on zoning, in general, not even for a specific project—*development;* and, the rest of the mail addressed to the rest of the family, such as clothing catalogs addressed "*to the resident of.*" I take the insurance bill with me to the dining room table, place it next to my regular spot, and then place a napkin from the napkin holder down to mark my dinner territory. Back into the kitchen, I get a larger-sized glass before putting it back on better thought from thinking about the upcoming meeting: I don't want to have to leave the meeting to use the restroom, so it's better to try to limit things. I fill a medium-sized glass with refrigerator-water filtered with a red warning light that's been on since 2011, and I get into a different cabinet to get out my treat of canned, lightly-salted mixed nuts for a side dish.

The house sure is quiet, I hope Corinne's upstairs in her room and not *not-here* without me knowing about it again.

The beeping of the microwave means dinner's ready, so I open the micro door, take out the steaming tray, peel off the plastic cover, place the tray on the empty plate, and drip condensation onto the floor in getting the cover into the trash can. Shuffling the plate, the water glass, and the mixed nuts all at the same time over to the dining room, I then hear the front door lock snap and the creak of opening as I place the last of the three items down. Walking back towards the kitchen, I exchange "hey" again with Michael and he works on freeing Tivoli from the leash. I then come down the stretch with the plate occupied by the hot enchilada tray.

"Dude," I urgently engage him, sitting down at my place at the dining room table. "I just got into a car accident out here at the alley, some guy in a pickup truck backed into me doing a turnaround at the alley onto our street. I can't believe it, he just didn't look what he was doing, just *backed* right into me as I waited at the alley to turn onto our street…there's no damage though, to either of us. But I'm, like, 'come *on* (!)'…"

"Oh yeah…?" Michael says, almost engaged.

After a hefty sigh from my mania, I dive into eating, focusing on consummation with no time to rifle through a few pages of a travel magazine on the table. I'm too into my mission of eating for the next ten minutes to show the normal proactive but passing interest in Michael's school day, since I have to be out the door by 5:45 p.m. But Michael's ready to talk, apparently, and he smiles his cerebral grin in thinking of something it looks like he's been wanting to tell me, or someone, about, probably for hours.

"Alex…did you hear about the migrant crisis in Hungary?"

"Uh, yeah…?" I say questioningly, focusing primarily on getting my meal into my system but looking up at him and doing my best to stay engaged in what he wants to talk about, forcing through the tiredness, the stress of the business day that's past, and the business evening ahead.

"So, on Comedy Station's *Old But News*? They had on Senator Marek, from Texas? You know? He was born in Hungary, but he opposes the U.S. getting involved in helping to resettle the migrants, from Syria?"

"Uh, yeah…(?)"

"Yeah? Well, he was on the segment '8½ Questions,' and John Lessard, the host, asked him," smiling into a barely-laugh, "if he was--if Senator Marek was a political refugee from another country, would he want to stay at the foreign train station and wait for assistance; or, would he want to be interred at a camp with other refugees behind a fence, but the guards constantly played the song 'Texas Commonwealth Anthem' for twelve hours non-stop a day," Michael laughs a full single laugh.

"Uh," I tiredly slightly-smile, not getting the reference or the joke. "No, I dunno…?"

"Well, because, you know," Michael explains, still smiling, "it was--the song has the phrase 'Despite being a stranger in a strange land, I was elected by the people to give everyone a hand'…you know? The anthem--the song, 'Texas Commonwealth Anthem," is by 'Border Crisis,' they're from Austin?"

"Oh, okay, no, sorry, I didn't know that one…but that's funny, though, I haven't seen that show much, but it *is* too-funny sometimes, the few times I've watched it…?"

Michael doesn't break his smile as he's pleased with the recognition of the humor. Like most seventeen-year-olds, he's much more interested in when his mother's coming home and what's for dinner tonight, anyways, not dissecting with insecurity his relationship with a stepfather-to-be's reaction to his news.

"Alex…so, do you--do you know what time…Jenny's…coming home, or…?"

"No, no I sure don't. Probably by around 6:00…"

"Do you know what we're having for dinner?"

"No…no, I sure don't. That's why I'm eating dinner now, actually, is 'cause I have to work the Disability Action Network meeting tonight at 6:00, I'll leave here in a few minutes by 5:45."

"Oh yeah," he says, then hums a song while walking into the kitchen.

I hope that I'm not just acting like a robot and coming off as too dismissive. *He's a good kid*, I think to myself. And so's Corinne.

Oh--(!)

"Michael, is your *sister* here?" I say loudly from the dining room, in order to try to get him to answer over the tap water he's pouring himself in a new glass.

"Um…I don't--well, I don't--uh, wait, *yeah*, she is, she's upstairs."

Mama mia…

"Okay just checking," I say semi-parentally. "I haven't seen her…"

Tivoli knows it's dinnertime for me, and if he wasn't so dehydrated and exhausted from his 94-degree-fahrenheit-and-humid walk, he'd be putting his giant head on my dress pant leg, slobbering me from the water he'd have drank, thereby giving me a temporary tattoo for the evening meeting on my thigh. For now, though, he's just laying in the kitchen, looking ahead at nothing and lost in his own thoughts, panting heftily with the largest grin mixture of happiness and elderly struggle to support his big mass, in the air conditioning escape from the summer heat.

A few more bites from the tray and the can of mixed nuts, and I'm done after gulping down the rest of the glass of water. My routine-oriented thought is to now have my nightly caffeine-free hot tea, summertime or not, but that'll have to wait until tomorrow. I'm so dehydrated from the lack of good sleep/perceived internal organ failure, combined with the summer heat and humidity, and the adrenaline crash, that I take a moment to just sit in my dining room seat looking ahead at nothingness. Getting up, I shuttle the dining room items to the kitchen where Michael is putting his empty glass down on the opposite counter to the sink and concluding his rifling through what looks like a University of Kentucky freshman orientation seminar update magazine from the mail pile.

"Okay, man," I update, "I'm gonna go upstairs and finish getting ready, Jenny should be here by 6:00 but text her if you have any questions or anything…"

Michael says nothing, already heading for the living room to take his regular seat on the couch and to contemplate the environmental impact of the television, video game, laptop computer, and living room lights he left on when he went to walk Tivoli. Or, he just assumes the couch position and is back into cyborg-mode.

I unzip my black work bag side-pocket and get out my city government identification badge, head upstairs, leaving the bag on the dining room table, and I knock on Corinne's closed bedroom door to see if she's actually there. A loud blowing fan from behind the door is a positive sign.

"Yeah…?" I hear behind the muted roar.

"Corinne, this is *Alex*, you okay…?"

Pause.

"Yeah…?"

"Okay, just checking," I almost-yell. "I have to go to the meeting tonight, I'll leave in a few minutes but Jenny should be home around 6:00 or so, text her if you need anything…I'll be back around 8:00 or 8:15."

"Okay…!"

Oy…

On to the second-floor bathroom, I open the cabinet, get a new small paper cup, run tap water over my toothbrush head, put whitening toothpaste on the brush, run the head under the tap again, then stand back while leaning forward to avoid getting anything on my tie, dress shirt, and dress slacks, to the extent that the inches of clearance space inside the small bathroom permit such. Then, it's a shot of mouthwash for a 60-second count in my head, killing the time by going into the bedroom and grabbing and using an eyeglasses cleaning cloth. Rinsing, I then ridiculously take the time to position the Louisville Metro Government identification badge as if I had pride in working for the Mayor's administration.

Back in the bedroom, the clock radio is black, with red digital font, and a red dot is on (at the bottom-left of the time), indicating 5:45 p.m.

I have *got* to go.

I quickly head downstairs and grab the black work bag from the dining room, slinging it over my shoulder.

"Okay Michael, I'm heading out, I'll be back around 8:00 or so, unless it gets done early…"

"Okay…see ya," he says, earnestly and quietly in looking up at me from the living room couch before then going back into game mode.

Tivoli is still looking ahead in the kitchen in the same, panting, trembling, exhausted position. His mind and body are as stressed out as mine, but he gets to crash now, staring straight ahead for hours if he wants…I never thought that I could be so jealous.

I open the front door to the outside oven and turn back to lock the door with a double-check tugging pull. I start to walk down the front concrete brownstone-like stairs but stop in my tracks to allow two women, one pushing a stroller with a small baby, past the front steps of the house. I smile an apologetic "oops, sorry" as they seem to smile back the same without saying it, too, and I wait for them to go past. I see and hear across one of the cul-de-sac closure stoops a standing male yelling loudly and gesturing wildly at another male sitting on a concrete bench there. I guess that the commotion is just slanging; animated drunkenness from being at the bar across their end of the street; or, always a possibility, symptomatic mental illness. Or, some combination thereof. I shrug off the interest that slightly wells up in my brain in order to focus on getting into my car, looking at the front bumper again before getting in and immediately locking the driver's side door once inside.

I start the ignition, I exchange my regular eyeglasses for sunglasses, I kick on the warm air conditioning full blast, and more Mexican film soundtrack comes on, reminding me how well the music matches the heat and humidity. I then put the car in gear and drive the short few yards around forward and to the left, to the end of the cul-de-sac, near the concrete bench with all the commotion. Silently hoping that the fracas doesn't spill over to, or attempt to involve, or *actually end up involving*, me, I hastily but prudently get the car turned around by driving backwards a few yards, then ahead left about a dozen yards up the street. I then make a right-hand turn onto the part of the alley where truckhead originally turned into in order to try to make his ill-advised turnaround.

I immediately see three males walking together in a line my way, and two of them are looking around the area, so I proceed down the alley against my better judgment in hopes to just drive past. I'm driven in part by defiance, in part by conceded exhaustedness, and in part by timeliness to get to the meeting. Driving to a slow crawl when reaching near them, one of them splits off from the other two towards my car's left side of the alley, while the two split off to the right side. Their walks are now a crawl. As I slowly motor past them, intentionally looking ahead with tunnel-vision to convey minding my own business, I catch the two on my right look at me piercingly in the eyes from the side of the road while the one on my left side then slaps the backside of my car. Now past them, I immediately look in my rear view mirror and see the other two look back my way, the solo offender appearing to just be moving along forward.

God dammit…

Too angry and tired, combined, to say anything, I make a right onto South 6th Street and head north about half a mile, confused as to the emotions inside me all working together but, at the same time, conflicting with each other, and bringing me down into internal chaos. I start breathing heavy, then heavier. It's all getting the better of me. Driving north on what's now turned disjointedly into South 5th Street, there isn't any traffic around. Breathing even heavier in the heavy, choking air, I almost-erratically pull over to the side of the road into what passes for a parallel-parking lane.

The car idling, I sit there, I wait there, with the music on.

I then feel the internal world and the external world zooming into my eyes, my brain, my soul, and my being, completely through physiology, and I erupt in primal scream from the front-middle of my chest leading into my lower head, cursing in a mechanical vortex of blinding, heated rage that shakes the windshield, rattles the car, throttles my body, and throttles the earth into swirling, open-mouthed decibel-screeching desperation of a million black holes exploding into the nihilism of universal destruction.

“GOD
D
A
M
M
I
T
!
!
!
!
!
!
!
!
!
!
!
!
!
!
!
!
!!!!!!
!!!!!!!!!!!!!!!!!!!!
!!!!!”

I pause.

I sit there and pant.

I sit there, and I pant.

I wonder if I'll scream out my curse again.

I sit.

I hit the cd player with my palm to turn off the music, downturned face exhaling.

I pause.

I pause, and I breathe.

I curse under my breath, and I pant.

I sit.

I breathe.

Somehow, I recover quickly enough to make another decision.

I put the car back in gear, and I slowly drive on.

No music.

No distractions.

No noise, and hoping for continued silence driving.

Turning onto York Street eastbound, I pass the Jefferson County Public Library main branch. Instantly, even though I've passed countless times recently without thinking about it, I remember how I used to drive down to this urban superstructure in the late 1980s and early 1990s to escape suburbia and transfer my disaffected mental health to the relative anonymity of a major city's signature downtown library facility. It may all be coincidence, but, just now, I fleetingly-remember those teenage years of soul-searching, chemically-imbalanced bodily hormones, and up-until-that-time life trauma. I found solace inside those walls. I think about how this was one of the few non-substance-abuse-filled escapes I'd had, then or since. I may have been confidence-starved, disabled enough physically and mentally and emotionally--well, rather, I felt like I was absolutely so, I had severe-enough limitation in my own worldview, if nothing else. But, it was a sanctuary-city for me at the time.

And, it's still here.

In 1980 Los Angeles, he wore shorts as a new eight-year-old out in public to the detriment of society, the beginning of the time in his life when he appeared to be starved of nutrition despite his parents feeding him a healthy diet of regular family food and, at one point, heavily-caloried protein shakes.

"Look at those skinny-ass legs!" the older boy yelled out at him at the public park, with malice and cruelty and anger, looking at him in the eyes while roaming past with a friend.

***

He occasionally snuck sips from his parents' bottles of amaretto and coffee liqueurs, possibly emboldened by the "Whiskey, Honey, & Lemon" he drank as a remedy from his mother when sick as a young child.

***

He drank his first few beers in high school, slowly accelerating his tolerance until a vomitous blackout at a party ruined his taste for years.

***

At about 6'2" and bottoming-out at 107 pounds as a junior in high school, he began to wear sweatpants underneath his bluejeans to attempt to mask his grossly-underweight frame. When he dressed in a formal tuxedo one day in a practice run for a chorale invitational, a classmate pointed out to everyone the grey cotton pantleg climbing out from under the black overpants; an athletic, beefy, male-catalogue model acquaintance then walked over, sat down next to him, looked him in the eye, and said questioningly in soap-opera-star delivery, with ambiguous motive, "Are you anorexic?"

***

Alone in his seventeen-year-old bedroom, the depression oozed and flooded, from head-to-toe fluidity, a rush like injection from a syringe. The isolation, the ruined self-confidence, the implosion of a body form that matched the exaggerated misshapenness in his mind with the reality of complicated mourning of his mother's death years prior, and overactive metabolism, all manifesting at once into his own body's liquid serum of despair throughout. Suicide was now in the picture, against his better nature and his better reasoning, and it was all chemical, not rational.

"I'll do it!!!" he literally cried out in soulful pain to the silent contemplation, looking up into the half-hearted idea of a God.

Not that he wanted to end his life with any plan, nor with any throwing-in of the towel, but just to stop the awfulness of the natural chemical imbalance.

***

As a high school junior, he tripped on LSD after only trying alcohol and snuff tobacco, inadvertently bypassing the typical gateway drugs of weed, mushrooms, codeine, etc. That first time, with the experience of chewing gum becoming a malleable tire reverbing inside his mouth; the empty nighttime high school parking lot turning into an ice hockey rink; the ground shadows and puddles appearing to be infinite holes into the Earth; and, classic rock music sounding backwards, legally-insane or not, was as profound an experience as might ever have been.

***

He arrived at his senior prom and, personal demons of insecurity and inability to relate to his contemporaries continuing, he left after an hour and drove from Louisville, to Lexington, to Cincinnati, and back to Louisville again. Alone.

***

He was prescribed an antidepressant that wired him up for the day, another that wired him down for the evening, and, some lithium, all at the same time mid-way through college. A year later, he'd just smoke marijuana heavily again for fun instead of living in the cartoon world of pharmaceutical physiological regulation.

***

He didn't need much convincing when his friend said that she had attention deficit disorder and dyslexia after she borrowed his telephone to order the pizza: he watched as she misdialed the numbers repeatedly until she got through, even though she and all the other college students knew the local number by heart.

***

He'll likely never forget the moment he cross-addicted from marijuana to alcohol, trading in three years of THC use for fifteen years of alcoholism. He did stay sober from drinking for one year during the run, ironically through an informal group-meeting program he didn't quite believe in as opposed to the outpatient rehabilitation he voluntarily signed up for, completed, and relapsed from, on Day 69.

***

At one point, he was prescribed disulfiram when he was desperate to stop his alcoholism. He at least found the humor to show off to a friend how lobster-sunburned red his face turned when drinking just one beer after taking the pill.

On other occasions, he just retched when attempting to circumvent the cure, or blacked out.

***

For his 36th birthday, between-romantic-relationships and a little desperate in being alone again, he sought out, found, and smoked, salvia.

***

The director of human resources assigned him a personality test that he suspects was not assigned to other candidates for the supervisor position he applied for, and he swears it was because his supervisors thought him mentally unstable (despite his superhuman job performance…55 active investigations, on top of all the other job duties, would make anyone insane for staying).

CHAPTER EIGHT

Parked near the university building main entrance on South 3rd Street, I gather two nickels out of the compartment-change from the car to get ready for a parking meter, even though the effective time period is scheduled to run out in five minutes. I'm still loyal to the idea of Louisville Metro Government, at least currently for this one facet. I exchange my sunglasses for the eyeglasses, I turn the vehicle ignition off, and I sit for another pause in silence with a frown. I then shake it off enough to grab my black work bag, exit the car after looking around for pedestrian traffic and uniformed, walking city government traffic citations, and then I put the nickels in the meter. Waiting for the meter to read a confirmation of the money deposit, slow as a sun-dial in turning from red to green, I see a Transit Authority paratransit bus for persons with disabilities drive past and then go around to the back of the university building. *They're here for the meeting*, obviously.

Composing myself while walking across the West Breckinridge Street crosswalk to the university building entrance, I pull open the university building main front door and briefly think about how heavy the door is. The lobby is filled with waiting and socializing students, all lining chairs, vending machines, walls, and hallways, and a security guard post is helmed by someone talking in jest to a student. And all appear to be able-bodied, or, in my current mindset, "TABs": temporarily-able-bodied.

I whirl around to the right hallway, dodging nineteen-year-olds, and walk past a computer lab with a few students and a teacher talking and possibly going over paperwork. I continue on down the hall, then make a left down the far end of the hallway where I then see ahead the destination classroom at the end of the far hall, open, lighted with conversation inside, right next to the closed back door of the building. Halfway on my way, a hard knock on the back door diverts me in a bee-line diagonally towards the door instead of the class. I push the back door open by almost slamming into the push-bar with my sprint, concurrently seeing that it's a paratransit bus driver accompanying Jonathan Earl, the latter who smiles up at me bright-eyed from his motorized wheelchair.

"Okay, y'all ready, then?" the paratransit driver asks loudly.

"Yeah, thank you," Jonathan says. "Alex, how ya doin'…?"

"Hey, Jonathan, I'm *surviving*, how about you-man?"

"Me too," he slight-laughs, "I just rode the TA, you know?"

"Yeah, I can only imagine," I say with an exhale-laugh in leading us into the classroom. "Hey, everybody, this is *Alex…*?" I announce to the group.

"Hey!" and "Hey, Alex!" come from three or four of the seated attendees who appear to look up diagonally, scattered about large round tables pushed together, and with chairs intermittently at tables, and not at tables, haphazard all over the place.

"Hey, y'all," Jonathan says to the crowd, eliciting similar response from the group.

I push one chair on wheels while pulling another chair on wheels, clumsily trying to make an accessway for not only Jonathan to navigate, but for myself, and my black work bag dangles and drags off of my shoulder in the awkwardness. One of the able-bodied Disability Action Network board members gets up and moves some chairs, and in a collision course with her, I say hi to Angelica Shea as she greets me, warmly placing a chair for me. She then quickly hands me an agenda for the meeting, causing me a little more struggle with the encumbrance. Jonathan motors around to an empty space at a table closer to other DAN board members. I place my black work bag down on the table at the Angelica chair, which coincidentally but welcomely places me a little removed from the board I'm not formally a part of.

Walking into the room then comes Russell Stallings, wearing an apron and a chef's hat while holding a two-liter of orange soda in one hand, a two-liter of cola in the other. Placing them both on a counter far away from the grouped tables along a side-wall of science class clean-up sinks and faucets, Russell efficiently organizes plates, cups, ice, napkins, utensils, corn chips, and other picnic dinner items until there's another knock at the back door just outside the room hallway. Getting things out of my black work bag, I hesitate and almost act as if I'm to get up to get the door, before Russell walks a restaurant-trained walk quickly out a second door closest to him to the hallway and around to launch the back door push-bar open.

"Hey, hey…!" Russell says, ushering in another Transit Authority paratransit driver with Bertrice Gowins, a person with a vision impairment, arm-in-arm. Russell greets with "Hey, my man" in taking

Bertrice's arm from the TA driver, and follows up with "And how are *you* this evening, young lady" in looking to finish her escort, slowly and patiently, to the closest open seat to the door.

"I'm good, is this my favorite Russell…?" Bertrice asks quickly with a smile to the open room.

"It *is*, yes *ma'am*. But you still don't get any extra dinner tonight, young lady…"

"Oh, okay, now, that's what I've been tryin' to *tell* y'all…You wait 'till I tell Pastor Glenn on you this Sunday, Russell," she says lightning-quick.

"All *right*, now…" and "Here we go…!" complement the half of us in the group slightly-laughing.

"Mmm-*hmm*, yes *ma'am*, that's *right*…" Russell says, swinging back to the food station after depositing Bertrice successfully to her seat.

On my 8½" x 14" yellow legal note pad, I write the header "*Disability Action Network*," and underneath "*6:00 p.m. @ University, 5:45 p.m. -   p.m.*" The next line, I write "# *of attendees:*" and count fourteen people currently in attendance, including myself, so "*14*" goes next to it.

I then hear a robotic, voicemail-default-sounding voice state out loud to the group, "*It's. Six. Oh-four. PM.*" I then see Samuel Banks, eyes closed but looking out to the open room, put his recorder back in his pocket.

Jonathan then says personably to Lester Bishop, a person with a vision impairment, seated at his immediate right, "Think it's time we started, Lester…"

"Yeah," Lester says personably back. "Okay…"

With the exception of Russell, busily entering and exiting the room working on his banquet, the Disability Action Network straightens up to begin. Everyone is at attention for Lester. I hold my pen in my hand, looking at him, then smile a small smile to Angelica when she catches me with eye contact.

"Okay then, well…" Lester sensitively begins, before speaking with perfect commanding but accessible charisma. "Welcome to the monthly meeting of the Disability Action Network board of directors, and general membership meeting. If we could go around, and have introductions, I think we may…we may all know each other here, but we have a guest speaker on the agenda for later, I don't know if she's here…"

"No, she's not here yet, Lester," Angelica says.

"O-kay, well…um, I'll begin. I'm Lester Bishop. I'm current Chair of the Disability Action Network…"

Pause and silence.

Angelica then gives the assist. "Do you wanna go around to your right, Lester, that would be Phoebe. Phoebe?"

Phoebe, eyes closed, looking up, and head-at-attention with a slightly open mouth, speaks quickly. "Phoebe-Carver, Secretary…"

"Sam," Angelica prompts delicately.

"Samuel Banks…"

"…Angelica Shea…"

I'm next, sitting a few spaces away.

"Alex, Calderon, the Louisville Metro Civil Relations Commission…"

"…Trisha Evans, Louisville Independent Living…"

"…Alberta, Taylor…"

"…Bertrice Gowins. And I'm gonna go ahead and say Mr. Russell's name since he's busy making me *two* plates tonight instead of one, thank you, Russell…"

"Now hold on now, young lady," he says, turning around from the makeshift buffet as we start slightly-laughing again. "Russell *Stallings*, Flaget Baptist Church…" he smiles out to the group, before then going back to his focus on food preparation.

Entering the room now is Matt Whitworth, fast food bag and large fountain drink cup on his front motorized wheelchair tray, and walking behind him talking to him is Jonah Penzik. I quickly cross out the "*14*" on my yellow legal notepad and write "*16*" in replacement.

The flow of the introductions disrupted, Angelica intervenes as the two quickly get settled.

"Okay, hey Matt, hey Jonah, we're doing introductions and we're on Robert. Robert?"

"Robert Davidson, Kentuckiana Vision Council…" Robert says, eyes closed and head-at-attention looking up and out.

"…Joyce Barnes…" Joyce says while adjusting in her motorized wheelchair.

"…Jonathan Earl, Vice-Chair of DAN…"

"Martha…" Angelica directs.

"Martha, Lane, Washington," Martha says. "And I'm here again with Tobey," her black Labrador retriever laying on the ground next to her, head on his paws, giving a quick lick of the chops as if on cue for the introduction.

Also using a motorized wheelchair is Mason Richards, who revs up his internal motor to say his name. "…Ma…Muh…Muh…Mu…Ma… May…Muh…May…sn…sn…Ruhy…Ruh…Ruhy…Ruhrd…Rns!" he caps with authority.

"Hey, *Mason…*" Angelica slightly-laughs in a tease to him, prompting him to smile open-mouthed and wide while tossing his head back.

Another pause in the action prompts the final two stragglers.

"Uh, yeah, Matt Whitworth, Independent Living…"

"…Jonah Penzik…"

"And, yeah, Jonah, we all know *you*," Angelica says in slight jest to a slight laugh or two from the board. "Okay…okay, Lester, that's everyone."

"Uh-*huh*," Lester says, "All right…Okay. Well, I guess--is there an agenda this evening?"

Angelica again is at-the-ready. "Yes, Lester, next is the reading of the minutes…"

"Okay, so…Joyce?"

Joyce again adjusts in her motorized wheelchair. "Yes, Lester, I have them here, I'll read the minutes. For the July 2015 meeting, 'The meeting was called to order by Lester. Those in attendance were Lester Bishop, Phoebe Carver, Angelica Shea, Jonathan Earl, Martha Lane…Washington, Sam Banks, Russell…Stallings, Joyce Barnes, Louise Collins, Alex…Calderon, Theresa Ford, Trisha Evans, and Dale…' I didn't get the name of the Public Works speaker who was here, the inspector…?"

Mason then starts motoring himself over towards me.

"Mr. Rollins." Lester clarifies. "Dale, Rollins."

"Okay, Dale…Rollins."

"Uh-huh…"

"Okay thanks, Lester," Joyce says.

Mason wheels up to the empty space at the far table alongside me and looks in my eyes, where we both exchange silent hellos. He readies a board with printed numbers and an alphabet on his front motorized wheelchair tray with a closed right hand, indicating that he's going to have something to say tonight (as he almost always does, he's no shrinking violet), and he's chosen me to be a messenger.

Continuing, "…'Joyce Barnes read the minutes…Angelica read the…Treasurer's Report, then Committee reports were given… Jonathan…gave the Accessibility Committee, report, with updates on the lawsuit filed against Downtown Bar & Grille, and our meeting with Public Works. Lester talked about his…perception of the meeting, with Public Works, and how the Mayor is unresponsive, to disability issues. Alex spoke on the work that the Civil Rights, Commission, is doing, in housing and public business places. And he said that his supervisors do not allow him…to attend the ongoing Rights Commission meetings with the Disability Action Network and Public Works at the Commission…so he is unaware of what happens in those meetings. Trisha gave the Conference Committee report, and said that mailers sent out in June might need a follow-up reminder, as only…31 people, have confirmed registration for the Achievement Awards, and the deadline to register is September 30th. Taylor Children's Hospital is catering the Awards, and they have to cater…the event, since they are hosting the conference at their facility. We had no Membership Committee report, since Theresa was not here, but Lester asked that members pay their $10 dues by the end of October. Our guest speaker, Dale, then--Dale Rollins, Public Works, then spoke on accessibility in Louisville, and the Public Works 20-Year Action Plan. The meeting was adjourned at, about, 7:55, p.m.'…Are there any corrections or changes that we need to make, to the minutes?"

"Yeah," Trisha eagerly begins. "It wasn't that Taylor Children's Hospital said that we had to go with *them* for the food, just that if we didn't go *with* them, then we'd have to pay a hosting fee, and after we all discussed it here, we agreed that it was, like, Taylor Children's almost makin' us have them to do it. We can still get the outside caterer, we just have to pay, but we're so close to the deadlines to get the Achievement Awards done, we just need to decide…I'm just sayin'…"

"Okay…" Joyce says, looking around the group.

"Yeah," Lester says. "Yeah, uh-huh. I think, what the discussion was, was, yeah, like Trisha said, Taylor Children's Hospital is donating the facility for *free*, and they're more expensive to cater than an outside vendor. But when you add the hosting fee that Taylor Children's charges, to get the outside vendor in, then we might as well go ahead with Taylor Children's. But that would also show loyalty for them hosting us this year, if we went with them, and they've donated to us before, so we don't have to go with them, but…you know…I think we should, it shows good faith between our two agencies and all."

Jonathan adds, "Yeah, I think the consensus was that we go ahead with them, even though we're not in love with the idea of the hosting fee."

"Yeah," a few other Disability Action Network members say.

"Okay," Joyce notes by hand onto a copy of the minutes. "Okay. Anything else…?"

"Yeah, if I may," I add. "My agency is the Louisville Metro Civil *Relations* Commission, not the Civil *Rights* Commission."

"Okay," Joyce writes. "Okay. Anything else…?"

Silence. I struggle to hide a yawn.

Lester himself asks, "Anything else, anything someone wants to add…"

Nothing from the group.

"Well," Lester shifts, "speakin' of Louise, I called for her, about the Achievement Awards, and I got a call back from her daughter, and Louise, she's in the hospital again, after complications from her diabetes." Pausing for the collective reaction of exhales and "*oh, no*" from the group, he continues. "So, I just want you all to pray for her, maybe visit her over there, at Urban Care Hospital…we all know she's had problems with transportation, with her daughter as the only one to care for her, and havin' to work long hours to support the both of them, so maybe we can get a card, or visit, or at least call her over there *at* Urban. I know she'd really appreciate the Network membership being with her right now, thinkin' of her…"

Phoebe quickly announces, "I'll-get-her-a-card, if everyone wants to sign it, sign it, everyone, and I can give it to her, I was gonna go down there this Saturday."

"What room number is she in?" Alberta asks.

"I…you know, I don't remember," Lester thinks. "I think they said…731…room 731. But don't--you might wanna call first, they move people around down there, you know, you-know-how-they-do. I do think it was 731, though…"

"I hope she's okay," Alberta says.

"Yeah, me too," Lester continues. "I mean, we all know she's had this problem, and battled with it for years, and she's come to these meetings here before, and told us of *her* fight, and her fight trying to get the appropriate transportation to her doctor, with the Transit Authority, things like that. All we can do is pray, and go see her, call her, you know…hope for a speedy recovery, and all…"

Nods of approval and earnest come from the Network board members.

Lester wraps up. "Okay, then…well…next, is it the Treasurer's report? Angelica?"

"Okay," Angelica says confidently. "As of July, 2015, we have a total of $6,784.26 in our account. We paid for the Achievement Award conference mailers in the amount of…$932, and we collected $780 in registration money. So far. Oh and $30 in dues. And that's pretty much it, there'll be more to report as we get closer to the Achievement Awards…"

"Okay…alright, that sounds good…okay. So, what's next, Committee Reports?"

"Uh-huh, yes," Angelica says.

"Okay…Jonathan…?"

"Okay," Jonathan starts. "Well, we have no new updates on the suit against Downtown Bar & Grille. But my sense is, just like I said last time, is that the defendant will settle, it's just a matter of how much remedy we should get. We obviously want the structural changes to the entrance so that it's accessible, which the defendant is prepared to do, but we also want George Dillon to get the remedy *he's* due, since he's the real litigant here that was damaged. You all already know, he said that when they refused to accommodate him and assist him into the bar over the threshold at the entrance, they got angry at him when he asked to be assisted, and then threatened to call the police on him, all while he was outside in the rain--in the *cold* rain. I mean, you don't have to be a business designed accessible if the date of construction is before the effective date of the Americans with Disabilities Act, but that doesn't excuse providing reasonable accommodations for persons with disabilities, when it's readily-achievable to do so. George isn't asking for a million dollars, he just wants compensation for the refusal, and the embarrassment, the humiliation--there were people outside smoking at the time, who saw all of this, and the one who supported him with the deposition as a witness to what happened…it's a small miracle that she followed through with her contact information when he asked for it at the time, that's maybe the key to the case. So, we'll just keep tabs on it, I'm hoping it gets resolved before the holidays, but if we have to go before the judge, we do, and so be it. I like George's chances, and our chances as the public interest agency working with him, as the Network, so…I think that's it, for now, really, for the Downtown Bar & Grille case update, unless there are any questions…?"

No one responds with anything verbal, or even a head-shake. I'm writing notes.

"Lester," Jonathan asks, "do you wanna go ahead and get into our meetings with Public Works?"

"Yeah," Lester affirms. "Yeah, uh-huh. *Well*, like we've been talking about, we've had a--a series of meetings, with Public Works officials, some with the assistance of Brenda McCoy, with Louisville Civil Relations, hosting some of the meetings at *her* offices, mediating things. Last week, we had another meeting with Brenda, and the Assistant Director of Public Works, Susan Cunningham, and we talked about the lack of accessibility with sidewalks, with Transit Authority bus stop locations, with public and city-owned facilities not *bein'* accessible, and that sorta thing…I think the biggest concern of the Disability Action Network, as *we* always talk about, is the backlog of work orders to *make* sidewalks more accessible, in Public Works repairs to existing sidewalks, both with those dilapidated sidewalks, and dilapidated curbs, that can be turned into wheelchair and mobility-accessible curb cuts. Susan, with Public Works--they always say that they just don't have the money to make *everything* accessible that they wanna make, citing the budget, and cuts by the Mayor's office, and the city council, but I know I--I've called in, to report sidewalks out where I live, in the West End, and they *say* they'll fix it, and then I wait, and nothing happens. So, I call in again, and then they say that's it's still in the queue as a work order, but they have all these other projects going on with the new bicycle lanes, and things like that, and there should be a *preference* for these projects and work orders that affect accessibility, and persons with disabilities like you and me. You know, this Mayor's administration, it's like pulling teeth just to get the communication going about these issues, much less the action that needs to be taken. Brenda's set up these quarterly meetings, but, it seems that when we finally got the Mayor's office somewhat-engaged a couple-few years ago now, we keep talking about the same things, the same inaccessibility problems all over the city, goin' around, and around. Brenda's gotten people to the table, but, at this point, we don't seem to be getting the results--*any* results, really, and that's why I think the Disability Action Network needs to think about a different strategy. Maybe more litigation, in order to get things done. As some of you--some of you all remember, we asked the state Civil Rights Commission about filing the administrative complaint against the city, to look at these issues in an investigation...you know, force the city to do what needs to be done. We invited them to speak here at a meeting about a year ago, but we've had trouble ever since then, getting them to take--they don't seem to *take the complaint* (!). They were supposed to get back to us after their representative came to give that presentation here, and if you all remember--some of you may remember, when we had Susan with Public Works over here at the meeting before that, along with Brenda, and Calvin Barber, the Director of the Civil Rights Commission himself, to talk about what Public Works is doing, or *could* be doin'..."

Pause. I'm writing notes. And yawning inadvertently, of course, fighting.

"Yeah," Jonathan says. "Well, like Lester says, there's communication here, which is ahead of where we were before the Civil Relations Commission got involved, but it's still slow getting the results we all want. As you all know, I sit on the Civil Relations Commission Advocacy Board as a Commissioner, and we've talked about some of this stuff as an advisory board to the Mayor's administration. We're asking for resources to be diverted, with the budgetary process, *to* Public Works, to help with the backlog. Like anything with government, change comes slow," he slightly laughs, "but I think that these meetings *have* helped to address some of the issues we've been concerned with as a coalition, as a Network. I think we are moving along, and it's gonna take some time, but I like where we're headed so far. We can always do better, and the Mayor's office can always do better, but I feel better about where we're moving towards, with Public Works, lately..."

Pause. I still take notes.

"Mr. Chair...Mr. Vice-Chair...if I may..." Jonah methodically asks as a statement, since he's about to address the board and the membership, ready-or-not. "--Excuse me, Jonah Penzik, advocate, professor, Disability Action Network board member, *and* a person with a disability…I hear what you both have been saying, Lester, Jonathan… and, I know I've missed the last meeting or two here, so please forgive me if I've missed some key things while I've been gone. But, what I'm *hearing*, is that the Disability Action Network is having meetings with the Civil Relations Commission, and Public Works, and even trying to do so with the state Civil Rights Commission. And maybe talking is good, or can *be* good, with what's going on, I don't know, since I haven't been able to be at the last meeting, like I said. But, what I do know is that--Jonathan: I, myself, have been a Chair of the Civil Relations Commission, back in the 1980s, when there was just an Anti-Discrimination Panel of Commissioners. And, what I learned at that time, was that sometimes, all the talk in the world may sound like things are good, sound like things are going somewhere, and everyone gets their assignments from the meeting, or their promises are made to everyone, or there's a commitment to change…and *then*, they all meet again for the next meeting (!)."

Jonah rears up some in his seat, breaking no stride. Same with me on my notes.

"What I propose, Mr. Chair, Mr. Vice-Chair…Disability Action Network membership…what I propose is, is that this coalition retain an attorney, or maybe even a team of attorneys, and, quite frankly, if nothing is being done, substantive, as it sounds like to me, then, we *sue* the bastards (!). As many of you know, I was a lead Complainant in the 1970s in one of the first lawsuits filed under the Rehabilitation Act against the federal government, back when the federal government was discriminating against us, as people with disabilities. And this was *long before* the ADA, the Americans with Disabilities Act, before the ADA was passed, through our efforts to lobby Congress, when we got *out of our wheelchairs*, when we got *on our hands and knees*, and we climbed the steps of every god *damn* federal building in Washington, to make our point, that people with disabilities have rights. We *have* rights, we *are* people who are discriminated against, just like our other brothers and sisters who've been oppressed throughout recent history in this country, based on their race…their color…their religion…their labor exploitation. People with disabilities, we're looked on like *garbage*--pardon my language, but it's the *truth*, and we have to empower *ourselves* first. And when those agencies, like the ones that--excuse me here, Alex--Alex here, he works for the Civil Relations Commission, and the other agencies like the state Civil

Rights Commission, the Mayor's office, Public Works...when they don't do *their* jobs, then you sue *them*, too!" Jonah pauses. "Now, I know we, as a Network, have limited resources, and at this point, not to be offensive to anyone, but I don't know how viable we are as a coalition, to engage in litigation, to force these do-nothing agencies to make these changes. Jonathan already spoke about the lawsuit in the public accommodations case, the Bar & Grille, that treated George like crap, and action *was* taken, and through the *courts*, not through talking. We as a coalition have to decide where the best course of meaningful action is to be taken, and the whole time that we talk, in meetings with the Civil Relations Commission, and here at these monthly board membership meetings, the streets: they are crumbling. And literally: they're falling apart, and *here*, we--I advise us, Mr. Chair, to go ahead and make the enforcement efforts. Public Works is not gonna do it. The Mayor's office is not gonna do it. The Civil *Relations* Commission is not gonna do it. We *know* that, because we've talked, and we've asked, and we've begged, and nothing gets done. And this is nothing against Alex, we all know he's committed to do his work, we *hear* him at these meetings, and efforts. But he's beholden to the Mayor. Just as Brenda is, and Civil Relations Commission staff. And, Jonathan, you're appointed by the Mayor to be on the Commission Advocacy Board. And of course, Public Works, they're *also* city government...and the state Civil Rights Commission is beholden to the Governor--and don't get me started on *him*--and these politicians work together, states and cities. It may be time to file with the federal government, and stop the banging of our heads against this Mayor's wall. So...that's what I wanted to say here, tonight. Mr. Chair."

I'm furiously note-taking.

"Well, Jonah," Jonathan slightly-laughs, "just because I'm on a Mayor-appointed board doesn't mean that I advocate for us any less. There definitely *is* the role of enforcement, and, as you and anyone should know about me, I'm an attorney, I work directly with the courts, and litigation can certainly work in some instances. The problem with the courts, and with the administrative law processes, as you know, is that it can take years to get a judgment on a case, and by that time, all the original players are gone, moved on, moved out of state, or, in some cases, have even *died*," Jonathan continues with a slight laugh, "before someone can even think about getting the remedy for the damages they've incurred. I know talk can be cheap, or can be viewed as cheap, but at least a few of the issues we used to talk about here at these meetings have been addressed. And some for the better, just by open lines of communication with the respective agencies and their directors. And that includes with the Mayor's deputies, or at least a few of them…"

Mason rocks back and forth with his body almost wildly in his motorized wheelchair next to me, and he moves his communication board more over towards me on his front tray with his curled right hand. I stop the note-taking. He then nods to me, and I look down, and he starts to spell by moving his hand over the letters.

"Mr. Vice-Chair, Mr. Chair? Mason would like to address the board," I announce.

"Okay, uh-huh," Lester says. "Mason…?"

I watch as Mason moves his hand to "*I*," then to "*A*," then "*G*," "*R*--"

" 'I…Agree,' " I voice to the group. " 'With…Jonah.' "

Mason nods and we both continue, with Mason all-in to make his affirming point.

" 'Like…Jonah…Has…' Seen?--" I question.

Mason quickly shakes off a negative with his head, immediately proceeding with spelling again.

"S…'Said'--Oh-ok-sorry-Mason. 'Like Jonah has said… We…Don't…Have…To…Talk…We…Should…Sue…Instead… Of…Talk…ing. Instead of talking.'"

Angelica jumps in.

"I couldn't agree more, we can't keep having these meetings with Civil Relations and expect anything else. I mean, I was at that meeting-- at the last meeting, too, and Brenda and Agnes were there as moderators, not mediators. It was like it was us against Public Works. We've asked the Civil Relations Commission to intervene, to talk with Public Works, to talk with the Mayor, and the only callback we get from the Mayor's administration is a Deputy Mayor…Shonda, Shonda Heyward. And Shonda just said that Brenda would be calling us and arranging for these meetings. Shonda is Brenda's boss, so obviously Shonda was responsive in *that* regard, but that just created another meeting, not an enforcement system doing something about what needs to be done. And that was two years--a-year-and-a-half ago, and since then, no word from the Mayor's office on any of our requests to have Public Works do their jobs making things accessible. So, I honestly think we've done all we can do with these meetings, I just don't see any meaningful movement on these other issues, which are the real important ones (!). I mean, discussing who does what in city government, and citing data and reports, and statistics…it's not gonna get *me*, if *I'm* a person with a disability who needs to get from point A, to point B, *any* assistance whatsoever if a sidewalk is broken, if there's no curb cut, if there's an impediment to *me* crossing the street to get to the *maybe* accessible side of the route and walkway…"

"Mr. Chair," Jonah pushes, "I'd like to move that we now hold a brief discussion of what the Disability Action Network should do next. But what I think we should do is do this in confidence, away from city government officials. And that means that I'd--Alex, this is nothing against you, okay, but I'd like to ask to you leave, so that we can conduct some discussion without you being present. *This is not meant* in *offense*, you *must* understand…"

"Okay," I respond slightly-smiling, stopping my notes. "I mean, sure, yeah, that's no problem, I don't mind…?"

"We *must* talk about the status of the Network," Jonah continues, "and we *must* begin a plan of action against the city. This is nothing against Alex, again, he's a good man, and he does his best, I've seen his work with the Commission. But you all must understand: he is here to *report.* He's here to report to Brenda, report to the Mayor, and report to all the powers that be, so we must have an honest, frank conversation and discussion on what we're doing, and what we can accomplish here…"

I sit up at attention to get ready to leave the classroom.

"Well…okay," Lester announces. "I think we have a motion on the floor from Jonah, so…all those in favor, say--all those in favor of Jonah's motion, to have Alex excused from the meeting, for discussion, say 'aye'…?"

In a waterfall of concurrent affirmation, about five Disability Action Network board members, and maybe even one or two non-board members, vote with Jonah. Bringing up the rear, I announce to the group the same vote for Mason after seeing his hand land on the "*Yes*" on his communication board as he gives bright-eyed and open-mouthed directions to me in conveying no offense.

"All opposed…?" Lester asks the group.

No response after a short pause.

I start putting my yellow legal notepad and ink pen into my black work bag quickly.

"Okay then…" Lester says. "Alex, don't leave the building," he slightly-laughingly says as I get up. "We need you here at the meetin' later, don't go nowhere…!"

Smiling tiredly and saying okay to Lester and the group in general, I walk out of the classroom on autopilot with what feels like all eyes on me, but in reality is probably not the case, with the group ready to engage each other instead of focusing on my presence and making it all about me. And if nothing else, I welcome getting up for the stretch, and to try to get at least a little of the all-consuming tiredness out of me for the next few minutes, or however long it'll be for me to wait.

I walk out of the second classroom doorway Russell's been shuttling in and out of, going to the right and completing a rectangle from the time I entered the front lobby near the building entrance. Student traffic has oddly cleared out, with just one undergraduate attempting to use a vending machine and no security guard present at the security post. I sit on one of the two lobby couches pushed together near the front entrance doors along the wall, black work bag resting on my lap as if I was waiting for a job interview. I look at the black seconds-hand of a 1980s white circular wall-clock behind the security desk go around, and around, right now indicating that it's 6:33 p.m. I just think about sitting here to rest, and I hope that the temporary banishment doesn't result in an extension of the meeting past 8:00 p.m.

Realizing that I haven't text-messaged Jenny in hours, I dig the domestic lifeline out of my front pants pocket and flip the phone open. I text slowly while yawning.

just got banished temporarily from the meeting so they could speak in private (!), dunno if ill be home soon or later, ugh, so tired :(

I flip the phone closed with a snap, put it back in my front pants pocket, slump back on the couch, and huff a sigh, both hands on my black work bag. I think about how I'm on the clock, getting paid by Louisville Metro Government to not do any real work, sitting there in limbo. I also think about how awfully, awfully tired I am, again exhaling and slowly shaking my head. And I think about the embarrassment of the meltdown in the car on the way over here.

There's nothing in my work bag to take out to study, there's no smart-phone at my disposal to surf the internet, there's only just me in the lobby, no one to converse with, waiting. I welcome the break to just sit there, though, and I'm a lot more at peace with just sitting and staring ahead, thinking all of my crazy thoughts while awaiting word on what my Disability Action Network fate is, next.

But then the anxiety of doubt creeps in.

What if they don't come back to get me, concluding their confidential discussion and leaving me in limbo without the courtesy or awareness to let me know that I'm permitted to go back in…or, that I'm relieved of my Disability Action Network duties and should just go ahead and call it a night?

Since I now think about how I'd better document my current status with the meeting, looking for something to do with my tired jitters, I dig out the 8½" x 14" yellow legal notepad and ink pen and write under the current notes "*6:32 p.m., AC asked by DAN to vacate mtg. re: confid. discuss., AC in univ. lobby.*" Fidgeting and a little insecure, I fumble the notepad back into my bag and put the ink pen in the bag, too. I then sit still.

I sit.

A student getting a bag of chips heads down the hallway I originally used to go towards the meeting, opens a side classroom door halfway down, goes in, and shuts the door behind her.

I sit.

I sit and make "*Well, here we are (!)*" mock expressions in silence.

I sit.

The clock above the security desk indicates 6:41 p.m.

I sit. I look out the glass lobby doors to South 3rd Street, seeing intermittent clustered vehicle traffic mostly timed to the changing of stoplights out of view. Occasionally, a pedestrian, or groups of two or three pedestrians, walk past.

I sit and look ahead down the hallway which connects to the hall that dead-ends to the classroom where private DAN discussions are being held.

I shift in my seat.

I must be very pale.

I lean forward sitting on the couch, forward at attention for whatever in my slovenly stretching.

I think about how unbecoming I look when I remember that I have a Louisville Metro Government identification badge posted on my dress shirt, so I lean back to sit with one leg crossed over the other in a more dignified pose. Since the sitting-style isn't me, I just then sit back with my black work bag on my lap as if waiting for a human resources professional to come tell me with near empathy that they're sorry, but I didn't get the job.

I exhale.

I dig out my flip-phone, and there are no texts received at 6:48 p.m. I look at the clock above the security desk again, and it appears to be one minute slow compared to my cell-phone service provider time.

I then hear steps from an adjacent hallway to the lobby behind me to my left, and not from one of the two rectangle hallways-leading-to-the-hallway leading to the Disability Action Network meeting. It sounds like high heels approaching, and I straighten up with my black work bag as if waiting for her to say hi with a big smile my way. Entering the lobby area then appears an able-bodied man in a suit and dress shoes, who continues to walk down the hallway past the vending machines and security desk, continuing down the hall leading to the hall that leads to the Disability Action Network meeting. He rounds the corner and I hear a door open before he would've reached the DAN meeting, shutting it hard. Then silence.

I sit, grimacing with sarcasm again.

I sit, watching the black seconds-hand go around the clock at the vacant security desk.

My cell phone then vibrates two short buzzes, so I eagerly dig out the messages.

Sorry baybee, hang in there

We're having tilapia and asparagus for dinner. And ice cream :x

I text back, thumbing the number pad like lightning with the only parts of my body that feel like they function properly.

K…im still in the lobby here, no word yet on whats going on for me…so exhausted :/

After the text appears to have sent, I delete the multiple-text conversation and put the flip-phone away.

Sitting and looking vacantly ahead, I then get my attention to one of the building front doors off to the right. A woman has appeared on the street outside, slowly making her way with an oxygen tank she pulls behind her with her left hand, and, slowly, ever so slowly, she reaches out with her right hand to pull one of the front doors open. I sit up at attention, like a dog with its ears perked that's just had its name called but doesn't get up, and I exhale my tiredness. The woman looks unaware and not self-conscious at all as she slowly stops, giving up on pulling open the door. I'm about to finally do the right thing and start to get up, and start to walk over, but the woman's found the disability-accessible entrance automatic door button and pushes it slowly. Both the external building entrance door and the internal entrance lobby door open up wide. The woman then slowly begins to enter.

Fearful that one or both doors could close on her, I move quickly from the couch and hit the internal disability-accessible entrance automatic door button in the lobby for assurance. The doors are still open, so it may be moot, but I hit the button repeatedly though not incessantly. I smile a new-acquaintance smile to the stranger, who's breathing with difficulty, and I then hold my arm out against the interior lobby entrance door to make sure that she can have enough time to pull the oxygen tank in with her.

Not looking at me and still navigating her entrance, the woman clears the entryway and stops just past the doors inside the lobby.

"*Eve*ning," I say politely and softly before turning and walking back to couch-sit in limbo again.

"Hello," she says in the meantime.

The woman stands in the center of the lobby for a few seconds, then looks herself up and down and adjusts the oxygen tank and cords. She looks around a few directions with quick looks, then stands there to compose herself internally after the physical composition has already been completed.

"Young man," she says to me like a teacher. "Do you know where the meeting--a meeting for disabled, people is, I'm supposed to be there…?"

"The Disability Action Network meeting?" I ask eagerly, standing up again but not stopping for a formal response. "Yes, it's down that hallway to the right there, then to the left at the end of that hall back there, and then it's at the end of that hall," I say, directing with my right hand.

"Okay," she says slightly-feebly, looking down to again check on her status.

"I can lead you down there if you like, but," I exhale a laugh, "they've sorta *banned* me from a portion of the meeting they're having right now, until later. I work for city government, and they're talking about my employers."

"Okay, well, no, that's okay, I can find it," she says, almost without missing a beat.

"Okay…" I say pleasantly, not knowing what else to really say.

The woman tugs on and straightens her fleece-like long-sleeved sweater-shirt, then looks to her right and slowly turns to proceed down the hallway. I sit back down and watch as she slowly, slowly pulls her oxygen tank again, and moves on towards where we both want, or need, to be. She now looks familiar, or at least I get the sense that we're familiar…for some reason.

I'm resigned again to sit there on the couch.

So, I sit.

But then, a younger, able-bodied woman appears at the university building front doors, quickly pulls open one of the outer, then inner, doors, and looks around a brief second inside the center of the lobby.

"Excuse me," she asks me as the only person around. "Have you seen my mother--an older lady come through here?"

Eagerly, I respond while again getting up. "Yes…! She went on to the Disability Action Network meeting? It's down that hallway to your right, then make a left down that far hallway, and it's at the end of that far hall, in the classroom there, at the end…"

"Okay, thanks…!" she says quickly and immediately walks away down the same hall.

I sit, looking down, around, and then straight ahead, lost in my thoughts once again. It's 6:58 p.m.

It's 7:03 p.m.

7:05 p.m.

7:06 p.m.

(No defiance in avoiding looking at the clock. Too tired.)

I should write down those two ladies as attendees on my legal note pad…

At 7:15 p.m., I'm gonna go check on them, I don't CARE if I interrupt them…(!)

And of course, that's just when I hear footsteps coming from down the far hallway leading to the meeting. Around the corner walks Angelica to the hall leading to me, in a fast walk, politely but almost sarcastically smiling and looking my way.

"Alex, we're ready for you to join us again…" she says as she stops.

"Okay," I say to her with the earnest half-smile.

I get up from the couch slower as Angelica already has turned around and turned the corner back, not waiting to escort me. My black work bag draped around my shoulder, I tug on and straighten my long-sleeved dress shirt, then look ahead to proceed down the hallway. I seem to be walking slower than my normal sprint…I may even be wheezing a little…

His parents were instructed by a doctor to have him wear braces on his legs for a year, until a second-opinion cleared his mobility enough for him to walk without them. His right leg would dangle a pointing of the left foot to the right, if he was held upright in the air, and even as an adult he'd occasionally stumble on the street while walking forward, causing him embarrassment since the world still hasn't invented a good-enough way to play something like that off to the public.

***

Diagnosed with asthma as a five-year-old, his younger brother took over for their parents rubbing his back at night when he had asthma attacks. He sat up on the edge of the bed, hunched over, slowly choking breaths, and his brother gently, dutifully, fearfully, and earnestly did the work that his brother, himself, would need just a few years later in also being diagnosed severely-asthmatic.

***

His young chest had an extreme dent in the center, pectus excavatum, making his heart beat very pronounced visibly to the naked eye. Compounding fears that his heart might be further strained or even deformed with abnormality similar to his chest, his asthmatic lungs put pressure on his body's front cavity and made his overall physical constitution very weak. After heart scans as a pre-teen concluded likely negativity for potentially-deadly marfan syndrome, he shyly opted not to have reconstructive chest surgery with the thought of his hospital-ridden mother's deadly cancer in the back of his then-fragile mind.

Conquering the physical limitation of his central physique, he'd struggle into his early 30s with poor body image.

***

He first learned what a basketball "rebound" was from his father's wheelchair-using co-worker and best friend who lived with polio, and who coached him as he shot toy basketballs into a toy basket inside an apartment.

***

When his mother came to pick him up on the playground after school in 1981, he noticed that her hair was now jet-blackish brown, and thick, not the thinning dark grayish hair that it was earlier in the day.

"Mom, you got your new wig!" he excitedly yelled out.

Ducking the excitement with a little humor and no anger, she told him publicly in private response not to announce it to everyone in the vicinity. She didn't want to be embarrassed.

***

Having a nightmare overnight, he was jolted awake in the light of the morning to a crashing body on top of his parents' bed where he'd sought comfort, maybe partially on top of him. His mother lay stiff in front of him, arms to her sides, in stoic agony.

"Go call Sharon," she said.

He ran to the kitchen slightly disoriented and very confused, and then picked up the wall-telephone. Dialing for Sharon, she answered and he told her that his mother was in pain and sick and laying on the bed.

"Go back to her, and if she needs me to call an ambulance, I'll call for one," Sharon responded.

Hanging up, he then ran back to the bedroom and asked his mother if she needed an ambulance, relaying that Sharon would call for one. His mother said after a slight pause that she did need one, so he ran back and dialed Sharon again.

Tearfully and fearfully, he told Sharon that his mother did need the ambulance.

The only other thing he remembers about that day was he and his younger brother standing across the street outside his best friend's house gate, friend on the other side, watching as the ambulance took their mother away. It was the only time he'd shed tears for his mother without the assistance of alcohol years later. The most painful memory of her was not when she was in a coma hooked up to machines and tubes, but, rather, one of her last days at home, after the initial hospitalization and the using of a walker, when he accidentally caught her standing naked, covering herself appropriately with her arms, looking in horror in a mirror at the metastatic breast cancer deconstruction of her own body.

***

He prided himself on the uniqueness of being violently-allergic to "regular" fish, like whitefish, but not allergic to shellfish, which was, of course, his favorite dining order out.

***

In middle school, a food particle chunk, or what he thought was a food particle chunk, hit him in the face when a classmate with a severe cognitive disability spit-blew forward into the air from a classroom seat.

***

In his early 30s, he was single and lived alone in one of his Louisville apartments when his flu-like symptoms took a turn for the worse. He remembered talking to his father, and then his bodily functions quit cooperating. His father drove down from Indianapolis and immediately checked him into an emergency room. Despite major delirium and minor hallucination akin to some of his more infamous substance abuse episodes, the nurses and doctors seemed intent on treating asthma. They questioned him on everything except what non-asthmatic symptoms he currently experienced, and he attempted to convey such to them.

Laying in wait for staff to return again, he snapped.

"I'd get better treatment in Abu Ghraib prison!" he shouted out, prompting his father to slam the thin room curtain shut in frustration.

Three days later, he'd be discharged by manual wheelchair from the hospital with an informal prescription of weight gain and a formal diagnosis of "other" (for insurance purposes).

***

He gets more and more eager to sign up for permanent disability insurance coverage as he gets older.

***

He's always had sufficient hearing, he's only ever had to wear glasses, he has all of his appendages, and he's never broken a bone in his life.

CHAPTER NINE

It's almost slow motion, physically and in my mental view, both, as I complete my final few steps and re-entry into the Disability Action Network meeting in the classroom. Walking in self-consciously, but with awareness of folks in the room, I notice out of the corner of my eye that Jonah and Matt are gone from the meeting. The two ladies who came through the lobby are seated by themselves at a far table off more towards where I was sitting before my exile.

Only Angelica and Joyce look at me as I move to sit where I was seated before, next to Mason, and near the two latecomers, and I don't make any eye contact with anyone in slightly-sheepishly and with all-intent to just getting to my seat. I successfully pull out the chair where I sat before without making a loud howl-of-a-scuff on the tiled floor thanks to the chair wheels.

It's silent. I'm tired and feel no mercy from a day that's not going to end. Russell is the only activity going on, efficiently and amicably taking the plates from those who are done eating and refreshing the drinks of those who want them as the meeting lulls.

"Okay, Lester, Alex is back," Jonathan prompts.

"Okay, well…" Lester begins again. "All right…Alex, we had our discussion, so, we're ready to move on in the Accessibility Committee report. Do you have anything for your committee?"

Eager to get in the Disability Action Network good graces, I jump in, tired as I am. "Yes, I do have a few things this month--"

"Wait Alex: Lester…?" Angelica interrupts. "It's already ten after seven, do we wanna go ahead with our speaker since we're running late?"

"Yeah, I think--" Jonathan jumps in. "Alex--Lester, if you don't mind, maybe we could go ahead and allow tonight's speaker to speak first…"

"Yeah, uh-huh," Lester agrees.

"Sure…" I quickly agree to accommodate. "Absolutely, yeah, for sure, no problem…"

"Okay, well…" Lester transitions. "Okay, well, you all know that we try to have a speaker every month, to talk about different issues, affecting the disability community, and this month I invited Ms. Daisy, after talking with her at our church. As I think you all know, at Flaget Baptist, there's a disability ministry, and we talk about issues that affect us as a community--"

"--Mmm-hmmm..." Bertrice affirms.

"--All-right-now..." Russell says in fleeting past, continuing in and out of the room to his invisible cooking station somewhere else in the building.

Lester smiles, looking diagonally-up in continuing after a pause.

"So, after talking in our meetin' last Sunday, Daisy said that she would meet with us, to talk about her experiences over there, livin' in Woolridge Park. She's had experience working to try to get changes made for herself, and for the neighborhood, and the area, regarding disability issues, so...I think she's here with her daughter tonight, Macey..."

"Yes, *Lester*," Macey says, messing with him.

Half of us slightly-laugh to break the ice and most of us smile, including Lester throughout his turning over the floor. "Okay, well...on *that* note: Ms. Daisy...?"

"Yes," Ms. Daisy says in an elderly-gravelly voice. She appears worn out, and she slowly rises from her chair while Macey looks her up and down with the familiarity of a daughter's slight contempt, but also ready to assist her with any needs.

I draw a line under my current notes on the 8½" x 14" yellow legal notepad and under the line write "*guest speaker: Ms. Daisy* ________."

"Hello, everybody," Ms. Daisy begins. "I appr--" coughing-clear her throat, then continuing delicate speech, "appreciate Lester, asking me to be here tonight...I had no idea that you all meet, to talk about things regularly, like we do, at Flaget. I hope I'm not taking up too much of everyone's time here tonight..."

"No, Ms. Daisy...!" Lester encourages, smiling.

"No, you're fine..." Angelica affirms.

"No, ma'am," Jonathan also encourages, smiling humbly with a small laugh.

After a pause, Ms. Daisy continues.

"I guess, I wanted to talk about some things I've experienced, some things I'm going through, where I live. It sure isn't easy getting older," she says with a single laugh, then pausing. "So...I've lived out in Woolridge Park for about...oh, I'd say...ten years, now...maybe eight, or--I moved into my apartment in 2006. I was on a waiting list for

Section 8, and I wanted to live in the West End, because it's where I grew up most of my life, the only time I didn't was when I lived downtown before I met my husband, who passed away. When *he* passed, I couldn't afford the house we had any longer after 25 years, even with the help of my daughter here…Macey…and my other two children couldn't help. So I applied for Section 8, and they put me on the waiting list, and after a few years--well, more than a few years, I think, it was six years, maybe…six, or, what--how long was I on the list…?" she asks, looking down at Macey.

"Six years--*more* than six years, mama…"

"Okay, well, *more* than six years…and, well, I haven't even been sick *that* long. But, anyway, I was on the waiting list, and I finally got in, they approved me for a one-bedroom apartment over at The Woods, The Woods of Woolridge Park, on the second floor of one of those apartment buildings over there. Which was fine, I could walk the steps fine back when I moved in, there's no elevator, but I wasn't sick, and I could walk long distances and walk up and down the steps fine back then. It was nice to have a newer apartment to move into, in a newer community, after living in my house for 25 years…I was scared going *on* to Section 8, and getting public assistance, I was thinking it would be like some of my friends said, with roaches, and all kinds of maintenance problems…you know, things like that. So it was nice when I got to move into a nice community in the West End, since there are so few new apartments where I live out there. Anyhow, I moved in, and things were fine for the first couple years, but then, in 2008, I was diagnosed with lung cancer. Which I know was my fault, because I smoked like everyone else growing up, and my husband worked for Corn Island Tobacco for 25 years before he passed. But I got sick, I started going for treatment, chemotherapy, and all that, you know--I was just so *tired*, it was so hard walking, especially when it came to those stairs, there are about--well, there *are*, sixteen steps, from the ground up to the second floor, I think, where my apartment is, and, like I said, no elevator--" Ms. Daisy is slapping her tongue more to the roof of her mouth as she speaks, with cotton-mouth.

Wait a minute, I think she may be…hold on…is she…maybe…?

"So, I asked my landlord about what I could do, to not have so many steps to go up and down, asked them if--could they allow me to transfer to one of the other apartments out there, so I wouldn't have such a hard time. They--it's not the Housing Authority, it's managed by some company in Chicago, but the management people here said that they'd look into it, but that all the first-floor apartments were taken, in the phase where I was--where I live at, right now…"

Back in the room, Russell wastes no time noticing Ms. Daisy in between his volunteer chef duties. "Hey, now, Ms. Daisy, can I get you a glass of water, or something to drink, I shoulda got you somethin' before you even began, young lady…"

"Yeah, can we get you anything?" Jonathan asks.

"Oh no, no, I'm okay, I'm fine," Ms. Daisy says politely.

"Mama, you sure, you know you're supposed to drink lots of water," Macey pushes.

"No, no, I'm--well, okay, well, a small glass of water'd be *fine*, okay, yes…"

"Okay ma'am, lemme get that for you right now, ma'am…" Russell says, shifting his course to go back out of the room quickly.

"You sure we can't get you anything else, Daisy?" Angelica asks.

"No, no, you all are fine, I'm okay," Ms. Daisy says.

"I can't believe she even agreed to have you all get her some water…" Macey half-jokingly tells the group, to a few polite reciprocating laughs.

And that's when it hits me: *oh my god, that's right, this is Daisy Jones, my Complainant from the end of 2010…or maybe it was 2011.*

Embarrassed internally, I try to take solace that I don't think she recognized me, either, and we both appear worn out with exhaustion for our own reasons today. At least I'm deluding myself into thinking that. And I immediately try to think of the facts of her case, and internally shake my head wondering why I can remember *all* the details of an active housing discrimination complaint investigation to its most minute piece of information, yet remember almost nothing when the case is disposed of and not active, especially when I'm this tired. I curse myself.

"So," Ms. Daisy Jones says. "Yes, I was--I asked management, at that time, it was this Chicago company called 'Development… Venture…' or something like that…"

Development Ventures, Inc.

"They kept saying that they'd get back with me, and they never did tell me if I was on the waiting list with them to transfer, or what. I asked Mr. Tony--Tony Davidson, the manager, if they'd put me on the list, and he said that they would, but I never received anything in writing, or was told by him, or told by any of the office people, if I was there on the list, and when I could move…"

"Here you are, young lady, ma'am," Russell enthusiastically and slightly-teasingly says, giving her a small clear plastic cup of water, no ice.

Slowly using her right hand to get the transfer from Russell, she says politely, "Thank you," and even more slowly takes a sip. Macey then reaches out and up and takes the cup from Ms. Jones. "Mmm-hm," Ms. Jones says softly, repositioning herself to continue.

Tony Davidson was the manager, the Respondent representative was attorney… Pappas. Donald Papp--Dwight, Dwight Pappas.

I'm even more at attention now that I feel directly involved, and my tired gears are spinning again as I adjust in my seat.

"So," Ms. Jones continues, "I called the corporate office, in Chicago, and they told me to talk to Tony, and he kept saying the same things, so I called Section 8, and they told me that I had to call Tony back, and the landlord management. And so I kept getting the run-around, and I finally called HUD, and they took my complaint. HUD said that because I was disabled, they should transfer me. So, I filed the complaint, and the HUD inspector met me at my apartment, and he helped me sign the complaint that week, back when I was having a *real* hard time during the chemo…"

That was me, I met you in your apartment…you had a hospital bed up there in your second floor unit, with grab bars to help you get up, and Macey wasn't there, it was your niece (?) who was there with you, I forget her name…

"So, HUD then had Human Rights investigate things, and then they sued the management company, and forced them to say that they had to transfer me. It took forever, but they had us all sign an agreement, back in…I don't know…2013…I think? 2014? And that was supposed to resolve everything. Then, the new management company came in, and I--Tony was gone, and I think the new management, they ended up being just like the old management. They said--the new manager, Lorraine, she told me they'd get right on it, but they never did transfer me. They showed me a copy of the waiting list, said I was second on the list to be transferred, but that was last year, and then I *know* they had people moving in from the senior building they have over there, I saw people moving in and out, and I know people over there. I live in the apartment buildings for families, but the senior building they have over there, the tower, it always has a vacancy. I asked about the senior building before, but they told me I wasn't old enough, 'cause I was 60, and you had--they said you had to be 62 years old, so I didn't qualify. But they had--they have all these other types of apartments over there, too, not just that senior building, they also have townhouses, other houses like homes, and other apartments, you know, and with the same manager. They have The Woods where I live, then they have...The Glen, The Townhouses, something like that, and other Section 8 or public housing over there." Ms. Jones stops and looks down to Macey. "Mace, hand me that again..."

Macey hands her the water cup, which again Ms. Jones takes slowly, then drinks the smallest of sips slowly...

The group is silent, waiting for more. I've been taking notes.

"Mm-hm, thank you," Ms. Jones says in slowly and carefully handing the cup back. "So, I still--the point of all this, I guess, is that I still haven't been transferred yet. I have my good days, and I have my not-so-better days, and it's so hard, sometimes, walking up these steps, and even just walking down the steps. I'm not on chemotherapy right *now*, but I'm scheduled to go through it again next month, and sometimes, I just can't make it back and forth from my apartment..."

Macey, both hands stretched out on the table before her, is getting visibly upset with tears. Incredibly, after the incident in the car on the way over here, I'm welling up with rage again, and not only at the fact that Ms. Jones hasn't yet been transferred, but because there's an apparent violation of the Housing Conciliation Agreement for the case. I'm angry at the role of the Civil Relations Commission's complicity in this, politically, when it comes to the Housing Authority and our agency lack of enforcement, as we share the same Mayoral boss. And I'm upset at HUD's lack of accountability over the Commission in all of this, not making us do our job to enforce the Agreement by threatening our federal money, much less HUD's own lack of enforcement with those other federal laws that apply here. And, I'll explain this in a nuclear tirade if I'm given five minutes, just *five minutes*, to speak here. After Ms. Jones is done, and with permission from her, and the Disability Action Network board.

"So, when Lester told me about the meeting here tonight, I was--he asked me to talk to you all about the things going on."

"And what you all need to know about," Macey says tearfully, "is how mama struggles with this every day. She has to go up and down those steps, up and down, up and down, and otherwise, she's a prisoner. She's a prisoner in her own home, her own apartment. Just because she doesn't have the money to move, she shouldn't have to be in such *pain* all the time, physically struggling. She has--" Macey almost sobs, "--she has to get down on her butt--" Macey gets up from her seat, then crouches down in a seated position near the tiled floor, "--she has to go, like this, she has to slide down, on each step, one at a time, and I'm holding her oxygen tank, while she goes down each step in pain…it shouldn't have to *be* like this…!"

Winces and groans from a few in attendance, and if Jonah were still here, he'd make the 11:00 o'clock news in retaliation against the current management company rental office.

After a pause, and after Macey dabs her eyes with a tissue from her purse, and while Ms. Jones slowly sits down, Lester moves forward.

"Yeah, so…so, we all talk a *lot* here, about the lack of accessibility here in the city, and we wanna help people like Ms. Daisy, and her daughter Macey, and those others of us struggling with this kind of issue, the problems in what can, or can't, be done, with reducing inaccessibility for persons with disabilities…Alex, you're the housing guy, do you wanna--you wanna offer some advice, or see how the city might help, you know, talk about this issue…?"

I pause, wondering how to begin, but since there's not a lot of time, and I have so much to say, I make the pause a breath. I'm gonna speak rapidly.

"Okay, well, yes, Lester…Ms. Jones, I thought you looked familiar before, and I'm so sorry I didn't recognize you in the lobby there," I bridge with one tired exhale-laugh. "I *do* wanna say that even though the case that you filed with us--with the Civil Relations Commission--was *supposed* to be resolved, obviously, it is *not*, and that is a moral outrage. So, what I first wanna do, is apologize on behalf of the system, the--the lack of empathy, the *apathy*, from the system. This is infuriating to me to hear this, personally, and I'm gonna take action starting tomorrow, tomorrow morning. Or actually, I have a lot to say quickly right now," I say, frustration, fatigue, and anger somehow giving me a third wind that causes me to physically quake a little. "Ms. Jones, I'm bound by confidentiality with regards to your specific case that you filed with us, but that doesn't mean I'm prevented from speaking on the procedural breakdown it sounds like has occurred here. With your permission, I can speak to your case specifically on some of the allegations, and I'm eager to do that, but, in theory, I can't be your advocate like an attorney and represent you…"

"No, that's fine. You can talk about it all, I know you have your job to do, and you were very helpful when we met," Ms. Jones graciously says.

I sure wish I had a little bit of water…Russell…?

"Okay, well, thank you, Ms. Jones. I do wanna say that Ms. Jones' case is egregious and--well, here I go, I guess I may not be so neutral, anymore (!). Ms. Jones' case is egregious, but unfortunately it's not unique. And I don't mean in a scholarly sense, I mean in a *real*, meaningful, tangible, systemic way. Her case is what happens when you don't just have problems with the landlord management company and their agents, but also with local and federal government, both with the subsidy administration *and* the enforcement agencies like mine. So, with Ms. Jones' case, she filed alleging unlawful discrimination in her housing based on disability when the *Respondent*, or the original management company, refused to transfer her by just placing her on a waiting list, and not accommodating her physical disability. She filed with HUD--or, the United States Department of Housing & Urban Development--or, in other words, the feds, and then HUD transferred the case over to us, the Civil Relations Commission, to investigate. But my agency only has jurisdiction over the private market, or so my bosses would have the public believe. So, with Ms. Jones' case, she lives in a dwelling--an apartment, that uses federal subsidy, it's project-based Section 8 for *her* unit, which means that the subsidy is tied to the unit itself, not like a voucher, or what most people still call a 'Section 8 voucher,' where you can go wherever you want with the voucher, and as long as the landlord accepts it, then it's portable. In *this* case, though, the subsidy is tied to the property, but also, the entire *community* is owned by the Housing Authority, which administers those voucher-based subsidies and, they also own the unit that has Ms. Jones' project-based subsidy. So, you have this entire community with all these different types of subsidies and such, from vouchers, to project-based, to low income housing tax credit units, to just regular private-market-non-subsidized units. And the Housing Authority owns *all* of the units…Well, the Housing Authority denies that, and they just say that they own the *land*, and not the units themselves, but my investigation indicated that they do own all the units in a bunch of different incorporated entities they set up, to carve out all these tax liability and operating schemes--well, schemes is a bad word, I don't mean necessarily that they're doing anything improper *that* way. At least with non-disability-related stuff…"

Jonathan laughs a little, Lester has a big smile.

"So, where the alleged discrimination comes in, is that the Respondent, the management company--and *not* the Housing Authority, which manages the subsidy on Ms. Jones' unit and all the other subsidies in the community, or at least manages the federal subsidy regulations--the Respondent management company just throws people on waiting lists, different lists carved up according to the different subsidy types, and keeps them all separate. So, when an apartment or a unit comes available at one location, or phase, then the person on the waiting list in a different location or phase is not permitted to transfer…they're just still stuck on the waiting list for their little section. Which, in my mind, is fine, if you're looking at the different subsidy terms for each tenant. *But*, and this is the *huge* caveat to all this, and why I'm going on and on with all this regulatory bureaucratic explanation," I slightly-laugh. "The *issue* is that, if you're a person with a disability, federal subsidy regulations *mandate a preference* for you to transfer, compared to others, if the accommodation--if this transfer is to accommodate your disability-based condition. So, this means that if you need the transfer, you aren't just stuck at the bottom of the waiting list: you're to be bumped up, with that preference, to towards the top of the list, *ahead* of those tenants who are waiting for transfers *not* to accommodate a disability. And even further, there are also waiting-list regulatory preferences for life-threatening conditions for a tenant: *so*, if your disability is not just in need of accommodation, but it's a life-threatening health-and-safety issue for you, like, end-stage renal failure, or, let's say, *lung cancer*, then you *need* to be transferred as soon as possible, with a preference like for someone who's been displaced through a natural disaster."

"Alex," Angelica interrupts at the pause, "I hear what you're saying, but I know that the apartment complexes are just gonna say that they don't have any units available, and that's why people are placed on waiting lists. They just say, 'Oh, well, we understand, but we really don't have anything open right now,' like Daisy's been saying."

"Angelica," I go on, addressing her directly, "I know. They say that, and that may be true with the different programs, like, at Woolridge… occupancy for subsidized communities is very tight, for sure. *But*, here's the issue for me, and in theory for the feds, for HUD: just because one 'program' is full, the reasonable accommodation, which is what's at play here, can maybe cross over from one program to another, one different project, different *community*, to another. What I mean by this is that because the management company works with the Housing Authority to administer all the different subsidy programs, why doesn't the management company transfer the person with the disability accommodation need from one unit, in one program at the same community, to another unit, in a different program, at the same community? 'Oh, well,'" I mockingly say, "'because HUD won't let us do that,' or, 'Our investors lose money with the low income housing tax credit program if we try to flip unit designations from one program to another.' Okay, so, we get responses like that, and even if--let's say, even if that's *not* a reasonable accommodation, with a nominal loss of income, or an administrative burden that trumps the reasonableness test that applies here, to switch programs--and I'm highly suspect of that--let's say, that burden *is* met, fine: then, *then*, what the management company should do, is look at other options outside of that entire community, with all of its programs: Are there other communities operated by the same management company that she could transfer to? No? Well, then, how about calling the Housing Authority, and ask about transferring her to another Housing-Authority-controlled--excuse me, 'owned,' property or community? And that's even if the current tenant with the disability doesn't even *wanna* move from the current community at Woolridge. If the management company and the Housing Authority work together here at Woolridge, then they can work together to permit transfer to another community that has the same subsidy, or, hell, even a different subsidy program. There doesn't even have to be a penny in income lost by the management company, much less the Housing Authority: if people *'just don't move'* and the waiting list is a mile long, like they say, then there's a replacement tenant ready to go, so there's no vacancy for long, no losing money on the unit. And you just have to *offer* the different community: if the tenant doesn't take it, to move out to somewhere else managed by the Housing Authority, fine, responsibility over. But, as you can see *here*, *none* of that was ever done, it's just limbo and purgatory on the damn waiting list (!)."

Lester smiles and says after a pause, "Well, Alex…we know--we know you're tryin'…"

And that seems to be all anyone can say after the rant.

But I want to keep going, even though I'm so exhausted, now-riddled with worse cotton-mouth than Ms. Jones, and sore internally from half my organs seemingly failing.

"If you all can indulge me, I just have one or two more things to say about how the system is failing here, I promise I'll make it quick. I just need to trash-talk my employer and HUD for a second…"

"Okay, yeah Alex," Lester smiles, "We know that's what you need to do, that's why--we're here *hopin'* you'll turn on your employer…!"

Smiling, too exhausted to lighten the mood with a laugh, and saving my strength for one final push, I dial into any last remaining eyes-half-open energy.

"So, in a case like Ms. Jones' case, our agency can find Probable Cause, initiate litigation, assist with a Housing Conciliation Agreement--or, negotiated settlement, like we did in this case, with the help of the Jefferson County Attorney's Office litigating it. But, what happens when the agreement is signed, the Complainant maybe gets some money to help with the remedy owed to her, but the dang transfer hasn't happened, and continues to not happen?"

"You received money…?" Trisha asks out loud to Ms. Jones.

"Not enough!" Ms. Jones snaps back non-feebly.

Everyone laughs, and I drone on with exhausted smiling and continue fading energy.

"I mean, the Civil Relations Commission should immediately petition court with a violation of the Agreement, but also, HUD's supposed to affirmatively further along this fair housing issue by threatening to withhold the federal subsidy--to the Respondent *and* us for not doing our job enforcing it (!). Again, though, our office only has jurisdiction under local ordinance and, in being substantially-equivalent, only one federal law: the federal Fair Housing Act. With receipt of federal funding, there are also other laws that apply to a discrimination issue, like Section 504 of the Rehabilitation Act of 1973, the one Jonah talks about. HUD's supposed to withhold, or at least threaten to withhold, all that federal funding as a result of discrimination, and for all those laws that the Commission doesn't have jurisdiction to make a determination under, HUD is the enforcement agency. And HUD knows about these cases, we document the details *ad nauseum* in data entry like you wouldn't believe. So, *two* enforcement agencics should be cracking down on things like this, local *and* federal authorities. And, the icing on the cake is that the Director of the Housing Authority, who I truly believe is a good man who works to address these things when he finds out about them, he--"

"Mr. Goss," Ms. Jones says.

"Yes…*Jason*, that's right," I concur. "Jason Goss…he's dealt with this kind of bureaucratic problem before, and he understands that classifying a tenant with a disability as needing an emergency transfer when it affects the health of the tenant is a way to immediately get someone transferred to the accessible unit. Why it didn't happen or hasn't happened in this case, I really don't know. I guess he wasn't made aware of it by his subordinates again, maybe. I shouldn't speculate, but…okay, since I'm dominating the meeting now and I'm exhausted, lemme just promise you, Ms. Jones, that, at this point, I have on my list to address this, on an *emergency-preference* basis, with the County Attorney's Office, my supervisors, and with HUD. I don't control much outside of the investigation, but I have a role that I can and *will* play in getting this case where it *still* needs to go…"

"You can't fight city hall…" Samuel quotes with a slight smile looking diagonally into the air.

A knock on the building back door outside the classroom diverts the always-walking Russell for response. Opening it with the push-bar, a Transit Authority driver exchanges only half a pleasantry to Russell's as-always full welcome to anyone. Russell then leans into the classroom.

"Beatrice, young lady," he announces and assists. "Your chariot is *here*…"

"All right, Russell, everybody…" she says.

Various smiles and goodbyes are exchanged while I pause long enough to re-group my dwindling thoughts about what I need to get in for the crowd.

"I have much more to say, but let me leave it at this, if I even can (!)," I start conceding, a little above the shuffling from a few board members. "I was gonna tell the group in the Announcements part of the meeting that the Mayor's Disability Forum is confirmed for this Friday, which is September…uh…"

"Fourth," Angelica and Phoebe both confirm separately.

"Yes," I repeat with their mercy, "the fourth. The fourth, at 1:30 p.m. at city hall, room 101. I know I mentioned at the last meeting that it was tentatively-set for September 4th, but now it *is*, as of last week, at least, confirmed. 1:30 p.m. at city hall, and many Louisville Metro Government departments, and associated agencies, including some Directors, have already confirmed they'll be there. I'll be there, Brenda's scheduled to be there as my department Director…I dunno if Mr. Goss will be there, I was involved in the planning for this but I wasn't in charge of confirming attendance. Deputy Mayor Shonda Heyward will be--is *scheduled* to be there, and, hopefully, the Mayor, too, who didn't show up for the last one, if you all remember, but…there ya *go* (!). So, in theory, we'll all be there to discuss disability issues with Louisville Metro Government, and to present on what we've done, or are doing, or, in my case, what we *should* be doing, with housing, transportation, public accommodations, Public Works, all that stuff. Call me if you all have any questions, but I know some of you have confirmed being there already, and I e-mailed the Disability Action Network e-mail listserv about it once or…twice. Maybe once. I dunno," I conclude flippantly.

"Yeah, it did go out to DAN membership, and some of us have already called in confirmations for Friday," Jonathan adds.

"Uh-*huh*…yeah, I know I'll be there," Lester says, "Jonathan will be there, and…"

"Yeah I'll be there too," Phoebe says lightning-quick.

"Phoebe, uh-huh," Lester continues. "Some others will, too. So, we'll do *our* part, as the Network, and keep the city's feet to the fire, pushin' those city leaders to do what they're supposed to do, and also to support the work that Alex does, and the other good people inside city government, few and far between as they may be, sometimes" he slightly-laughs. "And then, you know, we'll go on from there…so, do we know what time it--"

"--Yeah, I was gonna say, Lester, it's 8:00," Angela says.

"*It's. Seven. Fifty. Nine. PM.*" Samuel puts his recorder back in his pocket.

"Okay, then," Lester says. "Any other announcements, or…?"

No one speaks, with half the membership still preparing their personal belongings, checking with each other, and engaging in low small-talk.

Jonathan reads the crowd correctly. "Well, Lester, I think that's *it*, then..."

"Ok, well..." Lester concludes. "Our next meetin' is September 28th, 6:00 p.m., here at the university..." he says loudly as everyone trails off, and/or out, me included and/or especially.

"Thanks, Lester, thanks Jonathan...Angelica..." I say to the Disability Action Network board core, getting up. "Phoebe, Mason, Robert, see you at the next Transit Authority Accessibility Committee meeting..."

"Okay yeah Alex see ya," Phoebe says quickly.

"Alright, see you then," Robert says professionally.

Mason opens his mouth wide at me, bright-eyed, while motoring his wheelchair away to the Transit Authority rendezvous locked side-door.

I look at Ms. Jones and her daughter, and they're both standing and talking to Lester. I sheepishly extend my hand out in a half-wave to them as I leave the classroom, mouthing the word "bye," too tired to wait around to talk more about the case. Shame on me, but my body is now broken. I'll take care of this, or, rather, do what the hell I *can* about it, in the morning. *If* I don't call in sick, of course. I probably won't, since I usually don't. These Disability Action Network meetings rev me up into action instead of bring me down like city and departmental meetings.

Fatigued, but with a bare, fourth wind, I sprint yawning with my black work bag holstered over my shoulder with my right hand and arm, making my way down a hallway which leads to the hall which leads to the front lobby. I see the sunset approaching outside, and since this is Old Louisville, I be sure to look left, then right, before walking to the right on the sidewalk towards my car: crime has always been a part of my residential neighborhood area here. No red flags coming my way, so I cross the crosswalk north over West Breckinridge Street. I always half-expect to see the lime green parking ticket envelope under my driver's side windshield wiper when I leave the Disability Action Network meeting, but there's never anything there.

Too tired to be very nervous, I again look around for clearance to unlock my driver's side door, and then quickly get in the car with a locked-door finish. I turn the headlights on at the same time I turn the car ignition, and the lights come on but the ignition won't turn over. I grimace in frustration as I then rapidly keep trying to turn over the ignition switch, blocked by whatever manufacturer defect caused the first two recalls on it that I had fixed and making it now not work a third time. Paranoid again that the key will break off in an eleven-year-old car that I now wish was a new car payment instead, I stop and sit in silence. I sit like a statue, face drooping. The hot summer evening air has now brought out two questionable-looking males ahead on the horizon, walking down the sidewalk, headed my way. Not quite a slasher-movie dread of terror, but I *have* to be alert. Unless I can get the damn car started…

My face curls and my hand turns and flicks and jimmies, and again, turn-flick, turn-flick--*finally*, it starts, and only after twenty seconds of trying.

I need any energy I can get, since I'm leaning forward in the driver's seat desperate for just-enough to get home. I dial up the air conditioner heat, and I hit the knob on the dashboard car radio/compact disc player…the Mexican film soundtrack has no trouble coming on, and is again loud, and I zoom away from the meter since the green light's in my favor. All the stoplights should be coordinated to turn green down South 3rd Street, all the way at 35 miles per hour, until I make the right turn onto West Ormsby Avenue, so I should cruise home within five minutes.

Sure enough, and despite orange plastic traffic cones and a big lightbulb-marquee arrow directing the sparsest of 8:10 p.m. vehicle traffic to the right from the forever-blocked left-hand lane ("*It's Not Showtime, Folks!*" Public Works states every night), I make it to West Ormsby and then to the right turn. My car now turns right onto my residential street, and I make my way towards the no-parking-anytime section of the block by our house. All on-street parallel parking spaces are occupied except for frustratingly-just-too-small spaces here and there, and, of course, the maximum number possible of four cars parked in violation of the no-parking-anytime signs at the end of the cul-de-sac.

Cursing the parking offenders the entire time, I want to do a turnaround at the cul-de-sac gate, and I have to look around for pedestrian offenders, but there's less space to do both now that the no-parking area's filled up. I throw the car in reverse while turning the steering wheel to position the tight turnaround between the lined cars on both sides of the street, and then drive forward again a yard or so to almost one side of the street-lined cars, near the concrete bench with all the now-former commotion from earlier loiterers. I hastily but prudently get the car turned around with a back-and-forth, drive about twenty yards back the way I just came, and then make a right-hand turn onto the part of the alley where truckhead originally turned into in order to make his turnaround, and where the roving trio of madness passed me with their warning of the streets.

Crickets chirping, urban light pole lights dancing with random spotlight flashing and buzzing, I make my way down the alley to the end, at South 6th Street, and I stop to look for pedestrians and vehicle traffic, both ways. And with double-checks. There's a pedestrian across the street, but unless they dart across towards me after seeing me eye-to-eye, like two wild animals engaging, I should be fine to make my right turn.

Turn successful, I drive the short way down to the corner of 6th & Wild Wild West Oak Street, waiting for the no-right-turn-on-red light to turn green and welcome me towards one of the most infamously-troubled stretches of Old Louisville: the Oak Street Corridor. I may have no choice but to park along West Oak, at one of the non-metered on-street parallel-parking areas, since my residential hideaway street is all filled up so late in the evening, and that's even *if* there's a space available this late on Oak not occupied by the overflow from my street. Only two shootings on this stretch of Oak here so far this year…at least, that I read about in the news, because I certainly heard gunshots three times as many times as that, coming from what sounded like this direction.

Pedestrians all over the place, I get the right turn done, and…I think--yes, a spot back here, it's available, but there's empty space up there towards…the…house…I can't tell if it's…it may be the Transit Authority bus stop; I'm chancing it.

Driving up to the gated cul-de-sac area at my street and Oak Street on the right, yep, it's an illegally-parked car cutting off half of the Transit Authority bus stop space, so no real parking space there. Two men and a woman talk to each other sitting at the gate concrete bench while turning their attention to look at me creep past.

Cursing, I speed up a little bit and keep on driving to the red stoplight at 4th & Oak, ground zero for Old Louisville anti-social, inebriated, dare-you-as-I-look-you-in-the-eyes chaos, and a few hardworking folks just needing to take the bus. I turn my music down in hopes of not inciting anyone, and intermittent pedestrians walk back and forth across the street at the crosswalk, not at the crosswalk, and back and forth, in-and-around the bus stop there. No turn permitted on red, so I wait for the green to get me out of here, looking at the light but all-around with my peripheral vision. And it does turn green, so I turn onto South 4th Street headed again towards West Ormsby and then make a right-on-red there, which is oddly permitted. I drive down Ormsby again, and try again down my residential street, hoping that someone's pulled out their car and freed up a space.

Slowly, I make my way headed towards the cul-de-sac dead end, and headlights come on up ahead on the left-hand side of the street. I drive past the headlights to the same alley I've been down three times before already today, turn into the left side half-way, then do the correct backwards turn-around everyone is *supposed* to do when violating traffic laws, by backing into the L-shape from that alley (!), and head back up the way I just came, slowly.

I see the red tail lights and vehicle turn left out from the on-street parallel parking space now on my right ahead, and I also see a new car's headlights coming my way now from a turn onto the street from West Ormsby. In a panic that somehow this new vehicle could miraculously speed up, spin out to its left side in turning the car around while kicking up street blacktop and soot, right into the just-freed-up (read: *my*) parking space, turn off, and permit a 24-year-old accountant to jump out of the driver's side, in a flash of smoke, holding the car keys in a 1980s fashion-magazine grin looking at me in a dare, I speed up my car; I pass the space to a smart stop; then, divinely, I parallel-park in the space. I turn the ignition switch to be off, and it works, followed by the headlights. I grab my black work bag, open the driver's side door, manually-lock the door, slam the door shut harder than I intended, and walk a city-walk across to the other side of the street and onto the sidewalk after the other car goes past, looking all ways to make sure I don't have to be ready to fight someone with punches in the air during a collapse from exhaustion.

It's quiet, and vacant, for pedestrian traffic along the street and the sidewalks, though a yell is heard from West Oak Street ahead and either to the left, or right, out of view. Cicadas are chirping and rattling along the brownstone-like and mini-mansion-like Victorian-era houses along my street, I guess replacing those yells from people I expect to hear in a hot, end-of-August night. A few dogs are barking in the neighborhood, but are coming from back yards and hopefully not the side-alley I need to cross ahead. I cross the alleyway and see no people or dogs closeby, so I continue with a walk and almost a skip towards, and up onto, my house steps, right before a male's "Hey! Hey…!" is yelled, likely thrown my way from Oak Street towards me. I'm not stopping, no matter what, though. I get my key quickly into the front door lock and open it with one eye trying to look to my back left behind me to see who's coming. I snake in and lock the door behind me with one motion.

Inside, I see the foyer, living room, kitchen, and dining room lights all on. The air conditioning cools me instantly.

"He*yyyyy*…" I dwindlingly eek out in announcement.

No response.

No surprise.

I exhale a lumber into the kitchen, and see along the short way that no one's in the living room except an empty cereal bowl and a used spoon on opposite sides of the same rectangular living room table in front of the couch. No one's in the kitchen, no one's in the dining room. I get the mail I left on the kitchen counter and give it a second leaf-through…didn't miss anything earlier…then unzip my work bag side sleeve and walk into the dining room to place the auto insurance bill I left on the table earlier in the sleeve, without zipping it back up. I then flip off the dining room light, the kitchen light, and the living room light before achingly ambling up the stairs painfully-slowly, each creak of each stair matching the silent response of each creak of each limb, each step going slower and slower.

At the top of the stairs, I arrive with a mild, almost-exaggerated thud of my right foot and see that Michael's bedroom light is on according to the transom window at the top of his closed door. I also see a light under the non-transomed, closed bedroom door for Corinne. I shuffle the epic three steps over to the left to the master bedroom, door propped open with a small plastic trash can, overhead light on, overhead ceiling fan on, and Jenny's in bed, laptop resting on a cheap, wooden serving tray, watching a likely-British television miniseries with a headphone likely in her ear. I also hear the large floor fan in the room out of view going full-blast like a warehouse exhaust. Entering the room, there's Tivoli, lying down to the right, and he immediately whips his head up and around from the left <*clink*> to see what I'm doing.

"Hey," I ache out as loud as I can to Jenny, looking at Tivoli and then looking away quickly so that the eye contact doesn't elicit from him an explosion of required attention.

"Hey sweetheart," Jenny says somewhat-sincerely and somewhat-loudly, maybe as a test, and not looking at me while pausing her show and removing her earbud.

I pull out the insurance bill and place it on the wall ledge under the big mounted mirror, under my wallet and keys to prevent the whir of the tall floor fan and the overhead ceiling fan from blowing it around the room. Then I place my black work bag on the floor too close to Tivoli, who launches up in scrape on the hardwood floor, and he slowly goes to move, scratching his collar while wagging his tail at me. Ignoring him, I grunt out loud once and I start taking off my outer dress clothes, dropping the tie in a small plastic basket on the floor designated mostly for dry-clean items, putting my belt and shoes in the closet, and pitching my unbuttoned dress shirt and dress slacks into the tall hamper next to the covered non-working fireplace. I don't get relief from the humidity yet, but it doesn't matter anyways since my extremities are slightly cold from so much internal body-trauma.

Tivoli walks out into the hallway slowly and pantingly, where he collapses in the middle of the walkway to stare ahead and continue to pant from the heat, the humidity, and the elderliness. I almost do the same in slowly collapsing onto the bed next to Jenny, me half-seated against the wall in my white undershirt and boxers with not even enough strength to grab the netbook at the bedside table in routine, easy motion.

I don't say anything, I just stare ahead breathing hard in a stun.

Jenny and I both know that she's sick of my complaining, of course, so I see that she's already switched to the happy medium of checking her personal e-mail account instead of talking with me about my day versus just continuing on defiantly watching her miniseries. We're both just waiting to see who'll speak first, and whether it'll be the predictable negativity from me or just continued silence and passive attention-getting from us both.

A few seconds…

A few more…

"I love you Jenny," I say routinely and submissively, looking straight ahead towards the large mirrored wall and ledge and fireplace in the room.

"I love you too," she says robotically, reactively, and without feeling...and with e-mail clicking.

Wanting to speak like a parent, but instead coming off as a methodically-whining adult, I explain, "I just needed to get through today, okay? It's all over now for the week, probably."

"Al*right*..." she again speaks impassionately, except for her own slight frustration.

"Well, except for Friday," my analytical, can't-help-it soul forces out.

Jenny says nothing.

A few more seconds...

"You want me to sleep upstairs...?" I throw out as bait.

"You do what*ever*, darling..."

I lay there, half-seated, fully-defeated, still staring ahead. I know what the right thing to do is right now, I just am *so* tired, so sore, so exhausted, I just don't wanna do *anything*. Hoping it all somehow goes away...

I hear, and then listen to, the whir of the large floor fan while looking up at the revolving ceiling fan. The moaning roar of the standing floor fan sounding up and down, the ceiling fan more silent except for the intermittent clink of the pull-chain hitting in oval orbit.

Whirring...quiet overhead swooping...conversational silence...

More silence, more waiting, more laying and sitting.

I finally turn to Jenny, assuming the position, and she has mercy on me: she turns to me, puckered up, and I kiss her gently, kiss-to-kiss.

"I love you, honey," I almost, but of course, not quite, break down.

I lay back to the achiness that envelops me, and Jenny goes back to watching her show by clicking and putting in the ear piece again but placing a hand at my side. We're back to being a couple after we both, at the same time, turn towards one another again, Jenny with the forgiving lead. And thankfully, because I don't think I can fight anything anymore.

On Tuesday morning, despite being near-stifled with guilt, he took the advice of his wife and finally called in sick to work. After e-mailing the office manager to start arranging for a language interpreter for the walk-in complainants the day prior, he called in to his supervisor. The two-hour-and-45-minute non-paid flex-leave from working the night before alleviated about 2:45 of guilt from his lying in bed while doing laundry most of the day at home.

***

On Wednesday, despite being nearly-conscientious with guilt, he returned to work with the small dose of vengeance that came with the security of working the same job for a dozen years in the same location, combined with his mission of planning for Friday's seminal presentation. Juggling his workload from the domino effect of missing just one day out of the office, he managed to put out fires and supervise applicable staff in a two-days-for-the-price-of-one bargain. He even found a way to outline his Friday presentation to the mayoral administration and the general public.

***

On Thursday, he told one Complainant that interviewing her minor children could be put on hold after the Respondent's attorney called and e-mailed a conciliation agreement for the sexual harassment housing discrimination complaint, for her review without admitting any liability; he offered her $3,000 and full confidentiality if she were to vacate her dwelling at the end of her lease agreement term. He told another Complainant by telephone, consistent with agency procedure, that their housing discrimination complaint was dismissed with the director's finding of No Probable Cause; he then withstood the barrage of insults to the agency, though not towards him, personally, about city government laziness, inefficiency, bias, and uselessness. Speaking diplomatically, as he almost always did, to the latter Complainant, he wished in hindsight that he'd have openly agreed with the diatribe (with the exception of applicability to the housing discrimination complaint investigation, of course).

Thinking obsessively about the next day's mayoral administration public meeting, he worried about his planned presentation, city government supervisory response, and current and subsequent standing with his employment. Would he at least get a good night's sleep, which was the only thing he asked for from the powers that might, or might not, be? All he seemed to have wanted out of his life, rightly or wrongly, was the peace of a full night's sleep, free from half a dozen reasons waking him up overnight; free from professional and personal anxiety; free from decades of substance abuse radiation; free from life event traumas, big and small; free from his general insecurity; and, free from his general lack of firm faith in the nature of existence.

He had no doubt, however, about his required accountability to the general public scheduled to be in attendance at the next day's meeting. Not for a second. And if he was honest with himself, he'd have had no doubt whatsoever about his family who helped make his success the following day, the current day, and many--rather, most, previous days.

***

Fading in, a moody, low-note synthesizer bubbled into the darkness as a tune.

Disoriented, he fumbled his right hand towards the right in the blackness.

Feeling a plastic and top-metal inhaler shape, he moved his hand on, reaching a small egg of plastic-encased metal. Picking up the sounding object with a slight palsy, he pulled it to his face, unconsciously flipped it open in two connected halves, and then lightning-quick thumbed through the tiny keypad on one half in order to stop the mumbling science-fiction alarm upon seeing "5:25 AM" on the other half digital screen.

He laid there, item in hand.

He couldn't get up.

He was disoriented, his mouth was frozen open, his eyes were half closed, and his head was coma-heavy.

He didn't know where he was.

***

Later that early morning, after half his early-morning routine was completed, and after drinking at least half of his first cup of coffee, he'd then shrug off the imbalance to realize that waking up in such a way impossibly meant only one thing: he finally got a good night's sleep.

CHAPTER TEN

Friday.

I go through the daily work-week routine in the morning, including breakfast and Tivoli-walking, and have to fight the urge to talk almost constantly to, not with, Jenny, with the coffee lubricating and augmenting the inner re-set button activated overnight.

Forcibly deviating from my rotation-based work dress of whatever-comes-up-next clothing-item-matching compulsion, I put together a uniform that enhances my already bubbling cauldron of self-confidence. At least, based on what I interpret from the mirrors at home under substandard bathroom and bedroom lighting. Delusional about my looks or not, I have no self-consciousness today…

I drive to work, going through time and space in my car: the starlight matter of the entire universe shoots into and through my eyes, my brain, my warm chest, and my newfound, emerging embryology as the stereo compact disc player abandons swirling, swarming music in favor of a deafening shower-scream roar of sound of a monstrous laundromat wash-cycle black hole, in an expansive cosmos of eternal being. I forgot what it was like to be human, I forgot what it was like to be ready for anything.

Here I come, here I come, here-I-come…

I exchange have-a-good-weekends with Walter outside the garage; I small-talk and gossip with Janice upon office arrival; I trade weekend plans when Sherry arrives; I return Briana's good-morning as she bustles past me, in my office, like a freight-train; I exchange "It's Friday" pleasantries with a few other co-workers throughout my morning orientation; and, there's no diamond-lit voicemail message in my office desk telephone to process and/or return. All my focus can now be on reviewing and practicing for 1:30 p.m. at Louisville Metro Hall, room 101, today, September 4, 2015.

Last-minute-logistic e-mails go back and forth between me and representatives of other city government departments for finalized plans for the Mayor's Disability Forum: from the Office of Aging & Disabled Citizens, to Louisville Metro Parks & Recreation, to community-beloved Louisville Metro Public Works. I play my office desktop computer keyboard like a piano as I work to quell the collective nervousness of the rest of the group's final itinerary for the hour-and-a-half afternoon schedule.

Around 11:00 a.m., I reluctantly decide to walk around to Brenda's office at the end of the west wing to see if we'll have the uneasy conversation, on both ends, of agreeing to carpool together over to Metro Hall; or, if we can both delicately find that way around ridesharing in making it a team effort to *not* make it a team effort this afternoon. Zooming fast-forward towards her office, I see her door open and the light on, and I hear a public radio show host speaking clearly as I end my quick descent. I knock on her office door frame.

"Hey, Brenda…?" I project into her office, from the outside. Stepping in with one foot, my head peering in around the door frame almost concurrently with my address, I see that she's on her office desk telephone. She raises her eyes towards me while holding the receiver with a hand over the mouthpiece, not speaking, and I mouth "*Sorry*" while putting my left hand palm up to her before scooting outside the office door to wait while doing an "*Oops!*" face.

The next office over to my left, and where I decide I'll wait, is Roberta's: she's there sitting with her right hand on her desktop computer mouse and is looking at the computer screen…no radio noise.

"Hey Roberta," I say to kill some time, keeping an ear out for the plastic office phone receiver hang-up to my right.

"*Hey*, Alex," Roberta smiles, turning to me. "Whatcha got goin' on today?"

"Nuthin', just waiting for," nod-head and eye-roll to my right.

"Got any plans for the weekend?"

"No…no, not really, just chores and rest. This week has been rough. It *may* be rougher, depending on how nuclear I go this afternoon at the Mayor's Disability Forum…"

"Oh that's right, is that today?" Roberta perks up in her seat.

"*Yeaaaaah…*" I say half-sarcastically.

I then hear the click of the telephone receiver.

"Oops, Roberta, hold on--" I say in cutting things short, not giving her a chance to respond.

Knock-knock.

"Brenda…?"

Brenda's somehow already gotten back on the telephone. I visibly wince without her looking at me, and I decide to abandon the likely cat-

and-mouse futility in trying to speak with her and just hit my next stop. I retreat again, back to Roberta's office.

"Sorry, Roberta, I gotta go check in with Agnes about all this, talk to you later on…?"

"Oh--oh, yeah, okay (!), sure, no problem," Roberta says in a corporately-trained conclusion response to our quick conversation.

I walk like a laser-beam back along the west wing towards Agnes' office, where she sits in her office chair, two computer monitors actively facing her, but with her looking down at her smartphone. I announce my arrival with her name well in advance in order to act like I don't notice that she's on her phone, and also to stick to the professional framework reasons for stopping by. "Agnes," I say again, "hey, are you going to the Mayor's Disability Forum this afternoon?"

Looking up and putting her smartphone away in one stroke with her left hand relatively-discreetly, she says politely to me that no, "Brenda's going, she said…"

"Okay," I continue. "I just wanted to see who and what to expect, I have intake scheduled for the afternoon later on, and I just wanted to see if I needed to change my lunch hour at all…"

"No," Agnes reacts sharply in changing her tone. "We've all covered that, you should be fine."

"Okay, just checking…I'll just walk on over to Metro Hall on my own, I'll see Brenda over there, I guess."

"All right, okie-doke," Agnes confirms with almost disregard.

Since we both agree that this is not, and won't be, a social visit, I move on out of Agnes' office and around the front receptionist desk, unstaffed with Friday social abandonment in favor of Sherry's office hosting applicable staff conversation. Since the Mayoral administrative staff here at the Civil Relations Commission is a dead end on any prior instruction or logistical planning for my being out of the office this afternoon, as always, I just study a few presentation points; triple-check my disability-accessible (read: large print only) Commission brochures and annual reports; and, try not to talk anymore in order to save my voice for the verbal delivery. And, to be ready for the more-valuable question, answer, and concerns portion of the Disability Forum. And, for anything else I might initiate at the event…

The morning has flown by. Time for lunch already, which instead of a plastic burrito and sides today is a frozen microwave meat pasta dish, and, only three-quarters of a refilled crinkly plastic water bottle in order to try to *not* need to use a restroom at the assembly. I eat quicker than I normally do, incapable of giving myself the normal allotted lunch-hour time that's afforded by office policy, and in considering it only takes fifteen minutes with inconceivable heavy traffic to walk down to Louisville Metro Hall, room 101, a half-mile away. The anticipation of my presentation and last night's rest propel me through the restroom routine of cleaning myself up, posting my Louisville Metro Government identification badge on my dress-shirt breast, and preparing my black work bag with all the essentials of documents, cough drops, and the empty crinkly plastic water bottle for-the-ready.

Out the door with sunglasses on after the sign-out sheet I prepared upon arrival this morning, I ignore the elevator traffic, pedestrian traffic, vehicle traffic, and heat and humidity as I walk confidently northbound, intoxicated with a slight smile rolling my eyes almost into the back of my head, four-and-a-half long city blocks to the back entrance of Metro Hall. The building today is a colosseum for potential altercation with every departmental director I have grievances against, including because it houses the Louisville Metro Human Resources' Mayoral-drenched impediment to my career with city government. *What a grand location, a beacon of light for the public*, I think with petty snarkiness when looking to approach the security doors at the back.

Maybe not so confidently, I've checked my cellular telephone four-and-a-half times on the way over to check on the time.

Ahead of me near city hall are two Transit Authority paratransit buses, one of which is unloading with a male who uses a motorized wheelchair while a female behind him looks like she's holding onto the open door frames from the inside for dear life. Some persons dressed in professional gear walk the sidewalks around Louisville Metro Hall quickly with important business, while others dressed in professional gear walk in groups slowly with important casual-Friday business. Dressed-down people also walk around nearby, and some of them are looking around lost, others slowly walking confidently as if they've been downtown many, many times before, such as to the courthouse across West Jefferson Street.

It's 1:05 p.m.

I pause near the back entrance to allow a paratransit bus driver ahead of me to arm-escort a person with a likely vision impairment into one of the double-doors. I see that there might not be enough clearance space in the right door of the double-doors that the TA driver holds open with one hand, so I launch over into pulling open the left double-door with an eye to not have it open outward in a way to hit the arm-locked duo. I grimace with a polite, not-intended-to-be-sarcastic smirk as the two slowly go through the entry. They both then stop at the security scanning station immediately in front of the double-doors inside. I release the left double-door in favor of holding open the right door after they get inside, keeping it open with my right foot as the two ahead get processed by two security guards in the limited lobby entry space.

The person with the vision impairment slowly but effortlessly removes a wallet and a smartphone from his pants pocket, with the Transit Authority driver and the pre-scan security guard competing for assistance in placing the items in a small, round, plastic bowl. Slowly shuffling through the security full body scanner, which goes off upon TA driver entry assistance to the person with limited vision but with a wave-through of disregard by the guard standing behind it, the two then retrieve the items from the bowl while I say "Morning" and then "I-mean, afternoon" to the outer guard.

The guard, humorless, asks for an identification despite my Louisville Metro Government name badge posted clearly on my chest. I dig out my wallet and remove my city government plastic ID card, which has a picture of me laughing with shoulders hunched up since Janice and Sherry were with me that day at the photo shoot, cat-calling at me. The guard responds upon review that I didn't need to go through the security station and could've gone around the full body scanner to the left, since I was with Metro. *I'll remember that…thanks (!).*

After I quip to the outer guard that I just wanted to follow procedures, I briefly straighten myself up and go around to the left instead of going into the full body scanner. I'm paranoid that the second, interior guard will shout "Hey, wait…!" as I dart towards the building center foyer, so I grimace with raised eyebrows to him but try to convey no sarcasm. He doesn't notice me, anyways, instead looking straight ahead of him to check out the male in a motorized wheelchair who's now at the outer security scan treadmill with the first guard. I move on, trying to look professional to guards who aren't looking at me, and I check the cellphone time: it's 1:09 p.m.

At the circular foyer, the center of the pinwheel-designed building, I stop in my tracks trying to assess which corridor to go down in order to reach room 101. I've been here half a dozen times before, but I'll never remember, for whatever reason, that it's off to the 90-degree right hallway. After looking diagonally-left, then straight ahead, a quizzical look on my face, I just go ahead and instinctively walk straight-ahead. I see that to the left, towards the inexplicably-always-locked front entrance of the Hall, is where notarization applications are sworn; marriage licenses are issued; and, city government business is conducted where I *don't* want to be. I convulse to a stop and then turn back towards the way I came, now trying a left turn down the closest hallway. I see large doors open at a room down near the end of the hall on the right side, so, a little cautious and tentative in my sprint, I gain hope hearing a few voices. I think that's it.

In slower and slower cinematic motion in my head upon the approach, I walk almost head-first into the bright, large expanse of room 101 with an internal driving force and a slight deep breath. I see the face of Louisville Metro Parks & Recreation's Recreation division, Jamie French, walking around a series of plastic folding tables she, by herself, likely set up in a horseshoe U-shape to cordon-off half the room; the other half of the room has three rows of mediocre-grade plastic chairs, with three patient guests already seated including the Disability Action Network's Lester Bishop & Phoebe Carter, and two stacks of chairs along the back wall for overflow-reinforcement. Sufficient space is set up between the chair placement to accommodate navigation by persons with limited vision, persons using wheelchairs, and other strategic accessibility organization, all also likely arranged-for by Jamie. In the center of the inverse, mechanical U-shape of the table set-up is a laptop computer resting on a small black wheeled cart, facing a screened wall. Off to the immediate left inside of the room is Claudia Marks, Jamie's Administrative Assistant, who sits at-the-ready for attendee sign-in.

"Hey, Jamie…" I say while looking to claim my spot around the sorta-roundtable, also gauging for easiest-access pathway to approach the head of the class during my presentation.

"Well, *hey* there, Alex, how are ya?" Jamie stops.

"I'm alright, I'm-here…" I say brightly with a little sarcasm, walking around to the back-end row of seats at the U-tables to seat myself with a view to face who enters and exits the room.

"Good…you ready to lead this meeting?"

"*Gawd*, I hope not--er, I *could*, I guess, sure, why not…" I say, misunderstanding her joking wit at first but then going into the sarcasm.

"Aw, you'll do fine…you seen Janet yet?"

"No…No, not yet," checking my cellphone, 1:12 p.m.

"Okay. Well, Shonda is on her way, the Mayor is still supposed to be here…I haven't heard from--oh well look, there he is, Nate…Nate… *hello*, Nate…?"

Nathan Blair, Louisville Metro Public Works, analytically and efficiently has gone over to sign in with Claudia, focused on his signature and with carrying a functional and almost-stylish briefcase that's likely full of portable electronic media. After signing in, he doesn't thank Claudia but responds to Jamie in time.

"Okay, hey Jamie," he says, looking for, then grabbing, a chair to bring over to the laptop computer on the black media cart facing the wall-screen.

"We know *you're* ready, Nate…" Jamie teases.

"Now, hold *on*, Jamie, I haven't even got my presentation up on the screen here yet…you may wanna see what I have for ya up on the screen before you approve of everything," Nate banters, sitting and scooting the chair close to the computer cart while looking it up and down.

I again look at my cellphone: 1:14 p.m.

In walk the Transit Authority driver and the woman with the vision impairment I saw outside on my way in, followed by the Assistant Director of Louisville Metro Human Resources who I've seen at a meeting or two previously but can't remember her name. Claudia wrangles all three immediately to go over to her to sign in, then two more folks show up thinking they'll be seated before being stopped in their tracks, too, for Metro sign-in and tracking: another woman who I've seen before, a brain injury survivor advocate; and, a guy who I think works for the Commonwealth of Kentucky Cabinet for Health & Family Services.

The Disability Action Network's Jonathan Earl then wheels in; followed by the Director of the Transit Authority walking in, Thad Wethington; a Louisville Metro Police Department officer, who I don't know, walks in almost invisibly despite her uniform; the Director of Louisville Metro Inspections, Permits & Licenses, Ted Nicholson, amicably shuffles his feet into the room; Matt Whitworth, Louisville Independent Living, zooms in with his director, Margaret Zoeller; then, after a pause in the action, Trisha Evans of Independent Living wheels in separately from Matt and Margaret, giving me the same sense of familiarity-breeds-contempt relationship I have with the Louisville Metro Government mayoral administration since she is staying away from her co-workers too.

And, speaking of which, in walks Shonda Heyward, Deputy Mayor, smartphone guarding her wildly-animated eyes and sharp demeanor. Exuding confidence and no nonsense, she concludes her telephone call with a drop of the hand and immediately smiles a verbal greeting to those Louisville Metro Government and associated-Metro agency Directors already present. She exudes to any layperson in the public the image of the Mayor's workhorse and top henchwoman.

Jamie's familiarity instructs Shonda, instead of the-other-way-around, however.

"Shonda, sign in's over there…" she says to her like a teacher, still walking around the room.

"Yes, okay, we all have to sign in, Mayor's open data sets, I know…" Shonda jokes professionally while immediately going over to Claudia.

Shonda doesn't look at me. Maybe *hasn't* looked at me, but probably *doesn't* look at me.

My self-confidence has dropped a hair, as reluctant as it is for me to admit…I look at Shonda's wiley eyes and respect her almost impossible confidence that's mixed with instant judgment and reaction towards people. But I do forcibly toughen-up to be ready.

Another look at my cellphone and it's 1:27 p.m.

Finally, Janet Radcliffe, the one-person Louisville Metro Office of Aging & Disabled Citizens, enters slowly with two large bags, one in each hand, dropped to each of her sides. I walk over quickly from my seat to Lester & Jonathan, who are now sitting front-back to each other in rows, and I say hi, then also tack on a quick greeting to Phoebe, which they all reciprocate in appreciation of acknowledgment. On my way back to my seat, I see that Janet's off towards a corner seat near the closed back section of the U-shaped tables, near the wall screen opposite my side, but still standing with her armed bags at her side. She's frozen, and she looks mortified and like she's about to have a panic attack in her distress.

Instead of sitting, I walk over to her.

"Janet…hey, you *okay*…?" I ask, looking at her still standing there.

Janet breathes heavily, standing while encumbered. "I'm…I'm… yes, I'm fine…"

I can't tell if she's really okay or not, but I'm guessing that she's arrived later than she wanted to. That, on top of the anecdotal word I've heard from others in Metro Government that Shonda, as her boss, has ripped into her on occasion. It's getting the better of her.

"You *sure*, Janet…!?" I say with sincere concern, since she's one of the few departmental director supports I have here with Metro.

"Uh…yes. Yes, Alex, I'm fine," she says, holding back the slightest sob breakdown.

Shonda's now made her way to where she was going to sit upon arrival, one chair over from Janet, to whom she grants a quiet hello, just over to where my facing left of where the Mayor will likely sit at the head of the inverse-U tables near the wall-screen.

"Okay, everyone," Shonda says in authoritative announcement. "It's just about 1:30, and I've received word that the Mayor is running late, he will *be* here, though. Let's just wait two more minutes for the rest of our folks to arrive, and be seated, and then we can begin with presentations. Jamie, is that okay, are your folks ready? Janet?"

Jamie says without hesitation but amicably, "Yep, that sounds good."

Janet hesitates. "Um, yes…yes, that would be fine," shuffling her belongings to a chair now away from Shonda, more near me on my side of the tabled U at a corner.

Assistant Director of Louisville Metro Public Works' Susan Cunningham then walks in, as does Brenda, my Director, Louisville. Metro. Civil. Relations. Commission. The two are talking to each other upon entry before quickly seeing that the attention should go to their boss, Shonda, so they diverge to her in ignoring, or being unaware, that Claudia beckons for sign-in. I intentionally ignore all three while the trio converses about likely non-Mayor's-Disability-Forum business. At the break in their huddle, Brenda says ambiguously "Hey, Alex" in formality as she and Susan walk around to sit next to Transit Authority Director Wethington, without meeting with Claudia. I remain eternally grateful that Brenda telepathically took from our meeting this morning that we should sit separately at the Forum.

I check in with Nate at his laptop wall-screen presentation control panel.

"Okay, Mr. Public Works, I've decided that I'm not gonna do an electronic presentation today, so after Jamie gets done with your all's presentation, I'll just stand up and go into the civil rights stuff…"

Squinting at the laptop computer screen with a chuck-jaw, Nate responds, "All righty Alex, sounds good. Let me know if you change your mind, and I can move along the slides on the screen for you, if you like."

"No, that's okay, man, thanks," I graciously reinforce.

A few more professionally-dressed persons arrive for the audience seats and the roundtabled U, including one who sits next to Shonda like another Mayor's administration heavyweight. And then one or two more people quickly slide into the room.

Shonda, also known as the Mayor's Disability Forum 2015, will now begin.

"*Alright everyone*, we're going to go ahead and be*gin*, we want to talk today about what Metro Government is doing to address those issues facing people in the disability community here *in* Louisville Metro, and we have here today directors and Metro department staff to give presentations; provide you all information; answer questions from you, the audience; and, see what we're *currently* doing as a government, and maybe even what we can do better. This is the Mayor's Disability Forum, and the Mayor *will* be here, but I've been informed that he is running a bit late. We do have a full schedule for you all here today, so let's go ahead and start presentations from those departments at the table here--"

"Well, Shonda," Jamie jumps in. "Maybe, we could do some--"

"*Yes*, Jamie, you're right…Let's go around the table here and give introductions, so that everyone in the audience can get an idea of who's here from Metro. And, audience: if you could please hold your questions and comments until the end of the presentation, we *promise* there'll be time for you to give your thoughts, ask *your* questions, give *your* ideas, as stakeholders in the community…I'll begin, I'm Shonda Heyward, the Mayor's Chief of Community Building…"

Shonda then firmly gestures her head and fights the sarcastic smile to get Janet to lead us subordinates by going around the tables to Shonda's right.

"Um, yes. Janet Radcliffe, Office for Aging & Disabled Citizens…" she says to the table and the audience, succinctly bridging any communicative gap between the narcissists at the roundtable and the unsuspecting passive audience, as a professional social worker.

"…Jamie French, Louisville Metro Parks & Recreation…"

Slight nerves. Longer pause than I thought I'd make.

"…Alex, Calderon, Investigator, the Louisville Metro Civil Relations Commission…" I annunciate to the table and the crowd, giving the quickest looks to Shonda; to a stranger or two across the table; and, to the crowd members off to my far right, all in one periscope motion from left-to-right.

I see Shonda lean over to the unidentified Mayor's administration person seated next to her, Shonda's eyes looking up into the air whispering to her side, "*That's who was…*" I miss the rest of the sentence, but I have my suspicions on what's being said.

"…Shane McCord, Planning & Design Coordinator, Develop Louisville…"

"…Brenda McCoy, Director, Louisville Civil Relations--and not *McCord*," she quips, to a few small polite laughs.

"Hi everyone, Susan Cunningham, Public Works…"

Identifying with his finger along the previous line, "McCord, McCoy, Cunningham…Wethington! I'm Thad Wethington, Transit Authority…"

And on and around the tables, until the last bureaucrat, to the left of Shonda, identifies herself as Jo Niederhauser of Louisville Forward--also known as Mayor's Think Tank Department of Federal Grant Money Pass-Through to Private Sector. Department.

"Okay, now, the audience--well, let's wait on audience introductions," Shonda reins. "If folks could identify yourselves when you ask a question later or make a comment, we want to be sure to have time for our presentations and for the Mayor, who, like I said, is on his way…So: who's our first presentation," Shonda scans around the tables very quickly, ready to judge. "Jamie, who's first…"

"Janet," Jamie says, "she's first-up today…"

"Yes, uh-huh," Janet stands, looking towards the room's large door entryway. "Okay. If we could get the lights, please…?"

Claudia gets up from her sign-in station and flips the wall light switches on the side nearest her, a seamless continuation for Janet to begin. All lights now out in the room, Janet prompts by nod to Nate, who doesn't need prompting, since his electronic presentation for Janet has been at-the-ready in front of him in the middle of the U-shaped tables since before introductions, before Janet even arrived here.

"Oh, Nate, we didn't get you introduced, did we," Shonda announces.

"No, that's okay, I'm running the IT Department here," he says, turning his head to his right to address Shonda before then crookedly to his left trying to address everyone else. "Nathan Blair, Public Works... Master Control Panel..."

After one or two polite chuckles, including from Janet, who latches onto the lighter side of the Forum after her stressful arrival, she begins after Shonda looks at her with a silently-sharp look commanding such.

"Okay...hello, everyone...? I want to talk this afternoon about what I know is a problem near, and dear, to the hearts of many of you, especially you in the audience: the problem of our roads and our sidewalks, and how we have parts of town that...well...doggone it, just aren't quite *up to snuff* when it comes to being accessible for persons who are disabled. I think I speak for a lot of us here in Metro Government when I say that we don't have the budget, the staff, and the resources sometimes to fix all the roads, all the sidewalks in town, at a moment's notice, but...*we hear you*," she slightly laughs in leaning in. "We hear you, and the good news is that we *have* addressed some of the trouble-spots. Many of you all have called my office to report barriers, and issues, around the city, and we've worked with Public Works here to try to get things fixed, get the problems cleared up, and what-have-you. One of the great things that we've been doing this fiscal year is that our office received a grant from the RTC last year, to be in--excuse me, the Ronald T. Comer Foundation--they gave us a $10,000 grant, one of only ten given out around the country to make cities more accessible, and Louisville was chosen as one of the ten to get one. So far, we've done some neat things with the grant, like identify those trouble-spots that weren't necessarily on our radar before, and were brought to our attention by you, the public. So, here on the screen, we have some of those trouble-spots of inaccessibility..."

Janet continues, looking at the screen and then at Nate. Nate nods his approval and already-readiness.

"Here we have our good friend, Dixie Highway," she smiles, "where the sidewalk, contrary to popular belief, *does* end: as you can see, right there, *into* the grass..."

While a few chuckles and headshakes go in Janet's favor, I get lost in my thoughts of what I'm to say in my presentation, since I'm scheduled to be next. I think about the Civil Relations Commission general function briefly as an outline, but now I'm more concerned on how I'll come across with my conveyance of governmental, systemic dysfunction; the Commission's theoretical Departmental impartiality delicate-dance, paradoxically with advocacy for the general, public interest; and, explaining how a civil rights complaint can be filed against the private market or, more insidiously on my part, the public sector, such as a municipal government. I want my audience to be not just the public attendees today, but the surrounding Metro Government agencies. I'm nervous circling my wagon of one.

Janet goes on.

"And here--here is a photo, taken by you, the public, of a large, large bush, hanging over the sidewalk, blocking a person in a wheelchair from walking down the street…"

I'm getting a little more nervous, to say the least, than when I was walking over here from the office. I go through the typical overanalyzing my presentation format and content, thinking about how I'm interviewing for my own job out here, even if to a limited extent. Or maybe to a large extent, again considering the formal complaints I've made to the feds, and are still hopefully investigating Metro Government, though who knows. I'm certainly no darling to some key people sitting at these tables, and to a key person allegedly on his way to the Forum.

Janet still goes on, and she's a little inflammatory to Public Works… though Nate, with his engineering background, his engineering mind, and his engineering job function, appears to take no personal offense to the calls for public service Janet implies is needed from his department. Assistant Public Works Director Cunningham, sitting next to my Director a few spaces down to my right, might feel a little differently, of course.

Shonda, looking mostly at her smartphone screen and scrolling with her fingers during Janet's explanation, now decides that Janet's time is about at an end. Shonda scrolls Janet out of the picture, literally circling her finger in the air, to move things along.

"Okay," Janet says, regrouping, "and that's…that's what we've been doing. Time's up, I'm told. So, again, *we have you on our radar*, we assure you! And, we have more from Metro today…"

"Thanks, Janet," Shonda bridges succinctly. "Okay, we're still gonna hold questions, and go on with the next presentation, unless Public Works--Susan? Do you have anything you want to add to Janet's presentation--well, actually, before that, Susan: let me remind, everyone, that the Metro Council also has a role to play with this. The Mayor is committed to accessibility for all of us, and that includes working with Metro Councilmembers with their discretionary funds to fill the gaps in budget that might be an issue with the general fund appropriation for Metro Government departments. These kinds of initiatives by the Mayor may not make the headlines, but the bottom line is, at the end of the day, we want to work with the Council to also fulfill the needs for people with disabilities, and work with community groups, so that there's a multi-layered attack on getting the job done, and moving forward with some of the kinds of things Janet referred to in her presentation."

Claudia has creeped up from sign-in and kicks on the room lights.

"Yes," Susan adds, "and we have as part of our--sorry, Susan Cunningham, Public Works--we have as part of our Americans with Disabilities Act Transition Plan our analyses of data, action steps, and regulatory mandates from the Department of Transportation to look at sidewalks, curb cuts, roadways, and other areas where Public Works can, and should, get involved. Nate here can probably go into this better than I could, as our resident expert for Public Works' ADA Transition Plan, but we also have Brenda's group," she gestures to her side, "and, we've been in talks recently to try to smooth out those regulatory barriers once we identify from the public what's an ongoing problem, when it comes to the disabled. We want to get the word out that people should go ahead and *call* MetroCall, report the pothole, report the broken sidewalk, report the trees and the grass being overgrown, and Public Works will then address it. The Mayor has instituted in his Strategic Planning some mandated tracking systems for these calls from the public for service, and we have to be accountable to get the job done…"

Shonda gestures with her head "*Yes, next*" to Brenda.

"Yes," Brenda says authoritatively in standing. "My staff, has worked--sorry, Brenda McCoy, Civil Relations--my office has met with members of the Disability Action Network over the past few years to discuss this, as well. Alex here goes to their meetings every month, and he reports back on what needs are there in the disabled community. With Susan, here, and the Civil Relations Supervisor, Agnes Britton, and myself, we've discussed things with the Network, and worked to address those regulatory problems and issues that Susan talked about--I see Lester and Jonathan over there in the audience, we've all talked formally about what can be done better. I also have a list of things here that the Civil Relations Commission has done over the past year to address issues facing the disability community…"

With that, Brenda takes out a folded up piece of paper, creating a pause that goes on a second too long as she prepares herself to read through her list. I wonder how the Forum agenda will continue, and if it'll even include my presentation at all, at this point, since the Mayor's still on his way, as well. There's a little bit more frustration, a little bit more high-strungedness, and a little bit more insecurity for me since my planned address might be getting derailed.

Reading carefully and dryly, Brenda begins.

"…'In 2014-15, Fiscal Year, the Civil Relations Commission had the following cases filed: Twenty cases based on, disability in employment… eighteen, cases based on disability in housing…three cases based on disability in public, accommodations…and two, in hate crimes. The Commission had…the following cases closed, with a No Probable Cause finding: Eleven cases in employment…twelve housing…no public accommodations, and three hate crimes. The Commission had, the following cases closed with a finding of Probable Cause: No cases in employment, two cases in housing…no cases in public accommodations, and no hate crimes. In the two, closed housing cases, the cases are currently in litigation over at the County Attorney's Office.' " Brenda pauses. " 'The Commission had…five, conciliation agreements, for cases based on disability, during the fiscal year. No cases were, conciliated in employment…five of the cases were in housing…no cases were public accommodations…and zero hate crimes. In the five housing cases, the Complainants received affirmative…relief: Three of them Commissioner complaints, affording relief for the general public, and two… Complainants from the public, who received personal relief, themselves'…"

Shonda's still on her smartphone until she quickly and suddenly gets up from her seat, and she swirls her right hand around in the air to indicate "*continue on*" while she walks towards the front room entryway and then on out the room door.

Brenda continues her slow reading while not noticing Shonda leave the room.

"…'Members of the Civil Relations Commission, Public Works, and the Disability Action Network, had quarterly meetings during the fiscal year to discuss, what can be done, to address the following: Calls to MetroCall, and Public Works, not being addressed. Sidewalks in Louisville, are not usable by persons in wheelchairs…people with limited vision, cannot navigate unmaintained, sidewalks, and crosswalks. Training for Public Works service call and response staff, is needed…it was suggested, that Independent Living, do training for staff. The Civil Relations Commission will continue, to host, meetings, and encourage Public Works, and the Disability Action Network, to continue to work together to make problems known, and address the issues affecting the disability, community--' "

Shonda then quickly re-enters the room, walks over to and leans over to speak in Jo Niederhauser's ear, then places her smartphone down on the table as she takes her seat, not looking at Brenda.

" '…Civil Relations staff will continue to attend--' "

A large male with a sharp, not-necessarily-distinctly-modern suit then walks into to the room and stands off to the left side of the large doorway, looking straight ahead at no one with chin up and hands folded in front of him in exuding his silent, reactive will to the room. He is not, but could or should be, wearing sunglasses. A business-dressed woman then enter the room, speaking to someone behind her.

" '--on our Advocacy Board, members can talk about disabilities issues…' "

A conservatively-suited, average-sized male, with a barely-oversized silver belt buckle, then walks into the entryway with a slight strut, a complete bliss, and, a half-listening attention to the professional female who just entered. More imposing than his somewhat-slight frame might typically yield, he passively-listens to the female escort as his eyes are wide into the room, not looking at anyone in particular but using peripheral vision to compensate for a lack of standard visible visibility. He then scans to his right, seeing Shonda and co-hort Niederhauser, where his eyes go up in unspoken recognition that he is, in fact, in the right place. All eyes in the room, including from a paused Brenda, are to the man who's currently being led to his position to the empty chair to the right of Shonda, who now stands, and assists, with a directional open-palmed hand gesture to the table seat.

The man looks to his left, and then further back to his left, mouthing near-silent hellos and heys to a few seated around the tables rapidly and efficiently before looking back and seeing Brenda, then raising his eyebrows with politeness. He shuffles on to his reserved seat with a more-grinning demeanor than upon his immediate entry. He does not see me, or, he does not visibly reveal such, in his short quest for his place at the Forum despite my natural, pre-selected line of view. Sitting at the head of the U-shaped table set-up, Shonda slides him a few papers and leans over to speak in his ear. He nods briefly with professional approval to Shonda while Brenda concludes her information.

" '…Fiscal Year 2015-16.'…So, we welcome questions later, as Ms. Heyward said before. Thank you." Brenda stiffly puts her once-folded piece of paper down onto the table to signal the end, and Shonda again drives the train as Brenda seats herself.

"Okay-thank-you-Brenda," Shonda projects loudly. "*Okay everyone*, we want to *now* go ahead and welcome…a very special guest this afternoon…!"

"Justice Delayed is Justice Denied!"

***

"What Do We Want? Justice! When Do We Want It? Now!"

***

"Open Housing Now!"

"Not In My Back Yard!"

***

"Black Lives Matter!"

"Blue Lives Matter!"

"All Lives Matter!"

"White Silence Is White Consent!"

"White Privilege Is White Achievement!"

"Soy Chicano!"

"U.S.-Occupied Hawaii!"

"My Existence = Your Subsistence!"

"Columbus Was an Illegal Alien!"

***

"Immigrants Yes, Illegals No!"

"No One Is Illegal!"

"Secure the Borders!"

"We Didn't Cross the Border, the Border Crossed Us!"

"I Don't Have a Chinaman's Chance!"

***

"Stand Up for Religious Freedom!"

"Freedom of Religion is Not Freedom to Discriminate!"

***

"Keep Your Rosaries Off My Ovaries!"

"Keep Amy Out of Army!"

***

"Head Start is the Best Start!"

"Don't Mess with the Old People!"

***

"First Class Autistic, Second Class Citizen!"

"12 Steps to Ruining Neighborhoods!"

"Our Homes, Not Nursing Homes!"

***

"Out of the Closets & Into the Streets!"

"God Loves Homosexuals, Not Homosexuality!"

***

"Love Has No Gender!"

"A Moral Wrong Cannot Be a Civil Right!"

"Trans Parent!"

***

"I'm With the Government & I'm Here to Help!"

"No Government Can Ever Give You Freedom!"

***

Effective Government Matters.

Value Systems Matter.

Civil Disobedience or Criminal Disobedience?

CHAPTER ELEVEN

"Well, hello…"

Mayor Stephen Hoch stands, speaks dryly and slowly, looking out ahead, walking over slowly through a break in the back of the roundtable U-shape to the center of the room where Nate's backed-out his control console like a theatre technician.

The Mayor does not look at me, he does not look at anyone in particular, before continuing his stance.

He continues slowly, and sounding almost as if he has a cold.

"Thank you all for being here today, especially my colleagues here with Metro…I see here today Brenda, Thad…hello," he says, turning back to the left, "Shonda, Jo…But, again, thank you *all* here today, citizens of Metro. We're in an exciting time here right now. It's become a new era for Louisville, or what we now call 'Louisville Metro,' of course, which is fitting since it's not the same city, not the same Louisville, that we've known the past several years. It's not the same city *I* grew up in, as I'm sure it's not the same city you all, most of us, grew up in. What we have here today is a city on the move, a progress, a renewed spirit of entrepreneurship, a 're-boot,' as our young people say, to give the city a presence that, quite frankly, it hasn't had in some respects for decades, when we look at the world, our competitor cities out there…What we're actually *becoming* now, is the Louisville of Tomorrow, not just putting slogans in place, saying, with hope, that we're the Louisville of some future that hasn't arrived yet. Louisville is now on the world scene. We've always had the Kentucky Derby, we've always had some industry here in Louisville, but now Louisville, itself, Louisville *Metro*, is becoming a *brand*, and a lot of these local institutions that we all grew up with are changing along with us, continuing to lead us into the 21st Century. There's a new excitement to the city scene that my administration is proud to be a part of, leading the way, leading the charge, and--heck, even before going any further, let me say that it's also not just confined to the city limits. Our partner cities in the Metro area have been key to some of this growth, this progression, making this area a regional hub for setting trends locally, throughout the Commonwealth, and nationally, internationally…you know, parts of our area, from the south parts of Jefferson County to cities across the Ohio River, they've complained for years that they haven't been brought to the table with Louisville, that they've had little say, or no voice, in how we continue to transform our city and our area into a major destination for business, a major destination for our new citizens…just this morning I was down in Valley Station, and as I'm sure many of you know, a few of our residents down there have been vocal and active about how they feel, that this area is underserved by Louisville Metro when it comes to a variety of things, from perceived lack of service from our local government, to advocacy for business relocation down there…my administration is committed to working with *all* stakeholders in the Commonwealth, across the River, and from anywhere else, but especially in those areas that don't feel like they're given a fair opportunity to make their areas succeed. In Valley Station this morning, we dedicated a new craft beer company, Ohio Bend, started by some of our younger prospective industrialists here in town, a few college friends from our own Bellarmine University here. These young folks used state tax credits through programs we started here in Louisville Metro to streamline the process, cut through the red tape, get their small businesses *going*, and my administration's creation of Develop Louisville was specifically designed to help these businesses get started, find that path of least resistance, in the public-private partnership. Ohio Bend is also using a small business loan to rehabilitate an old, 100-year-old warehouse for their headquarters here, so, sustainability, and historic preservation, both get utilized in additional programs administered by the city, with little impact to the taxpayers in continuing to grow our local economy here…"

Adjusting his stance, Mayor Hoch puts both his hands onto his belt: thumbs across the top of the silver belt buckle, other fingers clutching up underneath the belt itself.

"…And this is just one example of how we're competing in the 21st Century, with new industry, and not just with the traditional things we're known for here in Louisville. But that doesn't mean, of course, that we're not supporting and expanding those institutions we've had here for decades. There's a continued international push and presence for our own Bourbon Tourism, as you all know, and this includes expansion to the Bourbon Network throughout Louisville and our surrounding cities and counties. We're working with the Louisville Metro Tourism Bureau to attract more conventions to the city, and retain those ones we've had here regularly for years. And, we continue to work with the Bureau and developers, nationally and internationally, to expand our hospitality industry. You know, we have five new high-rise hotels built here within my first term as Mayor, and we currently have a plan, and are in talks for, another half-dozen to be constructed, not just here downtown, but one in the East End, one in the South End…major players in the international hotel scene. And not just the standard box-cut highrise design you might expect with these things, I might add: unique architectural designs planned, with world-class features, by renowned architectural design firms, including one from right here in town, with green design, and sustainability, that's more environmentally-friendly with more trees throughout the property, renewable sources of energy, things like that, all those cutting-edge elements incorporated into the working function of the building…"

Mayor Hoch shifts his stance again during the pause.

"Lots of excitement, lots of *challenges*, ahead, for this second term of my administration. But, as you can see here, with your representative departments here today, we're committed to open government, to give you all a voice, to give you all a seat at the table, and a review of what we do as a Metro Government. I'm proud to work with all of you here, the Metro Council, Governor Mercer, *and* the President, as we continue to transform Louisville Metro into the best city government in the nation, and also into the world class city those of us who've lived here forever have already known it is…so…let's get to work!"

With the attendee applause, mine reluctantly included, I uncontrollably smirk my entire face in sarcasm.

"I'm building a phallic highrise hotel skyscraper in downtown Louisville at the expense of the taxpayers, and that'll be my legacy!" is pretty much all I heard from the Mayor in my overawe. *That, and a request to "put a bottle of bourbon between my legs."*

Looking back to Shonda, who animates her face while mouthing something I can't quite make out while not clapping, the Mayor walks back with his chin up, his own muted smirk indicating that he's dealt with crowds more important than this, back to where he sat before. The two then lean in quickly to each other to bullet-point in review as the applause from most of the crowd, of course me excluded, wraps up. Now I wonder what I'll get to say, if anything. Maybe it's the people's turn to ask questions.

"Thank you, Mayor…!" Shonda projects to everyone while standing from her seat. "Okay, we wanna go ahead and do--I see a hand or two out there up: let's hold off on audience questions, and go ahead with the next Louisville Metro Government department presentation, we heard from Brenda, who's…"

Jamie with the assist. "Shonda, that's Alex, we had him next, I think."

Without pause, the Mayor's hatchet and head coach shoots her eyes at me and nods without smile. "Okay, Alex…?" She then leans over back to the Mayor and they discuss more in confidence.

Okay…The pit of my stomach drops, and I stand at attention for the briefest moment before turning towards those seated in the crowd as my body, not my head, surges with mercurial physiological change and I effectively turn away from the heads of the roundtable.

"Thank you, Shonda, *Mr. Mayor*, *and* Brenda…Okay, hi, everyone, my name is Alex Calderon, and I'm an Investigator with the Louisville Metro Civil Relations Commission…Brenda over here is my boss, and--well, and Shonda, and the Mayor here, are my bosses, as well, as the heads of the elected and appointed Executive Branch of your Louisville Metro Government. We're here today to talk about *disability*. And, *with* that, *accessibility*, and how Louisville Metro Government works to address accessibility for Louisville Metro. We have department heads here, associates here, that need to be accountable for providing good customer service when it comes to reducing barriers for persons with disabilities, and that's why a few of us have worked to 're-boot' the Mayor's Disability Forum from the previous Mayoral administration that created the Forum. Jamie here with Metro Parks, Janet here from the Office for Aging & Disabled Citizens, Nate here with Public Works…we've worked over the past couple of years to get disability issues to the forefront of your Metro Government service response. And we have a few things implemented that hopefully have yielded some real results…"

I shift my stance but don't break the rhythm, which I guess is what I get for actually sleeping a good night's sleep for a change.

"For example, we've created a Disability Referral Portal to streamline those complaints from the public about disability-inaccessibility, sending those inquiries to my department of Metro, the Civil Relations Commission, for vetting and referral, and getting the concern where it needs to go. As many of you know, or might imagine, you can call in a complaint about inaccessibility to a Metro department, or to MetroCall, and the service call request gets bounced around to multiple departments and agencies. So much so that you don't even get a response from the right agency until a month, two months, later, much less a fix to the problem *affecting* a person with a disability. So now, all those calls, all those e-mails, all those complaints, come through us, Civil Relations, which is *your* city civil rights agency. And, we either assist with the filing of a discrimination complaint, such as in housing, employment, public accommodations, or a hate crime, *or*, we refer the complaint on directly, ourselves, to the right agency for assistance. Referrals can go to another Metro department, or a Metro-associated agency, or to state or federal authorities, or to the private market, whatever's appropriate…"

Looking out during a pause, it registers that the crowd may or may not be engaged. Since I've started into a rant, it's welling-up and it's going to continue to steamroll.

"But look: if you leave here today with *one thing*, aside from all the presentation of what Metro is doing, or not doing, just remember that accessibility for persons with disabilities is fundamentally a civil rights issue. It's *not* charity, of course, it's not just good will, it's *not* just the right thing to do: it's a person's fundamental right, and, many times, a *legal mandate* to be assisted and served in a manner consistent with getting the job done. A disability is not, and should never be, a, quote, 'handicap.' We always hear when we talk about 'discrimination' that, 'As long as I treat everyone equally, then everything's okay.' Well, not when it comes to a person with a disability who needs a reasonable accommodation *for* that disability, in order to make things accessible. You have to throw all that 'same' treatment out the window. I mean, aside from a good customer service issue, not only are these laws on the books to ensure access for persons with disabilities for the private market, but, as a municipal government, we have to, many times, go *further* than a private business, and maximize the accommodations and structural modifications to reduce barriers for persons with disabilities. All this robust federal money Louisville Metro Government gets, and uses, mandates further accessibility. And *affirmatively*, not passively…"

I shift my stance, internally moving forward.

"Need an interpreter for a hearing impairment? We, Louisville Metro Government, should work to get that for you. Need large print materials for written documents to help with a vision impairment? *We* should get that for you. Need a curb cut installed in the public right-of-way on a sidewalk, or leading to a street, to accommodate your wheelchair? *We* should get that done for you. Need an assistant on your behalf because you have an emotional, mental, or cognitive impairment? We should help you by working directly with that assistant, that proxy. Need a transfer from your second-floor apartment to a ground-floor apartment when you live in public housing, or federally-subsidized apartment communities, to accommodate physical disability? *We* should get that done for you, *and*, not only that, we should prioritize it in the queue as a top priority since you're a person with a disability and need it to *live*. No 'budget prevents us' talk, and referrals to outside social service agencies, to non-profits, trying to pass the buck, and make the challenges go away. *We* should do it. Us. Louisville Metro Government. So, we have some work to do, like the Mayor says, and that especially applies to some of the people sitting around the tables in this room…(!)"

Seeing no one stopping me, including out of the back of my head from Shonda and the Mayor, it's time to push it towards a conclusion after a pause short enough to not allow an interruption.

"So, you're being treated unfairly, you're being discriminated against, and you wanna sue, but you don't have the money, you don't know where to begin. Well, the Civil Relations Commission is here. And we're--some of us are not a bunch of empty slogans, a bunch of self-righteous words on a sign, a bunch of hashtags on the internet, almost all of which are out-of-date and, *worse*, as divisive as they are trying to be unifying. The elder persons with disabilities walked, and rolled, and marched, and climbed, the inaccessible steps and stairs, and they did the protesting, decades-ago now…that got the laws passed. *Now*, the issue of civil rights, with maybe a few…notable, exceptions, is getting law enforcement agencies like mine, and governments, to do *their* jobs. That's the civil rights issue. It's assembling evidence, and litigation, not these academic discussions we hear time and again. It's bureaucracy, it's apathy, and it's systemic dysfunction. You start enforcing the law against these individuals and, especially, these agencies, hitting them in the pocketbook, and then you'll *see* more compliance. And it doesn't have to cost you, the taxpayer, a penny. Administratively, government's supposed to take Probable Cause cases and fast-track them to legal proceedings on a Complainant's behalf, in the public interest. *Administratively*. As in, we have leeway, as the law enforcement agency, to get it done quicker. That means no court filings back and forth, if the Complainant doesn't want; no enriching the attorneys in costing *you* more than the case remedy should be. It's not about the same government reports, and studies, that sit on a shelf, collecting dust with each new administration and funding cycle, touting that '*we have a plan*'…it's about Probable Cause cases. Charges. And we've had them: some of us investigators have had them based on disability. And race, and religion, and national origin, too, things like that. But I can go to half of the new-construction multifamily housing developments here in Louisville and find design-and-construction violations by architects, developers, builders, and, as far as I'm concerned, local code enforcement here, since we as a government sign off on plans here looking at a less-restrictive standard under state, quote, 'ADA' law, instead of the federal Fair Housing Act, which mandates *more* accessibility. And the disability protection means that just the *refusal* to engage in the negotiation for an accommodation, or a modification, can be discrimination, much less an outright refusal to accommodate…This is all *civil* stuff, for god's sakes, or at least it's *supposed* to be. It's not like we're locking people up over this brand of social justice for the public good. Although, when it comes to wanton discrimination against persons with disabilities, maybe we *should* lock some people up. And, hey, look: if someone isn't doing their job in providing you, or someone you know, accessibility, then call. And we'll get you where you need to go, if it's not us to take care of it. Hell, and if it's *us* that's not providing accessibility, if it's Louisville Metro *Government*, call us, and we'll refer you out for proper enforcement if we're not doing *our* jobs right. 'Cause sometimes we don't, I can assure you of that, " I exhale-laugh out once. "And if it's *me*, *I'll* forward you on to my boss, or the Mayor's Office, for complaint. Or to the Metro Council, which is the legislative checks-and-balances branch, like Congress is to the President. Seriously. There can be no *compromise* here, you understand… Discrimination against persons with disabilities is immoral, it's bad for business, and *business* is what this administration says it's all about…"

I sense from diagonally-behind me that Shonda is now convulsing in twirling her finger in the air, trying to get me to conclude.

"Okay, so, if you have any questions, I'll be happy to answer any you may have when the green light's given. Or, after the meeting, individually, or you can contact me at the Commission…Thanks, you all, I appreciate it, it's certainly my pleasure to serve you at this *Mayor's*

Disability Forum," I conclude, providing the most earnest humility-smirk I can muster after the frustrated channeling is halted.

And I sit.

My bright, wide eyes stare ahead in looking around with peripheral vision to see what'll happen next after the shell-shock.

Is the silence shell-shock?

Where's the question-statement-accusation from someone, anyone, saying, "You're full of cynicism, huh?" or, "You're so full of resentment," where I can then go into the rebuttal of "Yes, I *am*, I'm cynical, and full of resentment, towards a broken system I'm forced to work with…"

Where's the Mayor, or the administration saying, "You're fired!" and "Get ready for civil litigation, Alex!"

Shonda pauses, then speaks to the crowd, professionally and courteously.

"Okay, thank you, Alex…and we do have a lot going on to help people with disabilities. You've heard some of our departments here, and I do want to assure you that we *are* listening, we *are* helping. And the Mayor makes this a priority with his administration. I know last month, I not only attended my first wheelchair basketball game organized by Jamie and Metro Parks, hosting out-of-town players visiting Louisville, but I used a wheelchair to play a pick-up game, myself…lemme tell you, it was *difficult*," she says, slightly-laughing. "It was difficult, but it was fun, and my kids loved that, and really got into it, yelling and cheering on the players, like I did. These are some *athletes*. I was wiped out in the first five minutes, and they played full games--Mayor, we're working on luring the annual tournament here to Louisville next spring, hundreds of participants…don't tell Nashville, though!"

A few sparse laughs, and a smile inside the brooding Mayor.

Oh, he just looked at me, albeit the quickest of glances and a nod-shrug of contemptuous disapproval.

"Okay everyone," Shonda bridges. "So, the Mayor has another engagement this afternoon, and he wishes that he could answer all your questions, but he does have time to answer maybe one or two questions from the audience…one question, maybe?"

A few in the audience raise their hands.

"Matt…?" Shonda selects quickly. "Independent Living?"

"Yes," Matt says, adjusting himself in his motorized wheelchair. "I just--oh, well: Hi, everyone, Matt Wentworth, Outreach Director, Louisville Independent Living…and I'm here with Director Margaret Zoeller. Shonda, we want to thank the administration, and you, personally, Mayor, for city government's response to what happened this past winter during the weather events here in Louisville Metro. When the city had its state of emergency announcements with the January snows, and then again in February with the ice storm, Independent Living constituents had a difficult time getting notice from our local TV stations about what was going on, as far as accessible formats, in real time, on the TV screens, when it came to things like road closures, and school closures…things like that. But when we called your office, you all responded by providing interpreters with your press conferences, and it's our understanding that you all contacted the media about it, and made them aware that more accessibility was needed from them, and that--you know, it really helped get the word out on how dangerous the situation was for some of our folks, those people who had medical and doctor's appointments, who needed to adjust their Transit Authority paratransit reservations to get to those appointments, or to their workplaces. And we appreciate that the city has plans for making the roads and streets more accessible, especially for persons with vision and mobility impairments…I dunno if you all *knew* this, but I, myself, am a person with a mobility impairment, so…"

The crowd laughs some, me included.

"But I'm not into playing any wheelchair basketball anytime soon, 'cause it'll just cut into my cigar-smoking and bourbon-drinking on the sidelines…"

(He's not joking, I've seen him cruising The Highlands and NuLu during Louisville street festivals.)

"Matt's not joking," Margaret says, not even slightly-laughing. "This is Margaret Zoeller, Independent Living. As most of you know, we're the local, private, not-for-profit agency working on disability-related issues across the state, and into southern Indiana. So, Mr. Mayor, like Matt says, thank you, and we'd like to present you with something today, it'll only take a second because we know how busy you are…"

And at that, and seemingly on someone's queue, Margaret pulls out a certificate-sized plaque and rises from her audience seat, as Matt and even the tentative Trisha Evans zoom their wheels up towards the front tables with her. Shonda smiles, and then she and the Mayor stand up. Back in the back, an ambulatory male who I'm unfamiliar with brings up Margaret's rear towards the front, digital camera in his hands ready.

"Mayor Hoch," Margaret announces to all, "for all your work helping people with disabilities here in the Louisville metropolitan area, we have here Louisville Independent Living's Person of the Year award for 2015. It reads: '*The Honorable Mayor Stephen Hoch, awarded this achievement for his always addressing the needs for persons with disabilities. September 4th, 2015.*'"

The Mayor stands there appearing dumbfounded and amazed and drunken and happy-go-lucky after a double-take, open-mouthed half-smile. I sit there and half-smile incredulously with a half-smirk, internally shaking my head at the series of events as the crowd applauds enthusiastically. Thank goodness for the photographer, since he blocks my view that administration would have seeing me squirm in my seat. I do summon up a few polite claps. The Mayor and Shonda shake hands with Independent Living and exchange smiles amongst the small group. The fracas goes on a minute too long before the seats are taken and the Mayor gets half-way out the room's front door.

"Okay, everyone," Shonda again bridges, "Mayor Hoch has to leave, but we--Bye Mayor, *thank you*, thank you again!--"

Saying thank you and goodbye inaudibly to Shonda, the Mayor waves and smiles open-mouthed at a few of the department directors at the roundtable, gliding out the room's front door on his magic carpet with the large sharp-suited male stoically right behind him. The small Louisville Independent Living parade disperses not to their former places at the Mayor's Disability Forum, but in a march right out the door after the Mayoral lead. I sit in disbelief, but I'm also coming down from the energy of my onslaught to the room.

Shonda continues.

"Okay, everyone, we have a few more minutes, how about we go ahead and get another question…comments?"

Nothing but silence from attendees, which surprises me considering the assertiveness and complaint-driven sessions of the Disability Action Network monthly meetings. Maybe if Jonah Penzik was here to take the lead, there'd be more than just myself to wield a big stick to these department heads…?

"Well," Shonda begins to wrap up, "Nothing…? No one out there…? You're not asleep, are you…? Okay, well, it's Friday afternoon, then. Jamie, why don't we finish by telling folks about our upcoming events…"

"Sure, yes: Louisville Metro Parks & Recreation has scheduled some fall events with our programming this year. We've adapted many of our programs to be inclusive for persons with disabilities, including beginning archery classes, which start meeting every week on Tuesdays at 4:00 p.m., uh, starting *next* week, at our Camp Taylor location, and you have to be age 18 or older, there's a $10 registration fee…We have water exercises that've been going on for the summer, and they'll continue on through the end of the month, meeting on Wednesdays every week at--also at 4:00 p.m., at a few different locations around Louisville Metro, only a $1 fee to participate…We have coloring book exercises every day after school, which are free, also at various Parks locations around town… And, like Shonda mentioned before, we're working on bringing a national wheelchair basketball tourney to Louisville next spring, and we hope to have more information available on that here in the next few months, but especially at the next Mayor's Disability Forum…"

"Yes, Jamie, good stuff…and, like I said," Shonda polishes, "we have a *lot* going on, this tournament is going to be big, you all really must experience it if you haven't before…my family loves it, and we hope you all discover it, too, if you haven't already experienced it yourself. *Okay*, well, I think that's all the time we have for to*day*…I do want to thank you all, in the audience, for attending, thank you to our directors and department representatives, we look forward to everyone back here in about six months for the next Forum. Okay…? Alright, thanks again, everyone, have a great weekend out there."

And, with that, it's at what seems like an abrupt end.

I immediately stand up to stretch, and I smile graciously and awkwardly to try to be welcoming to anyone who wants to approach the bench here. Brenda and Susan stand while chatting to each other, other department heads and representatives are up and trying to make their way out of the open front doorway, when, suddenly, Shonda gestures firmly and animatedly to Brenda that she wants to speak with her but, at the same time, sprints out after another director to speak in the hallway in a diversion. Neither Brenda nor Susan wish to speak to me, certainly, but that gives me more freedom to speak with audience members individually to address their concerns and questions.

Still standing and making impromptu stretches, no one's approaching.

I check in on Janet, finished with slowly gathering her papers together.

"All *right*...thanks, Janet, as always...!"

"I'm retiring," she says.

Laughing a little more than I should, in part due to the insecurity of no one approaching me with questions or comments, I try to latch on to her for conversation but also for her comfort, all while keeping an eye out.

"Well, don't ask *me* to fill your position, then..."

"Would you want to be the Director, or--rather: would you want to be the city Americans with Disabilities Act Coordinator, if they brought that position back?"

"Oh my gawd, no *way* would they ask me to be that," I scoff.

"Well," Janet says amicably, tiredly, and matter-of-factly, slinging one of her bags over her shoulder and carrying one dropped down to her side, "I think you'd be good at it. I mean--administration notwith*stand*ing, of course..."

"Heh, thanks, Janet, I appreciate you being one of my biggest supporters--*only* supporters..."

"Great job, Alex!" Jamie chimes in with seeming-sincerity, as Janet now slowly makes her way to the room front doorway.

"Heh, thanks Jamie! Good job to you, too," I affirm.

"Shonda's gonna *get* you, Alex...!"

"Jamie, you let *me* handle Shonda...but if I somehow get in trouble with her and can't handle it, I'll call *you*, obviously." I look around to see if Brenda's still around, grimacing that I'd be in yet more trouble. But, she's gone.

Not concluding the conversation with any formality, Jamie quickly walks over towards Claudia to check on the Forum sign-in data. I continue to stand, looking out over the expanse of the emptying room of just a few folks who've stuck around, and I'm almost desperate for eye-contact. The Disability Action Network members who attended have filed out, some with Transit Authority paratransit driver assistance, some without, leaving a few people I don't know except for Victoria Schrader, the former Chair of the Transit Authority's Accessibility Council.

And she's now looking at me. And she approaches in her motorized wheelchair.

"Hey, Alex," Victoria says, reaching the end of one of the U-ends of the roundtable.

"Hey, Victoria!" I walk a few steps over to greet her at the U-end and lean in towards her. "Thanks for comin' down…!"

She professionally but with courtesy dives right in.

"Hey, I wanted to thank you personally for what you said about reasonable accommodations for disabilities. You know, I had this problem with my landlord out in J-Town, who wouldn't respond to me when I was asking for a grab bar to be installed, in the bathroom of my apartment. I asked them, and the management there wouldn't respond, but then I heard you speak earlier this year, talking about reasonable accommodations, and modifications, all that, and then I wrote my landlord a letter about it, and they responded with an attorney sending me a letter, saying that they'd even pay for it…"

"*Oh*, yeah? Back in April, for National Fair Housing Month, over there at Horizon Development?"

"Yeah, so, that really helped, I was having a devil-of-a-time getting that approved. I guess they realized that they were wrong after I wrote that letter, based on what you said, about fair housing, you know, the Fair Housing Act, and not the ADA, and how there's a difference between the two."

"Wow, great (!)…Yeah, disability issues are the biggest reported problem in housing these days, when it comes to civil rights issues. Half--no, wait, more than half, of all housing discrimination complaints filed these days are based on disability. Here in Louisville, we're about tied, with half disability, half race, though."

"Well, yeah, no-kidding-it's-a-big-problem (!). I know a friend of mine also had a *big* problem with her parking situation where she lives, with the TA paratransit bus not being able to pick her up for her doctor's appointments. Not that it was TA's fault, you know, it was her apartment complex not accommodating her with a parking space big enough--or, an area for the paratransit bus big enough to pick her up, unload her back at home, and all."

"Yeah, the most frequently-charged, or Caused, cases I've had, as far as a trend, is the failure to provide a reasonable accommodation for parking in housing due to a disability. Like, no *reserved*, disability-designated parking space for a rental tenant, things like that…I mean, have your friend call us if she's having problems with that, and we can investigate, and get it where it needs to go, you know?"

"Sure…"

"So, are you--by the way, I appreciate the work that you've done with the Transit Authority Accessibility Council…"

"Yeah, you know, I can't get back on there right now, the by-laws make you drop out for a year after being on for three years. I hope to get back on there, we'll see what happens at the end of the year. I dunno that I'd want to be Chair again (!), but you never know with these things, no one else may wanna do it, and then I might be right back on there leadin' the thing again."

"Heh, yeah, I can only *imagine…*"

"Okay, well, Alex…Just wanted to tell you that, I guess I'll see ya at the next meeting, or wherever…"

"Yeah, it was good seein' you, Victoria, seriously, you just made my day, I couldn't be more thrilled about the good news on your housing situation…*seriously…*!"

"Yeah, no, thank you…Okay, bye now…" she says, motoring off to the left from me, towards the open front room door.

After Victoria leaves, Claudia, finishing her packing up of the tracking materials, also leaves, half-polite smiling at me with a quick raising of the eyebrows indicating "*We're done here.*"

I stand there another moment, in the room by myself, before then gathering my few materials from my place at the roundtable and putting them in my black work bag. I walk slowly over to the open door entrance of the room, which is now an exit, and, stopping in the doorway, lean over to the light switches, flick them off, walk backwards inside the room a step to grab the door, and I pull it shut with a click-thud behind me.

Race

***

Color

***

Religion

***

National Origin

***

Sex

***

Familial Status

***

Disability

***

Sexual Orientation

***

Gender Identity

***

Apathy, the most recent protected class from unlawful discrimination.

CHAPTER TWELVE

4:03 p.m.
The clock on the desktop computer is in digital font.

***

4:33 p.m.
The clock on the desktop computer is in digital font.

***

4:44 p.m.
(In defiance, I will *continue* to look at the clock.)

***

I sit at my office desk, slumped over and staring out, and up, into nothingness.

I was supposed to make reservations for our favorite restaurant tonight, but I'll come up with an excuse that Jenny will see right through again when we meet back at the house. Long-gone are any Fridays of excitement awaiting the beginning-of-the-weekend evening…all that remains is the duty to have a meal out, and, then, what really doesn't pass for an elation of crashing into bed to possibly sleep in the next morning, a little peace.

I look at next week's schedule on my office desk calendar, probably for the fifth time since my office telephone has been silent this late afternoon. Monday's schedule is an 8:00 a.m. Complainant interview, one housing discrimination tester scheduled to come in the morning on a tentative basis, and then a site-visit in the afternoon for the housing discrimination complaint investigation *Barnett v. Oxmoor Multifamily LLC*, a race case alleging disparate treatment in lease non-renewal/eviction for an African-American tenant in a low-income housing tax credit property, but with no federal subsidy. So, nothing to take home for study or preparation for the weekend.

Despite all the confidence of an end-of-the-work-week Friday, a twenty-year career in fair housing, and a head-clearing night's sleep, I still have the doubt of my entire profession right now while I semi-wait on an interoffice call from Brenda to come to her office. Or, an interoffice call from Agnes, more likely, as Brenda's sergeant-at-arms, calling me into Brenda's office where she'll already be stationed after a closed-door session they had together just prior. Since it's 4:46 p.m., I wonder how late they'll try to keep me after normal work hours and, again, on an epic-week Friday. I've kept my ear on the Civil Relations Commission front door and receptionist desk after getting back to my office, and I know that Agnes is here, but I don't know if Brenda's here. My better sense and reasoning should know that Louisville Metro Government's administration couldn't possibly get my termination papers ready by the close of the day, anyways, since they'd have to go through Human Resources and my bosses. So, like the six months it took to hire me on, I probably have another six months here to get word that I'm formally let go by the administration. And that's probably giving them too much credit.

I hear nothing but silence from the other offices, the front receptionist desk, the back east wing, the administrative-oriented west wing…half the staff is gone for the day already, as they, themselves, have had meetings during the week's off-hours, allowing them to flex their schedule and get off early today. The other half of staff, like me, are likely just traumatized zombies sitting at their desks, zoned-out to their computer screens or talking on city government telephone lines to family and friends.

I sit there. I exhale.

4:49 p.m.

I get up, I go to my office window, I lean over onto the interior ledge, and I look out at the traffic, heavy for a Friday but typical for a late-summer, hot and humid day downtown. Vehicle exhausting, vehicle acceleration-rumbling, vehicle rap-music-rumbling, vehicle classic-rock-'n roll blaring, vehicle horn-honking, overhead airplane sky-mowing, pedestrian soloing, pedestrian grouping, pedestrian shouting…office window rattling, shaking the street scenes below. I put my right hand to the back of my head and push while arching my back backwards for a stretch, before returning to my seat in a crash like the dogged Tivoli to the hardwood floor, waiting.

I sit, staring at my document-and-file-covered desk, looking slightly diagonally down at nothing.

4:53 p.m.

I hear Janice up front shuffling some bags after she's come around from her west-wing office, either going to the receptionist desk or setting the bags down on the front lobby chairs to adjust herself and wait for the small office staff land-rush out of the building for the weekend. I then hear clunking and drawer-shutting in Sherry's office next to mine, then rustling bags, then a hard click of a wall light switch. Sherry's had enough.

"Have…good weekend…" I hear from far down the other end of the hallway east wing offices, followed by distant-approaching rustling, walking, and slight huffing. It's Briana, saying goodbye to Chad in the kitchenette and tearing on out of here carrying, in my sixth sense of knowledge that comes with working with her for a dozen years, a large bag in one hand to her side while securing a large purse with the other hand.

"Bye…!"

She swoops past Bonnie's office, who yells back at her from her office seat.

"Briana…!"

I still hear the approaching rustling, walking, and slight huffing.

"Briana…!" Bonnie yells again, seemingly at random, from her office chair.

"Bye…Bonnie…!" Briana huffs out loud to Bonnie's office, now behind her, while she struggles to steamroll to the front receptionist desk area outpost.

"Oh, *lord*, *Briana…*" Bonnie says directly from within her office.

"Ha ha! Bon-*nie*…!" Briana laughs back, still moving forward, not stopping.

4:56 p.m.

As much as I love to joke around with Briana, Bonnie, Sherry, Janice…after this afternoon's clinic I performed for the public and the Mayor's administration, I'm gonna not-leave until 4:59 p.m.

Briana moves past my office door. "Bye Alex!" she huffs.

"Bye Briana, have a good weekend…!" I throw out from my seat.

From the front receptionist area rustling: "Come on, Briana…(!)"

Janice, as always, is leading the getaway.

<dong!>

"I'm. Comin'…" Briana ambles.

"See, Briana's leadin' us today, not you, Janice," I hear Sherry quip hard.

"Briana's not *nothin'* but a *secretary*, Sherry, I'm an *officer*, an *Intake Officer…!*" Janice is openly joking and goading the within-earshot supervisor Agnes, and to ultimate supervisor Brenda, via-Agnes if Brenda isn't even here.

"You can *have* your title back, Ms. Janice," Briana says, as the trio exit the front door with a double-thud closure.

4:58 p.m.

Complete silence.

Forget it, I'm outta here.

I use the computer mouse to clickly shut down the operating system, before then thumbing with a jerk the button turning off the computer monitor in slight contempt for my job. I grab my black work bag resting on the floor and sling it around my left shoulder, at the same time getting my sunglasses out of the side-pocket and replacing them with my regular glasses. I give my office a quick once-over to see if I'm forgetting anything. I flick off the light switch with a thud to turn off my Civil Relations Commission life and head on down the hallway, trying to slow my walk to the front door so that I make it out no earlier than about 4:59:45 p.m. But, I'm also trying to mind any awkwardness that would result in me being paired up with a leaving Agnes, or another co-worker that I don't want to share the elevator with who's also leaving for the day. I hear rustling in Chad's office behind me down the hall in the east wing where I just came from, so I double-step it back to my normal retail-service walk to try to make it out by myself, where I can be alive on my own. Not that there's anything wrong with Chad or anyone else under the Executive Branch.

<dong!>

I launch my right hand out leading with my thumb and hit the elevator-down button in one graceful swoop after exiting the Civil Relations Commission. I'm about to start worrying about how long the wait for the elevator will be, with at least Chad likely on my tail, but there's either divine mercy or random karmatic order.

<ding!>

The left of the three elevator doors lights up above, and I can't remember if it's the wild-card elevator car that takes people up to the seventh floor without provocation; if it's the slow elevator that crawls down each level until about six inches from the floor, when it then creeps gently enough to make passengers wonder if the car will ever reach the floor to open at all; or, if it's the jackpot-elevator running pretty much like it's supposed to run. I lean my head around when it opens, checking to see if someone is hiding along the wall-portion where the buttons are located, and I see that no one's there. I then leap onto the elevator car and quickly and desperately thumb the "1" button approximately 534 times…hitting the "*Door Close*" button has never done a thing my whole tenure here, probably ever, really, so I don't bother with it.

Down on the first floor, the elevator doors open and I see the security guard outside the front double-doors off to the right looking out at the street traffic three lanes thick and stalled, cigarette in his left hand to his side. Individual and group pedestrians walk in front of the building from east to west and west to east, some professionally-dressed and some professionally-dressed-down and some professed to be linked to formal, and informal, counter-culture underworlds that now pass for mainstream culture. The lobby has a twenty-something woman waiting there at the security desk, looking like a visitor to the building in complete casual dress, and she doesn't turn to see me exiting the elevator or walk to the disability-accessible automatic door. I push the large metal disability-designated entrance/exit sign square button and the heavy outer door automatically springs open. I walk through, and the rush of the early September, more-like-early-August heat and humidity oven-bakes me in its swamp, almost immediately.

Trying to avoid pedestrians and going against the traffic-grain along the side of the building to the left, instead of to the right, to the parking garage ramp, I briefly think about how I'd be cursing at me if I was one of the walkers on the right side of the sidewalk since pedestrian traffic lanes should mirror vehicle traffic direction. I glance up at a posted circular mirror, diagonally-attached at the empty garage monitor station, to see if a car's coming down the garage ramp, and then I tentatively stick my head around from my body to look directly up the ramp to my left in order to double-check that no vehicle's going to plow right into me if I round the corner and proceed up the ramp to the second level.

No traffic.

Gambling on the ramp, I walk double-time up the slope and towards the right turn-off to the second level parking area. A white subcompact sport utility vehicle has just exited backwards from a parking space, and it'll meet me before I'm able to sneak into my driver's side car door entry. I submit to the inevitable encounter and walk over to the right side of the garage parking lane, walking close to the few parked cars still left in their spots this late Friday afternoon. The small white SUV then comes slowly towards my way and the exitway, and I see that it's Briana.

I shake my fist and mouth a curse at her with mock rage, and she laughingly says "Bye!" without attempting to slow down or to stop as she motors past, laughing with both hands on her steering wheel. Smiling, I make it to and into my car.

Closing the driver's side door while throwing my black work bag onto the passenger side seat, I immediately lock the door manually but then sit a second instead of going through the routine, graceful, all-in-one motion of Friday-at-5:00-p.m. exuberance in tearing out of the garage with euphoria. It's a moment of silence.

I grab my 1995 vinyl cd-rom-case-turned-cd-music-holder and get out a late-70s/early 80s in-its-prime music group's 1979 disc that only *I* would like these days, changing out the current disc in the broken-digital factory-installed cd player. I look as the new cd enters the system, sliding into the receiver automatically with a revolving spin sound which turns into a whir. Hitting the lottery, the digitized "Track 1" appears with no foreign-looking random characters on the screen, so I click on the forward button on the cd player fully expecting the system to freeze up again. "Track 2" appears, so, taking advantage of the opportunity to get to a track I want to hear right away, in the order that I want to hear it, I click ahead while hoping: "Track 3," "*Track 4-5-6-7-8*," until I reach "Track 9."

"Track 9" is a staple, reminding me of my high school junior angst of playing a greatest-hits tape collection of the same band while sorting through all the regional college and university postal mail brochures I'd ultimately throw in the trash and not submit applications for. The track takes me back to the *sense*, though not the complete memory, of such time of mixed hope and despair. Rediscovering the music as a middle-aged adult now more than a quarter of a century later, it's constantly a reclaiming of at least a part of my identity. Or, at least until I likely get sick of playing the track, two or three more times ahead of now. But at this point, it's still the bridge of bringing back raw youth talent after wiping away the traumatic somewhat-misdirection of what my life might've currently become. Professionally, at least.

The longer-than-typical-radio-cut "Track 9" ends in a fade, and I hit the stereo system on/off dial-button to kick the entire system off. I want and hope for the song to be the evening musak in my head, because now I'm just about home.

Jenny's car isn't here yet.

I do a turnaround at the end of the gated cul-de-sac, seeing loiterers at both concrete benches bookmarking the gated cut-off on West Oak Street, and then I get to park the car with the end-bumper at the beginning of the designated no-parking sign across the street from the house. I turn the car off, exchange my glasses, grab the black work bag, exit the car, lock the door, and walk with a spring to the front brownstone-like steps.

On cue, the front door opens before I get up the concrete stairs. Michael appearing with Tivoli on a leash, it's now about 5:15 p.m.

I say hello to both, with Michael responding in his head but not out loud, apparently, while Tivoli starts wagging his tail looking at me with his big headed smile and small ears up from his huge head at attention.

"Be careful, Michael," I warn, based on my skimming-scan of the neighborhood. "I'll lock the front door for ya..."

Michael follows Tivoli's lumber down the steps and I make it inside the house, locking the door behind me. Instead of walking immediately into the kitchen to look for the United States Postal Mail stack on the stove, I look out of the stained-glass front door window to watch Michael and Tivoli lumber across the street towards the front of my car, and then they go on out of view to the left.

Zooming into view from the left on the street now is Jenny, in her handpainted-decoration, compact, art-car hybrid, Corinne in tow in the front passenger seat. Jenny appears to be singing, or, well, maybe rapping, as Corinne wears large headphones in silence. I stand and watch as the car does the same turnaround I did, though a little quicker and less disjointed compared to mine, and it drives on back to the left out of view. I stand there, watching now the brief neighborhood inaction except for a pedestrian walking from the right to left on the opposite side of the street near my car.

Then, back into view starting with the rear of her car, Jenny and Corinne parallel-park right in front of my car, slowly. The pedestrian turns his head looking at them while strutting along quickly, stops, and I then get more at-attention. Suspiciously, the pedestrian has something in his hand, but then, as sudden as his stop, he proceeds on again, along the sidewalk, out of view past Jenny and Corinne. I drop my black work bag onto the steps inside the house leading to the second floor, then open the front door and look for the suspect passing by as I slowly walk down the front steps. Jenny and Corinne exit their car out of the lesser part of my vision. The pedestrian's not looking back and continues an urban walk down the street, thankfully, and Jenny and Corinne are retrieving bags and items out of the car trunk.

"Heya, baybee…!"

Jenny is happy, and Corinne's head is in a recording studio in New York City as Jenny slams the trunk closed. They then walk towards me and the house as I stand guard in the middle of the steps.

"Hey-*ay*," I say back to both dryly and sarcastically.

"Hey," Corinne acknowledges in her strut.

Jenny sighs.

"Need me to help with anything…?" I ask, almost in earnest.

Jenny sighs again when earnestly responding that she's okay.

"Michael's walking Tivoli, did you see 'em?"

"Yeah hunny," Jenny says in working her way in the street up to the house stairs.

I sway the two to go up the steps past me with a leading right-hand chaperone, remaining a few steps behind to bring up the rear while looking around the area, and down Michael & Tivoli's route briefly, before then following them into the house. I lock the front door behind me. Corinne is in the kitchen selecting which drinking glass she'll leave on the counter after use, Jenny's leafing through the postal mail that Michael left spread out on the stove.

"Everything okay?" I ask Jenny.

"Yeah…" she says, leaving open for interpretation whether she wants to talk about anything from work or anything else.

"You know, you can talk about work if you want, Jenny, you listen to *me* vent all the time…"

"I *know*, I just don't want to dump everything from work on you…"

"It's okay…"

"Well," Jenny reservedly says, "I was named Interim Director this afternoon by the Mayor and Shonda…"

!

"Oh *my god*, that's great, Jenny (!), I'm so proud of you…!"

"Yeah, it's good," she says with almost half-doubt and definite half-exhale.

"Well, I think it's great, heh (!). You're now 'Director of the Jefferson County Public Library,' all your hard work has paid off, Jenny, you really deserve it…obviously…Let's go celebrate our victory against the administration together by going out to eat, you can choose where we go…"

"It's *Interim* Director, sweetheart. And I already told you where I wanted to eat, did you make the reservation?"

"No, I wasn't sure when you'd be home, so…"

"Well, I *told* you when I'd get home, so…"

"Okay, well, sometimes you're late, but, anyways, if we go *now*, or when Michael gets back--let's just go right away, then we can get in, maybe--"

"O*kay*, jeez…!"

"*Sorry*, okay?! I'm still in work mode, okay? I tried to calm down, I will when we get to dinner. I have to tell you about the Mayor's Disability Forum this afternoon, and you have to tell me about your meeting with Shonda and her good-buddy *Stevie Hack*…"

"Alright…"

"Maybe we can sleep in tomorrow morning…"

I walk over to Jenny's face, and she reluctantly puckers up while looking away from me as I kiss her cheek.

"We bettah…!" Jenny says after a pause.

<lock-snap…creek…>

A stumbling, struggling, smiling, hyper-panting Tivoli leads Michael through the front door. Corinne's nowhere to be found inside the house. Jenny and I will argue about my high-strung driving over to the restaurant, wherever that may be tonight. But once we get to bed after dinner, we'll be in bed looking online by 8:00 p.m., probably. Tonight, we'll just be lazing, consuming local and national news, social media, watching an internet-streaming television show or two, or watch half of, or no more than, a two-hour movie. We'll research vacation packages online, because, this time, it's *my* turn to choose where we go, and it's *gonna* be Europe, or South America. (Well, or Canada again.) All the preparation in the world for the next non-business-day's work. Eyes shut at around 9:30 p.m. Falling asleep usually within twenty minutes, but then the hourly open-and-shut case of insomnia after a long night's nap, or, since tomorrow's Saturday, going back to sleep after 5:25 a.m. for another hour, maybe even two…but then there's Sunday, and I may not even do a damn thing, with civil disobedience to any clock that tries to make me reconsider routine…in complete apathy for my usual system of doing things.

ACKNOWLEDGMENTS

This work could not have been written and published without the guidance, counsel, mentorship, and influence by many, including Tony B., Galen Martin, Kevin K., T.I., Sandra B., Bobbi S., Linda H., Rotonia S., Dinah C., Art C., Naima H., Sarah M., Kungu N., Tony S., Kentucky Housing Corporation, Geert Kliphuis, and Joe S.

ABOUT THE AUTHOR

After surviving a twenty-year Kentucky career investigating civil rights complaints, including extensive, groundbreaking fair housing work leading to established United States case law for multiple protected classes from unlawful discrimination, Nick Valenzuela now lives in Indiana.

28260777R00143

Made in the USA
Columbia, SC
09 October 2018